SOMEONE SPECIAL

SOMEONE SPECIAL

Sheila O'Flanagan

headline
review

First published in 2008
by HEADLINE REVIEW
An imprint of HEADLINE PUBLISHING GROUP

COVENTRY CITY LIBRARIES	
201635477	
HJ	07/08/2008
F	£12.99
CCS	

Cataloguing in Publication Data is
available from the British Library

ISBN 978 0 7553 3219 9 (hardback)
ISBN 978 0 7553 3220 5 (trade paperback)

Typeset in Galliard by Palimpsest Book Production Limited,
Grangemouth, Stirlingshire

Printed and bound in Great Britain by
Clays Ltd, St Ives plc

HEADLINE PUBLISHING GROUP
An Hachette Livre UK Company
338 Euston Road
London NW1 3BH

www.headline.co.uk
www.hachettelivre.co.uk

The usual array of people worked behind the scenes to keep me on the straight and narrow while writing *Someone Special*.

So much thanks as ever to:

Carole Blake and Marion Donaldson, my agent and my editor, who are always so helpful and supportive

The team of people who look after me so well around the world, especially everyone who has translated my books into so many different languages – I really appreciate the commitment you put into each book

My fantastic family who look after me at home

Colm, my Someone Special

During the writing of *Someone Special* my ever patient neighbours had to put up with the fact that I decided to do some renovation work to my house. I moved out but they were left behind – so a massive thank you to everyone who cheerily asked me how things were going even though I'm sure you were driven demented! Special thanks to Bert and Priscilla; and to Shay, Tara, Mark and Cian who helped get Djin through the trauma.

I have an ex-neighbour to thank too: Ciara Travers was wonderful at explaining the work of a forensic archaeologist and brought me on some very cold but interesting digs to see first-hand the work that they do. I'm grateful for the time that everyone I met gave to me when I asked stupid questions! Any technical errors are naturally mine and not theirs. I'd also like to thank Ciara's mum, Marjorie, for being so lovely.

The builders did (eventually) leave me with more space in which to write . . . so, for all their hard work, many, many thanks to Charlie, John, Barry, Corey, Fred, Martin, Robert, Ken, Declan, Eamonn and the rest of the crew; as well as to Tom for making the design work so well. I've no excuses for not sitting at my desk now . . .

Last, but so very definitely not least, my biggest thanks goes to all of you who read my books and get in touch with me through my website www.sheilaoflanagan.net. It's always a real pleasure to hear from you. I do hope that you enjoy *Someone Special.*

Chapter 1

On the night before she was due to travel back to Ireland, Romy Kilkenny went to dinner in a stylish restaurant overlooking Sydney Harbour. The restaurant was the current in-place to eat in the city, but its astronomical price tag as well as its lengthy waiting list for tables meant that it was normally out of her reach. Romy's usual haunt when she ate out was the rather less glamorous and significantly less pricey pizzeria at the end of her road. She liked the checked tablecloths and Chianti bottles as candle-holders, and that the staff welcomed her warmly as a regular customer. Right now – despite the spectacular views of the illuminated Harbour Bridge and Opera House from the curved picture window; and despite the carefully designed mood lighting, elegant place settings and amazing floral arrangements of the restaurant interior – she was rather wishing that they'd gone to the pizzeria after all. She wouldn't have felt so bad about not enjoying herself if they'd been having the two-for-the-price-of-one pepperoni and double-cheese special at Luigi's.

She'd wanted to have a good time tonight. Keith had gone to an enormous amount of trouble to ensure that the evening would be memorable and he'd had to pull in a huge favour to get a prized table by the window. But even as Romy gazed unseeingly at the leatherbound menu she was thinking that they should simply have stayed at the Opera Bar where they'd previously downed a couple of beers, crushed between a raucous hen party and a group of muscular rugby players who were hell bent on having a good time. Caught up in the midst of the fun-loving crowd she wouldn't have had any time to feel sorry for herself. She probably would've drunk too much beer, had a laugh and then tottered home on her impossibly high-heeled shoes which Keith had seen for the first time ever that night. He'd been startled by the sight of her in them, not having previously thought of her as the kind of girl who wore glamorous footwear and more used to seeing her in either desert boots or flip-flops. (The Australians called them thongs. She'd been taken aback at Keith talking about her lovely thongs when he meant flip-flops. It had, she told him, almost moved their relationship on to a whole new level.) He really had been stunned by her one and only pair of high heels, which brought her up to the approximate level of his shoulder. She was averagely tall at five foot four (and, as her father had once told her, sturdily built), but Keith was a towering hunk of a guy who made her appear small and fragile beside him. It was one of the reasons she liked being seen with him.

She'd been laughing and joking in the Opera Bar, trying really hard to be cheerful and carefree, but now – surrounded by whispering waiters and overwhelmed by the sheer elegance of her surroundings – she felt suddenly deflated, knowing that in twenty-four hours she'd be on her way home and knowing too that even though it was home she didn't want to be there when Keith was here. And she wondered why it suddenly mattered to her, because they'd said goodbye to each other before and she'd never felt like this about it.

She was dreading going home. Not just because of leaving Australia and leaving Keith. But because she was going home to be with her family. And in the last few years, as she'd worked her way around the world, she'd hardly spared them a thought. Which, she reckoned, was probably just how they wanted it. It was certainly how *she* wanted it. As far as Darragh and Kathryn and Veronica were concerned (especially, ironically enough, as far as Veronica was concerned), the more time they spent apart the better.

While they waited for their food to arrive, Keith (oblivious to her mood and always in sunny humour himself) chatted about his plans for the following week. He was going to the Gold Coast and meeting up with some of their friends there for a few days of scuba-diving, water-skiing and surfing. She'd expected to go with them and was disappointed at missing out on the trip. He was filling her in on the schedule and she knew that he wanted her to feel included so she told him as sincerely as she could that it sounded great. But at the same time she couldn't help wondering whether Keith (or indeed any of them), caught up in the sparkling blue ocean waters and the beach-front lifestyle, would even notice that she wasn't there.

She poked at her roasted barramundi, not hungry even though it had become her favourite fish in the world and was the expensive restaurant's signature dish. Then she rested her fork on her plate and stared out of the window.

'Don't you like it?' Keith looked at her in consternation and she picked up her fork again quickly.

'It's fabulous,' she said as she dug it into the fish once more. 'I was just . . . you know . . . thinking.'

He nodded in understanding. 'I know it's difficult for you,' he said. 'We'll all miss you when you go back. *I'll* miss you, you know that. But it might not be for long and . . . well, what choice do you have?'

'None,' she said, although part of her was thinking that of course she had a choice. Saying no was a perfectly acceptable choice, wasn't it? She could have told them that it was impossible to come home right now, that she'd been offered an extension to her contract (which was true) and that she needed to accept it for the sake of her job (which wasn't really true and which they would have known was just an excuse). Or she could have said that she'd met someone important to her and that it was impossible to leave him (not true either, even if she was having unaccustomed feelings for Keith tonight, wanting to throw her arms around him and beg him to ask her to stay). She told herself that these thoughts were generated by her unhappiness at leaving Australia, not her unhappiness at leaving Keith. But she was having them all the same. She could have even told them the absolute truth and said that she didn't care what the emergency was, that there was nothing on earth that would drag her home.

But of course if she said that they'd simply think she was being selfish. And she was certain that they thought of her as selfish already – the girl who had swanned (she just *knew* they would use the word swanned whenever they talked about her) around the world for the past four years, not even telling them until the very last minute on the few occasions when she'd come home at all and then not bothering to meet up half the time but spending it with her father instead. Veronica herself might not think she was selfish, of course. Her mother would understand only too well why she didn't want to come home because Romy had made her feelings very clear about it in the past. But now circumstances had changed and Romy had been surprised when she learned that Veronica had agreed that her return would be the best solution all round. All the same, being in the same house as her mother again would be . . . challenging. To say the least! She took a slug of Sauvignon blanc (about three times as expensive as Luigi's so, she told herself, she should savour it, not chug it back), then played with her food again.

Ask me to stay, she thought, as she nibbled at the fish (truly gorgeous, how on earth could she not feel hungry?) and glanced at Keith through her long, dark eyelashes. Ask me! Tell me you love me and you don't want me to go and I'll ring them now and say that I've changed my mind and hang the consequences.

She swallowed the flakes of fish, thankful that Keith couldn't read her mind. Wanting him to tell her he loved her was a ridiculous notion. He didn't love her and she didn't love him either, but that hadn't stopped her mind going into overdrive with the notion. It had been her middle-of-the-night alternative for the last few days when she'd lain in her single bed, separated from him by a plasterboard wall, and tried to come up with reasons for not going home. She'd wondered why it was that he'd never once, in all the years she'd known him, shown the slightest bit of interest in her. And why it was that she'd never before thought of him as the kind of guy she'd like to spend the rest of her life with either. She'd only started thinking like this since she'd got the phone call and she knew that she was clutching at straws in her efforts to find reasons not to leave. In the clarity of daylight she didn't want Keith to fall in love with her and she didn't want to fall in love with him either because that would mean losing one of her best friends, and she'd seen *When Harry Met Sally* so she knew that letting other feelings in ruined male–female friendships. And she really didn't want to ruin her friendship with Keith. (She conceded that Harry and Sally eventually got it together at the end of the movie. But she bet that they would've split up again later.)

Anyhow, there'd been no chance of ruining her friendship with Keith because there was no chance of him or, indeed, of anyone else falling madly in love with her and begging her not to go home lest it break his heart. There hadn't been anyone in her life for ages. So no broken hearts at her departure. Anyway a broken heart still wouldn't have been enough to get her off the hook.

Keith looked up and saw her staring at him and she blushed. He grinned at her and she smiled back before swallowing a forkful of fish. He was, as usual, being sensible about it all whereas she was being buffeted around by her unreliable emotions. It wasn't all that unusual; in their circle she was known as the emotional one – hot-headed and fiery-tempered but (she hoped) usually good-natured and cheery too. It was bugging her, though, that she couldn't find the good nature and cheer tonight no matter how hard she tried.

She wondered whether she'd fallen in love with him unknown to herself. but she was pretty sure that was impossible. Her relationship with Keith was comfortable and easy and one of the constants in her life. Love, if she'd read all the novels and magazines correctly, was the complete opposite of how she felt with him. It was about being on edge all the time; waiting for a phone call, unable to eat or sleep for thinking about the object of your desire, wanting to kiss them and hold them and touch them . . . love was those things, not the sort of relationship she had with Keith where they sat in the back garden with a couple of tinnies and shared news about the day.

Their kind of companionship would only turn into love if mind-blowing sex was an option. And there had never been the option of mind-blowing sex (it probably wouldn't have been mind-blowing. It probably would have been damp-squib sex, which she didn't want to have with Keith – or anyone). So she was cool about it, no worries, but it was just that tonight it would have been nice to have something more. To be with someone who did love her, who truly would be heartbroken and who would definitely have begged her not to leave.

Although they were in Australia together (and he was a genuine Sydneysider) she'd actually met Keith Barrett in Ireland. On her very first dig, in fact, outside Galway, when she'd been new to everything and excited about what she was doing and terrified of getting it wrong. She'd stood in the empty field and thought about what might be lying under the soil and she'd told herself that she was as qualified an archaeologist as anyone else there even though, quite honestly, she'd just felt like a kid let out of school for the day despite the fact that lots of people on the dig were nearly as young as her.

She was wearing her hi-vis jacket and her pristine new boots (bright pink and trimmed with fake pink fur – her dad had bought them as a joke but she'd decided to wear them anyway, although two days later, after it had rained, they were the same muddy colour as everyone else's) and she was ready to get going on the site, which was close to a proposed new motorway and which was being excavated to see what historical significance it might have.

It wasn't a particularly big site or a particularly big project but she'd loved every minute of it, even the back-breaking actual digging of the damp Irish soil (very few people realised how physically demanding archaeology could be!). She'd been overcome with excitement when she'd found her first skeleton and identified it as a young woman – finding the pelvis early on had been fortunate; a woman's pelvis was, unsurprisingly, different from a man's – and she'd called Keith, the supervisor, to show him.

'Hey, cool. Well done.' This was Keith's second dig in Ireland; he enjoyed working in the country because his grandfather was Irish and because he liked the idea of being somewhere so small after the vast expanses of Australia.

Thanks to the rampant development all over the country there was plenty of archaeological work and there were lots of non-Irish people on the digs. Keith's main interest was in maritime archaeology, although – as Romy said to him one afternoon as torrential rain had again filled the ditches and the dig had turned into a mudbath – Ireland was doing its best to give him a genuine underwater experience.

He'd been great to work with but after the digging had been done and Romy had been assigned to do some post-excavation work, Keith had headed off to an underwater site in the Baltic Sea. Romy had been sorry to see him go because she'd got on well with him, but she hadn't been heartbroken. After all, he was just a friend. Besides, she'd had a boyfriend then, although like most of her relationships it was short-lived and they'd split up soon afterwards. Nevertheless she kept in touch with Keith because, as with so many of the friends she'd made on her first dig, she'd added him to her email list and every so often he sent her a message which wasn't copied to the hundreds on his list and she sent him ones that weren't copied to the hundreds on hers. There was nothing special about their emails to each other but she liked the fact that, among their gang of archaeological friends and students, they had a connection, a deeper friendship. She valued that because she didn't really have many close friends. She'd lost touch with most of the people she'd known growing up, except Colleen Rafferty, who'd studied archaeology too before she'd been forced to change her plans abruptly. Romy kept in touch with Colleen because Colleen knew more about her than anyone else in the world. But by now she was probably closer to Keith.

After finishing the post-ex work on the Galway site she'd volunteered to work on a site in Arizona for the experience of a very different sort of dig and then she'd gone to Lisbon, where she bumped into a lot of people who had worked on the Galway dig, including Keith. After that she'd spent a few months doing more post-ex work in Egypt, which had been fascinating, and in Eastern Europe, which had been completely different (more like Ireland, she'd thought, what with the medieval burials and Bronze Age artefacts, so different from the Egyptian treasures). Keith had popped up in Eastern Europe too, although only for a short while, and that time she'd been really sorry to see him go because for some reason that had been the loneliest dig for her. Eventually she'd come to Australia. Not because of Keith, although she knew that he'd returned home himself. But because there had been an opportunity to do some work on a more recent site, an unearthing of a previously unknown convict settlement outside Sydney. Romy liked the idea of urban archaeology and she also liked the idea of spending a few months in the southern hemisphere. So she'd emailed Keith, who was now working in a private maritime archaeology company, and told him to break out the barbie, she was on her way.

Romy had been stunned to see that he had cut his hair (in Ireland and in Romania he'd worn it in a thick ponytail, but now it was short and styled and made him look a million times more handsome) and that he'd changed his ancient Levis and bedraggled T-shirt look for designer jeans and snow-white tees. He still wore a small stud in his right ear but, she told him, he'd gone all grown-up. He laughed at that and said that he was doing a lot of liaison work with various government bodies and he liked to look professional. All the same when they went for drinks at a harbourside bar the night after she'd arrived, she was relieved to find that he was still the same, easy-going Keith. Even if he had started to take life a bit more seriously.

'I'm right.' She'd looked at him gloomily. 'You've turned into an adult.'

'Maybe a little bit,' he said as he reached out and ruffled her long dark hair, which he used to do on the site in Ireland and which always drove her nuts. 'You know what it's like usually – roaming around the place, never staying anywhere for more than a few months, living in terrible conditions . . . So I'm doing more research and consultancy stuff and less digging and diving and it's working out fine for me.'

'I like digging and I'm perfectly grown-up myself, thanks very much.'

He laughed. 'You know what I mean. There's only so many times I can dive a wreck. Only so many times you can dig a ditch. It's not like being Indiana Jones, after all.'

She grinned at him. 'Did you ever think it would be?'

'I guess.' He smiled. 'I guess everyone wants to be a hero.'

She snorted with laughter. 'That'll be the day!'

However, he did turn out to be her hero when the girl she was house-sharing with suddenly asked her to leave because she wanted her boyfriend to move in instead. Keith offered to let her stay with him and she'd jumped at the opportunity.

His house was small but cute and close to the beach, which was its biggest selling point. She moved in one Friday evening and by Sunday felt as though she'd been there for ever.

The rest of the gang – all involved in some way or another in archaeological or heritage work – accepted that they were sharing the house but not a bed, even though once or twice Marnie Jones had asked her whether anything had happened between them.

'Of course not!' Romy had looked at her in disgust. 'It would be like sleeping with my brother.' And then they'd both laughed because everyone had heard about Romy's brother or (more accurately, and although she didn't generally use the term) her half-brother, who, as far as she was concerned, was hell on earth.

Sometimes she wondered if she thought of Keith as the brother she'd never had. But if that was the case then Colleen would be the sister she'd never had and she didn't think of Colleen as a sister. The problem, Romy admitted to herself, was that she never knew exactly how she should feel about anyone. My emotional development, she told them all one day when they were sitting on Bondi Beach and chilling out, was stunted at birth. And they'd laughed and told her that she was fine emotionally except when she'd had too much beer.

But tonight . . . tonight she hadn't had too much beer (not even that much wine really) and she knew that mentally she was all over the place because she just had no idea how she was supposed to feel about leaving her best friend and going home, or how she was supposed to feel about seeing her family again. And she had no idea how they felt either, other than relief at the fact that they'd managed to get her to return at all, thus solving the problem of who would look after Veronica.

And it seemed totally unfair that just because the word 'family' was used, she was supposed to be (and, in fact, was) overwhelmed by guilt and feel obliged to leave everything she had here behind her simply to fulfil some ridiculous sense of duty to someone who probably didn't really want it anyway.

Every time she thought of that, she snorted under her breath. A sense of duty! To them! To Veronica! It was actually laughable. It really was.

And yet she couldn't get away from it. Even Keith had been definite about it. You had to help out when it was family. And when she'd told him that she didn't really get on terribly well with anyone in her family, he'd looked uncomprehendingly at her (after all, he had a great relationship with his parents) and said that it was up to her to get on with them and it was all a matter of attitude.

The way she looked at it, the best way to get on with her family was to keep some distance between them. It had worked for the last four years. But maybe she'd feel differently when she went home. The only trouble was, she couldn't quite believe it.

Going home had been the last thing on her mind when her mobile had rung a couple of days earlier. She'd been sitting at the computer entering details of the bones they'd found on the site (Romy specialised in forensic archaeology, which rather disgusted Veronica – the idea, her mother said, of digging up old bones and studying them was utterly revolting) when the phone had vibrated on her desk.

She'd let the call go to her message minder because she was too absorbed in what she was doing to talk to anyone. This was because the notes she'd been looking at had been about the skeleton of the young woman which she'd uncovered at the site. She'd seen the bones straight away and had gone over to look at them. And then she'd gently brushed the earth away and realised that she was looking at a young woman and – poignantly – a young woman who'd been pregnant at the time of her death, because there was also the skeleton of a foetus inside her.

Whenever she uncarthed bones, Romy always thought about the living person they had once been. And seeing the bones of a young woman in the convict colony had been surprising. Seeing that she was pregnant had been distressing. She knew that mostly she could put her emotions on hold when she looked at them, but she'd cried that day for the woman she'd never known and the child that had never been born and had told herself how lucky she was to have the life she had, even if she sometimes asked herself if she'd been altogether right in some of the decisions she'd made.

She was still wondering about the dead girl and her unborn baby when she went home that night. Keith was out at rugby practice and so she cracked open a beer and sat outside gazing into the tangle of garden behind the house where hot rose-berries fought for space alongside slender green bamboo grasses. And then she started wondering – as she always did when she was on her own for any length of time – about the people who had lived in this house before them and who'd lived on this land before the house had been built, and she wondered what it was about her that made her think of the past more often than the present.

And then she remembered her missed phone call.

She put the bottle of beer on the deck and retrieved her phone from her bag. Then she dialled her voicemail and listened to the message which had been left for her.

'It's me.' She recognised the voice of her brother (half-brother, she reminded herself, the pompous half!) Darragh. 'Listen, we need you to stop faffing around the place and get back home for a while. Mum's going into hospital soon for surgery on her back. You know – or maybe you don't, because you're not exactly good at keeping in touch, are you – that she's been in pain for a while and that it's been getting worse. Well, they want to operate on her. She's going to need help. Ring me.'

She'd replayed the message a few times. No how are you? from Darragh. No questions about her job or her life or anything about her. It was a command to come home. So damn typical of him, of course. Thinking that he was in charge of everything. Thinking he was in charge of her! She felt tendrils of anger wrap themselves around her. He'd always had the power to make her angry. They all did really. Darragh. Kathryn. And, of course, Veronica herself.

She wondered whether she should have picked up a hint from Veronica about the state of her back, but thinking hard about it, she didn't think her mother had made a big deal about it. She'd moaned about a bit of backache in her emails and on the very rare occasions on which they'd spoken to each other, but then Veronica's normal conversations with her were always one long moan. It usually began with the hypochondriacal whinge about her migraine headaches or an unspecified virus or some kind of ache or pain. (Whatever it was, it was forgotten the next time they talked.) Then Veronica would move on to her more general moan, which usually included Romy herself – the sulkiest girl on the planet; and her father – if he'd given Veronica half the attention he was giving his new wife, maybe they'd never have got divorced; and being on her own – nobody really cared, did they, that she was in that big house all by herself?

Romy usually managed to stop herself saying that Veronica was the healthiest woman she'd ever known; that she was never on her own and that she had hundreds of friends and a brilliant social life, because she knew that saying so would only cause a row and she didn't want to row with her mother any more. She liked to think that she'd grown out of rowing with Veronica, that she was mature enough to put their differences behind her (even if she was perfectly right in thinking that all those differences were Veronica's fault!). Anyhow, rowing was futile; all that happened was that guilts and grievances got revisited all over again and opened up old wounds, and what was the point in that? It was easier to just stay away and keep the conversations brief. So when Veronica started moaning at her she'd simply say that if she was in pain she should take ibuprofen and if the house was too big for her she should sell it and buy an apartment. Veronica would then call her heartless because, she'd say, her whole life was in that house and Romy knew it. Whatever else, she couldn't sell it.

A whole kaleidoscope of memories and emotions flooded through Romy's head as she contemplated Darragh's message. She couldn't ignore it but she had to build up her mental reserves to return it. And so eventually she dialled his number even though it was early morning in Ireland and an awkward time to call. But she was sure that he'd be up and about already. Darragh was a businessman. He described himself as an entrepreneur, although Romy didn't think it was a totally accurate description. After all, she reasoned, entrepreneurs were supposed to be the kind of people who set up businesses and took risks. Darragh had inherited his business and she didn't think he'd ever taken a risk in his life. Nevertheless he saw himself as the second-generation entrepreneurial Dolan.

'What's this about Mum?' she asked when he answered the phone. 'And why do I have to come home?'

'You took your sweet time about getting back to me.' His irritation was clear, even over the miles. 'I was beginning to think you were ignoring me.'

'I was working,' she told him. 'I couldn't answer the phone straight away.'

She certainly wasn't going to tell him that she hadn't been bothered about answering it. Darragh wouldn't understand that. He was always on the phone himself, talking to clients, to employees, to suppliers . . . He was incapable of letting a phone ring for more than two seconds without answering it.

'Up to your armpits in muck?' he asked.

'Sort of.'

'You're nuts.' He said it in a matter-of-fact way. 'You'll never make your fortune at that lark.'

'I'm not in it for the money,' she said. 'Look, I'm really busy at the moment and I don't—'

'I thought you said you had a three-month contract?'

'Yes, but—'

'And it's up now, isn't it?'

'Almost, but—'

'Which makes it perfect timing,' said Darragh. 'You can't hide away from your responsibilities for ever, you know. Mum needs you.'

'She doesn't need me,' objected Romy. 'Mum never needs anyone, and if she did I'm probably the last person she'd choose.'

'Romy, you're going to have to take that chip off your shoulder at some point.' Darragh sounded impatient. 'She needs someone and that someone has to be you.'

'Why, exactly?'

'Like I said, she's having surgery on her back. Something to do with her discs; I'm not entirely sure, to be honest. You know how I hate that sort of stuff and so does she, so she's fairly typically vague about it. All the same, it's the only option for her. The last couple of months she's been finding it more and more difficult to get around.'

'Oh come on!' Romy couldn't get to grips with the idea of Veronica having difficulty in getting around anywhere. If anything, keeping her in one spot was more of an issue. (Perhaps, she thought in sudden amusement, that was something they had in common. She wasn't good at being in one place either.) 'You can't tell me that Mum is laid up at home! I can't see her sitting there with her feet up while her friends go socialising without her. And if she has a bad back it's probably from dirty dancing somewhere!'

'Don't be so facetious. Dr Jacobs laid it on the line for her. Surgery or a wheelchair.'

'You're not serious!' Romy couldn't help being shocked. The image of her mother in a wheelchair was an impossible one. She felt a stab of guilt at having been so dismissive.

'Hopefully it's avoidable,' said Darragh. 'Apparently it's a fairly straightforward procedure but she's going to be in a lot of pain for a while as well as needing someone to help her around the house because she'll be pretty limited in what she can do afterwards. She'll need someone with her until she recovers.'

'How long will that take?'

'A minimum of a month. But realistically, given what she's having done, it could be more.'

Romy shook her head even though she knew he couldn't see her. 'Look, I'm sorry this has happened. Hopefully she'll get over it quickly. But Darragh, I can't come home for that long. She wouldn't want me anyhow. You know she wouldn't. I'm sure she'd think I'd only make things worse. And the fact is that I have the opportunity to work in Melbourne as a supervisor on another dig when we're finished here. It would mean a hell of a lot to me because it's a promotion and it's about time I got the recognition. Besides, I can't afford to give up work, I haven't exactly got the Dolan bank balance, you know.'

'You won't spend money living with Veronica,' said Darragh dismissively. 'But I'm sure we can organise an allowance. And as far as your job is concerned, isn't everything you do contracted and short-term? I'm sure you'll have no problem getting back into the swing of your mud-digging again.'

She ignored the slight to her career. 'This is my chance to get on,' she told him. 'It's important to me. Like I said, it's a promotion.'

'And promotion is more important than your mother's health?'

Romy sighed. Of course it wasn't, but as far as she was concerned Veronica, as well as Darragh and Kathryn, weren't part of her life any more. She didn't see why he needed to drag her back across the world when there were other people nearby to look after their mother.

'Why can't Giselle help out?' she asked. 'She and Mum are best buddies, aren't they?'

'For heaven's sake! Giselle and I have enough to be doing. Mimi is three, in case you'd forgotten. She's a handful in her own right.'

'Yeah, but Mum loves her and—'

'And Giselle's pregnant again,' interrupted Darragh. 'So she can't spend that much time at Mum's. I'm at work. It has to be you.'

'Well, how about Kathryn?'

'Now you *are* joking!' Darragh snorted. 'She really *does* have a career! And a husband! You can't possibly expect her to come home indefinitely and leave both of them, can you?'

Romy had always known that asking Kathryn, six years Darragh's junior and five years older than her, would be a waste of time. Kathryn should have been the real entrepreneur in the family. These days she lived and worked in the States and had too many ties there to allow her to come home. Romy was vague about the exact nature of Kathryn's current job, which had something to do with financial fraud but which brought in a telephone-number salary, thus making her – at least in Darragh's eyes – immeasurably more successful than Romy would ever be. Darragh judged everyone on how much money they earned which was why Romy was so low down in the pecking order and why she was the obvious choice to abandon everything and come home to look after Veronica (even if Veronica wouldn't be exactly thrilled by the prospect). Nevertheless, Kathryn would still have been a much better choice than her for the task, Romy knew. Kathryn, cool and unflappable, could cope with Veronica. Romy, passionate and quick-tempered (and with the chip on her shoulder that Darragh knew was there although he didn't know what had caused it), just couldn't.

'What's wrong with home help?' she asked desperately.

There was a silence at the end of the line and she winced.

'Do you really want me to tell our mother that you suggested paying for help?' demanded Darragh. 'When she expected that you'd be coming home anyway? You did say, didn't you, that you'd be back after Australia?'

'I said that I'd be back in Europe. I was thinking of Lisbon again. But as I explained to you, I've been asked to stay here and I have commitments and . . . and a boyfriend.' She crossed her fingers because, of course, Keith wasn't a boyfriend but hell, she was thousands of miles away and Darragh couldn't see her blush.

'A boyfriend!' He snorted. 'You won't come home because of a boyfriend?'

'Would you leave Giselle?' she demanded.

'Giselle is my wife. It's totally different and you know that. You haven't been home in over a year and now, when we need you, you're too bloody selfish to come and you're using some beach bum as an excuse.'

'It's not that!' cried Romy.

'What then?'

She couldn't give him an answer to that, of course. There were a million reasons why she didn't want to go home and none of them were simply that she didn't care. But if she looked at it objectively she could see why he thought she was being selfish. And Veronica was her mother after all, wasn't she? No matter how crap she'd been at that.

'It's not that I don't want to help out,' she said as reasonably as she could. 'But it seems crazy to come home just for a few weeks . . .'

'We don't know how long it will be yet. Mum will need constant care after the operation.'

'Oh, you know Mum,' said Romy lightly. 'I bet she'll be up and about and going to her salsa class in no time.'

'For crying out loud, Romy, this is a serious operation. And she's not as young as she used to be. It'll take her some time to recover. I'm sure she won't want to have you fluttering around for any longer than necessary either, but she'll need someone. You're *so* self-centred it's hard to believe sometimes.'

'I'm not!' Romy cried. 'And you know what Mum's like about her age. She might be in her sixties but absolutely nobody would guess that she was over forty! She'd freak out if she thought you were telling me that I have to come home because she's old.'

'That's not what I said,' Darragh told her impatiently. 'Now are you going to behave in a reasonable manner or are you just going to be incredibly selfish about it as usual?'

Romy bit back the retort that was on the tip of her tongue. She was fed up with Darragh assuming that she was selfish.

'Of course I'll come if it's totally necessary,' she said. 'If there really is no other choice. And if Veronica herself is OK about it. Because, Darragh, she might not want me in the house.'

'Oh, don't be utterly ridiculous,' said Darragh. 'I know you and her spark off each other something shocking, but blood is thicker than water when it comes down to it and she'd rather have you than anyone else.'

'Are you sure about that?' asked Romy. 'I mean, have you actually spoken to her?'

'Yes,' said Darragh.

'Oh.' Romy was surprised.

'And so you can take time out from drifting around grubby sites and spend some quality time with your family. It might even do you good.'

'Great, thanks,' she said. 'I'm so glad you still think of me as the loser among you all.'

'It's obviously in the genes,' said Darragh. 'Me and Kathryn take after our father. You take after yours.'

Romy could feel herself clench and unclench her fist. She was tempted to hang up now and let Darragh think what he liked. How dare he imply that Dermot was any less worthy than Tom just because Dermot's driving force hadn't been making money, like Tom's had.

'Oh look, I'm sorry.' It was Darragh who broke the silence and his apology surprised Romy. 'That wasn't fair.'

'No,' she said shakily. 'It wasn't.'

His voice took on a persuasive tone. 'Look, Ro, it probably won't be for that long. A couple of months at the most. Then you can return to the outback and Giselle and I will keep an eye on Mum. To be honest with you, if it wasn't for the fact that me and Kathryn have responsibilities of our own, I wouldn't have asked you.'

'It's not . . .' She swallowed. 'You're right. I'm the young, free and single one in the family. I'm the one who should look after her until she's back on her feet. But it just seems so weird that I'm being told to give up everything and come back. I have this opportunity here . . . I was hoping . . .' She swallowed again. 'I guess there'll be others.'

'Sure there will,' said Darragh dismissively.

There was an awkward silence which Romy couldn't sustain.

'I suppose . . . congratulations on the baby,' she said eventually.

'Obviously if it wasn't for being pregnant Giselle would have been only too happy to look after Mum,' said Darragh. 'I can't believe you didn't know she was expecting. I'm sure Mum must have mentioned it to you.'

'Possibly,' admitted Romy.

'You're hopeless, you know that, don't you?'

'I've agreed to help,' she said. 'Don't start getting at me again.'

'OK, OK. When are you coming home?'

'When does she go into hospital?'

'Two weeks.'

'Before that, I guess.'

'Great. Let me know your flight details.'

'Sure.'

They disconnected and she stayed sitting in the chair staring into the garden. She was still sitting there when Keith eventually came home from his rugby practice and asked her why she was all alone in the dark.

Chapter 2

Until the moment she stepped on board the Qantas flight to London she didn't truly believe she was going. Keith had come to the airport with her and she'd waited until the last possible second before walking through to the departure lounge. He'd hugged her tightly and told her to come back soon and she'd suddenly wanted to cry. She gulped hard because she didn't want him to see her cry – it would be going too far to dissolve into tears in front of him. But then she cried anyway and he looked at her in astonishment as she scrubbed at her eyes with the back of her hand.

'What's the matter?' he asked.

She shook her head. 'I don't know. I . . . it just seems so far away all of a sudden.'

'C'mon, Ro. It's not far at all. We'll be in touch anyway. We always are.'

'I know,' she said. 'I guess it's a while since I've seen them and I'm anxious about it.'

He did his hair-ruffling thing to her again. 'No worries,' he said. 'They're your family. It'll be fine.'

'I'm sure it will.' She tried to keep the doubt out of her voice.

'Skype me when you get there,' he told her. 'I'll probably be online.'

She sniffed and nodded and he smiled reassuringly at her. She smiled back and then, without even thinking about it, she kissed him on the mouth. It was quite unlike any kiss she'd ever given him before. They'd occasionally pecked each other on the cheek in a totally asexual way but this kiss certainly wasn't that. And she didn't know why on earth she'd done it except that perhaps she was trying to convince herself that she did have ties in Australia, she did have a boyfriend even if he was Keith and not really a boyfriend at all.

You bloody eejit, she thought, even as her lips registered the softness of his and even as she tugged him closer to her. What in God's name d'you think you're doing?

And then he kissed her back. At least he did at first but almost immediately she felt him pull away from her and unwind her arms from him.

'You'd probably better go,' he said awkwardly.

'I . . . know. I'm sorry, Keith, I . . .'

'Hey, no worries, it's cool.' He moved even further away from her.

'Yes, but . . .'

'You're upset. I understand that. It's fine.'

'Keith, I . . .' But she didn't know what to say to him. That she loved him and that he meant the world to her? She didn't. He didn't. He was her best friend, after all. Only of course you didn't go around kissing your best friend on the lips. And he was still looking at her in surprise, not suddenly confessing that he was crazy about her and that he didn't want her to go . . . She felt herself blush furiously. What on earth had come over her – behaving like a girl instead of a mate!

'You'd better go.' He gave her a gentle push in the direction of the gate.

'Yes, of course.'

'I'll – well, look, have a good flight.'

'Sure.'

'And, um, yeah – I'll miss you.'

She looked at him, trying to see if there was more to it than that but she couldn't tell. I've messed it all up, she thought miserably. He's my friend and I've kissed him and I can't believe I was so bloody stupid because it *is* like *When Harry Met Sally* after all only it's not going to work out that way.

'I'll miss you too.' She spoke brightly and cheerfully. 'But I'll call you and . . . hey, I'll be back soon and – look, sorry, I didn't mean to . . . you know. It was just . . .'

'It's OK.' He spoke definitely. 'Absolutely. You're heading home and your mum isn't well and you're a bit concerned and you needed a comfort kiss. So no worries about that.'

She smiled with relief. A comfort kiss. That was all it was. Perfect. Thank God he'd realised it.

'Have a good flight,' he said again.

She nodded and walked towards the departure gates. Then she turned and waved at him. He waved back and walked away. And she was on her own again.

The plane wasn't full, which cheered her up because it meant that she had a whole row to herself, and after their stopover in Bangkok she stretched out and tried to sleep. But she'd never been very good at sleeping on planes no matter how long the flight and her head was still too crowded by thoughts of Darragh and Veronica and Kathryn to allow her to drift into oblivion.

Darragh is such a shit, really, she thought; demanding that I come home and then making that crack about Dad which was mean and nasty. And apologising doesn't change the fact that he thinks that way. As though being Tom's son is so bloody brilliant! As if he'd have got anywhere if he hadn't been the one to inherit the business. Romy knew that Kathryn totally resented the fact that her brother was running the family company even though it provided her with an extra income too. Romy didn't know how much it was worth to Darragh and Kathryn but it didn't really matter because it had nothing

25

to do with her. She wasn't the one with the father who'd set his children up for life. Her dad was an entirely different sort of person. She loved her dad.

Romy sighed and pulled the light blanket around her shoulders. It shouldn't matter who was Darragh and Kathryn's father and who was hers. They'd lived together for a long time, just as though they were all part of the same family with the same parents, exactly like loads of other families in similar situations. Romy didn't know why it was that it seemed to matter to Darragh so much that there was a difference between them. But it did, and he'd insisted on pointing it out at regular intervals throughout her childhood and telling her that she wasn't as good as him or Kathryn because of it. Yet it hadn't actually been Darragh who'd first told her that she wasn't a full sister. It was Kathryn who'd dropped that particular bombshell into her life. It had been in an argument over a doll. Romy, aged four at the time, had taken it from Kathryn's bedroom. Kathryn had more or less grown out of dolls by then (she'd never been particularly fond of them anyway), but she'd been furious to see Romy playing with golden-haired Annabelle in the back garden. And she'd stormed out and told her to give her back, that Annabelle was hers.

'She's mine too,' Romy had protested. 'You never play with her any more. She's lonely.'

Kathryn made a grab for the doll. Romy held firm. Then Annabelle's arm twisted out of its socket so that Kathryn was left holding the arm while Romy clutched Annabelle's torso. Kathryn went crazy. She slapped Romy and pulled her hair and it was Dermot, who'd been sitting in the conservatory at the back of the house and who couldn't help hearing the commotion, who'd come to break up the fight.

'You can't tell me what to do,' Kathryn had shouted at him as he demanded that she let go of Romy's hair. 'This doll was a present from my dad. My real dad. You're just a blow-in.

And so's she!' At which she'd given Romy another shove which had left her sprawling in the flowerbed.

Dermot put his arms around a sobbing Romy and explained to her that while everyone was Veronica's child, Darragh and Kathryn had a different dad. Tom, he told her, was in heaven and she had to make allowances for the fact that sometimes Kathryn and Darragh missed him.

'Along with Titch?' They'd buried the pet goldfish the previous week.

'Exactly,' Dermot said.

'I hope he remembers to feed him,' said Romy.

Snuggled under the airline blanket, she smiled at her innocence. At the time she hadn't given the subject of different fathers another thought. As far as she was concerned it wasn't important although she suddenly realised that her name was Romy Kilkenny whereas Darragh and Kathryn were Dolans. That simply hadn't occured to her before. Veronica called herself Kilkenny too and so Romy couldn't help feeling that being a Kilkenny was better than being a Dolan, no matter what Darragh and Kathryn might think.

It was only as she got older that she realised that it was important and that it did matter. She hadn't known that Darragh hadn't been at all happy when Veronica made the decision to marry Dermot. At the time it was simply his opposition to anyone new taking the place of his dad. Darragh had felt, after Tom's death, that he was the man of the house and that he was in charge of things. (Veronica had said as much to him the day of the funeral and Darragh had never forgotten.) Dermot's arrival changed all that. Also – although Romy had been totally unaware of it at the time – there had been some opposition in Veronica's family and a certain amount of amusement among her friends that she was marrying a man six years younger than herself. As far as Romy was concerned, Veronica and Dermot were her parents and they were grown-ups and it didn't matter how old they were.

But every so often, at the infrequent family gatherings, she'd overhear a snippet of conversation about Veronica's baby-snatching of the stud-muffin photo-journalist. And an occasional remark about the unlikeliness of the pairing. She hadn't exactly understood it at the time, but she'd known it wasn't good.

She'd tried to talk to Kathryn but, of course, by then Kathryn was a teenager and not interested in having conversations with her younger half-sister. She was dismissive, saying that she didn't really care who belonged to who and that Dermot was the only father she'd ever known because she'd been a baby when Tom had died. But, she'd said, it came down to blood too and the fact was that Dermot wasn't actually related to her at all.

'But you call him Dad,' Romy had pointed out and Kathryn said, yes, of course she did. He treated her just like a daughter and it made sense to call him Dad. But, she added, she'd probably just call him Dermot when she was a bit older because the point was that he wasn't her dad after all.

Romy had agreed with her; yet later she couldn't help wondering whether there would always be a feeling of my dad versus your dad and a certain division between them no matter how close they were supposed to be. And she wondered whether her relationship with her mother would always be different too because of the fact that Veronica and Dermot were very different as a couple from the perfect pair that Tom and Veronica appeared to have been.

Over the years the divisions became even clearer as the business set up by Tom Dolan grew more and more successful. He had been the sole owner of it and he'd left it to Veronica, Darragh and Kathryn. Veronica owned half outright. The other half had been held in trust for Darragh and Kathryn until they were both twenty-one. Veronica certainly hadn't realised when she'd married Tom that he had started up something that would mean that years later she didn't actually have to worry about money. She herself had no special interest in the business but she was a shrewd woman and she made sure that the manufacturing firm was well run by other people. She employed an excellent managing director and insisted that the staff were looked after and that they received an annual bonus every Christmas. In fact she provided for a Christmas party every year at which she personally thanked everyone for their hard work over the previous twelve months, something which made her hugely popular among staff and management alike.

Romy remembered Veronica getting dressed up for the party, looking young and glamorous with her impossibly curly blond hair and artful make-up, wearing the latest fashions and a selection of her expensive jewellery. She remembered being enveloped in Veronica's scent when her mother kissed her as she was leaving. And she remembered Veronica saying that if they looked after the company, the company would look after them.

Only the company didn't look after Romy. It took care of Darragh and Kathryn. The rightful heirs. And no matter how often Romy told herself that it didn't matter, that she didn't care about the money and that Veronica loved them all equally, she still couldn't help feeling that one day maybe it would and that as far as her mother was concerned there was a difference after all.

She sat up in the darkened plane and opened the bottle of water in the seat pocket in front of her. She glugged some back and then decided to go for a stroll around the cabin to stretch her legs. Most people were asleep now, with only the occasional passenger watching a movie on the video screen in front of them. A mother and father, at either end of a row of four seats, were talking quietly to each other over the heads of their two children, both sleeping. First marriage? wondered Romy. Second? Married at all? Who knew these days. It didn't much matter any more, did it? Marrying Dermot had been a conventional thing for Veronica to do, even after finding herself to be a wealthy widow. Although that, Romy conceded, was relative. The real money didn't start coming in from the company until a good deal later. She sometimes wondered if that wasn't what had caused things to go wrong for Dermot and Veronica in the end and not the fact that they were actually two very different types of people. Not even the fact that they disagreed on so many things (though why, she often asked herself, why did they get married if that was the case?). Still, the money was a major factor no matter how much Dermot might have liked to pretend otherwise.

She returned to her seat but didn't stretch out this time. She leaned against the headrest and gazed unseeingly in front of her.

She'd known things weren't right for a while. She'd heard Veronica complaining to Dermot one night that she'd married him for love and companionship and to have somebody in her life, only he wasn't in her life, was he? He was hardly ever there. Veronica had been right about that, and that was what worried Romy as she strained to listen to her father's response. He'd said something about having to work and Veronica had made some fairly waspish comment about it not being work but an adrenalin rush. Romy hadn't understood what she meant by that but afterwards she'd looked it up in the dictionary and had to agree with her mother.

Dermot was an adrenalin junkie. Even Romy, who allowed her father the benefit of the doubt in everything, couldn't deny that. The reason that he had spent so little time at home was that he was covering the Gulf War and had been posted to Kuwait. Veronica would watch the TV in the evenings, her face taut and her lips narrowed, and she'd gasp every time they showed the devastating effect of a bomb or zoomed in on a dead body lying on the road.

Darragh occasionally commented that Dermot clearly had suicidal tendencies but Romy could hear a certain admiration in his voice when he said it which made her feel good about her dad. Kathryn would always walk out of the room when the news was on, saying that she couldn't bear to see man's inhumanity to man. And Veronica would say that Dermot was very brave but very stupid and that it was a pity he didn't have a brain for business in the same way as he had a brain for photo-journalism because then he could have worked in Tom's company and they would have been set up for ever.

Getting Dermot to work in Tom's company had been a mission of Veronica's for a long time, Romy knew. There had been other snatches of overheard conversation when Veronica had said things like 'advertising campaigns' and 'interesting photo-shoots' and Dermot had replied that you couldn't have an ad campaign for industrial components and would she ever cop herself on. There had been talk of his duty to her and the children and he'd said that he was doing his duty, earning a living, looking after them. She'd said that the money wasn't important, that there was always the company, and Romy remembered Dermot saying 'that fucking company' in a disgusted tone of voice. She'd been horrified at that. Veronica kept a swear box in the kitchen and nobody was allowed to use the f-word in the house.

And then there'd been a real row, a stand-up, shouting and screaming row which Romy had almost walked in on and which had left her ashen-faced and shaking.

'It's a good job,' Veronica had been saying, 'and you'd be crazy to turn it down.'

'I'd be crazy to take it!' Dermot's voice was firm.

'You'll get killed in the Gulf!' cried Veronica. 'Don't you give a shit about that?'

'I won't get killed.'

'Yeah, easy to say. I'm sure all you so-called macho guys think the same. But you could get killed and you'll leave me a widow for the second time and this time with an extra child, your child, to worry about. That's not what I want.'

'I helped you out once when you needed it but I'm not going to work in the company and that's final,' Dermot told her. 'The war won't last for ever.'

'And so you get through this one unscathed? What then? The Balkans? Africa? Some other trouble hotspot.'

'It's important work,' Dermot said.

'Oh, rubbish!' she yelled. 'It's just you getting a fix. Like bungee jumping.'

'Are you equating my work to bungee jumping?' Dermot's voice was dangerously chilled and Romy, who had stayed just outside the living room door where she could hear without being seen, shivered.

'Look, I married you because I wanted a stable family life,' said Veronica. 'I can't stand worrying about you every second of the day.'

'I thought you married me because you loved me,' responded Dermot.

'I did. I do!' she cried. 'But there's more to it than just love. There's responsibility.'

'Oh, and you take that so seriously?' He laughed. 'The Merry Widow is a responsible adult?'

'What's that supposed to mean?' This time it was Veronica who sounded chilly.

'C'mon,' he retorted. 'I'm married to a female Peter Pan. You seem to think you're a feckin' teenager still, what with the nights out with the girls and the clubbing and the skinny clothes from Topshop. Ever think of acting your age for a change?'

Romy could have told him that he'd made a big mistake by bringing Veronica's clothes and her age into it. She knew that her mother hated the idea of being over thirty and loved wearing up-to-the-minute fashions. Besides, she had a fantastic body and they looked good on her and nobody ever, ever thought she looked her age.

'What the hell d'you mean by that?' Veronica demanded.

'Just that you could be a bit more . . . appropriate.' Too late, Dermot knew that he'd said the wrong thing.

'I beg your pardon?'

Dermot was in the hole now but he still kept digging. 'It's not that you don't look great because you do but, well, you're not that young any more, are you? You've three kids, for God's sake! And those short T-shirts and skirts . . . they're more like something Romy or Kathryn should be wearing, surely?'

'So I can't get dressed up for a night out but you see yourself as some James Bond character,' Veronica had responded, her voice taut with anger. 'Out there in the danger zone, saving the world through pictures, some kind of heroic sex symbol? Get real.'

Romy hadn't waited around to hear the rest of the argument. She'd gone up to her bedroom and huddled, arms twined around her body, in the alcove beside the chimney breast. She knew that things would never be the same again.

And she was right. Dermot had gone off to Kuwait, where he'd been hit by shrapnel though not badly hurt, and a year later he and Veronica separated. Which was the beginning of another trauma as far as Romy was concerned.

They argued over custody of her.

Veronica had laughed at Dermot and said that if he thought he had a chance in hell of getting Romy he was more deluded than he thought. The courts, she snapped, wouldn't dream of allowing a man with a job like his to take responsibility for a little girl. And how, she demanded, did he intend to look after her when he was flitting around the globe?

'The Gulf War is over,' Dermot told her. 'I can stay home.'

'You'd do it for her but you wouldn't do it for me?' Veronica was furious. 'You are a selfish bastard, Dermot Kilkenny.'

Romy knew, because she'd seen programmes on the TV and read articles in *Sugar*, that the children were never to blame when parents got divorced. She also knew that both of them were still supposed to love her. And that was why they were fighting over her. But she couldn't see that Veronica and Dermot fighting was a good thing at all. And when either one of them would ask her what she wanted all she could say over and over again was that she wanted everyone to be together.

'That's not possible,' Kathryn told her one evening. 'You're twelve years old, Romy. You've got to grow up and face facts.'

Romy felt as though she'd been facing facts ever since the encounter with Kathryn over Annabelle. She was always surprised at how cool and analytical her half-sister could be, at how easily she was able to detach her feelings from everything that went on around her.

'There's no point in Mum and your dad staying together if it's making them miserable,' Kathryn pointed out to her. 'All that happens is that there are more and more rows.'

'But they're having rows over me,' said Romy. 'I hate it.'

'Then pick one of them and say you want to live with that person,' Kathryn told her. 'You should pick your dad. You're more like your dad than like Mum. Besides, Mum probably only wants you because Dermot does. It's not like she really cares.'

Romy had agreed with that. She'd never felt that Veronica loved her as much as Darragh and Kathryn even though Veronica insisted that she did. (She had to insist it at regular intervals because Darragh would sometimes call her the half-breed, and although it was supposed to be a joke Romy didn't really think it was. Whenever he said it Veronica was forced to remonstrate with him and defend her.) The thing was, Romy could understand Veronica not loving her as much. They were two completely different people. Romy wasn't tall and willowy like Veronica, nor did she have her mother's interest in clothes and fashion. She was a tomboy who preferred climbing trees to buying clothes and whose chunky build looked better in jeans than in dresses. Veronica simply didn't understand her.

Anyway, part of her did want to pick Dermot. She adored him. He was fun and adventurous and he didn't care if her

34

shoes were scuffed or she wore the same skanky jeans for the entire week. Veronica was forever trying to interest her in high heels and make-up no matter how often Romy told her that she didn't care.

Left to herself she would never have been able to make the choice. She might have wanted to live with Dermot but Veronica was her mother and it seemed wrong to walk out on her mother. And she knew that whatever decision she made it would be the wrong one.

Thankfully, in the end she didn't get the opportunity. Veronica and Dermot worked it out with their solicitors. She would spend weekdays with Veronica and weekends with Dermot. She would spend every second school holiday with Dermot and half of the summer holiday too. It was, she remembered Veronica telling her, the most sensible solution.

For them, maybe, but not necessarily for her. Being out of the house at weekends made her feel even more cut off from Darragh and Kathryn. Not that Darragh's opinions mattered much because at twenty-three he'd just started working in the family firm and he didn't take much notice of Romy any more. And as for Kathryn – well, Romy knew that she'd never have the kind of cosy relationship with her that she'd thought all sisters had. Kathryn was just too damn remote for that.

But shuttling between the two houses – Veronica in Rathfarnham and Dermot in Glasnevin on the other side of the city – reinforced the distance she'd always felt existed between them as well as totally messing up her time with her school friends. She didn't get to go to the birthday parties or other weekend events with them so she missed out on the camaraderie on Monday mornings in school when everyone talked about it. And she didn't have any friends in Glasnevin where Dermot lived on the top floor of a newly built apartment block which was populated generally by single people and childless couples.

She knew that she was closer to her dad than to her mother.

Dermot was hers and was special whereas Veronica was shared between them all, but she didn't like being in the apartment much. And so she was always horribly confused on Friday afternoons, wanting to see him but not wanting to leave her friends, knowing that he wanted her to be with him and she wanted to be with him too, but still feeling unexpectedly bad about leaving Veronica, who always looked so sad when she left.

Colleen Rafferty told her that it was more glamorous to be staying with Dermot in Glasnevin than hanging around Rathfarnham. Didn't Dermot bring her loads of places and didn't Romy get to see the latest movie releases as soon as they hit the screens? Didn't Dermot give her everything she wanted?

'Yes,' she said mournfully. 'But it's not the same.'

'Would you prefer if you never got to see him, like with Becky Murphy?'

Becky's parents had split up far more acrimoniously than Veronica and Dermot and Becky's mother was refusing her father access to the children, which had left Becky confused and disconsolate.

'Why are they so hopeless?' Romy demanded. 'They're grown-ups. They should know how to do things. They shouldn't fight and shout and hate each other. But if they have to have a row . . . if they have to get it all wrong . . . then they should have a better way of dealing with it.' She swallowed hard. 'Right now, Col, I hate them both. When I grow up I'm not going to bother with either of them at all. And I'm never, ever going to fall in love or get married. It's just not worth it.'

'I know how you feel.' Colleen grinned and hugged her friend sympathetically. 'Wait till I tell you what my stupid mother just did . . .'

The seatbelt sign lit up. Romy clipped hers closed as the plane was buffeted by some strong air currents. She slid the headphones over her ears and flicked through the video options. She was too wide awake to sleep now and she was fed up thinking about her parents. A blood-and-guts thriller would be far more relaxing.

Chapter 3

Romy was exhausted by the time her connecting flight landed in Dublin. As soon as she disembarked from the plane she headed for the Ladies' where she spent fifteen minutes freshening up. She cleaned her teeth and changed into a faded blue T-shirt before brushing out her dark hair and pulling it into a single shoulder-length plait secured by a tiny jet-black ribbon. Then she bathed her eyes in Optrex before spraying herself with the Calvin Klein perfume she'd bought on board the plane. She felt ready for (almost) anything as she collected her luggage and stepped out into the arrivals hall.

It was very busy and she looked around her uncertainly. She'd given Darragh her flight details but he hadn't said anything about collecting her and she somehow didn't think he'd be all that interested in taking time off to come to the airport. And although Veronica had sounded relieved (if somewhat wary) at her agreement to come back, she thought it was unlikely that her mother would show up, especially if she wasn't able to get around very well. Naturally she'd told Dermot that she was coming home and at least he'd been thrilled to hear from her. He would have picked her up and dropped her over to Veronica's (and run the gauntlet, he'd chuckled) but unfortunately he'd be in Kerry when she arrived.

'Interesting job?' she asked and he'd laughed and said no, just an ordinary old commission and that he'd be back in Dublin by the end of the week and couldn't wait to see her.

She was looking forward to seeing him too, although they'd met up seven months previously when she'd gone back to Arizona and he'd come to visit her.

She scanned the crowds again and finally saw the woman at the barrier. Romy didn't know how she'd missed her the first time. She was tall and beautiful with almost straight Nordic-blond hair which fell to her shoulders in a smooth sheet. Her eyes were a vibrant blue in a flawlessly made-up face. Her lips, full and pouting, were glossed in a soft pink. She was wearing a pair of loose-fitting white three-quarter-length trousers over Ugg boots and a pink gilet over a pristine white T-shirt. A white Louis Vuitton handbag was slung over her shoulder. She was holding a small girl by the hand. The girl was wearing a white broderie anglaise dress, pale blue shoes and a pale blue ribbon in blonde hair that matched her mother's.

'Giselle.' Romy walked over towards her. 'Thanks for coming to meet me.'

Darragh's wife leaned towards her and air-kissed her cheek. 'Welcome home,' she said in her soft, feathery voice. 'You look . . .'

'Tired,' Romy supplied as Giselle hesitated for a moment.

'I was going to say well,' said Giselle, though she didn't sound entirely convinced. 'You look well. The tan suits you.' She ran her fingers through her blond hair in an unnecessary tidying movement.

'Scruffy,' said the little girl beside Giselle. 'You said to look for someone scruffy.'

'Mimi!' Giselle looked down at her and made an admonishing face. Then she turned to Romy and shrugged. 'I'm sorry. You know what they're like. And she's so precocious. I think she already has the vocabulary of a six year old.'

Romy said nothing but smiled at the little girl. 'And how are you?' she asked. 'The last time I saw you, you were a baby.'

'Not a baby now.' But quite suddenly Mimi hid behind her mother.

'And, um, Giselle – congratulations.' Romy spoke doubtfully because she was finding it hard to believe that the woman in front of her was actually pregnant. The trousers were loose, but even so Giselle didn't seem to have the slightest of bumps.

'It's not been too bad so far,' said Giselle.

'You look great.' Romy knew that there was a touch of envy in her voice. Giselle always looked great. But to look so fantastic halfway through her pregnancy – Darragh had told her that the baby was due at the end of the summer – didn't seem at all fair.

'Come on,' said Giselle, blinking a couple of times so that Romy could see the full extent of her wonderfully long dark eyelashes. 'Let's get a move on. The traffic is, of course, utterly appalling.'

'I do appreciate you coming,' said Romy as she hiked her rucksack on to her back and followed Giselle to the car park. 'I wasn't sure that anyone would.'

'Oh, well, Darragh couldn't leave you to get across town on your own after such a long flight,' Giselle told her.

'Maybe he was afraid I'd skip off again,' said Romy as she got into the 4x4.

'You wouldn't,' said Giselle. 'Not after coming back. And you can't. Veronica needs you.'

No, thought Romy, you guys need me. So's you can get on with your lives and not have to worry about being at Veronica's beck and call.

'How is Mum?' Romy fastened her seatbelt.

'Oh, you know Veronica,' said Giselle effusively. 'She is such a wonderful, wonderful woman. Despite everything she looks absolutely fantastic. I do so love her.'

Romy choked back the impulse to snort loudly. She knew that her mother and her sister-in-law got on famously but she'd forgotten how gushing Giselle could be about her. But then Giselle was the daughter that Veronica had never had. She was truly beautiful and she made the most of it, so Romy could see exactly why the two women got on so well. Giselle was into beauty and fashion in a way that neither she nor Kathryn (who was prettier by far than Romy) had ever been.

'How's business?' she asked, wanting to divert the conversation away from Veronica and her bad back.

'Mine or Darragh's?' asked Giselle.

'Yours?' Romy was surprised. 'I didn't think you were working.'

'Sweetie, we all have to work.' Giselle fluttered her eyelashes again.

Romy stifled a laugh. Giselle certainly didn't have to work. With the money that Darragh was making out of the company, she doubted the other woman had to do anything she didn't want to.

'What are you doing?' she asked. 'Back at the company?'

'God, no!' Giselle laughed lightly. 'I've done all I'm going to do there!'

That was true, Romy thought. Giselle Forde had nabbed Darragh Dolan, a career move which was way better than anything else she could have come up with and an almost exact replica of what Veronica herself had done with Tom years earlier. Tom had employed Veronica as a receptionist in his newly opened company and Veronica, young and stunningly beautiful with her big blue eyes and gently curling blond hair (at the time she hadn't needed the champagne-blond Clairol she used now), had wooed him in an instant. Veronica had often told them the story of Tom taking her to dinner one evening after she'd worked particularly late and how he'd been so wonderful and nice to her and she'd suddenly started seeing him not as a much older man who was her boss but as a person she could fall in love with. (Romy did rather feel that there were a lot of men that Veronica could have, and had, fallen in love with over the years, in which case Tom wasn't really all that special.) Veronica's story about Tom had always been laced with lots of romance when she told it. The next day he'd left a red rose on her desk. And every day after that until she married him. After they'd married he brought her home a bouquet of flowers every week. Romy felt as though she'd actually been around at the time of Tom and Veronica's relationship because she heard so much about it – particularly after Veronica and Dermot had split up.

So she always felt it was interesting that Darragh had done almost the same as Tom when it came to finding a wife.

She actually remembered the day Giselle had been hired. It had been during a scorching hot summer when business was booming. Darragh had come home and told them that he'd found a wonderful receptionist, someone who would be an asset to the expanding firm. Romy had seen the speculative look in Veronica's eye as he spoke and she'd known that there was something more to the receptionist than just being a great asset to the company. A few months later, Darragh and Giselle were engaged. Giselle, when she met the family, told them that he was the most romantic man in the world and that she'd never had so many flowers from anyone in her life before. They'd married the month after Veronica and Dermot had separated. Dermot hadn't been invited to the wedding.

'So what are you up to?' Romy asked Giselle now.

'Makeovers,' said her sister-in-law. 'Corporate makeovers.'

Romy frowned. 'What do you mean? You redesign companies? How d'you do that?'

'No.' Giselle swung the car round the airport roundabout and headed towards the motorway. 'People in companies. I go in and give them lessons in grooming and make-up and that sort of thing. I'm a consultant and I do it in my spare time. You'd be surprised how lucrative it is. These days it's not just about having a good product. It's about the whole corporate image.'

Romy nodded. Giselle would be good at that. Giselle was an image woman through and through. Today's streetwise and sassy look could just as quickly be replaced by a sleek city image if that was what she wanted. Or by an elegant partner for a corporate dinner. She was (as Veronica had been) the ideal managing director's wife. Romy remembered a magazine article shortly after Giselle and Darragh had married which referred to her as Dublin's Latest Glamorous Socialite and the perfect partner for the successful entrepreneur Darragh Dolan.

'Not just our company,' Giselle clarified. 'Though I started off with that. The state of some of the girls in the office had to be seen to be believed. Belly-tops, far too much jewellery and terrible make-up. I told Darragh that if people came in and saw them wandering around they'd have totally the wrong impression of us.'

'Although the people that come in are all engineers, aren't they?' said Romy. 'It's not like Dolan's is selling a lifestyle choice.'

'You want everyone to look the part all the same,' Giselle told her. 'And we've redesigned the gear that the guys on the factory floor wear too. Green, with our logo. Looks fantastic.'

'Between yourself and Darragh you've done a lot of work,' said Romy.

'Yes.' Giselle sounded satisfied. 'And I got more work out of it and so, well, happy days!' She smiled as she overtook a white van. 'Tom built up a good company but Darragh has been taking it into the superleague.'

'What about . . .' Romy faltered as she tried to recall the name, 'Christian? The guy who had been the MD?'

'He's gone,' said Giselle. 'Well, there wasn't space for him once Darragh took over, and you know how it is, there'd only be some kind of power struggle. Better to get rid of him. Darragh looked after him and he's got a job in another company now anyway. No probs.'

'Good.' Romy settled back into the seat. It was funny, she thought, how the company dominated everything to do with the Dolan family. It was the most important thing in their lives.

Despite her lack of interest in the day-to-day business, Veronica still went along to the Christmas parties every year. Company talk had always been a part of life at home although Romy had been excluded from it. Dermot too. They used to go out for walks together whenever the family had what they called a company conference.

Romy had always thought the set-up was like the Agatha Christie novels that she liked to read when she was younger, dipping into Tom's hardback collection which he'd kept in the den. A family company where eventually members of the family would get bumped off one by one because someone else wanted all the money. She knew that this was just a wicked fantasy of hers, but she enjoyed imagining it all the same. Her money would have been on Veronica getting whacked first. Whoever got her shares would then have a controlling interest and be able to do what they liked. She smiled now at the thought. It was an improbable – no, impossible – scenario for the Dolans. Darragh was utterly devoted to Veronica, and although she knew that Kathryn and her mother had rowed monumentally over Darragh's appointment as MD, the idea of her hitting Veronica over the head with a mallet just to get her hands on the shares was pretty far-fetched. Nor did they live in the requisite old manor house of Christie thrillers, she reminded herself as they eventually exited the motorway and turned towards the old village of Rathfarnham and the family home. Their house was big and originally built in the 1940s but it had been completely modernised by Veronica, who redecorated every couple of years to keep up with current trends in home décor, and so it was badly suited as a setting for a murder mystery.

'D'you mind if I just drop you here at the gate?' asked Giselle as the car glided to a halt. 'If I go in I know I'll be there for ages and Mimi's got a ballet lesson in an hour.'

'Ballet?' Romy looked surprised. 'Isn't she a bit young?'

'You can never be too young to learn deportment,' said

Giselle. 'And she loves going to Little Belles, don't you, honey?' She turned to smile at her daughter.

'I have a dress,' said Mimi.

'They all have pink tutus,' Giselle explained. 'So cute.'

'Right.' Romy got out of the SUV and pulled her case on to the pavement. 'Well, see you again, Giselle. Tell Darragh I said hello.'

'Oh, we're hoping that we'll meet up for dinner some day next week,' her sister-in-law said. 'Darragh wants to talk to you about Veronica. He has his concerns about her well-being, you know.'

'Um, OK.'

'Be in touch.' And Giselle roared off down the road.

Romy stood at the double gates and looked at the family house. It was impeccably maintained, with bay windows either side of the front door and a short gravelled driveway leading up to it. Perfectly tended glossy green ivy grew halfway up the grey-brick walls. There was room for about four cars at the top of the driveway but only one was parked there now, a newly registered Volkswagen Golf cabriolet in metallic silver. Veronica loved soft-topped cars and always bought them in silver. The gates were electric but Romy didn't have a remote zapper to open them. She was about to push the bell to let Veronica know she was here when they suddenly began to swing inwards. The front door opened and Veronica stepped outside.

The first thing that Romy saw was that her mother had changed her hairstyle. Veronica had always been a fan of big hair. In her younger years she'd worn it in a Farrah Fawcett *Charlie's Angels* style, beach-blonde and flicked around her face. Then she'd gone for twisted corkscrew curls in more golden hues. Later the curls had been relaxed into gentle waves and Veronica had added caramel tones to her champagne colour. Now, though, it was poker straight and flicked up at the ends. It was shorter too, reaching to just above her shoulders. But still without a trace of grey. Still champagne blond.

She was wearing a coral kaftan embroidered with gold beads and multicoloured sequins over a pair of wide cream palazzo pants. Two gold chains hung from her neck while on her wrists she wore a matching link bracelet and a gold Omega watch. A half-hoop emerald ring glittered on her left hand. On her right she wore an oblong ruby.

She looked amazing. Her face was carefully made up and her naturally long and curling eyelashes were coated with a slick of dark brown mascara, making them look even longer. If she hadn't known better, Romy would have suggested Veronica's age to be anything between thirty-five and fifty.

Closer, though, it was clear that she was older. There were fine lines at the corners of her eyes and Romy could see that her skin beneath the make-up wasn't as firm as it used to be. Additionally, and fleetingly, Romy thought that there was a trace of the pain she was obviously feeling on her mother's face. But all these things were minor. Veronica Kilkenny was still a stunningly attractive woman.

As Romy drew closer, Veronica stepped forward. Romy saw that she was wearing a pair of coral sequinned loafers. It was the loafers that made Romy realise that maybe there was something wrong with her mother after all. In her whole life she couldn't remember ever seeing Veronica in anything less than a two-inch stiletto heel.

'Hi, Mum,' she said as she stepped into the porch.

'Well hello, stranger.'

Romy shrugged and the two of them looked at each other for a moment.

'Thanks for coming,' said Veronica.

'No problem.'

Her gold chains clinked as Veronica reached out and pecked her daughter on each cheek then looked at her contemplatively.

'Maybe we should go inside?' suggested Romy.

Veronica turned in to the house and began to walk slowly along the hallway. Romy was horrified to see that she wasn't walking easily and that each step was an effort. Veronica normally sashayed rather than walked. She didn't usually hobble (except on the very occasional times when she wore totally unsuitable shoes to a function and suffered for the sake of her appearance).

'Goodness, I didn't realise you were in such a bad way.'

'Thought I was faking it, did you?' Veronica asked as she opened the door to the living room.

'Of course not,' lied Romy. 'It was just that you look fantastic. So I thought . . .' She shrugged again. (A lot of her conversations with her mother ended up with her shrugging, she realised. She always found it impossible to talk to her.)

'I don't have to look a wreck just because I have a bad back.' Veronica eased in to one of the high-backed armchairs and arranged a velvet cushion behind her for support.

'You never look a wreck,' said Romy.

'I feel it,' Veronica told her.

'I was sorry to hear about your operation.'

We sound like a couple of complete strangers, thought Romy. And this feels so weird.

'Yes, well, I guess it's got to be done.'

Romy nodded.

'So how were things in Australia?'

Romy shrugged. Again, she thought. She'd have to watch the shrugging. She was beginning to feel like a teenager once more, like when she was sixteen and for a few months her entire method of communication with Veronica had been through shrugs.

'It was going well,' she said.

'In that case I'm sorry to have dragged you home.'

'That's OK.'

'Is it?'

'It's not for long,' said Romy. 'Tell me about this operation.'

'Stupid back,' said Veronica savagely. 'Stupid discs. Stupid, stupid bones.' She shook her head. 'Now that would be more worthwhile, if you'd studied how to fix creaking bones instead of spending your time digging them up.'

'What's wrong with you exactly?' asked Romy.

'Oh, I don't know.' Veronica was dismissive. 'One of my discs is out of alignment or worn away or something. I'm wearing this ridiculous – oh, corset I suppose you'd call it, to keep me in shape until surgery. I think they're fusing the bones or something. I don't need to know. I really don't want to know. I told the doctor just to get on with it.'

'Do they think it'll be successful?'

'You know doctors. Won't guarantee anything.' Veronica looked disgusted. 'It'd better be bloody successful. I can't live my life like this!'

Romy said nothing.

'You probably think it's funny,' said Veronica. 'You probably think I deserve it!'

'Now you're being silly,' Romy told her.

'Am I?'

At least a month of this, thought Romy, despairingly. A month if not more of skirting around things, of needing each other. She didn't know if she could take it. She didn't know if Veronica could either.

'How about a cup of tea?' she suggested.

'You know where everything is.' Veronica moved uncomfortably on the chair.

Romy walked into the kitchen and exhaled with relief. She'd promised herself that she wouldn't get into a flap when she saw Veronica and that she wouldn't let herself be riled by her, but the truth was that – even if they'd had a perfectly good mother–daughter relationship, unmarred by anything that had happened in the past – they would always end up sparking off each other. They were two completely different people and they found it difficult to see each other's point of view. And so the key thing from her perspective would be to keep her impulsiveness in check and to think before she spoke. To stay off the subject of age and illness – which she knew freaked Veronica out – and to let things wash over her. Keith was great at that. Nothing ever riled him and he always laughed at how easily she got upset about what he called trivia. But the relationship between herself and Veronica wasn't trivial, she thought as she took a couple of blue mugs out of the cupboard. Whatever else, trivial certainly didn't cover it.

Dermot's leaving had initially been the start of the somewhat more difficult times between them. There had always been arguments, of course, whenever Veronica had tried to style Romy's long, wiry hair, for example (which only ended in tears of rage from Romy and frustration on Veronica's part); or when her mother begged her to wear skirts instead of jeans or tried to get her to use the latest moisturisers on her face. But they were easy things to get over. Other things had been harder. And what Romy had always struggled with was Veronica's occasional mutterings whenever she did something wrong that she'd 'got that from your father'.

Romy knew that Veronica had been truly upset about the break-up of her marriage. For lots of reasons, including hating the fact that people (her own family especially) said things like 'I told you so' to her. Romy thought it was very unfair of them to comment on a marriage that had lasted for fourteen years and which was a damn sight longer than lots of other marriages. But she knew that some people had murmured that Dermot would now go off and find someone much younger and prettier than Veronica while she – by then in her late forties, yet more stunning than ever – would struggle to find someone new because in the end all men wanted younger women no matter what and Dermot, freed from Veronica, would revert to type.

She knew that those kinds of remarks incensed her mother.

Besides, Dermot didn't have time to find someone new; he was still working really hard because he'd bought the apartment and was trying to sort his life out. But that wasn't the point. And in the end people knew what they were talking about, because it *was* true that younger women were attracted to Dermot – over the years Romy had met a few of his new 'just friends'. Some of them she liked better than others but they all had one thing in common: they were younger than her mother even if most of them couldn't hold a candle to her in the glamour stakes. Whenever Romy met any of her father's new girlfriends she felt devastated on Veronica's behalf. But whenever Veronica raged about Dermot, Romy felt equally angry for him. Everything to do with her parents' split left her feeling split too. And as she grew older, she felt it even more.

When she went back to the house in Rathfarnham, Veronica would quiz her about Dermot's potential girlfriends and she'd feel incredibly uncomfortable about answering her questions, generally resorting to monosyllabic replies and the inevitable shrugs, which left Veronica feeling annoyed at her exclusion from Romy's glimpse into Dermot's new life.

All the same Romy knew that Dermot was also paying child maintenance to Veronica for her, which she thought was unfair given that Veronica was getting a good income from the company and that she didn't really need it, while Dermot struggled with his bills. (But, of course, income from Dolan Industrial Components could only be spent on Tom's family, at least as far as Tom's family were concerned.) And whenever she might mention that Veronica had gone out somewhere for an evening Dermot would remark, sourly, that it was easy for her to do, Merry Widow that she was. And then, of course, Veronica had begun socialising again and upping the glamour stakes higher than ever, which had been responsible for even more trouble . . . Romy winced again as she remembered and then immediately clamped down on those memories, focusing instead on how hard it had been to be stuck in the middle of Dermot and Veronica's disintegrating relationship.

She'd hated being part of it and she hated how it had affected her relationship with Darragh and Kathryn too. So, for lots of reasons, when she finally went to college she was happy to pick a discipline which gave her the opportunity to travel. She also changed her living arrangements, because Dermot was much closer to DCU where she was studying and so she moved in with him instead. Veronica hadn't been able to object at that point – in fact Romy knew that the whole thing had probably been a major relief to her. And six months later she moved into a rented apartment even closer to the college with three other girls from her year, which was even better. It was easier to be away from both of them. Easier to be away from it all. And although she'd mellowed eventually and even had a kind of reconciliation with Veronica over her mother's absolutely unforgivable behaviour at Kathryn's party – Romy gritted her teeth and reminded herself that she was never going to revisit that again; they had promised to put it behind them – reconciliation or no reconciliation, staying well away whenever possible was the best solution for everyone.

She brought the tea into the living room, then poured her mother a mug and left it on the small coffee table beside her.

'There *are* cups,' said Veronica, eyeing the blue mugs critically.

'Sorry,' said Romy. 'I usually use mugs.'

She poured tea into her own, added a splash of milk and then took a sip.

'So,' said Veronica, who eventually followed suit. 'You actually came.'

'I rang you. I told you I was coming.'

'Yes, but I was surprised that you agreed. I was perfectly prepared to manage on my own.'

'I doubt very much that you could manage on your own

after the op, especially seeing you now. Darragh called me, and of course I said I'd come.'

Veronica raised a carefully shaped eyebrow. 'And he didn't have to persuade you to return?'

'It was inconvenient,' said Romy. 'I'd been offered more work with Heritage Help, in Melbourne this time, and I really wanted to do it. But there'll be other opportunities.'

'I know that you don't want to be here. I know that I'm a burden. Don't worry. It won't be for long.'

'I'm not worried,' said Romy evenly.

'Have you talked to your dad lately?'

'No,' Romy said. 'Other than to say that I'd be home.'

'How is he?' asked Veronica.

'In Kerry at the moment,' Romy told her.

'On his own? Or playing happy families?' Veronica snorted.

'Mum!'

'He didn't ever find time to go to Kerry with us.'

'Mum, you never had the slightest desire to go anywhere in Ireland,' protested Romy. 'I seem to remember you muttering about the country being a nice place to get out of.'

'I'd have gone if he'd taken me somewhere nice,' Veronica said mutinously.

'He brought you to France and Spain and the Canaries and Morocco and a whole heap of other places.'

'That was completely different.' Veronica swept her hair to one side with a dismissive rattle of her bracelets. 'They were official holidays. Not getaway breaks.'

'I'm not going to argue with you,' said Romy as she replaced her mug on the table. 'I've made a promise to myself.'

'I see,' said Veronica slowly. 'Any other promises?'

'To get back to work as soon as you're on your feet again.'

Veronica grimaced. 'Digging in the dirt.' She sighed. 'I know it's what you like doing, but – honestly, Romy!'

'It's a serious job,' Romy protested.

'Yes, but what will it bring you, in the end?' asked Veronica.

'Satisfaction.'

'Money?'

Romy stopped herself from shrugging this time. 'Not as much as you'd like, I guess.'

'I suppose you could always marry well,' said Veronica.

'I can't believe you said that.'

'Kathryn did.'

'Kathryn also has a successful career.'

'Is there any man on the horizon for you?' asked Veronica. She tapped her long tapered nails against the arm of the chair.

Romy looked coolly at her mother.

'Oh for heaven's sake!' Veronica was impatient. 'If there is, he's six thousand miles away.'

'I have a boyfriend,' Romy said, thinking that Keith would freak out at his change in status for the sake of her family and hoping he'd got over the comfort kiss. 'He's great and he hopes I'll be back in Oz soon to be with him.'

'What does he do?' asked Veronica.

'He's a marine archaeologist,' said Romy.

'Fish bones?' Veronica was incredulous, and Romy grinned.

'No. Shipwrecks mostly.'

'Oh.'

'He's a nice guy.'

Veronica raised a sceptical eyebrow. 'Is this a serious relationship?'

'I don't know yet.' She wasn't able to lie any more. A comfort kiss could only carry it so far.

'Figures.'

'Better not to know than to marry him by mistake.'

The two of them stared at each other for a moment while the air between them crackled.

'Sorry,' said Romy, not able to keep up the silence.

'My marriage to Tom lasted for ten years and it would have been for a lot longer if he hadn't died,' said Veronica icily. 'My marriage to your father lasted for fourteen and would have been longer if he hadn't been too damn selfish for his own good.'

Romy shivered. There was that selfish word again. Was selfishness something she'd inherited from Dermot? Was it genetic? Was she really as bad as they all seemed to think?

'And my marriage to Larry was, I admit, a bit of a disaster.' This time Veronica spoke wryly. 'But I was hurt at the time and I mistook sympathy for love.'

Romy didn't reply. Veronica's third marriage had been a very short-lived affair. She'd met and married Larry Watts a year after her divorce from Dermot had eventually been finalised and she'd separated from him the following year – shortly before Dermot himself had married his beautiful new (and significantly younger) wife, Larissa.

The inadvisability of Veronica's third marriage was the one thing that Darragh, Kathryn and Romy had agreed on completely. They had been united in their belief that she was making a massive mistake and they'd begged her not to do it. (Well, Darragh and Kathryn had done the talking. Romy had sat in the room and said nothing until she'd been forced to spring to her father's defence when Veronica had had a go, as she'd known she would.) Anyhow, despite Darragh and Kathryn's best efforts there had been no dissuading Veronica. The wedding had taken place in the Maldives and had been gloriously romantic. But the marriage had been a disaster. Two days before their first anniversary, Larry had moved out. The only saving grace, as Veronica had admitted to all of them, was that he hadn't tried to stiff her for some kind of divorce settlement. It had been amicable in the end, Larry agreeing that they'd got it all wrong. He had been a bachelor before he married Veronica and didn't have any children. Which, Romy often thought, given the usually fractious relationship between herself, Darragh and Kathryn, was probably a good thing.

'Anyone else in your life at the moment?' Romy wasn't sure

she really wanted to know. She felt uncomfortable having this kind of conversation with Veronica for a whole heap of reasons, only one of which was that she honestly didn't think that daughters should have to ask their mothers about their love lives even though she accepted it was almost inevitable these days.

Veronica shrugged. 'Not lately. There have been a couple of guys I met through some of my social clubs. A nice man from bridge, but we didn't click as well as I thought. A widower from my salsa class – of course I haven't been back there since I did my back in. A bloke I met at art appreciation – only he was married and I'm certainly not at the time of my life when I want to be having some kind of clandestine affair! But these days it's more about friendship, as far as I'm concerned.'

'That's a change,' said Romy.

'Not really,' said Veronica. 'All I ever wanted was someone who could be a good friend.'

Romy looked at her sceptically.

'But if it turns to more . . .' Veronica grinned. 'So much the better. Which, now that you have a boyfriend of your own, you must realise.'

'I've had boyfriends before,' retorted Romy.

'Nobody I'd call serious. Was your current man upset at your coming home?' asked Veronica.

'He knows it's not for long.'

'Indeed.'

The look Romy flashed Veronica was challenging. 'I don't think we could hack it together for long, could we?'

'Probably not,' agreed Veronica.

'But let's do our best for the time I'm here.'

'I'm perfectly willing to get along,' said Veronica. 'I always have been.'

'Once getting along means getting your own way. Doing whatever you want to do whenever you want to do it.' As soon as the words were out of her mouth, Romy wished she hadn't spoken.

'Well, I'm hardly going to get my own way with you in charge,' Veronica said with amusement. 'And I suppose I'm going to have to get used to living the monastic life or face your disapproval. Still, I'm sure you have plenty of tips about living quietly. Despite the boyfriend.'

This time Romy did keep her mouth shut. She knew it was the better option.

Chapter 4

Giselle was watching TV when Darragh arrived home that evening. She was stretched lengthways on the sofa in her baby-blue Juicy Couture tracksuit and although she looked very comfortable she also looked very beautiful. Darragh's heart flipped, as it always did, at the sight of his wife. Giselle had always reminded him of the blonde one in Abba, and when he'd been six or seven, he'd had a crush on the blonde one in Abba.

'Are you hungry?' she asked. 'I've already had a chicken salad and there's more of that in the fridge, but there are some WeightWatchers meals in the freezer too.'

He groaned as he flopped on to the cream-coloured U-shaped sofa and kicked its base so that the integrated footrest came out.

'I need more than two calories a day,' he told her. 'Is there anything in the house that would be considered a bit more hearty?'

'I'm eating healthily,' she reminded him. 'For me and the baby.'

'You always eat healthily. And so do I, despite myself! I just need some decent rations from time to time.'

'You eat far too many carbs and too much salty food and—'

'All right, all right!'

'I'm just looking after you,' she said.

'I know,' said Darragh glumly. 'And I appreciate it. I do, really. But I'm starving!'

Giselle smiled at him. 'You could always pop a potato in the microwave and bake it with some cheese. Have it with the salad.'

'Hum,' said Darragh as he eased his hand-stitched shoes from his feet. 'We'll see.' He looked at his wife. 'So how did it go today . . . how was Romy? In a snit at having to come home?'

'You know what she's like,' said Giselle dismissively. 'Never very forthcoming. Sulked a bit in the car, but maybe that was because Mimi blurted out that she looked scruffy.'

'She didn't!'

'Little rip,' said Giselle. 'She's getting far too mouthy.'

'And was she?' asked Darragh.

'Scruffy? No more than usual. Not as chubby, actually, quite toned in fact. I suppose all that digging has to be good for something. Far too tanned, though. Her skin'll be like leather when she hits her forties. Dressed in her usual combat pants and ancient T-shirt. She looked more like a gap-year student than a working woman.'

'Yeah, well, working . . .' Darragh snorted. 'How she can call scrabbling around in the muck like that a job I don't know. And she earns buttons from it.'

'She once told me that she'd probably be better paid if she did forensic work for the police,' remarked Giselle.

'Maybe. But that'd mean her hanging around crime scenes and stuff like that instead,' said Darragh. 'I really wouldn't want my clients to know that my sister spent her days looking at murder victims.'

'You can't have it both ways,' Giselle told him. 'Anyway, I don't think she's cut out for police work. She's not in the real world, is she, with all her dreaminess about history and the past. It's all very well being a tree-hugging vegetarian environmentalist who probably doesn't even shave her legs, but the world can't survive on tree-hugging alone. And how she can be your mother's daughter and not give a fig about her appearance is absolutely beyond me.'

Darragh grunted. 'Well at least she's ensconced with Mum now and that's one less worry off my mind.'

It was one less worry off Giselle's mind too. Ever since Veronica had broken the news about her impending operation, Giselle had worried that somehow she would be the one who'd end up looking after Darragh's mother. It wasn't that she didn't like Veronica; in fact she got on well with her mother-in-law most of the time, but when Darragh had made suggestions about Veronica moving in for a few weeks Giselle had been utterly determined that would never happen. Giselle really wasn't into looking after people. She didn't like being at anyone's beck and call and she knew that being at Veronica's would be a step too far. Besides, as Giselle had said to Darragh when he first broke the news about Veronica's operation, she couldn't be expected to help Veronica with anything when she was pregnant herself. As well as which, it took her at least an hour to get ready every morning because she always washed and dried her hair and did her make-up and took time to select what clothes to wear – she couldn't do all that with Veronica in the house and she didn't like being rushed. It stressed her. And that wouldn't be good for the baby.

Anyhow, Giselle had better things to do than to run after Darragh's mother all day and she knew that Veronica would be a demanding patient. No, Giselle had thought as she suggested it to Darragh, the best approach to take was to get his feckless sister home from her pointless job and get her doing something for the family for once in her life. She hadn't actually believed that Darragh would be able to shame Romy into coming home but she was very, very relieved that he had.

'Anything else on your mind?' she asked Darragh now as she shifted in the sofa to make herself more comfortable. She hated being pregnant. Even though she never looked very pregnant she certainly felt it. And her back ached unbearably.

'Where do you want me to start?' demanded Darragh. 'We're having terrible trouble with absenteeism this week because of that damn football match in Stuttgart; Cahill's still haven't given us the order they promised last month; Jimmy McIntyre resigned this morning; the Belgian company is way behind projections and I'm going to have to fire that idiot in Operations who couldn't manage his way out of a paper bag.'

Giselle looked at him fondly. Darragh loved complaining about the company – about how people never lived up to expectations and how hard it was to get staff you could really trust these days. But she knew that he loved it really. He liked going to his endless conferences and meeting up with fellow executives and talking about business models and methods. And, like her, he enjoyed going to the business dinners and awards ceremonies where they had to dress up and look the part. Giselle knew that Darragh was always pleased and proud when they walked into a function together – she dressed impeccably in an expensive evening gown and wearing her favourite diamonds, and he in his well-fitting dress suit and gold cufflinks. They stood out, not just because of their clothes, but because they were both good-looking people. Giselle knew that. Having gone through a makeover herself before she'd met him, she'd known how to make the most of his dark good looks too by sending him to a beautician, who shaped his rather bushy eyebrows, gave him facials to deal with his spot-prone skin and regular manicures to keep his nails in good condition. Giselle thought that it was only right that the managing director of Dolan Component Manufacturers should look the part.

'Everything will be fine,' she told him. 'You know that there's no need to get into a state. Besides, Stephen and Alex look after things, don't they?' Stephen and Alex were the company secretary and the financial officer and they'd been with the firm for years. 'Right then, since you haven't asked, I had a crap day myself.'

'Why?'

'Meeting your sister, for one,' Giselle said. 'It took for ever to get to the airport and back. I'd planned to get my hair cut but I couldn't fit it in. We were late for Mimi's ballet and she threw a strop because Sinead Curtin has a new tutu with sparkles. She'll make my life a misery until I get her one too.'

'Don't!' Darragh's tone was so firm that Giselle was startled. 'For heaven's sake,' he said more mildly, 'the child has everything she could possibly want. She has millions of those tutu things.'

'Yes, but it's all about peer pressure,' said Giselle. 'If the other kids have stuff and she doesn't, she feels left out.'

'I just think that she needs to learn the value of money,' Darragh said slowly.

'Sweetheart, she's only three!' Giselle laughed. 'Time enough when she wants a Ferrari and you tell her she can only have a Micra.'

'I guess so.'

'It's not expensive.' Giselle snuggled up to him. 'Don't worry. I'll give her values and stuff when she's older. But right now I want to treat her. You know I hated not having things when I was a kid. Hated not being able to get the latest clothes or games or whatever like everyone else. I want things to be different for Mimi. And for Junior here.' She patted her stomach.

'I understand,' said Darragh. 'I guess that every so often I feel I need to be . . .'

'Manly.' Giselle giggled and buried her head in the crook of his arm.

He laughed. 'Too right. I am the man of the house and will be treated with all due respect! By the way, Sean Nolan rang to ask me if you were interested in giving one of your poise and personality classes to a gaggle of women in his company.'

'Sean Nolan?' Giselle sat up and frowned.

'The mobile phone company guy.'

'Oh, right! Him. Sorry, pregnancy brain in gear at the moment. I can't remember a thing. Unless you specifically want me to do it, I can't be bothered right now. It takes time to put together and I get tired really quickly. So I'm just going to finish up the two things I have running at the moment and then take it easy.'

'Sure, no problem. I'll tell him. What are your plans for the rest of the week?' Darragh looked at her enquiringly.

'Lunch tomorrow with Enya and the girls. Coffee morning the day after in aid of . . . um . . . can't remember actually, but some kind of good cause . . . Pilates, some shopping maybe, and on Friday I'm getting myself in shape for the dinner.'

'What dinner?'

'Darragh!' She stared at him. 'How could you have forgotten? It's the golf club dinner.'

'Shit.' He frowned. 'I had.'

'You're donating a holiday abroad for the draw,' she reminded him.

'So I am. I'll get Susan to sort it out. That's what PAs are for.'

'Great.'

Darragh got up off the sofa. 'I'd better find something to eat,' he said.

'There's some eggs in the fridge too,' Giselle called as he headed towards the kitchen, 'if you don't want the baked potato or the frozen option. I can't eat eggs so I don't know why I bought them. Or there's pasta. Or you can send out!'

He nodded and she leaned back on the sofa again. She should have stocked the fridge earlier in the week with stuff that Darragh liked. But these days she just wasn't hungry herself and the idea of cooking for him made her feel ill. When she did cook it was grilled salmon or chicken with some lightly steamed vegetables, which made Darragh sigh and mutter about starvation rations. The annoying thing, she conceded, was that he was in pretty good shape for a man in his thirties who ate mostly red meat and packets of Pringles. He hadn't started to develop a paunch like so many men who were drifting into middle age (not, of course, that thirty-six was middle-aged any more, but still!); he worked out regularly in the gym near the factory and he ran the Dublin City marathon every year. So generally speaking she didn't have to worry about him. On the flip side of things, however, they went to a lot of business functions because he was a member of a variety of professional organisations and on a number of their committees and so they had to show up at every event; he probably drank too much because it was hard to go to these things and not drink; he smoked – only the occasional cigar when he was with some of his business friends, but Giselle assumed that they must have some impact on his health; he had his Pringles addiction; and he was (no matter how much he told her he wasn't) under a certain amount of stress as the managing director of Dolan Component Manufacturers.

Giselle drummed her fingers lightly against the armrest. She'd wanted to change the name of the company and make it more modern and relevant when she'd gone in to help with the makeover two years ago. But Darragh had told her that his father had founded it as Dolan Component Manufacturers and that was how it was going to stay. Besides, he'd said, the name was hugely relevant. They manufactured industrial components. The name was perfect.

She moved to the other end of the sofa. She could hear the ping of the microwave so she guessed that Darragh had gone for the WeightWatchers lasagne after all. She'd do some food shopping tomorrow. Sometimes Magda, their child-minder, who worked four days a week, cooked for them. Darragh loved it when she did – Magda was from Hungary and her favourite dish was goulash, which Darragh adored. Even when she wasn't pregnant, though, Giselle wasn't into cooking. Food hadn't interested her since she'd shed three stone and turned from a tubby teenager into a leggy young woman. Losing weight had transformed her life. Nobody had noticed her great skin or blue eyes or blond hair before. They'd only seen her flabby thighs and wobbly stomach. Now it was a completely different story. When people looked at her they really saw her. Darragh Dolan would never have noticed her at sixteen but he sure as hell had fallen for her at twenty, and being married to Darragh was the best thing that had ever happened to her. So she worked very, very hard every single day to keep the pounds off and to look fabulous for him, and the reason that there was so little food in the house was that she was always afraid of falling off the wagon and stuffing her face with sausages and chips just for the heck of it.

The thought of sausages and chips made her mouth water.

She turned up the volume on the TV set and got back to watching the rom-com movie to take her mind off eating.

Darragh was sitting at the kitchen table eating the microwaved meal out of its cardboard carton. The food bore no resemblance to its appetising picture on the outer sleeve. Whenever he microwaved anything he either managed to incinerate the contents of the carton so that it stuck together in an inedible gloop or else didn't heat it enough so that there was a frozen core in the centre that he knew would probably give him food poisoning. But at least the microwave was quick. Which was the point. He'd erred on the overdone side of things tonight so the lasagne was crispy at the edges and tongue-searingly hot in the centre. In fact, having burned his tongue on the first bite, he couldn't taste what he was eating so it might have been anything, which was probably a good thing.

Although he didn't expect her to, and knew that it wasn't something she liked doing, he wished Giselle would cook for him. Of course he was perfectly able to grill a steak himself but it was too much of an effort after a day at the factory or out with clients. What Darragh dreamed about, although he knew it would never happen, was coming home to a hot meal placed in front of him a few minutes after walking in the door.

Veronica had done that for Tom. Darragh remembered clearly his father's routine when he came in every evening – his coat hung on the hook underneath the stairs; a kiss for him and Kathryn and one for their mother too, then sitting down to dinner with Veronica while he and Kathryn watched TV. It was kind of warm and satisfying, and even though he knew that Veronica didn't especially like cooking, he always thought that their family meals were perfect.

It had changed, of course, when Tom died. Darragh didn't think he'd ever forget his father's sudden illness. He'd gone into the bathroom one day and seen Tom holding a blood-stained towel to his nose and asked him what the matter was and Tom had said that he didn't know, that his nose was bleeding and it wouldn't stop.

It had eventually stopped, of course, but what was impossible to stop was the march of leukaemia through him so that within a few months of that day Tom was dead. Darragh hadn't been able to believe it. He'd stayed strong and brave, as Veronica had asked, in front of people but he'd cried himself to sleep every single night for months.

His BlackBerry beeped and he looked at the email application. The message was from Jim Cahill. It said that Jim was sorry, he wouldn't be able to place the order for the circuit setters with him after all. It was a question of price and delivery. He'd found someone who could provide what he wanted at a considerable discount to Dolan Component Manufacturers.

Darragh felt his chest tighten and the microwaved lasagne turn over in his stomach. He stared at the message. Jim Cahill was a long-time client – he'd even considered him a friend. It just wasn't possible that he had gone off and got a quote from someone else at a cheaper price and had accepted it without getting back to Darragh first. He took a sip from the bottle of Bordeaux he'd opened to go with his lasagne on the basis that even if the food was crap the wine was good and he was entitled to good things in life. Then he started tapping a message in reply to Jim, asking him to call him, suggesting that they could surely work something out. Darragh wasn't sure what they could work out but there was no way he was letting someone undercut him and take away one of his best customers without trying to do something about it. Then he forwarded the email to Stephen and Alex, his management team. Stephen had been the one to cost up the quote so obviously he'd made a complete mess of it – it seemed to Darragh that lately they'd been making a mess of quite a few quotes, because Jim Cahill wasn't the first person to talk about going elsewhere. He was the first to have done it, though. He'd have to have a meeting with them, Darragh decided, wave the stick around a bit. No point in paying them the big bucks if they weren't keeping the clients.

He scrolled down to the next email. It was from Norman Mulligan at the golf club reminding him about the dinner on Friday and his generous offer of a holiday for the draw.

Why had he offered that? Darragh wondered. What had got into him when he'd said that he'd pay for two people to go to Barbados any time in the next twelve months. He should have suggested a week in the Canaries or something, which was more than generous. But he'd been thinking big, thinking of the type of holiday he liked for himself and thinking that he didn't want to appear cheap in front of the hotshots in the golf club.

That was the thing about the golf club. Almost everyone was some kind of captain of industry and most of them were managing directors of multinational firms. Dolan Component Manufacturers was small fry in comparison, even though the company supplied many of them with plant and machinery.

He took another sip of the wine and felt its gentle warmth

ease the sudden bout of tension that had gripped him. He didn't normally get tense about the business. He knew that it was a strong company and that it was his birthright and that he was a good successor to his father. It was important to Darragh to be a good successor to Tom, who had been quietly brilliant in how he'd set up the firm. Tom hadn't been involved in quite so many outside activities as Darragh, but these days things were different and you had to play golf and belong to various management organisations in order to get ahead and at the same time stay in with the posse. He understood these things instinctively, and both the golf club and the management organisations of which he was a member had brought him lots of good contacts.

Veronica knew that he was the right person for the job, even if Kathryn didn't. He felt a sudden pang of tension again as he thought of his bookish younger sister who had been totally opposed to his promotion to managing director.

'You've got to see it!' she'd cried to Veronica as the three of them sat around the rosewood table in the tiny boardroom. 'He hasn't a business brain.'

'Your dad wanted him to take over,' said Veronica. 'And it's time. Christian isn't up to it and Darragh is the right person to replace him.'

'I've got plans,' said Darragh. 'Don't worry, Katy, you'll still get your dividends.'

'I'm not worried about my dividends,' Kathryn had said tightly. 'I'm worried about the future of Dolan's. It's not that you don't have ideas, Darragh. It's that you have the wrong sort of ideas.'

'Oh? And what would they be?'

'All this upgrading of the office. Glass walls and state-of-the-art furniture. We don't need it.'

'That's just where you're wrong,' he told her triumphantly. 'That's exactly what we need. A refit to prove that Dolan's is a progressive company.'

'Spend the money by all means,' said Kathryn. 'But spend it on the factory floor, not the offices.'

'You don't understand PR and image,' Darragh told her. 'You never will.'

'Oh, and I suppose the lovely Giselle does?' Kathryn had looked at him defiantly.

'Yes,' said Darragh simply. 'She's got a great eye and she's a beautiful woman and she might not have gone to college like you or me but she's street smart.'

'She is,' Veronica had agreed.

'She's a bloody drain on your resources,' said Kathryn sourly. 'What with all her clothes and her jewellery and her beauty products! But do whatever you like. I don't care any more. Dad was an old fool and you're no better.'

'Kathryn Dolan!' Veronica's cheeks were pink with anger. 'Apologise to your brother now. And apologise to me for what you're doing to your father's memory.'

'Oh for God's sake!' At that point Kathryn had got up and walked out. 'Dad might have been a great businessman but he married a fool of a woman and had a fool for a son too.' And she slammed the boardroom door behind her.

She was completely wrong, thought Darragh morosely as he looked at Jim Cahill's email again. Not all of his plans had worked out but he'd had some satisfying successes. The refit had looked fantastic (there was no doubt Giselle knew what she was doing when it came to design, despite her lack of formal qualifications). Admittedly it had all gone terribly over budget and he couldn't believe how much debt the company had, but there were loads of new businesses setting up all over the country who needed Dolan's products and expertise. So there were plenty of potential clients out there and he had the perfect company to deal with them. What was more, people were stunned when they walked into the office and saw how great it looked. And they were equally stunned by his glamorous wife.

He had it all, thought Darragh, his gloom lifting. He had it all and he'd keep the show on the road and one day that sarky cow of a sister would apologise to him for thinking for one second that she knew what the hell she was talking about.

Chapter 5

Kathryn sat on the terrace of the tenth-floor apartment on East 77th Street. She liked being on the terrace with the sounds of the city carrying through the air, making her realise that she wasn't alone – though how could she be alone? she asked herself. She was in New York, a city with a population of over nineteen million people, for heaven's sake! But being inside the apartment always made her feel insulated from the crowds of people and the cars which clogged up Manhattan's streets; being on the terrace, even at a distance from everything, made her feel part of it. The terrace was the nicest feature of the wonderfully located apartment; not everyone in the building had one, which made it extra special. The apartment was actually Alan's apartment, of course. She'd previously rented a much less desirable place downtown but had moved into East 77th a few weeks before they'd married and there had been no question of them ever moving anywhere else. Alan loved it and, truthfully, so did she. The rooms were big and bright and Alan's slightly masculine décor appealed to her. She loved the location and she loved the building. She also loved sitting here on her own.

The only problem was that she loved being on her own more than she loved being with her husband. In fact she didn't want to be with Alan at all. And that was why, despite the serenity she usually felt when she came out to the terrace, she wasn't moved by the views and the city lights and the feeling of belonging in the same way that she once had been. That was why she was sitting here with a cigarette between her fingers, worrying about her future. Worrying about the terrible mistake she thought she'd made. She didn't want to think that she'd made a terrible mistake with Alan. She wasn't the sort of person who made mistakes; she left that to Darragh and to Romy. Kathryn knew that she was the analytical one and so she was supposed to be able to read situations and know how to do the right thing. She'd thought she had done the right thing in marrying Alan. She'd thought that she loved him and that he loved her. She'd been so sure of it that she'd said yes as soon as he'd asked her. And he'd asked her very shortly after the first time they'd met.

That was in the boardroom of a midtown office building. She was there along with one of her colleagues to listen to the company's concerns that one of their employees could be falsifying records and defrauding the firm.

'If it's a fraud it's not very big,' Mitch Kraviz, one of the company's financial officers, told her. 'But we haven't been able to identify it. And obviously that's a concern to us.'

'Almost every big fraud starts out as a small fraud.' Kathryn smoothed back her fine dark hair; unnecessarily, because she knew there were no stray wisps escaping from her sleek style. She regarded the board members of the company with her clear blue eyes. 'Someone steals a few hundred dollars and you think it's not worth your while investigating. But they do it every week for years and then you're talking thousands of dollars. You don't deal with this, you're giving a green light to employees to fleece you.'

'The thing is . . .' Alan Palmer spoke for the first time. He had a deep, melodious voice which instantly attracted Kathryn. As did his movie-star looks. 'Our auditors didn't pick this up and we're not sure whether it's just an internal glitch. We don't want a PR disaster on our hands.'

'If what you say is true and this is possibly something quite small which you haven't managed to identify, then you can be pre-emptive,' said Kathryn reassuringly. 'Not doing anything about it would be a million times worse, in terms of both your profitability and your PR.' She smiled at him.

'You're right.' Mitch was suddenly decisive. 'Let's get this show on the road.'

It had been an interesting investigation (well, she'd thought it was interesting, but she knew that to most people accountancy, even her speciality, investigative accountancy, was almost impossibly boring). In the end she'd discovered that one of the employees had been falsifying records, and that so far he'd managed to siphon $68,000 from the firm.

'We can cope with that scale of loss.' Alan Palmer worked in the public relations area of the company and was always concerned about how things looked to its investors and its customers. 'And we can spin George's departure to make things look OK for us.'

Kathryn nodded.

'We appreciate your help in all this,' said Mitch. 'We also appreciate your discretion.'

Alan grinned. 'We'd like to take you and your colleagues to dinner but we don't want to be seen with you.'

Kathryn laughed. 'We're not that high profile at Carter Clarke,' she assured him. 'I don't think being seen out with us would be a major PR disaster for your company. But I totally understand it. Once you pay our bill we'll be quite happy.'

She left the building, amused by their concern, and returned to her own office building, where she opened her laptop and began work on a presentation she was giving to an industry group on how to prevent fraud in their businesses.

Kathryn knew that she was good at her job. She knew that she could winkle out discrepancies in accounts, that she often found things that auditors overlooked. Companies were usually horrified by this because they felt that everything that needed to be found should be found by the auditors, but as she pointed out, most auditors worked to a particular plan, not to uncover fraud. Her methods were completely different.

She'd almost completed the initial outline of the presentation when her phone rang.

'It's me,' said Alan Palmer. 'I've been having second thoughts about being seen with you in public.'

She chuckled. 'Oh really?'

'Yes, really. I'm thinking that perhaps if you wear a mask . . .'

'I think I'll pass, thanks all the same.'

'Perhaps not.' He laughed. 'Anyway, why should you hide that lovely face behind a mask?'

'Is that a flattery thing you have going there?' she asked.

'Yes.'

'You're doing quite well.'

'How about this,' he suggested. 'Dinner tonight. Four Seasons? No masks.'

'Can't tonight,' she told him. 'But tomorrow would be good.'

'Tomorrow it is.'

It had been a wonderful first date. That was what it had become, of course, because all through dinner there had been a subtext of physical desire between them. She'd never before felt like this about a man – in fact most people had regarded her as the cold fish of the family. She wasn't go-getting and arrogant like Darragh. Nor was she hot-headed and emotional like Romy. She was calm and decisive and she never did anything without thinking about it first. So she thought about it before going to Alan Palmer's apartment that night. But she didn't think about it for long. And the only thing she was thinking about as she got into his bed was that he was the most desirable man in the world.

There was a kilo bag of the finest Arabica coffee on her

desk when she arrived into work the following morning. She smiled when she saw it – she'd told him that it was her favourite coffee, that the aroma of it positively turned her on. They'd laughed about it and he'd told her that she was very different from the girls he normally dated. As she picked up the bag and inhaled the aroma, she thought that he was very different from the men that she normally dated. And that she had fallen in love with him. She knew that she had never really been in love before.

For Kathryn, falling in love had been cataclysmic. It had shaken her world completely. She lost herself in being in love with Alan, in finding someone who was more important to her than anyone had ever been, and in being the most important person in someone else's life too.

She'd never been the most important person when she was younger. How could she be when Darragh, her older brother, was being groomed to take over the family business and while Romy, her younger sister, was the baby of the family whose father adored her? She'd been stuck in the middle, overlooked by everyone, and she'd hated it.

But it was different now. She was on an emotional high for the first time in her life and she couldn't believe how lucky she was. Alan was all the things she'd ever wanted in a man. Strong. Dynamic. Forceful. And, of course, very successful. Kathryn liked being with successful people. She liked their drive and enthusiasm. She liked the way they didn't accept failure.

Success had always been important to Kathryn, both for herself and for the people around her. After graduating she'd worked for an international accountancy firm located in Dublin, and when the opportunity had arisen she'd applied to join their US office. She'd been offered a position in their audit department and had then concentrated on investigative accountancy. There, she'd been involved in a number of areas before specialising in corporate fraud, where she'd had to testify in a number of cases, all of which had favourable outcomes for her clients. Everyone agreed that Kathryn Dolan had the ability to make complicated things sound simple and that she cut a striking figure on the stand, always impeccably groomed, always completely in control of what she was saying.

She'd sent copies of the newspaper clippings from her first trial home to Veronica, who'd called her up and asked what exactly she was getting involved in.

'Number-crunching,' Kathryn said. 'Only the way I work is that I have to find the right numbers to crunch. It's very interesting, poking around financial statements, looking to see what comes up.'

'Forensic accountancy and forensic archaeology.' Veronica had sounded despairing. 'What is it about my daughters that you feel the need to poke around at all?'

Kathryn laughed. 'I never thought of that.'

'Well I do,' said Veronica. 'Why can't you do something . . . something fun with your lives?'

'This is fun!'

'That's what Romy says.'

'We're happy, Mum,' said Kathryn. 'We're doing what we want to do which is a good thing.'

'It's not what I'd expected for either of you,' said Veronica.

'Oh well,' Kathryn said lightly. 'Life doesn't always work out like you expect.'

Nor had being married to Alan.

She shook another cigarette from the packet on the wooden table beside her. She was trying to give up but she hadn't quite succeeded yet. So, she thought, a failure in my life even though it's not a critical failure. But still something I haven't been able to do even though I want to do it. I can succeed and I can fail. But I always want to succeed.

She stared into the distance as the blue-grey smoke furled in front of her and drifted on the breeze. The lights of the apartment blocks chequered the view and she wondered whether the people in them felt alone in the city of millions too. She shivered in the evening air even though it wasn't cold.

I should try harder to give up smoking, she thought. Maybe another success would make a difference to how I feel. She finished the cigarette in a couple of quick drags then stubbed it out and walked back into the apartment. She stood there indecisively for a couple of minutes, twirling her long dark hair between her fingers, before picking up the phone.

She didn't especially want to talk to Veronica – Kathryn hated talking about illness and frailty – but she did want to check that Romy had arrived and had taken over responsibility for everything. It was about time, Kathryn thought, that Romy took some family burdens and realised that Veronica was her mother too. Romy had always been so bloody conscious about the fact that she had a different father that she never seemed to take on board the fact that she had the same mother as both Kathryn and Darragh. Kathryn had to admit that she sometimes played up to Romy's insecurities about this but she always thought that the younger girl was far too easy to rile about it. After all, as she'd told her when Dermot and Veronica announced that they were separating, as far as she was concerned Dermot was the only father she'd ever known. There might have been a biological difference but she knew Dermot and she didn't know Tom.

She always felt a little guilty about that. About knowing (and loving) the man who wasn't her father (and about wanting him to love her as much as Romy) and not remembering a single thing about the man who was. It didn't seem right somehow and so she often tried to tell Darragh that she did remember things about Tom even though it wasn't true.

She wished he hadn't died. She wished that she could remember something – anything – about him so that she could be grounded in knowing who her biological father was. The reason she used to argue with Romy about fathers so often was that Romy was so damn smug about the fact that hers was there, with them. Romy, of course, had been kind of smug about everything when they were small. She was a superconfident child, always so sure of herself and what she wanted from life and completely unaware of how other people saw her. She was pretty too, in an outdoor, tomboy sort of way, with her untamed hair and olive skin and vivid blue eyes. Kathryn always felt prim and proper beside Romy because she wasn't an outdoor kind of person herself. Kathryn preferred being inside with her books to outside climbing trees.

Veronica had told her that spending her time with her nose between the pages was the reason she had to wear glasses. She told her that she'd lose her looks because of it too. Veronica had always been pleased that Kathryn, despite having inherited Tom's darker colouring and despite her glasses, took after her in the looks department. The possibility of losing her looks and having to wear glasses because of reading wasn't true, of course; Kathryn had always been short-sighted, but Veronica used to make sweeping comments with no basis in fact and insist that she was right. Kathryn sometimes thought that the reason she spent so much time reading and poring over factual books was simply to find out whether Veronica was right or not about things. She would wonder whether, if Tom had lived, there would be someone who understood her better than Veronica, who (in such an old-fashioned way, Kathryn always thought) insisted that women couldn't have it all and the best way to success was to marry a rich man. Kathryn never knew whether to believe Veronica when she came out with that kind of nonsense. After all, Tom hadn't been rich when she'd married him. And Dermot wasn't rich at all. Kathryn sometimes wondered whether Veronica's comments about rich men weren't, in some way, really just jibes at Dermot, who pretty much ignored them anyway. She knew that Romy thought the problems between Dermot and Veronica all stemmed from his time in the Gulf. Kathryn herself rather felt that they'd been there long before that. She sometimes wondered whether Dermot and Veronica had ever really loved each other or whether it had just been a passionate affair that had ended in an unsuitable marriage – even if the marriage had lasted as long as it did.

She listened to the ringing tone of the phone as she waited for someone to pick up and answer her. We are a dysfunctional family, she thought. We really are. We're not like the ones you see on TV where everyone is cutely dysfunctional and loves each other beneath it all. We're just messy dysfunctional. It's hard to know who loves who with us. If any of us actually loves anyone else at all.

'Hello.'

'Hi there, Mum.'

'Well, hello,' said Veronica. 'I'm getting overwhelmed by daughterly affection today.'

'I was ringing to check that Romy had arrived OK,' said Kathryn. 'I guess that means she has.'

'Turned up like the bad penny,' quipped Veronica. 'Full of concern about me, making me drink nourishing soup and insisting that I go to bed early and look after myself.'

'Really?' Kathryn sounded surprised.

'Of course not,' responded Veronica. 'But she's here.'

'And is your surgery still on schedule?'

'Yes.' Veronica sounded resigned. 'I wish they could offer me a guarantee that it'll work but they're so damn vague about it. If I end up going through all this only to be exactly the same afterwards . . .'

'It'll be fine,' said Kathryn.

'And you know? You have a medical qualification on top of everything else?'

'Of course I don't know,' said Kathryn. 'But you have to be optimistic. I'm sure they wouldn't suggest surgery if they didn't think it had some chance of success.'

'Hmm.' Veronica sounded doubtful. 'I told them if I

couldn't wear my Jimmy Choos afterwards it wouldn't have been worth it in my opinion.'

Kathryn laughed in genuine amusement. She and her mother were like chalk and cheese – a different type of chalk and a different type of cheese from Romy and Veronica, but two totally different people nonetheless. Kathryn didn't care about shoes and bags and the designer stuff that Veronica loved so much, although since moving to the States her own wardrobe had been significantly upgraded. But her mother could always make her laugh.

'I'm glad you think it's funny,' said Veronica sourly.

'I don't really. I hope it all works out for you. Honestly. Anyway, I just rang to check that everything was going OK with Romy.'

'Yes. She's here. D'you want to talk to her?'

'I guess so.' Kathryn wasn't very sure about talking to Romy. They rarely seemed to be on the same wavelength about anything and she was always afraid that she'd say the wrong thing to her and provoke an argument. It was a pity, she thought, that Romy was so touchy. About everything.

'Hi,' said Romy. 'How're things in the Big Apple?'

'Fine,' said Kathryn. 'And you? Everything OK?'

'Sure.' Romy's voice was guarded.

'I know you didn't want to come home,' said Kathryn. 'I talked to Darragh.'

'Of course you did,' said Romy. 'But it makes sense for me to be the one.'

'Is everything all right?' asked Kathryn.

'Sure.'

'With you and Mum?'

'Why shouldn't it be?' Romy sounded defensive.

'No reason,' said Kathryn quickly. 'I just wanted to make sure that you were settled in OK and that she hadn't got you wearing designer dresses or anything like that yet.'

This time Romy laughed. 'Nope. Still in scruffy combats. Which I guess will be a huge disappointment to her.'

'Probably,' agreed Kathryn. 'But you never know. Maybe after a few days you'll have succumbed totally and even have your own Manolos.'

'As if.' Romy was still amused. 'I do think that particular gene passed me by.'

'Still desert boots for you?'

'I wore high heels the day before I came home from Australia,' said Romy lightly. 'And I went to a flashy restaurant. So maybe I'm not a total lost cause after all.'

'Maybe not.' Kathryn chuckled, relieved that Romy seemed to be reasonably OK about being in Ireland even though she knew that her sister (she never thought of Romy as a half-sister) had probably freaked at the thought. 'So, listen, how's Mum really?'

'In pain,' admitted Romy. 'I thought it was her usual hypochondriacal thing but it's not. She's really struggling to get around and I feel sorry for her. She's so angry about it all. She's wearing flat shoes.'

'No!' Kathryn was astounded.

Romy laughed faintly. 'I know. That was what made me realise that she wasn't faking it. Sensible shoes! It's hard to believe. But the rest of her is as usual – she's in full make-up, looks great to be honest; you wouldn't actually think she's in pain or anything most of the time.'

'So what's the actual situation on the surgery?'

'Apparently they're fairly confident it'll work,' said Romy. 'Not necessarily that she'll be totally pain-free, but to an extent.'

'It's probably those damn high heels that caused it in the first place.'

'Possibly,' agreed Romy.

'So what are your plans?'

'Stay until she's mobile enough to do things for herself,' said Romy. 'A few weeks anyway.'

'That's not such a big deal.'

'I . . . guess not.' Romy's voice was suddenly edgy.

'Wasn't that job in Australia almost over?'

'Yes. They'd offered me another contract, though. And the chance to be a supervisor on the next dig.'

'There'll be loads of other opportunities,' said Kathryn dismissively.

'Is that what you say to your clients when something goes wrong for them?'

'Sometimes,' replied Kathryn.

'This is different,' said Romy. 'It's about getting interesting work. Doing interesting things. It's not like another great deal will come up. There are lots of people looking at limited opportunities.'

'If you're good you'll get the breaks,' said Kathryn. 'If you're not . . .'

'Muscle my way to the top?' asked Romy. 'Like you?'

'I didn't muscle my way,' objected Kathryn. 'I worked hard and made the right decisions.'

'How do you do that?' This time Romy sounded genuinely interested. 'How do you always do the right thing?'

'I don't always do the right thing,' said Kathryn blankly.

'Oh but you do! You joined the right company, you went to the States, you're really successful and you married a mogul!' She laughed. 'You always seem to land on your feet.'

Kathryn said nothing.

'I'm sure there have been down sides,' said Romy. 'But you're the poster girl for being a successful woman, aren't you?'

'I do what I do,' said Kathryn. 'It's not always as easy as you make out.'

'I suppose not. Still, you can rest easy in your corner office knowing that I'm here looking after Mum and that Darragh is here looking over my shoulder.'

'How is Darragh?' asked Kathryn.

'I dunno,' replied Romy. 'I haven't seen him yet. He's

dropping by tomorrow. The lovely Giselle picked me up at the airport.'

There was a sudden complicit silence between them.

'And how's the lovely Giselle?' asked Kathryn.

'As lovely as ever.' Romy giggled. 'It's hard not to like her but she's so . . . so . . . into the loveliness of herself, isn't she? I mean, you're sort of pretty yourself but she . . . well, you know!'

'She reminds me of Mum,' said Kathryn.

'Me too. And she sucks up to her like crazy. D'you think it's true that men are really looking for a clone of their mother when they get married?'

'I don't know.'

'And do women look for a clone of their father?' wondered Romy.

'I can't answer that either.' Kathryn's voice was suddenly very tight.

'Is Alan like Dermot?' asked Romy. 'Or d'you think he's more like Tom? I didn't get the opportunity to meet him, of course, but what d'you think?'

'It wasn't my fault you didn't make it to the wedding,' said Kathryn. 'And Alan is his own person. He's not like anyone.' Which was perfectly true, she thought. 'This is a silly conversation,' she added.

'I suppose so.' Romy couldn't help feeling disappointed that their moment of togetherness had evaporated so quickly.

'So, look, put Mum on the phone again. I'd better talk to her a bit more about the surgery. And I'll be in touch later.'

'I'll call you when she's out of theatre,' said Romy. 'Just to let you know that everything's OK.'

'Thanks.'

Romy put the handset down and called her mother, who had disappeared into the kitchen while her daughters chatted.

'I made tea,' Veronica told her as she picked up the phone. Romy thanked her and disappeared into the kitchen herself.

After Veronica had finished talking to Kathryn, Romy told her that she was going to bed. She was tired and jet-lagged and was up much later than she'd intended so she could hardly keep her eyes open.

Veronica said that she'd watch TV downstairs for a while and Romy asked if she needed her to stay up so that she could help her to bed later, and Veronica told her (a little shortly) that she'd managed perfectly well on her own for the past few weeks and that she wasn't a damn invalid. At which Romy apologised (reminding herself that Veronica was sure to be touchy about the subject) and said good night and went upstairs to her old room.

It had changed completely. She'd expected it to, of course. When she'd first left, to live with Dermot for her initial year in college, Veronica had redecorated within a month of her departure. She'd stripped away the burnt-earth wallpaper and the ethnic carpet which Romy had requested a few years earlier, replacing them with white walls and an off-white carpet. Now, the room had been painted in a soft fudge and the carpet was pale green. It was surprisingly restful.

Romy took her laptop computer out of its bag and put it on the bedside table. She opened it and switched it on and then realised that Veronica had wireless internet access in the house, which perked her up instantly. She opened her Skype application, stuck the earpiece into her ear and looked at Keith's name on her contacts list. He wasn't online so she scrolled to his mobile number instead. She took a deep breath and clicked to dial it.

'Hi, this is Keith.' His voice was clear and distinct. 'Can't take your call now but leave a message.'

'It's me.' She was half relieved that he hadn't answered. 'Just letting you know that I'm here and that everything's OK. Maybe I'll call you tomorrow. Hope you're all right.' She made a face at her own words. How silly they sounded! But it was so difficult to talk to voicemail, especially when you were still a little embarrassed at having comfort-kissed the person you were leaving the message for. Maybe he's forgotten about that now, she thought hopefully as she closed down the program. She clicked on her web browser instead and typed in the website address of Heritage Help. They had a webcam installed in the office and she was able to see Tanya Brooks standing over the big table where a full-sized skeleton was laid out.

'Hi, Tan,' she mouthed, even though she knew that her friend couldn't see her. It was nice to be able to watch them, though. Made her feel as though she wasn't so far away after all. She posted a message on the Heritage Help bulletin board, saying that she wished she was still there and that she'd see them all soon, and then she closed down the computer.

She'd unpacked, somewhat sketchily, before dinner. She couldn't be bothered to put anything away now; her eyes were suddenly very heavy and she felt as though she might fall asleep on her feet. So she simply brushed her teeth and undressed, before clambering naked into bed.

She had almost drifted off when her mobile rang. Her eyes snapped open instantly and she grabbed it from the bedside locker.

'Hi,' said Keith. 'How're you doing?'

She sighed with relief to hear his voice. She hadn't messed things up after all!

'I'm OK,' she said.

'How's your mum?'

'Her back is certainly a problem,' admitted Romy. 'But she's all right.'

'You guys getting along?'

Romy chuckled. 'More or less.'

'Take it easy.'

'I'll try.'

'Call me any time you need to talk.'

'I tried to get you on Skype earlier,' she told him. 'How about we chat online tomorrow, same time?' She flinched slightly. Tomorrow sounded a bit keen and needy. Saying she'd call him the following day had never sounded needy before. It's because of that damn kiss, she told herself angrily. I so so so shouldn't have done it!

'I don't have my computer with me,' he said.

She'd forgotten about Queensland. How could she have forgotten already? She closed her eyes and conjured up pictures of the beautiful coastline. Blue sea. Blue sky. Fluffy white clouds. Warm breezes.

'Are you all having a good time?' she asked.

'It's great,' he admitted. 'The surfing is superb.'

'Don't have too much fun without me.' Did that sound kind of proprietorial? she wondered. As though she wanted him to be miserable while she wasn't there? She groaned silently. She would have to get over this feeling that she was saying one thing and meaning something else and not being able to talk to him as she used to.

He laughed. 'Well, hopefully you'll be back soon. It's a cracker of a day.'

'Don't make me even more envious than I am already.'

'You're doing the right thing,' he said.

'I know. But the right thing isn't necessarily something you want to do.'

'You'll be glad that you did.'

'Hum.' Romy wasn't quite so sure.

'You will,' he repeated. 'Anyway, have a good day.'

'It's night-time here.' She chuckled. 'I was going to bed. I'm zonked.'

'Oh, hell, forgot you'd be shattered. Sleep well.'

'Thanks. See you.'

She closed her phone and lay back on the pillow. Already Australia seemed like a lifetime ago. It was weird how quickly you adapted to being in a different place. Weird and somehow disconcerting.

She closed her eyes and thought of Keith and of Tanya and

of everyone she'd left behind. But she only thought about them for a few minutes because she soon fell into a deep sleep and didn't stir even when Veronica poked her head around the door a couple of hours later when she went to bed herself.

Chapter 6

Giselle didn't need to go to a maternity shop to buy her dress for the golf club dinner. She'd found the perfect one at her favourite designer boutique in Terenure and, as she surveyed her reflection in the full-length mirror of her bedroom on the night of the function, she reckoned that there were a lot of non-pregnant women who would be very pleased to look half as good as her in it. The dress itself was soft black and gathered under the bust so that it flared out gently, disguising her five-month bump. As she turned slowly in front of the mirror, Giselle reckoned that anyone would be hard pushed to realise that she was expecting a baby at all. She'd visited the hairdresser's earlier in the day and her blond hair was now piled on top of her head in a mass of curls and waves and studded with diamanté clips. She was wearing a matching diamond necklace and earring set which Darragh had given her for their last wedding anniversary, and she knew she looked both elegant and a little bit vulnerable and that she'd wow the rest of the golf wives tonight.

It was important to Giselle to look good. She regularly scoured the pages of *OK!* and *Hello!* and a variety of other gossip and fashion magazines to see what the celebs were wearing and to find a look to copy. She currently liked Kate and Sienna for casual style; her glamour idols were Scarlett Johansson and Sharon Stone. She'd never dreamed, when she was younger and growing up on the sprawling housing estate off the Greenhills Road, that one day she'd be mixing with the rich and famous of the Irish social scene. Not that she hadn't been happy in her days of rummaging through the bargain bins in Penney's and Dunne's, but marrying Darragh had been a major step up the ladder of success for her and she was determined to enjoy every last second of it. And so these days her clothes came from Brown Thomas and Harvey Nicks as well as local designer stores; and whenever they attended a function she bought a new dress and new shoes because it didn't do to be seen in the same outfit twice. (She loved tonight's shoes – black satin studded with tiny Swarovski crystals, which she'd picked up in the Dundrum Town Centre mall.) Spending time and money on her appearance made her feel confident, and it was important to her to feel confident when she was out with Darragh.

She sprayed herself with Chanel and then shuddered because during this pregnancy she was finding that the scent of perfume made her feel nauseous. Nevertheless, she absolutely couldn't go out without it. She took a couple of deep breaths and the nausea passed. Then she went downstairs.

'You look lovely,' said Magda as she walked into the living room.

'Thank you,' she replied. She looked around for Mimi.

'She's in the playroom,' Magda told her. 'Playing with her doll's house.'

Giselle went into the playroom, where she hugged Mimi and told her to be a good little girl. Her daughter looked at her comfortingly and said that she was always good, which made Giselle break into a fit of giggles.

Darragh poked his head around the door to tell her that the taxi had arrived, so Giselle kissed Mimi and promised that she'd be home soon and then both she and Darragh left for the dinner.

'I wish we could afford our own driver,' said Giselle as she got into the cab, which was clean but worn and was filled with the overwhelming aroma of the pine air freshener hanging from the rearview mirror, making her feel slightly nauseous again.

'It'd be nice,' agreed Darragh, 'but Dolan Component Manufacturers hasn't quite hit enough of the big time for that.'

'One day,' said Giselle.

'Maybe.' Darragh shrugged. There was no reason why not, he reckoned. The economy was doing well and there were more and more industrial plants opening all the time, so that even though he'd lost one or two contracts (he was still raging over the loss of Jim Cahill's business), there was plenty of opportunity to build up more. He'd called Jim and asked to talk to him about the contract but Jim had been quite firm in his assertion that Dolan Manufacturing Components couldn't match the quote he'd been given, and that if they could, they'd obviously been ripping him off for years. Darragh had been furious with Jim – the man knew he hadn't been ripped off, that whatever pricing he was getting was a special deal just to lure him away. And Jim had allowed himself to be lured, despite his long ties with Dolan's. Every time he remembered the conversation, Darragh felt himself grinding his teeth.

He exhaled slowly and draped his arm across Giselle's shoulders as they turned along the Ballycullen Road towards the golf club. Jim Cahill didn't matter, he thought. He had a great company, a gorgeous wife and a lovely daughter. And soon, he hoped, he'd have a son. It wasn't that he was so tied up in old-fashioned ideas that he didn't think Mimi was the most wonderful child ever to have walked the earth, but it would be nice to have a son. Someone he could pass the business on to, like Tom had passed it on to him.

Well, more or less. Darragh felt the usual dull stab of annoyance when he recalled that Tom hadn't, in fact, passed it on to him entirely; that he'd left Veronica with the lion's share and divided the rest between his two children. He supposed that Tom thought he was being fair, but in fact all that had happened was that it was a complete nuisance because Kathryn, when she realised that she had a share in the firm which was equal to Darragh's, had insisted on coming to the board meetings too. Veronica, possessing fifty per cent of the company, had always told her that the meetings were a desperate waste of time and that there wasn't any real point in her being there because as a family they were always going to vote the same way anyhow. And Kathryn had said that she didn't see the logic in that, not if there were things that needed changing.

Bloody Kathryn, he thought, feeling his blood begin to boil. She'd caused nothing but trouble for a couple of years as she'd protested about Darragh's ability to do the job and freaked out about the cost of redoing the company offices. She had actually voted against him being made managing director. He didn't think he'd ever actually forgive her for such a vicious betrayal, but in the end it hadn't mattered because naturally Veronica had voted for him and that had effectively blocked any of Kathryn's plans.

'I don't want to be the bloody managing director myself!' she'd cried when he accused her of wanting to shaft him. 'I'm not interested. All I'm saying is that we need someone with a strategic vision for the company. One that doesn't involve the managing director getting his wife to tart up the premises unnecessarily.'

Darragh had been furious, but at least she'd been wrong. Business had gone up after the refit and sales of their existing stock were high. Admittedly profit margins were down, but if they managed to get the new customers out there they'd go back up again. Kathryn was intellectual, Darragh often told Veronica, and very smart but she knew nothing about business and how things really worked. And, he'd add, it was all very well for her to pore over the accounts and tell him what he should be doing, but theory and practice were two very different things. Later, when she'd gone to the States and done well there (which thankfully meant that she couldn't come to the board meetings any more, although he always sent her the minutes), he'd admitted that she did know a thing or two, but an accountancy firm was very different from a manufacturing company and all she was doing was offering advice, not getting down and dirty with plant and machinery.

Veronica agreed with him about that too. Veronica, fortunately, agreed with him about almost everything. And that was because he knew that he got on better with her than Kathryn and Romy ever would. Partly because they were both on the same wavelength – they liked the feeling of power that came with owning Dolan Component Manufacturers; they liked the social responsibilities that came with it too and both of them, above all, liked going to the various dinners and functions that they were invited to as board members. The other reason for their closeness was because he was the only one in the family who actually remembered Tom as a person and he could talk to Veronica about him, which neither Kathryn nor Romy were able to do. He'd tried, with Kathryn, to tell her stuff about Tom – how good he was with his hands and how he'd made Darragh the best go-kart on the road so that everyone wanted to have a turn in it; how kind and gentle he was at home and especially to Veronica – so unlike Dermot, who never let her have her own way about anything; and how determined he always was to do the best for his family.

Darragh knew that he wanted to be like Tom in as many ways as possible but most especially in doing well in the business so that he could look after his family in the same way. He didn't want Giselle and Mimi (and Junior when he was born) to want for anything and he planned to ensure that they never would. But he also wanted them to enjoy themselves when he was around – if there was one regret that Darragh had about his childhood with Tom, it was that his father had been so caught up in building up the business that his times of making go-karts and going out with Veronica and Darragh were actually very rare. Darragh didn't want Mimi to think that he cared more about the business than about her and so, despite the fact that sometimes – like this week – he worked long hours because he felt obliged to or because there was a flap on at the office, he liked to be home early whenever possible and at least in time to put her to bed. And he liked socialising with Giselle too because he was, actually, completely in love with her. It wasn't entirely fashionable, he thought, to be in love with your wife but Giselle was the perfect person for him and he wanted her to be happy. He knew that it was important to her that she didn't have to worry about money and that she could buy as many designer clothes as she liked and that she had Magda for help around the house. And because Giselle was happy, she would come to boring as well as fun events with him and look radiant beside him and everyone would envy him.

Darragh liked the idea of people envying him, both for his great business and for his gorgeous wife.

They were among the first to arrive at the golf club, but Darragh had planned it that way. He was on the club's management committee, so even though he had nothing to do with the organisation of the night's event he wanted to be there in plenty of time in case anything cropped up. He ordered a gin and tonic for himself and a soda water for Giselle and took up his place at the end of the bar, which was where he felt most comfortable. The room filled up quickly and soon there was a steady hum of conversation which ranged from people's scores at the most recent competition and complaints about the proposed changes to the course to discussions between various members who liked to talk business together.

Darragh was joined by Norman Mulligan, the captain, who was also a board member of a boutique European bank; Cillian O'Farrell, who owned a printing company and was a client of Norman's bank; and Maurice Bond, who was the financial controller of a shipping company. Darragh, Norman, Cillian and Maurice played a semi-regular fourball together on Sunday mornings and Darragh had the lowest handicap of them all. In fact, Maurice often told him, if he played more he could get right down into low single figures, maybe even become a scratch golfer. Darragh always beamed with pleasure when Maurice said this even though they both knew that there was no real chance of it happening.

'The bank is sponsoring the Madrid Open this year,' Norman told them now. 'Fancy some passes?'

'Absolutely,' Darragh replied. Madrid later in the year would be lovely.

'I should probably try to get some for the next charity do,' Norman said. 'But you can only give so many away, you know. By the way, Darragh, that holiday – very generous.'

'Thanks.'

'Top prize tonight.'

'Is it?' Darragh already knew that it was and he was glad now that he'd gone with the Barbados holiday instead of the fortnight in the Canaries, which would have been definitely less prestigious and wouldn't have made him look half as philanthropic.

'I'm rather hoping to win it myself!' Norman laughed. 'Business was down last month so a fortnight away would be lovely.'

'We had a downturn as well,' said Maurice, 'but it picked up in the first week this month.'

'All's well for me,' Cillian said in satisfaction.

'Me too,' said Darragh.

'Oh? I heard that Jim Cahill had gone with Insystems for his latest.' Norman looked at Darragh enquiringly and Darragh felt his stomach tighten. How the hell would Norman know about that? Of course businessmen were just as gossipy as their wives were supposed to be, so he shouldn't really have been surprised, although in their case it was exchanging information. Information was power, everyone knew that, and so everyone wanted to know as much as possible about whatever was going on. Nevertheless it was disconcerting to think that Norman had been discussing his business with someone else. And Insystems! Darragh felt another spasm in his stomach. Insystems was their main competition for industrial components but Jim had always professed to dislike Garrett Jones, its managing director.

'They're losing on the deal,' he told the other men. 'The pricing is cut-throat. I'm not going to keep business and lose money. That's madness.'

The other three agreed.

'Still,' said Cillian, 'whenever something like that happens you have to adjust your mindset, don't you? I heard that Insystems had bought a new business in Geneva. Perhaps that's allowing them to pass on some cost savings.'

Geneva! Darragh looked at Cillian in astonishment. What the hell was Garrett doing in Geneva? What possible opportunity was there that he didn't know about? He'd have to talk to Stephen and Alex and find out what his company secretary and financial officer were doing. They'd lost Jim's business. They hadn't told him anything about Insystems and Geneva. They were letting him down big time and he was going to have to throw his weight about the place a bit and let them know exactly who was boss. Get them to get their act together and keep properly in touch with what was going on.

As he thought his dark thoughts about his subordinates, the conversation switched to golf again. He gladly rejoined it, happy to talk about anything other than damn industrial components.

Giselle, despite her high heels and bump, was happy to stand rather than sit while people drank and she chatted happily to the wives of the other committee members as well as to the lady captain, Josephine Hewitt. Giselle had been amused by the fact that the men and the women had different captains and different playing times and sometimes (she thought) treated each other like people from different planets; but it didn't matter to her because she didn't actually play golf and her only real interest in the club was for its social benefits (and because Josephine had championed the installation of a sauna and steam room in the ladies' changing area).

'I must move on,' said Josephine during a lull in the conversation. 'It's important that I circulate.'

Giselle stayed with the group and listened idly while Mandy and Crona began a discussion on the most recent tournament, which Mandy had unexpectedly won. The prize had been a weekend in Paris and Giselle wondered if, despite her lack of interest, she should take up golf herself after the baby was born. It was getting very popular among her set and the prizes were really very good (though nothing as brilliant as Darragh's prize for this evening's draw), but in all honesty, she thought as she listened to Mandy's description of holing out for an eagle on the sixteenth (whatever that actually meant), the idea of tramping around the course for four bloody hours a day was too boring for words. And the clothes were just vile – there was a sports shop in the club and Giselle couldn't believe that the women actually liked those twee little V-necked jumpers and staid skirts in those revoltingly pastel pinks and oranges and simply dreadful checks. Fashion sense went out the window on the golf course, she thought. And there was no way she was going to lose her fashion sense for a stupid bloody game!

She was relieved when it was time to go in to dinner and Mandy and Crona ended up at a different table. Back beside Darragh she murmured that there were some very stuffy people here tonight and he pinched her unobtrusively on the behind to show that he wasn't one of them. She giggled and sat down, flanked by her husband and Cillian's wife, Carlotta, who had just returned from Paris. She spent a very happy time chatting with Carlotta about Parisian fashions and about the shopping opportunities on the Avenue Montaigne (she'd gone there with Darragh just before she got pregnant and spent a fortune on designer clothes which unfortunately now she wasn't able to wear) as well as the eclectic night life. They talked, too, about another charity lunch which Carlotta was organising and for which Giselle promised to provide flowers, they bitched a little about a couple of the group who had pleaded hectic schedules as reasons not to get involved and then they indulged in some very pleasurable gossip about Norman Mulligan's wife, who – according to Carlotta – was having an affair with a very well-known social diarist.

'No!' Giselle's eyes opened wide. 'You've got to be kidding me.'

'Not at all,' said Carlotta wickedly. 'Everyone's talking about it.'

'Does he know?'

Carlotta shrugged. 'They say the woman is always the last to know when her husband is having an affair. But I think men are a million times more stupid about it. They go off to work for sixteen hours in the day sometimes and they think we're going to sit around waiting for them to get home! I mean, come on!'

Giselle laughed.

'I said it to Cillian,' Carlotta continued. 'I told him that if he went twelve hours without coming home or contacting me then he wasn't to be surprised if when he did arrive back he found me in bed with the gardener.'

'Wow.' Giselle looked at Carlotta in admiration. 'I've never issued an ultimatum to Darragh in my life. But I must think about it.'

'Ah, but Darragh doesn't work night and day, does he?' asked Carlotta. 'He's a fantastic guy but he doesn't live and breathe it like some of them. And of course it's a family firm so that's different.'

Giselle nodded. 'I suppose you're right. He works very hard, though.'

Carlotta smiled. 'They all want you to think that. Whether they're doing anything useful is another question entirely.'

Well, thought Giselle, Darragh always seemed to be doing useful things. He was the strategic thinker in the company, that was what he told her. And he took it all very seriously. He was worried, she knew, about the fact that Veronica was going into hospital and that she might be out of action. He relied on Veronica's support. Giselle knew that Veronica frequently said that she wasn't interested in being involved, but whenever she and Darragh had a board meeting she was always keen to hear what he was up to and how the company was performing.

At least Kathryn didn't bother them any more. Giselle remembered the time when her sister-in-law had tried to muscle in and take things over but was firmly rebuffed by both Darragh and Veronica. Giselle disliked Kathryn intensely – much more than she disliked Romy. It was hard to actually dislike Romy; the truth was, Giselle just found her impossible to understand, with her complete lack of any feminine charms whatsoever. Kathryn, though, was too shrewd by far and condescending with it. If Giselle had to pick either of the two of them to be marooned on a desert island with (and that thought in itself was pretty horrific) it would have to be Romy. Yet she knew that Darragh felt a million times closer to the irritating Kathryn than to his scattier half-sister.

It was all about blood ties with Darragh, Giselle knew. She'd never before met anyone to whom family was so important. And that, for her, was a good thing. Because although Darragh felt that Veronica and Kathryn were important to him as family, she knew that she and Mimi and Junior were more important still. Darragh had already told her that when Veronica signed over her fifty per cent shareholding to him – as she was bound to do some day – he would divide it between her and the two children. But, he'd said, if Junior was a boy he'd have the biggest shareholding. He hoped she wouldn't mind but he wanted his son to follow him into the family business.

Giselle didn't mind in the slightest. She didn't want Mimi being caught up in industrial components – how boring could that be for any girl? She wanted her to have fun and maybe get involved in media or PR so that she could live a more glamorous life and rub shoulders with the really rich and famous. Or perhaps she could become a singer or a dancer (she was actually quite good at ballet) or – preferably – an actress (she was even better at acting, Giselle reckoned, the way she carried on sometimes!).

All the time these thoughts were going through her head she was nodding in agreement with Carlotta and the other people around the table until the draw took place and she was called on to pull the ticket out of the hat for the winner of the holiday in Barbados.

That turned out to be Crona, who shrieked in delight when she realised that the resort had its very own golf course. Giselle thought it was a desperate waste to schlep halfway around the world simply to play a game of golf when Crona could lie on the gorgeous white sand or go scuba-diving instead, but she didn't say anything like that as she handed the voucher to her and told her to have a fabulous time.

'Oh, I will!' Crona's eyes were dancing with delight. 'I totally will.'

'And very many thanks to Darragh Dolan for his generosity in donating our top prize tonight,' Norman said. 'Thank you all for coming and for supporting the event and we hope to see most of you on the tee in the morning!'

There was a round of applause and Giselle went back to the table.

'My hero,' she murmured as she slid into her seat beside Darragh. 'Everyone's really impressed.'

'Hey, why not?' He grinned at her. 'I like them to know they can depend on me for things like this.'

'I told Carlotta I'd do the flowers for the next one,' said Giselle, her glance flickering over to Cillian's wife who was now sitting opposite.

'Great. Save me having to top this by sending someone to Alaska.' Darragh grinned at her.

'Hmm, yes. The flowers aren't cheap, though.'

'By comparison,' Darragh told her. He looked at his watch. 'Do you want to head off?'

'It's a bit early, isn't it?'

'Yes. But to be honest I've got a slight headache and I don't feel like hanging around.'

'Oh. OK.' She stood up again.

'Thanks.'

They said their goodbyes and got a taxi home.

'Want a cup of tea before going to bed?' asked Giselle as they walked quietly through the darkened house.

'No thanks. I'm actually flaked.'

'You look tired.' She frowned. 'Everything OK?'

'More or less.' He almost told her about Jim Cahill and the lost business and Insystems and their new company in Switzerland but he stopped himself. There wasn't any point in offloading his worries on her. Stephen and Alex were the people to do that with.

'I was thinking,' she said as they lay side by side in the queen-sized bed. 'Maybe we should go to Barbados ourselves. Have a break before Junior comes along.'

'It's a nice thought,' said Darragh after a moment's pause. 'But it's not realistic. At least not until we see how Mum is doing.'

'Yes, but isn't that why Romy is back?' asked Giselle. 'To be there for your mother. So that you don't have to spend your time running after her.'

'I guess so.'

'I was only thinking of a week.' She snuggled closer to him. 'Before I'm not allowed to go anywhere. I'm tired and the weather here's been so awful lately . . . It might be spring but it feels like winter and I could do with a dose of sunshine vitamin D.'

'Yes . . . well . . . I guess it's a possibility,' said Darragh slowly. 'What about Mimi?'

'D'you think Romy could look after her too?'

'Are you joking?'

'Yeah, but if she's already keeping an eye on Veronica she might as well keep an eye on Mimi at the same time.'

'It's a thought. And Mum will be there to make sure Romy doesn't do anything really stupid.'

'We don't have to decide tonight,' said Giselle. 'Let's sleep on it and talk about it again tomorrow.'

'OK.' Darragh put his arm around her. 'Meantime, my headache has suddenly disappeared.'

'Oh, really?' Her tone was playful.

'Really,' he assured her.

'And isn't that good news.' She was laughing softly as her fingers slid down his naked stomach. 'Very good news indeed.'

Chapter 7

Romy was alone in the big, airy kitchen, leaning against the island worktop and gazing out of the enormous picture window at the garden beyond. It was funny, she thought, how being on her own in the house felt completely different from being there when there was another person somewhere else in it, even if she couldn't see them or hear them or didn't know exactly where they were. She'd stood in this kitchen on her own plenty of times before but then it was in the knowledge that Veronica or Darragh or Kathryn could walk in at any moment. Now it seemed to her that the tick of the ancient wall clock (a prize won by Kathryn in her science exams in her first year at secondary school) was louder than ever while the occasional creak of an expanding floorboard seemed to echo around her.

She'd brought Veronica into the hospital that afternoon, driving the silver Golf with her mother in the passenger seat and trying not to allow herself to be wound up as they slowly made their way through town. Veronica was a terrible passenger, sucking in her breath every time she thought that Romy was too close to the car in front or hadn't seen a pedestrian step out on to the road.

'Oh, look, I know I haven't driven this car before!' Romy eventually cried in exasperation as Veronica's right foot headed towards an imaginary brake yet again. 'But I've been driving SUVs in Australia and jeeps in Egypt and I really don't think that I'm going to ram some unsuspecting lorry driver in Ireland.'

'Traffic is desperate in Dublin,' Veronica told her. 'Legendary, in fact. Australia is all open spaces so it's completely different. You're not used to this.'

'Sydney is a city,' said Romy firmly. 'And as busy as any other city, including this one. I know you regard me as a hopeless case, but honestly, whatever else you think I'm crap at, I'm really quite a good driver.'

She was relieved when they finally arrived at the private hospital and Veronica was admitted. Her mother had a small room overlooking the garden area which, she said, at least made things a little less institutionalised. Then she opened her overnight case, took out her cosmetics bag and arranged all her creams and potions on the small dresser.

Romy looked at them in astonishment. 'I don't think they'll let you wear make-up in the operating theatre.'

'I know that,' said Veronica as she fluttered her luxuriously mascaraed eyelashes. 'But at least I have stuff for afterwards.'

Romy laughed. 'You'll be knackered afterwards,' she said. 'You won't want to be doing your face.'

'I've never felt bad enough not to do my face,' said Veronica.

'I guess.'

'So having my stuff helps. I hate being in this place.'

'It'll be worth it in the end,' said Romy.

'It better be.'

'Are you very worried about the operation?' Romy felt a sudden rush of sympathy for her mother.

'No,' said Veronica. 'I just don't like . . .' She shrugged. 'I don't want to be here. I don't want to have some stupid thing wrong with my back. I don't want to have a bit of arthritis in my hand. I don't want so-called laughter lines on my face and I don't want to have to wear reading glasses and grunt every time I get out of the armchair.'

'It's sort of inevitable, though, isn't it?' said Romy. 'Not that I think having to wear reading glasses and stuff is something to look forward to – but what can you do about it? And, you know, laughter lines can give you character.'

'Character my arse!' Veronica snorted. 'Oh, you can say that now with the indulgence of knowing that you're still in your twenties and you've perfect sight and no aching bones. Character is wildly overrated. Just wait and see what you think when you spot a few wrinkles of your own.'

'OK, OK!' Romy held up her hands. 'I know you're right. I suppose that I'll freak out when I see a grey hair. But the truth is, Mum, you're in great nick for someone your age. You really are.'

'But that's the whole point!' Veronica looked at her in exasperation. 'I don't want to be someone my age.'

'Well, the alternative is being dead,' said Romy lightly.

'You just don't understand. And I can't tell whether it's deliberate or not.'

'And you're obsessed!' cried Romy. 'Everybody gets tweaks and twinges when they get older. It's not a crime to be over sixty! I don't know what you want.'

'I want to be a person with no tweaks and twinges. I don't want to have to spend my time checking for new wrinkles! I don't want to be lectured by ageing movie stars about my "very mature" skin and how it loses precious moisture every nanosecond. I want to be – well – young again.'

'Being young isn't all it's cracked up to be,' Romy told her firmly. 'It's not the be all and end all. There's just as much trauma, you know.'

'But at least you have it with an unlined face and your natural hair colour.'

'As if you ever had a natural hair colour!'

'You think it's shallow and vain to want to look young,' said Veronica. 'But it's not!'

'I don't think there's anything wrong with looking good,' protested Romy. 'You always look good. But thinking that you need to look like a teenager again is just plain silly. I'd rather have a mother who grew old gracefully than someone who ended up with her face stretched so tight she looked like a Barbie doll. Plus,' she added, 'you can always tell who's had it done; it never looks natural and all you have to do is look at someone's neck or hands to check out their real age.'

Veronica glanced down involuntarily at her own hands. She used an expensive cream on them every morning and every night but they still had a few telltale brown spots, despite the extravagant promises on the jar.

'I always knew you thought I was a silly woman,' she said.

Romy looked at her in exasperation.

'As far as you're concerned I've failed you, haven't I?'

'We don't need to talk about the past,' said Romy. 'Not now.'

'Why not? What happens if I die under the knife and we don't say all the things that you're still itching to say?'

'You're not going to die,' said Romy, 'and there's nothing I need to say that I haven't said already. We've moved on, haven't we? Didn't we agree on that years ago? Not to go over old ground again? You're tense, that's all.'

Veronica shot a look at Romy. 'You're hoping that my back trouble puts a stop to my gallop. You're hoping that I end up like some fairy-tale grandmother with apple cheeks and a body like Play-Doh.'

'Of course I don't hope that.' Romy faced her mother in frustration. 'Besides, you'll never be apple-cheeked. Mum, honestly, I want you to look as good as always. I know you're in pain now. I can see that, and I'm sorry.'

'You probably thought I was making it up for sympathy,' said Veronica.

'You're driving me nuts,' Romy told her. 'It doesn't matter what I say, you're going to think whatever you like. And the truth of it is that I may not always have approved of some of your more bizarre fashion ideas . . . and . . . and other things, but I do think it's great that you look fabulous and that you've got a life of your own.'

'I work hard to look fabulous,' said Veronica. 'It matters.'

'It always did.' Suddenly Romy couldn't help herself. 'What's outside was always far more important to you than what's inside.'

Veronica said nothing but rearranged her pots on the dresser.

'I'm sorry,' said Romy after a moment of taut silence. 'Look, is there anything I can get for you? Books, magazines, fruit?'

'I'm not helpless and hopeless yet,' said her mother shortly. 'I'll go down to the hospital shop myself later.'

'OK, in that case I'll head off.' Romy knew that she couldn't stay. Despite their promises of putting the past behind them, she had a horrible feeling that one or the other of them would probably end up saying something that they'd regret.

'Fine,' said Veronica. 'Don't forget to move my stuff.'

Veronica had reluctantly agreed, the previous night, that it would be better when she came home if she slept in the down-stairs guest bedroom until she was feeling more able to tackle the stairs again. Romy had suggested moving everything there and then but Veronica had, quite suddenly, become upset at the idea, saying that she wanted to spend her last night at home in her own bedroom. Romy, dismayed and shocked by her mother's apparent vulnerability, had agreed to move things when Veronica was in hospital.

'I won't forget. I'm going to do it as soon as I get back.'

'No poking and prying.' Veronica spoke sharply.

'Mum, relax, for heaven's sake!' Romy opened the door. 'I wouldn't dream of going through your stuff and I don't want to nose around your room. I don't care what you've got hidden away!'

Veronica shrugged and Romy breathed out slowly.

'I'm going now,' she said. 'Good luck. I'll see you tomorrow.'

'Right,' said Veronica.

Romy hesitated for a moment, then walked out of the room.

When she glanced back she saw that Veronica was staring into the mirror beside her bed. She was pulling at the skin around her face. Romy wondered if she was going to ask the surgeon to have a go at lifting it while she was there.

She'd been exasperated at the hospital but now, back at the house in Rathfarnham, she was feeling sorry for Veronica again. She knew that her mother didn't like hospitals, even expensive private hospitals with individual rooms and daily menu options. Veronica didn't like illness full stop. She couldn't cope with reminders of her own mortality. As a child, Romy remembered that it was always Dermot who'd looked after her when she was unwell, Dermot who'd sat beside her and held her hand when she hadn't wanted to be alone. The only time she'd been sick when he'd been away on a job – a virulent tummy bug which had seen her practically take up residence in the bathroom – Kathryn had been the one to take charge. But, of course, Kathryn had done everything in her matter-of-fact way, dispensing medicine but not sympathy and reading a list of Romy's symptoms to her, comparing them to the medical handbook which was always kept in her room.

The kettle clicked off and Romy poured boiling water over the tea bag in the blue mug on the counter. She'd hardly drunk any tea at all in the past couple of years but now, back home, she was downing it at every available opportunity. Tea had been on the go all the time when she was small, and now when people talked so much about its antioxidant effects Veronica was cheered to know that she'd been a prodigious tea-drinker all her life, which, she reckoned, would stand her in good stead for the future.

Romy took a chocolate biscuit from the Tupperware box in the cupboard and put it on the plate beside the mug. The tick of the clock continued to echo around the kitchen and she turned on the radio to drown it out. It truly was totally weird being here on her own. She felt as though she was an intruder in the house, a stranger sneaking around to find out all its secrets. Because it wasn't home any more. It didn't feel anything like home.

But then it never really had. Not as far as she was concerned. Which was probably a little bit weird too.

She ate the biscuit in three bites and then, hands wrapped around the mug, walked out of the kitchen and into the living room. When Romy had lived in the house this had been the main family room, slightly scruffy and usually cluttered with schoolbooks or toys or discarded jumpers and coats, much to Veronica's perpetual frustration. Now it was painted in soft neutral shades and there was nothing out of place. It was a grown-up's room, adult and sophisticated.

Romy wondered how Veronica coped when Giselle and Mimi came to visit. Was she in a constant state of terror that the three year old would mark the walls or dirty the carpet? Maybe Mimi was the kind of child who didn't get mud on her hands and spill things and generally wreak havoc. Maybe she was the kind of child Veronica would have wanted for herself.

All traces of Veronica's husbands had been removed from the room. When Romy had lived at home there'd been a small family portrait in a silver frame on the sideboard. It had been taken by a friend of Dermot's and showed her father and Veronica standing beneath the flowering apple tree in the back garden, with Darragh, Kathryn and Romy sitting at their feet. Anyone seeing the photo would have assumed that they were a united family but Romy knew that Darragh had argued fiercely about it, saying that he didn't want to be in some stupid photo with Dermot. Veronica had had to bribe him (although Romy didn't know how) to be part of it. There had been a row with Kathryn too – Veronica had wanted her to take off her glasses but Kathryn had refused and it was hard to see her face, hidden behind the huge frames and her long fringe. Romy herself had argued too, although in her case because Veronica wanted her to change out of her raggy jeans and into a pretty dress. She, like Kathryn, had refused.

Poor Veronica, thought Romy. She so wanted to have daughters to share her life with and she ended up with me and Kathryn. Her only consolation is Giselle!

She continued to wander through the house – the den, which had been Dermot's study (and Tom's before him) and presumably had also been used by Larry, was still a masculine sort of room with its oak desk and no-nonsense bookshelves. The dining room, like the living room, had been thoroughly made over in a modern, minimalist style. The TV room was the most relaxed room on the ground floor and the plasma-screen TV on the wall was one of the biggest Romy had ever seen in her life. All these changes had happened in the last two years. Things had been different when she'd visited previously, but never as expensive and quietly classy as they were now.

Looks like Dolan Component Manufacturers is going from strength to strength, she murmured to herself. Looks like Tom Dolan still holds sway as the most successful of Veronica's husbands. Looks like no one will ever truly replace him, either in her heart or in her wallet.

She continued to sip her tea as she went upstairs. She would move Veronica's stuff after she'd finished and would abide by her promise not to pry in her room, but she intended to prowl around the rest of the house first. She hadn't been able to prowl when Veronica had been there – in fact she'd never really prowled through the house at all. Even as a small child she'd been wary about opening closed doors. She'd spent most of her time in her own room, or doing her homework in the den or playing outside. She hadn't been welcomed into Darragh's room, or Kathryn's, and she very rarely went into Dermot and Veronica's room either. It was as though big chunks of the house simply weren't anything to do with her, although surely, she asked herself now, surely she'd had a perfect right to go wherever she liked? Yet it had never actually felt like that.

She didn't really feel as though she had a right to open the door to what had been Darragh's room now either. But she did anyway. It wasn't Darragh's room any more. It hadn't been his room in years. It was just a room. And it too had been made over, she saw as she pushed open the door and peeped inside, in shades of ochre and brown. Kathryn's room had also been given the decorator's touch, although her colour was a soft blush. Romy grinned. Kathryn had never been a pastel sort of person. Kathryn liked definite colours. She did, however, have the best bedroom in the house, overlooking the big back garden with its apple and plum trees and with double doors instead of a window leading to a small balcony which got the evening sun. Romy had always been jealous of Kathryn's room. Her own, although sizeable enough and with a bigger en suite bathroom, didn't have either the views or the balcony.

I envied her all the time, remembered Romy. Him too. I envied both of them although I was never really sure why.

But not now. I'm doing my own thing now. I'm Romy Kilkenny and I was offered a supervisor's job in Australia which is where I'm making a new life for myself and where I really belong now, and I'll be back there in a few weeks and everything will be the way it's supposed to be again.

The doorbell rang and startled her so much that she dropped her mug and spilled the dregs of her tea on to the rose-coloured carpet.

'Shit, shit, shit,' she muttered, hurrying down the stairs, thinking that it was typical of her to mess up the house as soon as Veronica's back was turned and remembering that Veronica had often accused her of being hopelessly messy and uncoordinated as a child.

Darragh was standing on the doorstep, his key in his hand.

'I thought you weren't in,' he said as he walked past her.

'I was upstairs.'

'How's things?'

This was the first time she'd seen him. He'd called over the day after she'd come home but she'd gone to get her hair trimmed and there'd been a delay at the hairdresser's and by the time she got back, he'd left.

'I'm fine,' she said now.

He was as handsome as ever, she thought. He always had been – she remembered when he was a teenager and girls used to hang around outside the house hoping he'd notice them. He was averagely tall but his square face was strong and his eyes a brilliant dark blue. His hair had always been soot black but now it was lightly sprinkled with grey. It wasn't fair, Romy thought, that men looked good with grey hair. It suited Darragh. It gave him a look of gravitas that he hadn't had before. Made him seem more of a managing director type of person.

'How's Mum? Did she settle in OK?'

'Fine,' repeated Romy.

He looked at her appraisingly and she felt herself flush. She'd always been in awe of Darragh, eleven years older than her, almost a grown-up as far as she was concerned. And the condescending way in which he'd treated her had made her feel even more in awe of him. When she wasn't hating him, of course. She'd hated him quite a lot because he was always so horrible to Dermot. Not always overtly nasty. But horrible all the same.

She'd said it to her father once and Dermot had grinned at her and told her that it was difficult to have two alpha males in the house but that he wasn't bothered. She hadn't known what he was talking about. She'd asked Kathryn, who'd explained it to her – both of them wanted to be the top dog, she'd said. Both of them wanted Veronica to love them the most.

Well, thought Romy now, Darragh had succeeded in being the long-term alpha male. He'd seen off Dermot and Larry and Romy knew that Veronica adored him. Her only son. The eldest. The boy who could do no wrong.

'Sorry?' She'd missed what he'd just said, lost in her memories as she'd followed him into the kitchen.

'Any chance of something to eat?' he asked.

She looked at her watch. It was nearly six in the evening. 'Like what?'

'Anything,' he said irritably. 'Food. Hot food. You can cook, can't you? You did it in school. I remember you bringing stuff home.'

'Well, yes,' she said. 'I can cook. But aren't you going home to eat?'

'Giselle is at her Birthing is Beautiful class tonight,' he told her. 'She doesn't have time. Besides, she's eating healthily and I hate all those light meals.'

'Oh. Right. What about Mimi? Don't you have to feed her?'

'The au pair is looking after her. It's not her night to cook for me and I don't want to ask her. So – what are the chances?'

'I guess I can rustle up something.' Romy was disconcerted by his request. 'Chicken? Tuna?'

'Anything with red meat?' he asked hopefully, and she laughed.

'Actually, there are beefburgers in the fridge,' she told him. 'Real burgers, from the butcher's. I bought them the other day. I could do you a burger and chips if that's what you mean by cooking. Oven chips, though, I'm afraid, so the truth is that it's not really cooking, just sort of heating up.'

'Sounds ideal to me,' he said.

I don't believe I'm doing this, she said to herself as she took the meat out of the fridge. I don't think I ever cooked Darragh anything to eat in my life before. Even oven chips!

He hadn't been around much by the time she'd been allowed anywhere near the cooker and she considered him to be closer in age to her parents than to her. He spoke to Veronica and Dermot as though he was an adult, and of course by the time her parents split up, he was an adult and living in an apartment a couple of miles away. He'd moved back home after

Dermot had left, slipping back into the man-of-the-house shoes that she knew he felt Dermot had appropriated. That had been a horrible time in his relationship with her, because she felt as though he tried to take out his anger with Dermot on her, constantly sniping at her, always ready to argue with her over the slightest thing. She wouldn't have dreamed of cooking for him then.

He had a temper too – according to Veronica, it was Tom's temper only not as well contained. He would suddenly flare up over the silliest of things and somehow Romy always seemed to take the brunt of his anger, even if whatever he was angry about (like Mrs McArdle's Jack Russell puppy coming into the garden and digging up all the plants he'd just put down) had nothing to do with her. She recalled the Jack Russell episode now – he'd blamed her for leaving the front gate open!

But right now he was being perfectly pleasant to her, as though all those other times hadn't ever happened. She wondered how long it would last.

He wandered into the TV room and she heard the sound of the news. She popped the chips into the oven and the burgers on to the grill. Then she shook some frozen peas into a bowl, added some water and put them to one side to cook in the microwave. This is so not me, she thought. Being domesticated. For Darragh, of all people!

They ate at the kitchen table, where she'd set two places.

'Not bad,' he said as he tasted the burger. 'You were always quite good at this, weren't you?'

'Grilling burgers? It's hardly rocket science.' She shrugged. 'You never actually tasted my proper cooking.'

'Mum told me,' he said. 'She was surprised by it on account of the fact that most of the time you were climbing trees and stuff. She didn't think you'd be much for cooking.'

'Maybe it's the one thing I inherited from her,' she said drily. 'You always liked her food, didn't you?'

'I guess so.' He shrugged. 'So how are you settling in?'

Romy shrugged too. 'OK.'

'I was right to ask you to come home,' he said. 'You're the only one without responsibilities. It had to be you.'

'I know. But I don't like being railroaded into things.'

'There was no other way.'

'Maybe not.' She cut her burger into pieces.

'How did the boyfriend take it?'

So he'd taken on board the fact that there was supposed to be a boyfriend! She swallowed a piece of burger before she replied. 'He was understanding.'

'Men are,' said Darragh.

She looked at him sceptically.

'Will you go back to Australia?'

'I hope so.' She put down her knife and fork. 'Like I said before, I was offered another job there but I had to turn it down to come here. I guess it depends on what crops up.'

'If you're any good they'll offer you another job.'

'It's not like big business,' she said edgily. 'There aren't as many opportunities.'

'It's all what you make of it,' said Darragh.

'How's business for you?' She picked up her cutlery again.

'Excellent,' he told her. 'Dad sure built up a great company.'

'I guess at this stage it's you that's built it up.'

Darragh looked pleased at her words. 'True,' he said. 'But Dad was the concept man.'

She nodded.

'Anyway, the other reason I came over was to invite you out to dinner tomorrow night,' said Darragh, glossing over her silence. 'Giselle thought it would be a good idea. Welcome you home, that sort of thing. Nice restaurant, good food.'

'She mentioned something about it when she picked me up at the airport.' Romy had actually been hoping that they'd forget about it because she never knew what to talk about when she was with them.

I wish I was comfortable in his company, she thought. I

wish I felt like he truly was my big brother and he looked out for me and that going to dinner with him and his wife was something to look forward to. She glanced across at Darragh, knowing that they shared Veronica's genes but not seeing where. He still felt like a stranger to her despite the fact that they were sitting together in the house where both of them had been brought up. Why? she wondered. Why was it so hard to find a connection?

'That was great.' He'd eaten every last morsel of food. Now he stood up and stretched. 'I'd better get back. I normally see Mimi before she goes to bed and I haven't managed that the last few nights because I've been caught up in a business deal.'

'OK,' said Romy.

'So we'll see you tomorrow. What time did the doctor say that Mum will be out of surgery?'

'She's going to theatre early morning. He said to call some-time after two.'

'Fine,' said Darragh. 'You call, then call me. You have all my numbers, don't you?'

She shook her head and he reached into his pocket and took out a card. It was off-white, on linen-effect paper. His name, Darragh J. Dolan, was embossed in gold print above his title, Managing Director. It looked important.

'See you tomorrow then,' she said as she walked to the front door with him.

'Good to see you home,' he responded as he turned towards his car and clicked on the remote locking.

Good to see her home! She didn't think he'd ever said that to her before either. Everything about being back was strange.

She put the plates into the dishwasher and then went back upstairs, bringing some carpet foam with her to squirt over the stain left by the tea she'd spilt in Kathryn's bedroom. She wasn't sure whether the foam would be effective but she rubbed it in anyway, comforting herself with the thought that the room was hardly ever used and it would be months before anyone would notice it anyhow, by which time she'd be safely back in Australia.

Then she went into Veronica's room.

It was a huge room, taking up a quarter of the upstairs space and with windows facing south and west which made it bright and warm. A king-sized bed (no, thought Romy, bigger than king-sized; super-king, surely) was centred along the north wall and covered in a quilted satin duvet of pinks and creams along with matching cushions and pillows. The carpet was a deep pile in luxurious cream and the curtains were rose pink. A huge dressing table took up the space behind the door and there was a neat flat-screen TV on a stand opposite the bed. The room smelt of Veronica's signature Dior perfume and was, thought Romy, a total fairy-tale room. It had definitely been much plainer when her father had been around.

She wondered what it had been like in the year of Veronica's marriage to Larry. She also wondered whether or not women who lived with men had very different bedrooms from women who lived on their own. Would she herself go for Barbie pinks if she was in charge of her own bedroom? The small single room in Keith's house was painted in a neutral buttermilk, there were wooden floors and the duvet cover was bright blue. There was a small mirror and no dressing table for her bits and pieces, which she kept, along with her laptop, on top of a chest of drawers. Not very fairy-tale. Not even very feminine! But she was quite happy with it the way it was.

Veronica had said that there were bags in her wardrobe which she could use to carry down her clothes. Not everything, she'd told Romy; she could use her discretion. But all of her lingerie if Romy wouldn't mind.

She opened the double doors of the two large wardrobes and looked inside. Veronica's clothes were neatly arranged in what Romy reckoned were seasonal outfits and then subdivided by colour. She'd never seen such a neat arrangement nor so many clothes before! And part of one of the wardrobes was taken over by Veronica's shoe collection, each pair neatly stacked into what seemed like custom-made cubbyholes.

Romy slid one of the shoes from its home. It was a red satin slingback with a four-inch heel and a crystal brooch with a red stone on the front. The designer was Jimmy Choo. Romy could see that the shoe was a thing of beauty although she wondered how on earth Veronica managed to stand upright in it, even though she'd heard people say that it was perfectly possible to walk in high heels if the design was good. She slid the shoe back into its place. The next cubbyhole contained yet another pillar-box-red high-heeled shoe – more of a sandal this time, Romy decided – in suede and snakeskin. There were black shoes, grey shoes, blue shoes and brown shoes too – all with ultra-high heels and all breathtakingly beautiful. A sudden memory flashed through Romy's mind, of Veronica bringing her to school, an unseasonably wet and wild day in September, wearing red leather boots and a red wool coat with big shoulders and nipped in at the waist by a wide black belt. She'd worn a black Russian Cossack-style hat over her golden hair and sported her full make-up. The other mothers had been harried and wearing duffel coats or anoraks. Romy had been half pleased but also embarrassed by Veronica's glamour at the school gates.

She replaced the shoes. Veronica wouldn't be wearing any of these in the next few months. At the lower level of the cubbyholes was a selection of flat loafers. Some of them were plain but most had a detail on them – sequins or pearls or rhinestones – to jazz them up. Even in flat shoes, thought Romy, Veronica liked her glitz.

Romy scooped the loafers together and put them into one of the big carrier bags. She took a selection of trousers too (Veronica had worn only trousers in the few days since Romy had come home and she reckoned it was because her mother wouldn't be seen dead in a skirt and flat shoes). Then, from the chest of drawers, she extracted a variety of tops which she imagined might go with the trousers.

She brought all these downstairs and put them away in the less luxurious but carefully decorated guest room, and then went back to her mother's room to retrieve her lingerie. Romy felt incredibly uneasy and intrusive about opening the drawers that contained Veronica's bras and knickers and she felt herself blush as she took out the filmy lace and satin underwear. For God's sake, she thought, as she appraised a Janet Reger bra and matching briefs, I don't wear stuff like this! So why the hell should she? Who, she wondered, did Veronica wear it for? Herself? But would you be bothered wearing Janet Reger just for yourself? Or was Romy the one out of touch with things just because she preferred plain knickers? It wasn't as though she was mean about them; she did sometimes buy Calvin Klein, but somehow it wasn't quite the same thing!

Romy shut the drawer abruptly. She had enough stuff here to be going on with and she really couldn't face looking at her mother's intimate garments for a moment longer. She then went into the bathroom and gathered the beauty products that Veronica hadn't taken to hospital with her – a collection of creams, emollients, face scrubs and serums – and put them in yet another bag. She brought those down to the guest room too, where she shoved the lingerie into the drawers as quickly as possible but spent a bit of time trying to arrange the cosmetics in the bathroom so that they looked nice. She hadn't poked or pried. But she felt as though she had still violated Veronica in some way, learned things about her that she didn't want to know. As she sat down in front of the TV and drank a cup of hot chocolate, she couldn't help thinking of the wispy knickers and push-up bras and sexy shoes and wishing she didn't really know about them.

She's my mother, thought Romy. But she's a person too. She's entitled to wear that kind of stuff if she wants to. I shouldn't feel freaked out by it. I mean, think of Helen Mirren.

Everyone considers her to be one of the sexiest women in the world and she's older than Veronica!

But Helen Mirren's not my mother. Veronica is. And I *am* freaked out by her no matter what.

Chapter 8

She met up with her father the following afternoon. Having called the hospital to check that Veronica's pre-op tests were going OK she drove across the city to Dermot's house. He didn't live in the apartment any more. After marrying Larissa five years earlier they'd moved to a small redbrick house off Botanic Avenue, still on the north side of the city, from where Dermot ran his photography business. He'd given up on the photo-journalism and now concentrated on studio portraits, weddings and other events. He'd told Romy that it had been a bit like copping out really, but that he couldn't afford to go off to the world's trouble spots any more. He'd retired from it on his fiftieth birthday, saying that there were younger guys more suited to the job. And that he had to put his wife and daughter first.

Romy hadn't asked (although it had been on the tip of her tongue) which daughter he was putting first. Dermot and Larissa had a three year old, Erin, born a couple of months after Mimi. Romy hadn't known how to feel when she'd learned of Larissa's pregnancy. She'd never had to share Dermot before, even though Kathryn had called him Dad. But that had been very different. That had been allowing Kathryn to share. With Erin she didn't have the choice.

She was always surprised, too, when she thought about it, that she and Erin were related in the exact same way as she and Kathryn or Darragh. As much of an outsider as she often felt with them, she felt disconnected from Erin completely, even though she'd seen her as a baby when she was a few months old and had been totally smitten by her baby-blond hair and violet-blue eyes.

I wish it was simple, she thought to herself as she parked outside Dermot's house. I wish I felt like I was supposed to feel. I wish I *knew* how I was supposed to feel!

She rang the doorbell and Larissa opened the door. Romy smiled at her father's wife. Larissa was from Lithuania and she'd met Dermot when he was doing a story on the emergence of new states in Eastern Europe. She was tall (at five foot eight a good four inches taller than Romy), with caramel-coloured hair and the same violet eyes as Erin. She was thirty-three and didn't look much older than Romy herself. On the long list of things that freaked Romy out about her extended family, the idea that her father had married a woman who was younger than her half-brother (and by doing so had proved everyone who believed he'd find someone way younger than Veronica right) was probably the freakiest of all.

'Hello there!' Larissa's smile was wide and welcoming. 'It's good to see you. Dermot's been so excited at the idea of you being back.'

'It's good to be back.' And that's a lie, Romy said to herself. It's not good. It's not good at all.

'Hi, honey!' Dermot stepped out into the hallway. 'Sorry, I heard you ring but I was on the bloody phone! I hung up but Larissa got there before me. How the hell are you?'

She suddenly changed her mind about being home. Maybe it wasn't so bad after all. She'd missed her father. She'd missed his unconditional love. And she'd missed the warmth in his voice. Everyone else had welcomed her home. With Dermot she finally felt as though someone really meant it.

'I'm great,' she said, allowing him to envelop her in a massive bear hug. 'I'm great and it's ages since I've seen you and it's really good to see you now.'

Dermot hugged her even tighter. 'I'm sorry we weren't here when you arrived,' he said. 'But we'd planned the Kerry trip ages ago.'

'No problem.' She leaned back and he released his hold on her. 'How've you been?'

'Fantastic.' He led the way through the house to the sun-drenched kitchen and conservatory at the back. 'C'mon, let's sit down and chat.' He flopped into one of the wicker chairs and stretched his long legs, encased in faded denim jeans, out in front of him. He looked fantastic, Romy thought. More relaxed than she'd ever seen him.

'Would you like something to drink?' asked Larissa. 'Tea, coffee, juice?'

'Water would be good,' said Romy.

'Nothing else?'

She shook her head. Then she reached into the tote she was carrying and took out some paper bags.

'I got these for you in Oz,' she told Dermot. 'Stubbies. They're for putting on the end of your tin or bottle of beer. Makes it easier to drink.'

He laughed. 'Thanks.'

'And this is for Erin.' She looked around. 'Where is she?'

'Asleep.' Larissa's voice floated from the kitchen. 'She was up at five this morning and she suddenly flaked out.'

'Oh well, she can have it later.' Romy put the furry koala bear on the table. 'I got you some perfume, Larissa,' she called.

'Thank you.' Larissa came back to the conservatory and picked up the delicate bottle. She sprayed a little on to her wrist. 'Lovely,' she said.

Romy grinned. 'That's what it's called. It's the Sarah Jessica Parker one.'

Larissa sprayed more perfume behind her ears. 'I like her. I like this.'

'I'm glad.' Romy settled into the comfortable cushions of the wicker chairs.

'So how's Veronica?' asked Dermot.

Romy sighed expressively then told him of her shock at Veronica's obvious pain and how her mother was hoping that surgery would cure everything. But also how she seemed to think that it might turn back time. And she remembered again the filmy underwear and tried not to think about it.

Dermot grinned. 'That's Veronica for you.'

'Yeah, well.' Romy looked glum. 'I think it might be more difficult than that.'

'How long do you stay?' asked Larissa.

'It depends. A few weeks at least.'

'It's something you have to do,' said Larissa. 'She's your mother after all.'

'And then?' Dermot looked at her quizzically.

'I go back,' said Romy definitely. 'I have some good opportunities out there and I want to take them.'

'And men?' Larissa's eyes twinkled. 'Any men?'

'Sweetheart, not every girl thinks men are important,' Dermot told her. 'Romy is a career girl, not a marrying girl.'

'Oh?' Larissa looked at Romy, who scratched her head thoughtfully.

'It's not quite a career,' she told them. 'It's more a way of life. I don't know if I'll ever achieve anything brilliant in forensic archaeology.'

'Why not?' asked Dermot. 'I think you're doing great.'

'Thanks.' She smiled at him.

'But is there any man?' asked Larissa again, and this time Romy blushed. She thought again of Keith, of the comfort kiss, and suddenly she wished that it had been something more. The unexpected thought horrified her. Why? she asked herself. Why am I thinking of him like this now? I don't want to think this way. What the hell is the matter with me?

'I don't have time for men,' she said. 'Occasionally I go out on dates. But I'm not really interested.'

'You will soon be thirty,' Larissa said. 'You need to be married. Have babies. Like me.'

Romy laughed. 'I've a bit to go yet.'

This time Larissa pouted. 'You think I'm an old woman?'

'Oh God.' Romy groaned. 'Not you too!'

She told them how obsessed Veronica seemed to be with her age at the moment and how every conversation with her mother had centred around being in her sixties and unwell but still in her prime.

'She *is* an older woman.' Larissa said pointedly. 'It doesn't matter what she does. She is still old.'

'Darling – I'm not that far off it myself,' said Dermot.

'It's different for a man,' said Larissa baldly and Romy nodded in reluctant agreement.

It wasn't fair, she thought, that it should be different. But it definitely was. She'd thought it when she'd noticed how distinguished his greying hair made Darragh appear and she'd thought it too when she'd looked at her father and realised that, although he was now totally grey, he still looked great. Fortunately she didn't yet have a speck of grey herself but she knew that the moment she found the first hair she'd be lashing on the colour. You couldn't have dark hair as a woman and allow grey threads through it. It just wasn't acceptable any more. And she wouldn't want it anyway. She was a dark-haired person and she always would be.

'Do you want to stay here with us for a few days?' asked Dermot. 'While Veronica is in hospital.'

It was tempting. Romy wasn't really looking forward to being on her own in the Rathfarnham house. But neither did she want to stay with her father and Larissa. And Erin.

'It's OK,' she said. 'I'll be fine.'

'This is more convenient for the hospital,' Dermot reminded her.

'I know. But even so, I'll stay at . . . at Veronica's.' She'd been going to say at home, but on the basis that it didn't feel like home it was a stupid word to use, and besides, she felt reluctant about using it in front of Dermot, who might feel bad that she didn't consider Botanic Avenue home either. Although how could she? She'd never lived there.

She rotated her head slowly on her shoulders. It was all too complicated and messy and why the hell didn't people think of other people when they got married and had kids and divorced and married again and God knows what else? She loved her dad more than anyone in the world, but in the end he'd made things just as confusing as Veronica.

'You OK?' Dermot had been watching her.

'Sure,' she said. 'Just a bit tired. My body clock is still out of whack.'

'So tell me about Australia.' Larissa's blue eyes danced at her. 'Is it lovely? Is it as laid back as everyone says? Are there lots of men there with excellent bodies walking up and down the beach?'

Romy laughed. 'Sort of.'

Larissa swooned mischievously and Dermot grinned at her. Then she got up, put her arms around him and kissed him on the mouth.

Don't do that, thought Romy, squirming. He's my dad! I hate it when you act all lovey-dovey around him.

'Are you going to stay for dinner?' asked Larissa when she'd disentangled herself from Dermot. 'We're having salmon and salad.'

'No thanks.' Romy refused automatically although even as she said the words she thought she was being silly, that she might as well eat here as anywhere else. 'There's tons of food in Veronica's,' she added apologetically.

'So what?' asked Dermot.

'If I stay for dinner I won't feel like calling in to the hospital on my way home.'

'Does Veronica expect you to?'

'I'd feel bad if I didn't,' said Romy. 'It's only up the road, after all.'

'Why don't you drop in and call back here afterwards?' suggested her father.

'I'd love to. But . . .'

'Leave her be,' Larissa told Dermot. 'If she wants to relax on her own instead of being with us that's fine.'

I want to be with Dad, thought Romy. I don't want to be with you. And it's not because I don't like you, because I do, it's because I want some time on my own with him. To be like it used to be. Only that's not really possible any more, is it?

'Well, perhaps you'd like to have dinner with us tomorrow,' said Dermot.

'I think I'm having dinner with Darragh and Giselle tomorrow,' said Romy.

'Oh.' Dermot looked surprised and a little disappointed.

'Let's arrange it some other time. After Veronica is back from hospital. I'm sure I'll need to escape then.'

'OK. I'll have a chat with Larissa. We'll go out somewhere nice, although I'm sure Darragh and Giselle will take you to the best.'

She heard the thinly disguised sarcasm in his voice. Alpha males, she thought. They still think that way.

'I'm not actually looking forward to a night out with Darragh and Giselle,' she told her father. 'I mean, I don't really know him, do I? He never liked me.'

'I rather think it was me he didn't like,' said Dermot lightly. 'I don't think he cared much about you one way or the other.'

'Don't you?' Hadn't her father ever noticed the dismissive way Darragh had always spoken to her? Hadn't he noticed that he was impatient with her all the time? Hadn't he noticed anything?

'He was a teenage boy when you were growing up,' Dermot

said. 'There was nothing he liked at the time, except being out with his mates.'

'And talking about Tom,' said Romy.

Dermot's face reflected his agreement. Tom had been a constant topic of discussion in the home because it was at that time that Dolan Component Manufacturers had begun to break through into the big league with its first contract from one of the country's leading businesses to kit out its new processing plant. Romy remembered coming home and seeing Darragh looking at plans and documents which had been sent to Veronica for her consideration. Veronica always agreed to anything that looked like good business for the company. She relied on the advice of the management team and didn't bother reading up on the detail herself. But she liked getting the papers and being there while Darragh looked through them.

'It's not as though he has a clue what's going on,' Kathryn had said to Romy one night when she'd murmured that Darragh was really very clever. 'He likes to look good, that's all.' And Kathryn had pushed her big round glasses higher on her nose and stalked out of the living room.

'You OK?' Dermot's words broke into her memories.

'Oh, sure.' She smiled at him. 'So, look, tell me all about what you've been doing and I'll tell you about the last few months in Australia. Let's do the real catch-up thing.'

'I will do some household things,' said Larissa, getting up. 'Leave you two alone.'

Romy glanced gratefully at her. 'So?' she said to Dermot. 'Tell all.'

It wasn't as though Dermot had much news. Whereas once his stories had been exciting tales about dodging bullets in Kuwait, now they were anecdotes about wacky weddings or chaotic christenings. Romy wondered whether he liked the way things had changed for him, whether he wouldn't prefer to be in the thick of a war zone instead.

He shook his head when she finally asked him.

'Truly, no,' he said. 'I've gone past that. I'm happy now.'

'How come you're happy to do it for Larissa and Erin but you wouldn't do it for Veronica and me?' she blurted out.

He looked at her in astonishment. 'It's not like that. I was much younger then. It didn't matter so much.'

'It would've mattered to me,' she said shortly. 'To Veronica too.'

'Are you angry at me?' he asked in confusion. 'I thought you liked what I did.'

'I did. I do,' she said. 'I just . . . it upset Mum so much. Maybe if you'd given in . . .'

'If I'd given in on that, I would have had to give in on everything,' Dermot told her.

'Would that have mattered so much?'

Dermot looked at her incredulously. 'You're kidding me, asking that.'

'Couldn't you have . . . compromised?'

'There was never any compromising with Veronica,' said Dermot. 'You know that. It was her way or no way once you agreed to anything. She tried to sucker me in but I couldn't be part of that company. I would have lost every shred of my dignity and my independence.'

Romy smiled ruefully at him. 'I guess I'm just a bit frazzled what with Mum being in hospital and everything. My thinking is a bit off right now. I've been wondering . . . wondering what it would have been like if we'd all stayed together.'

'I love you as much as I've ever loved anyone,' said Dermot with intensity. 'Just because I wasn't always there didn't mean I didn't always care. Or think about you every single day.'

'I know,' she said. 'I do know. Really. But I think Mum always felt . . . well . . .'

'Your mother wanted me dancing attendance on her all the time,' said Dermot flatly. 'Which wasn't possible. Oh, she liked boasting about me when my pictures were used in the papers but she didn't like the attention I got.'

'Was it always that way between you?' asked Romy. 'Fighting for attention?'

'Of course not.' Dermot looked impatient. 'We just weren't the best people to be married to each other, that's all.'

'How come you stayed together for so long in that case?'

Dermot sighed. 'There were good times and bad times,' he said. 'And we had you to think about.'

'You stayed together for me!' Romy looked horrified.

'Not only for you,' said Dermot quickly. 'We cared about each other. But obviously not enough.'

'I don't like to think that you stayed together because of me.' Romy couldn't let the idea go.

'You were a factor,' Dermot told her. 'Children are always a factor. But not the only one.'

'Would you have left sooner if I hadn't been around?' asked Romy.

'I really don't know,' Dermot replied. 'We're looking at things in hindsight now and that's never the best way.'

'Why did you marry her?'

'What's with all this?' asked Dermot. 'You never bothered with these sorts of questions before. What's eating you now?'

Romy couldn't answer that. She couldn't explain that she was suddenly confused about her family, about what was real and what wasn't, about the whole structure of it. She shrugged helplessly. 'I don't know.'

'Don't worry about it.' He smiled at her. 'It's always unsettling when people split up, but hey, haven't we all made things work out marvellously?'

Marvellous for him maybe, she thought. But not marvellous for Veronica, who couldn't cope on her own right now and needed help. Not exactly marvellous for Romy either because the whole separation and its aftermath had really upset her, messed up how she felt about marriage and about commitment. Marvellous for Larissa, though, who seemed very content with her life. And for Erin, who would grow up with a father who adored her.

But he adores me too, Romy told herself. I do know that. I do. I can't expect him to have given up his work at a time when he loved it most just to keep Veronica happy. And so she smiled at her father and then changed the subject so that she was talking about her time in Australia and the work she'd been doing and the offer of the new dig near Melbourne which she'd had to turn down.

'That's terrible,' he exclaimed. 'I didn't realise you were doing that.'

'There'll be other opportunities.' She repeated the words that everyone else had said to her.

'You're being quite self-sacrificing about it all,' said Dermot.

Romy thought she detected an edge in her father's voice. 'There wasn't anyone else when it came down to it,' she told him. 'Somebody had to look after Mum. Anyway, hopefully it won't be for too long.'

'Let me know if they're imposing on you too much,' said Dermot.

Romy smiled crookedly. 'They already are – they made me come home, didn't they!'

'I didn't know about it,' said Dermot. 'Nobody called me until you did to say you were coming back. I was surprised but I thought you were doing it willingly. I don't like the idea that all of them have dragged you back—'

'Oh Dad, it doesn't matter.' Romy interrupted him. 'Of course a bit of me resents the fact that they've offloaded the issue on me while they get on with their lives and I've put mine on hold but, truthfully, it's not like it's going to be for months and it's not like Mum needs constant care. It'll be fine, and once I've done my bit I'll head off again and maybe then they'll stop seeing me as the useless half-sister.'

'They don't think like that!' Dermot was shocked at her comment.

'Maybe not,' said Romy doubtfully. 'But quite often I think they do.'

Dermot looked anxiously at her. 'Are you OK, honey? You've never said anything like this before. Why would you think that they regard you as useless?'

'I'm fine,' Romy assured him. 'Honestly. And there's always been a bit of a thing between Darragh and Kathryn and me. You know that.'

'Well, yes, but I thought it was the usual kids' stuff,' he said.

'Don't mind me,' she told him. 'It's fine, it is, really. Actually my biggest worry isn't Darragh or Kathryn. It's boredom. I've never hung around with absolutely nothing to do before.'

'Why don't you get a job here?' he asked.

'What's the point in that?' she said. 'I don't plan to stay for long enough. As soon as Mum is mobile I'll be heading back to Oz.'

'I meant why don't you come home for good?'

She stared at him. 'Why?'

'Why not? You've done lots of travelling. Maybe it's time to settle back here.'

'I like what I do,' she told him.

'You could do it just as easily in Ireland. I'm sure there's loads of work what with all the development going on. Plenty of sites to check out. It'd probably be more interesting too – older bones!' He grinned at her.

'What I'm doing *is* interesting,' she said.

'But I miss you,' said Dermot.

She laughed. 'Like I missed you when you went off to the Gulf?'

'I guess.' He looked at her ruefully. 'I don't mind you travelling, honey. I understand the urge to do that. But you're very far away.'

'Rubbish,' she said robustly. 'It's only a phone call. All the same, I agree that it's not quite the same as being home.

So maybe I should do it more often when I move away in future.'

'Maybe,' said Dermot as Larissa came back into the room again.

Romy thought of her own words later that night as she linked up her computer and opened Skype. This time she could see that Keith was online. She stared at his name wondering whether to click on it and call him. That stupid kiss at the airport was wrecking her head! If she hadn't done it she would just have called him the way she often did to talk through things that were bugging her. But now she wasn't sure what to do. Because despite all the times she'd told herself that you didn't complicate friendships by dragging sex into the mix (though it was only a damn kiss, hardly an orgy!), she'd gone and done it anyway, with the result that she didn't know what to say to the one person in her life who, up to now, she'd been able to talk to about anything.

An incoming signal startled her and she realised that Keith had decided to call her. She clicked on the answer icon, realising that she was actually trembling.

His face, jerky but still recognisable over the webcam, was a welcome sight.

'Hello there,' she said, feeling a wave of relief wash over her that he had been the one to call her and not the other way around.

'Hi.' The sound and the picture weren't in perfect synchronisation and so his lips were still moving as she heard his voice. 'Thought I'd check with you and see how you're doing.'

'I'm good,' she said.

'And your mum?'

'She's having the operation tomorrow. Hopefully it'll go well.'

'I'm sure it will.'

There was a silence in which she wanted to apologise to him again for kissing him. But she told herself that it would be better to put it behind her and stop obsessing. Kathryn had always told her that she obsessed too much. So she asked Keith about his weekend in Queensland instead.

'Queensland was great,' he told her. 'But not as much fun without you.'

Her heart thumped in her chest. Was he sending a signal by saying that? Was he suggesting that he would have liked her to be there so that they could have done something about the kiss? It was, she thought crossly, incredibly stupid to kiss someone for the first time just as you were about to put six thousand miles between each other.

'I'm glad to hear that,' she said.

'There was no one to tell me that it's not a crime to eat full-fat food from time to time,' he told her. 'Tanya and Emma kept dragging me into restaurants that only served lettuce leaves and vegetables.'

'Oh,' she said. She didn't want him to miss her for her love of food.

'I swear I lost weight,' he said plaintively, 'and I so don't need to do that.'

She giggled. Keith was forever ranting about the obsession that so many women had about their weight – it was one of the things that they laughed at together. He always enjoyed eating out with her, he would say, because she knew how to put away her food.

'Anyway, I thought I'd better let you know that I'm going to Perth for a while,' he said. 'Advising on a wreck they've discovered there.'

'Really? That's good, isn't it?'

'Yeah, I'm looking forward to it. Just as well you're back in Ireland – I've rented out the house for a few weeks.'

'That was quick work.'

'Got lucky,' he said succinctly. 'Put an ad online and got someone later that day. No worries.'

'Great,' she said.

'I love it when a plan comes together.' He laughed. 'Anyway, I just wanted to say that I hope it goes well for your mum and, you know, keep in touch, but obviously if I'm doing a lot of diving you might not be able to get me for a while.'

She said nothing for a moment. Although he was telling her that he might be out of contact for a while, she wondered if he was actually trying to say more than that. Something like 'I'm moving away so's you can't keep in touch with me, you demented cow. And just as well you're out of the country if you're going to start kissing me at every available opportunity.'

'How long are you expecting to be in Perth?' she asked.

'Dunno really. It depends. A few weeks.'

She could sense an awkwardness between them. It had never been there before and she hated it now.

'OK,' she said finally. 'Well, look, if . . . when I'm coming back to Oz I'll let you know. Maybe you'll be back in Sydney by then.'

'Maybe.'

'Enjoy Perth.'

'Enjoy Dublin.'

'Bye,' she said.

'Bye.'

She looked at the blank space where his picture had been and then reached out and touched the empty square, resisting the urge to ring him again straight away. I'm going bonkers, she told herself as she closed the computer with an angry snap. Really and truly bonkers. I don't need Keith. I don't want to kiss him again. He's just a bloke after all. And I've more things to worry about right now than a bloody bloke.

Chapter 9

She didn't sleep well that night, constantly jerking into wakefulness, convinced that despite the sophisticated alarm system, someone had broken into the house and was prowling around. At three a.m. she got up and checked every room to prove to herself that there was nothing to be afraid of. When she went back to bed she left the bedroom door open and the landing light on, telling herself that she was a grown-up and should be far away from having to have lights on to keep her fears at bay. But it made her feel a whole lot better to see the oblong glow of yellow light at the doorway, and at least she did fall asleep after that even though she didn't feel at all rested when she woke up again in the morning.

After she got up she loaded the washing machine with a selection of her underwear and T-shirts and spent ten minutes reading through the manual for Veronica's state-of-the-art machine before figuring out the best wash programme to use. It had been easier at Keith's where they left his ancient machine on the same programme for everything. (Naturally this occasionally led to whites suddenly turning blue or pink or sludge grey, but it didn't bother Romy too much. She rarely wore whites anyway.) She didn't really know what to do with herself once the machine started the wash cycle. She sat at the kitchen table with a huge mug of very strong coffee and read the newspaper while nibbling at a day-old muffin. It was disconcerting to have nothing to do. Every day for the last four years there had been something – digging, filling out archaeo-logical feature sheets, inputting information on to computer spreadsheets or interpreting it . . . Her days had been filled with activity, and even though sometimes it became boring (looking for shards of bone or other material in trays of soil with nothing more than tweezers could be mind-numbing at times), she always felt as though she was doing something useful and worthwhile. And although coming home to be with Veronica was surely worthwhile – at least in terms of daugh-terly duty – she wasn't feeling terribly useful right now. It would be different when Veronica came home after the oper-ation, of course. There'd be plenty for her to do then. But Romy was actually dreading that.

She finished her coffee and swallowed the remainder of the muffin. Then she wandered into the den.

She hadn't spent much time in it the previous day because it had been another room in which she'd felt like an intruder. When Dermot and Veronica had been married she'd spent a lot of time in here, sitting on the floor beside the big desk doing her homework while Dermot edited his photographs on the computer. She'd liked working there with him, both of them absorbed in what they were doing, conversation un-necessary. It had been their room, not just his room, and their space. She wondered whether it had become Larry's space while he was married to Veronica.

She'd been at college when Veronica had married Larry and had moved out of the house by then so she hadn't had any need for the den any more. Once she'd moved out, she hadn't bothered to return, although she'd come back reluctantly the evening on which the three of them, Darragh, Kathryn and herself, had begged Veronica not to remarry. It was Kathryn who'd put the pressure on her to turn up, telling her that it was important Veronica realised that *all* of them thought it was a bad idea. Romy felt that her presence would probably only annoy her mother further, but eventually she gave in, if only to make sure that Kathryn and Darragh didn't use Dermot as an example of how Veronica's marriages could end up.

'I love Larry.' Romy remembered the flash of anger in Veronica's eyes when Kathryn told her that he was totally unsuitable. 'And it's really not up to you to tell me who's suitable or not.' She laughed. 'Actually, you of all people! You don't have a boyfriend of your own; you'll probably never have one the way you carry on.'

'And what's that supposed to mean?' demanded Kathryn.

'Well look at you, for heaven's sake!' cried Veronica. 'You're twenty-four and you should be gorgeous but you look . . . well, I'd say fifty-four only I've seen fifty-four and I looked a million times better than you. You're dressed in that dowdy jeans and jumper combo that does absolutely nothing for you. And you're cross-eyed from reading so much.'

'I'm short-sighted,' Kathryn informed her. 'Which has nothing to do with reading or not reading.'

'You don't even wear contact lenses,' said Veronica. 'Instead you go around with those huge glasses on your face like a mask.'

'We're not talking about me here,' snapped Kathryn. 'We're talking about you and the stupid, stupid mistake you're making.'

'It's not a mistake.' Veronica looked mutinous.

'I don't know whether it's a mistake or not,' Darragh's tone was conciliatory, 'but Mum, you've only known him a short time.'

'He treats me well,' said Veronica firmly. 'He brings me places and he's there for me and God knows I need someone there for me. You lot aren't and Dermot was useless.'

Both Darragh and Kathryn glanced quickly in Romy's direction. She was normally like a wildcat when it came to defending her father and they could almost sense her rage at Veronica's words.

'My dad certainly wasn't useless,' she retorted. 'He was great to you.'

'Even you, with your blind adoration, can't believe that.' Veronica snorted. 'You know how I begged him not to go to the Gulf. You know how I told him that it would end in tragedy. And what happens? He goes and gets shot and then he has to come home and be waited on hand and foot.'

'You didn't wait on him hand and foot,' said Romy. 'I did.'

Veronica laughed. 'Proves my point, though. He always has to be the centre of attention.'

'So do you,' said Romy angrily. 'You did it before and see where . . .' She paused, her eyes locking with Veronica's. 'And . . . well, you're doing it again now,' she concluded lamely, looking away from her mother.

'I'm not marrying Larry to be the centre of attention.' Veronica looked away from her too. 'I'm marrying him because I want to have someone in my life who loves me.'

'We love you,' said Darragh.

'I want a man to love me,' said Veronica. 'I'm entitled to some love and happiness in my life. I was widowed at such a young age and . . .' She started to cry. 'You don't understand. None of you understand!'

Their original plan of a reasoned debate about Larry's suitability as a husband disappeared under Veronica's deluge of tears. Darragh put his arms around her and told her that he only wanted her to be happy; Kathryn looked at her with ill-disguised impatience and Romy was still too angry about the insult to Dermot to talk to her at all.

And in the end it hadn't mattered because she'd married Larry anyway and it had started to go wrong almost immediately and the only saving grace was that he'd been a fairly decent person and it had ended amicably.

She's no good without a man, thought Romy, as her eyes wandered over the photographs of Veronica on one of the den's bookshelves. She's right when she says that she needs someone. It's just a pity that she always seems to pick the wrong someone.

There had, she knew, been men after Larry, although thankfully Veronica hadn't wanted to marry any of them. But through her irregular contact with her family Romy had learned about Conal, Francis and Mel, all of whom had gone out with Veronica in the five years since she'd split up with Larry. At the time – so Kathryn had told her – each man was wonderful in Veronica's eyes and a potential next husband. But the Larry experience had scarred her and she was more careful about them. And whether it was because she gave less of herself or whether it was because of the men themselves, none of those relationships had ever gone the distance.

Romy wondered whether Veronica would ever meet anyone again. It was bad enough in your twenties (her own experiences proved that – plenty of friends-who-were-boys like Keith but no one who was likely to be any more than that) so it had to be a million times more difficult at sixty, no matter how much faith you put in anti-ageing creams and light-reflecting foundation and no matter how good you still were at shaking your booty! (The idea of Veronica shaking anything made her squirm.) The pool of available men for someone like Veronica must be fairly diminished by now. The good ones would definitely all be married, the bad would be too stuck in their ways and the ugly – well, Veronica would never go for ugly. And as for baggage – surely any available man of that age was carrying a whole carousel of it.

So perhaps there would never be anyone new to notice Veronica's gorgeous lingerie and share her fairy-tale bedroom.

Romy made a noise of digust. She would have to stop thinking about her mother as a sexual being. It was too horrible for words. She sat in the big leather chair behind the desk and drew her knees up beneath her chin. Then she spun the chair around until she was dizzy and had to grab hold of the walnut desk to stop it.

She wondered what it would be like to work in an office, behind a desk. What it would be like to be Darragh, the

143

apple of Veronica's eye and the heir apparent to Tom's legacy. Not actually the heir apparent any more now, of course. He had inherited. He was the managing director of Dolan Component Manufacturers. An important person in his own right. Who, despite Kathryn's reservations about some of his business decisions, seemed to be managing the company well and who would one day hold the controlling interest in it. Veronica had once said (to Kathryn's rage) that she'd probably sign over her shares to him when she was sixty-five because she wanted to spend the last years of her life having fun.

'Last years!' Dermot (he and Veronica had still been married at the time of the conversation) had laughed at her. 'Sixty-five, your last years! You'll still be going strong at ninety!'

He'd been paying her a compliment. Everyone knew that Veronica Dolan-Kilkenny was a fit and fabulous woman who looked a million dollars and half her age. It was one of the crosses that Romy and Kathryn had to bear, to have a mother who was infinitely more fashionable than either of them.

And probably would be for ever!

She rang the hospital early in the afternoon and they told her that Veronica was in the recovery room and that she could come in that evening to see her. She texted Darragh and Kathryn to tell them and Darragh responded with a message saying that he'd see her at the hospital later. Kathryn's reply was a terse 'good'.

At seven that evening she was sitting beside Veronica, who was still groggy although she'd made a stab at doing her make-up, which gave an illusion of colour to her pale cheeks and dry lips. She'd also put on her gold chains and rings again. She's incredible, thought Romy. If I'd just got back from surgery the very last thing I'd be thinking of would be how I looked.

'They said it went well,' said Veronica weakly. 'But I'm still in agony. I told them that I didn't think much of still being in pain at this stage.'

'You'll be in pain for a while,' Romy reminded her. 'That's what they told you.'

'I thought they were exaggerating.' Veronica clicked her pain-relief dispenser.

'I spoke to the nurse on the way in. She said you'd be fine,' said Romy reassuringly.

'That slip of a thing. What the hell would she know?'

At that point Darragh and Giselle walked in and Veronica perked up. Giselle had brought a bottle of Veronica's favourite perfume and Darragh gave his mother a box of expensive chocolates. Romy, who hadn't thought to bring anything with her, suddenly felt embarrassed at having arrived empty-handed although she felt marginally better when Veronica told Darragh that she wasn't able to eat yet and so the chocolates were wasted on her.

'How long do you expect to stay in the hospital?' asked Darragh.

Veronica closed her eyes and then opened them slowly again.

'Three days.'

'Mum! Dr Jacobs said at least four,' Romy reminded her. 'Possibly six.'

'I don't want to be here for six days.'

'There's no point in coming home too soon,' said Romy. 'You want to make sure that everything's OK, don't you?'

'You just don't want me there.'

There was an element of truth in what Veronica had said. Weird though it felt to be in the house without anyone at all, the time spent with Veronica had been mentally exhausting as they both tried to get over the fact that there was a gulf between them which was only partly due to their differing opinions on just about everything under the sun. The first morning, when Romy had eventually come downstairs after a deep and dreamless sleep, Veronica had asked her when she was going to get dressed. (Veronica herself was wearing a royal blue shirt over a pair of white tailored trousers with a narrow snakeskin belt and matching snakeskin loafers.)

'I *am* dressed!' Romy glanced down at her fatigue-green T-shirt and baggy cargo pants, an outfit which she thought was casual and practical.

'For a dig maybe,' Veronica said. 'Not for anything else.'

'For everything.'

'I wanted you to take me shopping,' said Veronica. 'We can't go shopping with you looking like that.'

She'd protested but it had been futile. And so in the end she'd given in and changed into a pair of jeans (Sass and Bide, so Veronica couldn't complain about them, even if she had bought them at a massive discount in the sales) and a neutral V-necked top. She'd ignored Veronica's remarks about a touch of make-up and had driven to the Dundrum Town Centre mall where Veronica – despite not being able to walk faster than a snail – insisted that they visit shops on every floor. Romy had almost gone demented with boredom, especially when Veronica asked her opinion on three identical blouses in Harvey Nicks.

'They're not identical,' Veronica told her earnestly. 'The detailing is quite, quite different.'

That had been the worst day. But the following ones hadn't been much better, with Veronica's various demands all punctuated by her saying that she didn't want to be a burden. And behind it all crackled the tension that had existed between Romy and Veronica for the past seven years but which neither of them talked about.

Romy had enjoyed being able to come downstairs that morning in her ancient grey pyjamas without being lectured on what was decent night attire and she'd revelled in having her morning coffee without a discussion about Giselle's pregnancy (Veronica was thrilled by it, which Romy thought was a bit weird – after all, another grandchild should surely make her feel even older!) and without the additional commentary on how fantastic Giselle always looked. On the first day that Veronica had said this, Romy had retorted that she too could look great if she was being kept in style by a bloke with limitless pockets and if she had nothing better to do than to worry about what colour lipstick to wear! Not that it was something that she would worry about. Not that it needed worrying about at all.

When it wasn't Darragh and Giselle being held up as examples, Kathryn's name was brought into the conversation. Kathryn, according to Veronica, was now combining style and savvy and had been featured in the *New York Times* in an article about business fraud . . . At that point Romy had been dispatched to the den to find a folder which was filled with clippings about Kathryn and how she'd testified in some corporate trial. There had been an accompanying picture, and Romy had been amazed because the girl in the photograph was a million times more chic than the girl she remembered and it was clear that, having ditched her glasses, Kathryn had actually inherited some of Veronica's style after all. She'd wondered then whether anything she did would ever merit a cutting in Veronica's scrapbook. And then she got annoyed with herself for caring.

And so no, she really wasn't looking forward to Veronica's release from hospital and all that her return entailed.

She was particularly dreading the overseeing of her rehabilitation programme. The nurses had told her, when she'd spoken to them earlier, that it could possibly take Veronica significantly longer than the four weeks she'd confidently expected to become comfortably mobile again. This was because the bones took time to fuse together, and according to the nurses, it usually took about six weeks before they could be sure that they were seeing positive results on an X-ray.

Romy had wanted to cry when they told her that. She'd been hoping against hope that Veronica's outwardly youthful appearance was a reflection of strong and healthy bones (despite her disc problem) within. As far as she was concerned she didn't want to spend any more time than she absolutely needed to in Ireland.

I am a bitch, she thought miserably. Everyone's right. I'm selfish thinking like this. Veronica is in real pain and all I can think about is that I want to be somewhere else. I'm a really shitty daughter who needs to learn to forgive and forget. Something I should've learned by now.

She sat on a visitor's chair and stared into space while Darragh talked to her mother about the company – something to do with the sponsorship of a golf tournament, which Veronica agreed weakly was probably a good idea, although how she could make any judgement on anything when she was obviously still a bit spaced out was beyond Romy. Then Giselle started chatting about the latest celebrity gossip, which made Veronica perk up again.

Romy felt excluded but told herself that it was her own fault. She didn't know anything about the company, had never shown the slightest interest because of the fact that she wasn't involved anyway; and when it came to celebrity gossip she was worse than useless because she only ever read gossip magazines at the hairdressers or the dentists when they were inevitably out of date and so the fairy-tale marriage she was reading about had probably already moved on to the acrimonious divorce.

I'm probably just jealous, she told herself, watching Giselle play with the ends of her sleek blond hair as she and Veronica nodded wisely about the upcoming marriage of someone Romy had never even heard of. If I was good at glamour then maybe I'd be more interested in it all myself. She glanced down at her worn jeans and black slip-on leather shoes. So far away from Veronica's collection it was a joke! She supposed that if someone like Kate Moss was wearing the slip-ons they'd look cool and stylish. But on her Romy knew they just looked as though she couldn't be bothered.

She heartily wished that she'd made more of an effort after they left Veronica for the night and arrived at the restaurant, which was far more upmarket than she'd expected with its dark wood interior, crisp linen napkins and array of crystal glassware and polished cutlery on each table. It reminded her of the flashy Australian restaurant and she felt a pang of loneliness. (Not for Keith particularly, although being here with him would be a million times better than being here with Darragh and Giselle, but she wished that there was someone like him with her. Someone who cared.) She slid into a seat with her back to the wall and hoped that nobody had noticed her lack of elegance but had instead been dazzled by Giselle's beauty.

She studied the menu and ordered soup followed by steak and kidney pie.

'Green leaf salad for me,' said Giselle, closing the menu. 'No starter.'

Crikey, thought Romy, no wonder she's so skinny.

She was relieved when Darragh ordered the steak and kidney pie too; it would have been so awful to be the only one tucking into the food. But, she remembered with amusement, Darragh liked his food. She had something in common with her half-brother after all! She smiled.

'What's so funny?' asked Giselle.

'Oh, I was just thinking of the last time I had dinner with Darragh.'

'Years ago,' said Darragh hastily and Romy looked at him in surprise. Then she realised that he hadn't told Giselle about his illicit burger and chips and she wanted to laugh.

'You should share the joke,' Giselle told her.

'It's nothing. Honestly.' But she couldn't stop grinning.

'I thought Mum looked well considering,' said Darragh, changing the subject to something safer from his point of view.

'Well enough.' Romy smothered her smile and embraced the new topic. 'But she's still in a lot of pain.'

'The doctors say that's only to be expected.'

'She'll be fairly laid up for a while,' said Giselle.

'I know,' said Romy. 'That's why I'm here, isn't it?'

'I would have taken care of her,' said Giselle. 'But in my condition it's not possible.'

Romy thought, but she couldn't be certain, that she detected a faint tone of relief in Giselle's voice. She couldn't blame her sister-in-law if that was the case. It was surely one thing to call in and see Veronica from time to time, or to socialise with her, but having to look after her was a different matter entirely.

'Have you been talking to Kathryn?' asked Darragh suddenly.

'I texted her when Mum came out of surgery.'

'She emailed me last night. Said that perhaps she should visit for a few days.'

'I thought she was far too busy to leave her important job and husband.' Romy knew that she sounded waspish but she couldn't help it.

'Don't be silly,' said Darragh. 'A visit is entirely different. And I'm sure Mum will be delighted to see her.'

'So tell us about your work, Romy,' said Giselle, breaking the silence which descended on the table after Darragh's words. 'What's new in skeletal remains?'

'Yeuch.' Darragh looked at his wife. 'Not a good dinner topic.'

Romy smiled, happy to discuss something she was interested in. 'Possibly not. But we don't have to talk about skellies if it freaks you out too much. I've been involved in excavating what seems to be a convict settlement. Nobody knew it was there. They were going to built a sports centre on the site.'

'And what happens now?' asked Darragh. 'The centre gets nixed just because of a few dead people?'

'You sound so callous,' said Romy mildly. 'No, the centre will be built but they've delayed it until we finish our work on the site. It's not that much of a delay and when the centre is built it will have a museum with some of the stuff we found in it. So it's a win-win situation.'

'Except that costs will have gone up,' said Darragh.

'Not really. They factored in certain delays and we've been as quick as we can.'

'I thought that all excavation work was painstakingly slow,' said Giselle as she poured herself a glass of water.

'Slow, but not necessarily painstaking,' replied Romy. 'We do our best.'

'I'm sure you do.' Darragh's voice had taken on a warmer tone. 'And we know that you're doing your best with Mum too.'

'Thanks,' said Romy.

'We were wondering . . .' Darragh cleared his throat, 'if you wouldn't do one extra little thing for us.'

'Oh?' Romy looked at him cautiously.

'Giselle and I want to go away for a few days,' he explained. 'Before she's unable to fly.'

'And?' Romy split a bread roll in half and buttered it.

'We need someone to look after Mimi for a few days,' said Giselle.

'She's no trouble,' Darragh assured her. 'She's one of the best kids in the world. And she'd be happy with you. You're her auntie, after all.'

'But . . . but I know nothing about kids,' protested Romy. 'I haven't a clue! Besides, Mimi hardly even knows me. Plus I'll be looking after Mum at the same time! You're crazy.'

'I hardly think asking you to give up a little bit of time to take care of your niece is crazy,' said Darragh.

Romy stared wordlessly at him.

'It wouldn't be so difficult.' Giselle spoke persuasively. 'Veronica can help you.'

'Veronica will be flat on her back!' cried Romy. 'I'll be helping her, she won't be helping me! When exactly did you think this might happen?'

'The week after next. Just for a week. We're thinking of going to Barbados.'

Romy felt as though she was going to choke. It was bad enough being put in the position where she couldn't say no to looking after Veronica, but being asked to look after Mimi too just so that Darragh and Giselle could go on an exotic holiday was too much! Honestly, she thought in annoyance, give her brother an inch and he took way more than a mile.

'I'm really sorry.' She tried to keep the shake out of her voice. She had never successfully refused to do anything for Darragh before. 'But I just can't do this. I'm useless with kids, I really am. I really and truly don't think that I'm the best person to look after Mimi. Anyway,' she added, 'don't you have a nanny for her?'

'It's not the same thing,' said Darragh. 'Magda is an employee. We'd never leave Mimi alone with her for a week. You're family.'

'Darragh, Mimi knows Magda. She doesn't know me. Family has nothing to do with it.'

'It never has as far as you're concerned! You act as though you're apart from all of us.'

Romy swallowed hard. Of course she was apart from them! She always had been.

'Look,' she said, wondering why she always had to make an effort to keep her voice reasonable when she talked to him, 'I don't know anything about kids. I'm not the right person for this. You don't want to leave your precious daughter with a scatterbrain like me. Really you don't.'

'You can't get out of pulling your weight just because you're a scatterbrain,' said Darragh.

'But I *am* pulling my weight!' she cried. 'I'm looking after Mum.'

'And it's about time. After all, you've been swanning around for the last few years and it's been Giselle who's been Veronica's support. She's entitled to her holiday.'

There, thought Romy, he's said it. Swanning around. I knew that's how they all looked at it.

'I didn't think Veronica needed much support,' she said tartly. 'She's not even retirement age yet and it's only because she's had the back operation that I'm here.'

'Looking after someone doesn't mean just looking after them when they're sick,' said Darragh. 'It's being there for them. Keeping an eye out for them. Making sure everything is OK.'

'I'm sure Veronica was fine.'

'A week with Mimi,' Darragh said. 'God almighty, Romy, it's not much to ask.'

Romy said nothing. She was fighting back tears of frustration. Not content with successfully ensuring that she came back from Australia, Darragh was managing to make her feel mean and horrible.

'Oh, look, leave the girl alone,' Giselle said to him. 'She's clearly not interested, and I'm not leaving my daughter with someone who isn't a hundred per cent committed to her care and attention. I thought some time with Mimi might be something that Romy would enjoy, but I was wrong.'

'Giselle, Darragh, I'm really sorry.' Romy had been feeling browbeaten but suddenly she grew determined. 'I don't feel capable of looking after Mimi for a week and I don't think it's right of you to ask me. If you want to go away for an overnight stay somewhere in Ireland then I'll certainly do my best, but otherwise it's no deal. And it's wrong of you to make me feel bad about this.'

'It was just an idea,' said Giselle. 'No need to blow a gasket.'

'Well it wasn't a good idea,' said Romy. She got up from the table. 'And this isn't some grand gesture on my part, but I'm just not hungry any more. So thanks for dinner but I'm going home.'

She walked out of the restaurant without looking back.

'Damn,' said Giselle. 'I would've liked Barbados.'

'So would I,' said Darragh. 'Why is she so hopeless? It's not like she has anything else to do. Selfish cow.'

'I would have loved to go away,' said Giselle wistfully. 'But if that's her attitude it's better not. I wouldn't leave my precious daughter with her anyhow. We'll think of something else. Not Barbados, obviously, but maybe we'll get away at home. Mimi could have a sleepover somewhere.'

'Good thinking,' said Darragh. 'All the same, I can't understand why Romy is so unhelpful. Gets it from her father, I suppose. He was hopeless too.' He stabbed the crust of his steak and kidney pie with his fork.

'We can't all be perfect,' said Giselle.

Darragh glanced at her. But her expression was completely serious and there wasn't a hint of irony in her voice at all.

Chapter 10

Kathryn stood at the bar of Manhattan's newest nightclub, dazzled by the strobe lights, deafened by the house music and anxiously wondering what would be the earliest time she could slip out without being noticed. She asked herself what self-destructive button in her body had made her come tonight, even when she'd already decided that it would be a terrible idea. It didn't matter that her immediate boss, Henry Newman, had ordered everyone in the company to show up because the owners of the nightclub were clients of Carter Clarke. Henry had sent around an email saying that it would be a sign of support for their clients as well as a good bonding exercise for everyone. But Kathryn was senior enough to make her own choices about what was good for her and for the company. And she hated bonding exercises anyway.

She hated nightclubs too. Well, perhaps hated was too strong a word, but she'd never been particularly fond of the idea of wall-to-wall music which invaded every pore of your body so that it was impossible to do anything other than lose yourself in it. Kathryn wasn't the sort of person who enjoyed losing herself in anything. She preferred to stay slightly detached, a little bit remote. She was, as Veronica had once told her, an observer not a participant. (In fairness Veronica hadn't been talking about nightclubs at the time. She'd been trying to get Kathryn involved in the game of Twister that Dermot had brought home one Christmas. But Kathryn had declined very firmly, saying it wasn't her thing.)

What was her thing? she wondered, as she watched the rest of her colleagues enjoy being part of the VIP set because they'd all been given passes to the nightclub's exclusive lounge. Most of them, having collected free cocktails, had since pushed themselves into the heaving throng and were gyrating on the dance floor to the thudding bass beat which pounded hard through the air. Beautiful girls – really beautiful, thought Kathryn, unlike my expensive grooming, which is entirely different – were spinning and twirling on the multicoloured glass floor, showing every inch of their long, tanned legs and giving maximum exposure to their surgically enhanced breasts. The club only allowed the hottest, trendiest, most exclusive people to pass its doors and these girls were all New York A-listers. Tonight, though, the NY A-listers were joined by some big celebrity names too – Kathryn recognised the latest supermodel striding across the floor as well as an Oscar-nominated actress and the slightly zany (and therefore media-friendly) daughter of a presidential hopeful.

Kathryn knew that she wouldn't have got past the gimlet eyes of the bouncers outside if she hadn't been with the company, even wearing, as she was, a short black dress and spiky high-heeled shoes and with her hair uncharacteristically gelled to give it an edgier style. It wasn't that she didn't look OK. It was just that she gave off the wrong vibes. The vibes of someone who knew that she should really be somewhere else.

'Cocktail!' shrieked Leonard, one of her colleagues, handing her a wide glass filled with a toxic-looking green liquid. 'Their signature . . . can't remember what it's called but it will blow your brains out!'

Maybe I could do with that, thought Kathryn, as she took a cautious sip. Maybe half of my problem is that I overanalyse everything instead of just accepting things the way they are and living with them. Maybe it's not that bad after all. Maybe it's all my fault. Maybe downing a few toxic cocktails will help.

'Good?' She saw the word on Leonard's lips rather than heard it.

She nodded and then finished the cocktail in a swift gulp. Leonard laughed and waved at one of the topless males behind the bar. 'More!' he mouthed.

Kathryn drank another toxic cocktail and then another. She wondered whether they were really toxic at all, whether they weren't just a mixture of juices with the merest hint of alcohol, because she didn't feel as though they were having any effect whatsoever. She reminded herself that she didn't actually want them to have any effect. That she wanted to be OK when she was leaving the club. And thinking about leaving made her worry all over again about the wisdom of having come in the first place.

'Dance with me!' Leonard dragged her on to the glass floor and began shaking his head in time to the music. Kathryn swayed, trying to keep up with him and realising that she wasn't succeeding, because whatever sense of rhythm she possessed had been hijacked by the cocktails, which had obviously contained hefty quantities of alcohol after all. She was actually finding it difficult to stay upright.

'Camille Carson!' She heard Leonard's voice pierce through the fog and she followed the direction of his pointing arm to where a stunning brunette was sitting in one of the booths. Camille Carson, the daughter of a daytime talk-show host, was currently the top A of the A-listers, even more popular than the supermodel or the Oscar-nominated actress or the daughter of the presidential hopeful. Her seal of approval for the club would make it even more desirable in the future. At least the short-term future anyhow. Kathryn knew that clubs went in and out of fashion nearly as quickly as A-list celebrities. She'd once done some work for an entertainment corporation that had counted a number of nightclubs in its stable and she knew how things were. Today's must-have was tomorrow's has-been all in the twinkling of an eye.

She shouldn't have had the third cocktail. She was finding it hard to focus on anything now and was annoyed with herself because she didn't like to let herself down in front of her colleagues even if that was meant to be part of the bonding experience. She hadn't let herself down yet; she tried to keep a knowing half-smile on her face every time Leonard turned to talk to her but she knew that if she spoke she'd only come out with complete rubbish. Although would it matter? Surely everyone here was off their heads on something? Being sober was probably a greater crime than being drunk or stoned.

But Kathryn didn't really want to be drunk or stoned. She'd knocked back the cocktails on a stupid whim, a vain belief that they'd make her feel better. What she had wanted just for a minute was to get back to a time when she could do stupid things and not worry about it. She hadn't often done stupid things of course (if, she thought suddenly, she didn't count marrying Alan, which hadn't seemed stupid at the time); it wasn't part of her nature. But she remembered, in her teens, going to a local nightclub and drinking cider out of a bottle behind the rather seedy-looking building before going inside and knocking back even more despite the fact that she wasn't crazy about the acidic apple taste. She'd known it was stupid but she'd wanted to do it because she'd wanted to prove to everyone that she wasn't as distant and as together as they thought.

She'd been truly drunk by the time she'd arrived home. It had taken her five fumbling minutes to put her key in the lock and open the front door, and when she'd finally stepped into the hallway Veronica had confronted her, demanding to know if she'd been drinking. Kathryn, swaying slightly in front of her, had dissolved into helpless laughter.

'Of course,' she said. 'Of course I've been drinking. You don't think I'd be like this if I hadn't been drinking.' And she'd toppled off the wedge shoes she'd been wearing and ended up in a heap at the bottom of the stairs.

She vaguely remembered Romy's eyes peering at her from over the banisters. There had been a look of horrified amusement on the younger girl's face as she'd watched what was going on with intense interest. Kathryn was glad to be the butt of her amusement, glad to be seen to be normal.

'I won't have it,' said Veronica. 'You can't stay out till all hours and come home in this sort of state.'

'Why not?' Kathryn's words were slurred. 'Darragh does.'

'He doesn't,' Veronica said. 'But in any event he's older. And he's a man. It's different.'

Kathryn snorted. 'No it's bloody not. Not at all. You pamper him, you know that. You think the sun shines out of his arse. Because he's a boy. So . . . silly. Silly.' She'd closed her eyes then and Veronica had helped her to bed, where she'd passed out without even getting undressed.

The next morning her head had felt like a quarry pit being mined by a squadron of JCBs. Veronica had been sympathetic but firm.

'I'm glad you got that out of your system,' she told her. 'Everyone needs to get drunk at least once even if it's only to stop you doing it again. But you've got to remember that it's not a good idea to let yourself get out of control.'

It was good advice from Veronica. Kathryn sometimes thought that her mother was capable of giving excellent advice only she never actually followed it herself. Kathryn had seen Veronica out of control on a number of occasions, like the Christmas after she and Dermot had separated when she'd drunk two bottles of wine at dinner and lectured them on the infidelity of men and the hopelessness of a woman's lot in general, then insisted on singing maudlin songs until she passed out on the sofa. (Kathryn remembered trying to make a joke of it to Romy, who had listened to their mother with increasing distress and anger because, of course, she'd badmouthed Dermot for much of the day.) And then there'd been Kathryn's twenty-first birthday party, a night that she had looked forward to even though she'd initially said that she didn't want to have a party at all. But Veronica was good at parties; she'd insisted on a total extravaganza for Kathryn and all of Kathryn's friends (who were generally like her, a little too studious for their own good, but who had suddenly come over all girlie and excited at the idea of dressing up). Unfortunately all Kathryn now remembered about the party was that it had been the catalyst for the break-up of the relationship between Veronica and Romy and that Veronica had eventually got absolutely blotto and had been found passed out in the hotel's residents' lounge long after all the guests had left. Kathryn had been the one to rouse her and get her home and even put her to bed, and she'd listened as Veronica had protested over and over that it wasn't her fault and that she hadn't done anything and that Romy just didn't understand. Afterwards Kathryn had thought about talking to both Veronica and Romy and maybe dishing out advice to them, but then she realised that she was hopeless at giving advice and that it was up to her mother and her sister to sort things out between them. It was better, she'd decided, not to become involved.

What advice would Veronica give me now? she wondered. What would she tell me to do? Actually she felt pretty sure that she already knew what Veronica's advice would be. She didn't need to ask her. She didn't need to see her – although she'd been thinking that perhaps her surgery was a good excuse to get away to Ireland for a few days and have some time to herself. She reckoned that visiting home because of Veronica's surgery would be something that Alan might understand and accept without thinking of it as a reflection on him and on their marriage. And she wondered why she was so worried about how he felt.

But I can't, she thought desperately. I can't go home, because if I do I'll surely end up telling them that my fairy-tale marriage isn't a fairy tale after all. I can't have Veronica look at me and think that she was right all the time, that I

160

haven't got a clue when it comes to men. I can't have Darragh and Giselle laughing at me for getting it wrong – me, who's supposed to be such an expert at getting it right.

And maybe it's not all wrong. She rubbed the back of her neck. I just don't know about that, do I? I can't seem to rationalise it properly. Because maybe Alan is right about everything and it *is* just me. I wish I could see it clearly, though. I really do.

She staggered slightly and grasped Leonard by the shoulder, pulling his ear close to her lips and telling him that she had to leave.

'But we're having such a good time!' he protested.

'I know. I have things to do tomorrow,' she lied. 'I have an early meeting and I need some beauty sleep. Tell the others I said good night.'

'Whatever.' He kissed her on the lips, a warm, moist kiss that would have made her shudder if she'd been in a fit state to shudder. She picked up her bag and walked out of the club into the cool night air.

She caught a cab on Tenth Avenue and sank happily into the back seat, closing her eyes, oblivious to the vibrant city around her. When the taxi stopped outside the apartment building she overtipped the driver and then stumbled into the marbled foyer. The concierge came from behind his desk and took her arm as he led her to the elevator and pressed the button for the tenth floor. She was embarrassed at being so obviously drunk in front of him, though she told herself that he must surely be used to seeing residents of the building under the weather. But usually not her. She groaned as she stared at her reflection in the mirrored walls.

Her hair was a mess. The fixing gel she'd used to hold it in its edgy style had lost its potency and it was now flattened against the crown of her head. Her mascara had smudged so that she had black circles beneath her eyes. They matched her expensive dress, which hadn't really been suitable for the nightclub at all, covering as it did far too much of her body despite the fact that it was way shorter than anything she'd normally wear. Mistake, she told herself, as she got out of the elevator. Big, big mistake. Might as well keep right on making them. What was one more in a long list? Even though it wasn't how she wanted it to be.

It only took her one attempt to unlock the apartment door. Once inside she slid her feet out of her high-heeled shoes and padded silently along the parquet flooring. It was funny, she thought, how quickly she'd managed to get hold of herself. Her head was pounding now but the fuzziness had disappeared completely. She blinked a couple of times in the dim light of the living room and then moved on to the kitchen, where she poured herself a huge glass of water. Water was always her salvation when it came to alcohol. At least two pints before going to bed. She knew that it meant that when she woke up, even if she did have a slight headache, she still wouldn't feel totally and utterly wasted and she'd be able to function almost normally.

She leaned her head against the white-tiled wall. Getting drunk wasn't going to make things better. She knew that. In fact it could make things worse. The truth was that she needed her wits about her now. She needed to know what she was doing and why. Drinking to paper over the cracks was weak. She wasn't a weak person. She swallowed hard as the words formed in her brain.

How could she say that she wasn't a weak person? She was allowing this situation to get out of control, and if that wasn't weak she didn't know what was. She was uncertain about her marriage and afraid to deal with it. That was incompetently weak. It was what some of her clients did. Not facing up to reality. She always told them that the most important thing was to face reality. It was, of course, easy to say. Not always so easy to do.

The apartment was so quiet that she thought she might

162

have got home before Alan. When she'd told him about the bonding exercise at the nightclub his eyes had narrowed but then (to her surprise) he'd smiled at her and told her it was fine, that he had a dinner engagement himself. She should go to the nightclub and have a good time. But she wasn't entirely sure that he really meant it. And she'd really, really wanted to get home early so that he wouldn't think she was deliberately staying out late. Even though that had been part of the reason for her going in the first place.

It's all so silly, she thought, as she sipped her water. I should just sit down and talk to him about it instead of trying to second-guess everything. I should say that we need to discuss this in a rational, adult way. It is, after all, only about setting boundaries for each other and knowing what's acceptable in our marriage. That doesn't sound so terrible, does it?

She sighed. It was more than that and she knew it. The balance of power in their relationship had somehow been skewed entirely the wrong way and it just wasn't possible to change it. There were no rational discussions that could solve this problem. Deep down, she knew that.

But if that was what she truly believed, then her marriage was over. The thing was, she thought, she wasn't sure how to deal with that. She wasn't sure about anything any more.

She rinsed the glass out under the tap and then walked to the master bedroom, picking up her shoes on the way. She pushed the door open gently. And then she froze.

'So.' Alan was sitting on the bed, fully clothed. 'You decided to come home.'

She stared at him wordlessly.

'What time d'you think this is?' he asked.

She bit her lip.

'And you're drunk.'

She held her breath.

He got up from the bed and walked towards her. She felt

herself stiffen. Then he put his arm around her and pulled her close to him.

'What the fuck is going on here, Kathryn?' he asked sadly. 'What the hell is happening to you? And what are we going to do about it?'

Chapter 11

Romy was thinking about Egypt as she stood in the supermarket queue. At first she didn't know what had catapulted her into her memories of Luxor and Karnak, visiting the tomb of Tutankhamen and wandering around the ancient temples, and then she realised that the piped music was of the Bangles singing 'Walk Like an Egyptian' and she grinned at the way her subconscious had linked the two things together.

She'd enjoyed her time in Egypt, where she'd been doing volunteer work with a forensic scientist who was writing a paper about bone health in ancient populations. The fact that the ancient Egyptians took so much care and effort with their dead meant that the bones were in a much better state than more recent finds from other countries, making them a good study for the forensic scientist. Romy had learned a lot from the experience and she often thought that it would be nice to do another study like that. But she couldn't afford to take the time out for a volunteer dig right now.

The music changed to Robbie Williams and the images of Egypt receded into the background as she began to load the shopping on to the conveyor belt.

I can't believe, she muttered to herself as she hauled a promotional pack of Veronica's favourite sparkling water out of the trolley, that I've turned into someone who does supermarket shopping. She normally only did her shopping at late-night corner stores and (on the occasions when Keith would text her and suggest firing up the barbie) at the local organic butcher.

She tried not to think about the barbies she was missing and told herself that coming home had been the right thing to do. She just wished that Veronica's recovery would speed up a bit. It was now over two weeks since she'd come home after surgery and she was still very frail. She was also querulous and irritable and sorry for herself, which was really hard to cope with.

Romy was particularly worried by the fact that in the last few days Veronica hadn't even bothered to do her full make-up. Oh, she'd slapped on some foundation and a smudge of lippy but she hadn't done her eyes or bronzed her cheeks and she hadn't bothered co-ordinating her outfits either. In fact she'd actually stayed in a pair of tracksuit bottoms and a T-shirt all of the previous day. (The tracksuit bottoms had been Lacoste, but despite their designer credentials Romy knew that Veronica wasn't really a tracksuit woman at heart.)

Romy found it difficult to believe that she was now getting as worked up about her mother not wearing make-up and spending hours over her wardrobe as she normally did when Veronica actually did spend all day at it. But there was no doubt that Veronica's lack of interest in everything was really, really worrying. Romy thought it was down to the fact that the surgeon had told her that she needed to take it slowly for the next couple of weeks and that she was to limit the amount of moving around that she did. It would take three to four months, he said, before there'd be substantial healing to her back, and so although there were plenty of exercises for her to do, she had to go easy during that time.

Veronica had looked horrified at the time frame of three to four months. Romy had been pretty horrified by it herself.

The incessant beeping of the barcode machine was still going through her head as she pushed the laden trolley back to the car. I'm now officially a drudge, she thought, as she loaded the shopping into the Golf. My entire life is revolving around going to the shops and watching *Emmerdale*. (She'd never been into soaps before, but Veronica loved them and they were the only things that seemed to interest her at the moment. Which meant that Romy now felt as though she'd known the characters in them all her life.)

Darragh was no help. Despite the fact that she'd expected him to call to the house on a regular basis as the family's alpha male (and had, in fact, been prepared to be irritated by his constant presence), he had only dropped by a few times and stayed less than fifteen minutes on each occasion, saying that Giselle wasn't feeling the best and that he needed to be home with her.

Romy knew that she was feeling very down in the dumps and sorry for herself that morning but she couldn't help it. She was also feeling resentful towards both her brother and sister, who were clearly relieved that someone else was worrying about their mother so that they didn't have to make any changes to their busy, more important lifestyles. The worst of it was that on the evenings Darragh had called by Veronica had perked up and become instantly chattier and more fun, which made Romy feel all the more hopeless. She wondered if this was how stay-at-home mothers felt when they'd been at home all day with truculent kids and the father returned from work to be greeted as a beloved hero figure. Veronica certainly seemed to hero-worship Darragh, although the atmosphere between her half-brother and herself was currently somewhere between frosty and glacial. He made no mention of her refusal to look after Mimi and she was determined not to raise the subject, but it was there between them and coloured everything they said.

Romy couldn't help feeling massively guilty even as she told herself that she couldn't have coped. She kept thinking that she should have said yes anyway, that surely there was a way of managing, even though she didn't know what it was. Then she would remind herself that there were other people who could help out, that Giselle had family too and that if she and Darragh were so set on going to Barbados they could surely leave Mimi with her maternal grandparents, who lived only about thirty kilometres away in County Kildare.

None of all her logical reasoning made her feel anything other than mean. And so when Darragh had turned up at the house she made herself scarce, bustling around in the kitchen while he chatted to Veronica. She made tea and coffee for them, feeling like a servant as she brought it in to them and then getting annoyed with herself for feeling anything at all.

Giselle had called around once, totally glammed up and looking utterly fabulous, but Veronica had been asleep at the time and so Giselle had just left a magnificent bouquet of flowers for her and said that she had to rush because she was picking Mimi up from class. (From what Romy gathered, Mimi went to drama, arts and crafts, music, early reading and 'personal development' classes as well as ballet. If the child didn't turn out to be a genius, she thought, it wouldn't be from want of her parents trying. Though how a three year old could do anything constructive in arts and crafts was utterly beyond her.) Giselle was less glacial with Romy than Darragh had been, but Romy had still felt the waves of disapproval coming from her sister-in-law. Veronica had been delighted by the flowers and Romy had been annoyed with herself for not remembering that her mother liked them around the house and not keeping vases of them on the go to perk up her spirits.

It was after Giselle's visit that Veronica spoke to Romy about Mimi.

'I believe they wanted you to look after her,' she said as the two of them sat in front of the TV, not particularly enthralled by the programme but watching it anyway. Veronica was wearing a loose top and a different pair of Lacoste bottoms along with her sequinned loafers. Romy was in jeans and an old grey sweatshirt.

'The idea of me looking after Mimi is just off the wall,' she said defensively. 'It was a ridiculous notion.'

'I know.' Veronica smiled slightly at her. 'I reminded Giselle that you were the baby of the family and that you had no experience.'

'You did?' Romy was astonished.

'And I told her that you'd be the worst person in the world to look after a small girl,' continued her mother.

'Oh.'

'Well, that's what you think yourself, isn't it?'

'Um, yes.'

'So she's OK with it,' Veronica said. 'She realises the insanity of entrusting their only daughter to someone who thinks that digging in muck is a sensible way of earning a living.'

'I don't—' Romy broke off and smiled suddenly. 'I guess that's as good a way to put them off as any. Make them think that their precious little girl could end up like me!'

'They're not bad people just because they suggested it,' said Veronica. 'I don't blame them. Being a parent is hard work. Sometimes you need a break.'

Romy wondered if Veronica was getting in a subtle dig at her but she was so pleased that the whole looking-after-Mimi situation had been somewhat resolved she didn't really care.

'Anyway,' Veronica said, 'Darragh has had to go to Switzerland for a couple of days, so any plan for time away has been put on hold.'

'Lucky him.' Romy sounded envious.

'It's business,' said Veronica.

'So what?' Romy looked at her dismissively. 'At least he's getting away somewhere different, isn't he?'

'I'm sorry you're finding life so monotonous,' said Veronica. 'Of course it's not exactly a whirlwind of excitement for me either.'

'It's not . . . I'm not . . .' Romy searched for the right thing to say. 'It's just that I'm used to doing my own thing. And so are you! Anyway, you can jazz up your life a bit – why don't you ask some friends around?'

'I'm recovering from surgery.' Veronica sounded horrified. 'I'm not fit to be seen. It'll take months.'

'Mum!' Romy looked at her with irritation. 'You're perfectly fit to be seen. You don't have to look like you've just come off a fashion shoot for your friends.' And then she sighed. 'Although maybe you do.'

She walked out of the room and went upstairs, disappointed in herself for letting herself get riled by Veronica and feeling that in the last few days the fabric of their relationship was being pulled very tight.

She took out her computer and logged on to read her emails. There weren't very many of them. Most of them were group messages – either archaeological interest ones from the newsletters she subscribed to or jokes from her friends. None of them were specifically sent to her as a person. She was just one of the '79 others' on the group email headings.

She desperately wanted to hear from someone. She kept taking her mobile out of her pocket and checking it for texts or on the off chance that she'd missed a call. But it remained resolutely devoid of any communication from anyone at all. It was horrible, she thought, how quickly you could fade out of people's lives. A few weeks ago she was a recipient of texts about weekends in Queensland or barbies on the beach. Now it was as though her life in Australia was nothing more than a dream.

The atmosphere between herself and Veronica had been more fraught than ever over the past few days. Which was why getting out of the house and going to the supermarket that morning had seemed like such a good idea.

Two hours after she'd set off for the shops, and with a ferocious headache pounding her temples, she turned into the driveway and saw the black Audi parked in front of the door. Who was that? she wondered. She frowned. Veronica would have had to make her way to the door herself to answer it. She wouldn't have been pleased about that, certainly not if she was still vegging around in her tracksuit and without any make-up. Romy opened the door and, laden with shopping, walked through to the kitchen.

Veronica was sitting at the table, her back straighter than it had been for a few weeks and a coquettish smile on her face. She'd changed from the comfortable top and tracksuit bottoms into a fitted blouse in jade green over a navy silk skirt. High-heeled slip-on shoes dangled from her feet. Romy's eyes widened at the shoes. There wasn't a hope in hell that Veronica could actually walk in them – if she tried she'd surely wreck her back completely! Her mother's face was made up too, and for the first time in her life Romy was relieved to see her wearing her full array of war paint. At least now she looked like the person Romy had always known. She looked like her mother again! But Romy was astonished at the sudden and dramatic change in Veronica's look and Veronica's mood.

The man opposite her mother was smiling too. Despite the fact that she was pleased to see Veronica up and dressed, Romy felt unaccountably uncomfortable at the idea of the strange man in the kitchen. (Why? she asked herself. She's a single woman. It's her house. What exactly is my problem? She was utterly unable to answer her own questions, which annoyed her even more.)

'Hi.' She looked uncertainly between them.

'Oh, hello,' said Veronica in the special husky voice that Romy knew she used with men. 'This is Will Blake. He's a patient of Dr Jacobs too and a friend of mine from the bridge club. Will, this is my daughter Romy.'

'Nice to meet you,' said Romy neutrally.

'Will had the same surgery as me a couple of years ago,' Veronica told her. 'He's been giving me advice.'

'Maybe you'll listen to him so.' Romy put the shopping on

the table between them and rubbed her own back, which she'd jolted lifting the bags out of the car, something which had made her snort with the irony of possibly ending up with a crocked back herself. 'You sure as hell don't listen to me. You didn't do your exercises this morning.'

'This is what I've had to put up with!' Veronica smiled brightly at Will. 'Romy is supposed to be keeping an eye on me at the moment.'

'I've heard lots about you,' said Will.

Romy looked at him mockingly. 'Nothing good, I'm sure.' She'd meant it to sound light-hearted but somehow she didn't quite succeed.

'Romy!' Veronica was annoyed. 'And watch that coffee, it's going to fall.'

Romy caught the jar which was just about to slide off the table and put it in the cupboard.

'I had the same procedure as Veronica,' said Will. 'It made a huge difference to me. I told your mother that she'll be glad she had it done.'

'Good,' said Romy. She stopped putting the groceries away, filled a tumbler with water and swallowed a couple of aspirin.

'Well, look, Veronica, I'd better go.' Will stood up and Romy could see that his movement wasn't as fluid as it could be. I hope I never do have serious back problems, she thought fleetingly. It would be murder on a dig!

She saw Will out and then came back to the kitchen. Veronica was still sitting at the table.

'You didn't have to be so rude,' she said to Romy. 'Honestly! Chasing the man out of the house.'

'I didn't,' protested Romy.

'Like you made him feel welcome.'

'I didn't do or say anything!'

'Exactly.'

'I'm sorry, I'm sorry!' Romy slammed a tin of tuna on the worktop surface. 'I've got a headache, I've spent hours in that bloody supermarket and at the chemist getting your stuff – and no they *still* don't have that Lancôme lotion by the way, why don't you switch to something easier to find? I didn't mean to be rude but it's a kick in the teeth to see that you make an effort for some bloke but you can't be bothered whenever I'm around.'

Veronica looked at her in amusement. 'You want me to dress up for you?' she asked. 'You hate the way I dress.'

'It's not that.' Romy looked at her mother in frustration. 'It's just . . . I put up with you every day and—'

'Nobody asked you to put up with me every single day!' Veronica interrupted her crossly.

'Oh really? And if I wasn't here how would you manage?' demanded Romy.

'Perfectly well,' retorted Veronica. She picked up the tin of tuna, stood up and walked awkwardly and uncomfortably in her high-heeled shoes to the kitchen cupboard. She reached upwards to put it on the shelf but it slipped from her grasp, fell on to the glass tumbler which Romy had left on the counter below, causing it to shatter into hundreds of pieces, and then rolled slowly along the kitchen floor before coming to a stop at the back door.

'Bugger,' said Veronica, sitting down abruptly on a kitchen chair.

Romy opened the door to the utility room, took out a dustpan and brush and began sweeping the glass into the pan.

'Stop behaving like a martyr!' cried Veronica. 'You think it's fun for me being stuck in the house with someone who despises me?'

'I don't despise you.' Romy emptied the glass into the chrome pedal bin.

'Yes you damn well do,' snapped Veronica. 'You always have! You hate the fact that I divorced your dad and you hate the fact that I love life – even if it's been hard the last few weeks. But who can blame me with you here looking down on me all the time. You're a snob, Romy Kilkenny. I don't know how it happened but that's how it's turned out.'

Romy put away the dustpan and brush and looked at her mother.

'I don't hate you for any of those things,' she said evenly. 'If I wanted to hate you – and I don't any more – I could pick far more likely reasons.'

'You'll never let it go, will you?'

'It's somewhat difficult to let go,' said Romy.

'I've apologised a million times.'

'And meant it. Huh.'

'He was too old for you.'

Romy started to laugh. 'And that's the best yet. It truly is. You did it for my own good, is that it?'

'Romy . . .'

'I don't want to talk about this,' said Romy. 'I don't want to rehash it all over again. All I'm saying is that I don't hate you because of the past. I got over that a long time ago. I guess I'm just feeling a bit bored and frustrated and maybe I'm taking it out on you. I'm sorry.'

Veronica looked at her. Romy's blue eyes were unwavering.

'Why don't you get a job if you're bored?'

'Dad asked me that too. But what's the point?' asked Romy. 'You need me here. And it would only be for a short period of time. I want to go back to Oz as soon as possible.'

'I know,' said Veronica. 'But . . . well, you've seen how things are. I'm struggling, I really am. I need someone for a bit longer. Maybe another month or two. Romy, I can't do things yet. I can't be on my own.'

'If I had a job you'd be on your own,' said Romy.

'Not all day, every day,' said Veronica. 'And not at night either. And maybe with you out of the house I could have people around and I wouldn't feel—'

'I haven't stopped you from having people around!' cried Romy. 'I want you to have people around.'

'I know. I know.' Veronica pressed her fingers against her temples. 'It's just that I'm used to doing things my way.'

'Mum, nothing you've done over the last week or two has been anything like your way. Not getting dressed. Not getting made up. You've been scaring me rigid.'

Veronica smiled slightly. 'Really?'

'Yes. Because you've never not bothered before.'

'I thought that if I didn't do too much of the make-up stuff you'd feel sorrier for me. And stay.'

Romy stared at her in complete astonishment. 'You're not serious.'

Veronica shrugged. 'So I told people not to drop by. That I didn't feel up to it. Only Will rang while you were out and suddenly I wanted to see someone again.'

'Honestly.' Romy didn't know what to say. 'You're nuts, Mum. You know that.'

Veronica shrugged again. 'I know that you'll always think of me as nuts.'

Romy swallowed. Of all the things she'd expected Veronica to say, admitting that she needed her wasn't one of them.

'Don't make me beg,' said Veronica.

'I'd have thought you'd be happy to see me go.' Romy's lip trembled.

'I'd be happy not to think that every time you looked at me you were judging me and finding me wanting,' said Veronica. 'But I'm not going to be too proud to admit that I need some help.'

Romy was silent.

'You don't know what it's like,' said Veronica tightly. 'Not being able to do things. Your body betraying you a thousand times every day. Being in constant pain.'

'You shouldn't be in pain by now.' Romy took a tissue from the box on the counter and blew her nose. 'You wouldn't be if you'd do your bloody exercises.'

'A constant state of discomfort,' amended Veronica. 'And

I'll do the exercises. I promise. I want to be able to wear shoes again. I thought my back was going to break in half with these.' She poked at her mules with her toes.

'Is that the Holy Grail for you?' asked Romy. 'Two-inch heels?'

Veronica laughed bitterly. 'Maybe.'

She moved position on the chair while Romy returned to unpacking the shopping. She watched her youngest daughter, supple and lithe as she stood on tiptoe to reach the highest shelves and bent without difficulty to pack things away in the storage area beneath the sink.

It wasn't fair, thought Veronica as she twirled her ruby ring around on her finger. It wasn't fair that her back had given way on her and left her like this. Dr Jacobs had assured her that she would be significantly more mobile in the coming months but right now she felt old and useless and scared.

She'd never felt old before. She'd always been an active person and one who'd made the best of herself. And while she'd acknowledged over the past couple of years that there were some things that were too much trouble to do any more (like intensive workouts in the gym; far too much like hard work!), she didn't feel any different from how she'd felt when she was forty or fifty. Or even twenty or thirty. She was still the same Veronica. Just because she had more candles on the cake didn't mean that she'd turned into an old person. She still liked the same things she always had. But what she didn't like now was having to depend on her children to take care of her. She hated the idea that Romy – of all people – had agreed to come home to be on hand. She hated the fact that she'd had to move to the downstairs bedroom because the stairs were too much for her at the moment and that Romy had been the one to bring her things to the spare room. Veronica knew that Romy had probably looked at her stuff and thought that she was an old fool. That only young girls should wear gorgeous, wispy things. But why? OK, so she wasn't young and lissom and smooth-skinned but they made her feel good and surely that was important? Besides, she was still attractive enough for men like Will Blake!

Romy had probably looked at her jars and potions too, at her wrinkle defence creams and collagen-rich products, and sniggered as she herself slapped on the most basic moisturiser she could lay her hands on. And the worst thing about that, thought Veronica, was that Romy looked great on it. Oh, her face was slightly too tanned for her own good. But her skin was as clear as a baby's and looked just as soft. Veronica wanted to scream at her to protect it in every possible way because when she was sixty she'd wish she had, but she knew that it was pointless talking to her. Because she knew that whatever she suggested, whatever she asked her daughter to do, Romy would always, always want to do the complete opposite.

She remembered their discussion about college, when she'd suggested to Romy that media studies might be something she'd enjoy. Romy had looked at her with ill-disguised irritation.

'Media studies?' She laughed. 'You want me to choose the soft option, the one you choose when you haven't a clue what else to do?'

'You said that you were interested in it,' Veronica protested. 'And your father can give you lots of information.'

'I'm not interested in media studies.' Romy's voice brooked no opposition.

'What then?' Veronica had been taken aback. She'd confidently expected that Romy would end up in some area of the media. Like Dermot she was endlessly interested in people and situations and wanting to know what was going on. And then in trying to analyse it afterwards. Dermot managed to do all of those things in his photographs. Even though Veronica hated what he did she knew that he did it well. She'd expected that Romy would do it equally well.

'I was thinking of archaeology,' Romy told her.

'What!'

'It seems like an interesting discipline to me,' Romy said. 'We don't know half enough about the people who were on this earth before us. If we're going to destroy it for future generations the least we can do is find out more about the past.'

'You're not interested in archaeology,' said Veronica flatly. 'You know you're not.'

'Actually, I am,' Romy told her. 'But you didn't know that. There's a million things about me that you don't know.'

'Look, I tell you what I do know,' said Veronica. 'I know that it's incredibly silly to decide to take a particular course just to spite me.'

'I'm not doing that,' Romy said.

'Yes you bloody are!'

Maybe she'd been wrong about that, thought Veronica, as she continued to watch her daughter. Maybe Romy had been right after all. Maybe she'd only thought she'd known what Romy wanted and had got it completely wrong.

And yet part of her didn't think so. Part of her knew that Romy loved TV documentaries and reading newspapers and how things were presented. She would have done well in media, whether it was as a print journalist or on TV herself. She'd chosen archaeology just to spite her mother.

But she seemed to like it. And she seemed to be good at what she did although Veronica was still somewhat unclear as to what exactly Romy's job entailed. But if she was good at it, thought Veronica, where would she go from here? Veronica had no idea what her daughter's career path might be. She couldn't see her digging up skeletons for ever, but she supposed it was a possibility. And if she spent her time trekking around the world, what chance did she have of finding someone to love? She thought that Romy might be in love with the Australian boyfriend. She could see the signs. The way Romy jumped expectantly whenever the phone rang. The way she constantly checked her texts and her emails. Veronica had a lot of experience of women being in love with men who didn't love them in return, and she rather thought that this was Romy's current situation. But Romy clammed up whenever she tried to bring the conversation around to it and Veronica knew there was no point in pressing her even if she wanted to. She wanted Romy to confide in her the same way Giselle did. Her daughter-in-law would chat about the most inconsequential of things. Romy only ever seemed to talk in order to argue with her. And she would never, ever confide in her.

Veronica shook her head. How the hell had she managed to get it all wrong with her youngest daughter? Was it because Romy had spent so many weekends with Dermot after the divorce? Veronica had hated seeing her rushing off on Friday evenings to be with him; hated the fact that Dermot got her during weekends and holidays when she was cheerful and free-spirited, whereas Veronica was the one who had to nag her to do her homework and go to bed early. Maybe that was it. But then, Veronica thought, she hadn't exactly succeeded brilliantly with Kathryn either. And Kathryn had been with her all the time. So what sort of hopeless mother was she?

The phone rang. It was Darragh, saying that he was home again and would swing by that evening.

At least I didn't get it wrong with him, thought Veronica. At least I managed to get something right as a parent – my clever, brilliant son!

While Veronica and Darragh chatted on the phone, Romy went upstairs and opened her laptop. She checked her emails and was delighted to find one from Tanya giving her all the latest Heritage Help gossip, although she bristled when she read that Pam had asked Tanya about supervising the Melbourne dig. If Pam was talking to her about it, she must think that Romy wasn't coming back.

She rattled off a rapid reply to Tanya telling her that she couldn't wait to get back and then sent another one to Pam saying that she hoped to be leaving Ireland very soon. She knew that she had no real idea when she would be leaving (she would have to think long and hard about Veronica's request that she stay for longer) but she wasn't going to have Pam think that she could simply parachute Tanya in to Melbourne ahead of her.

She clicked on the Heritage Help webcam but, of course, it was the middle of the night in Australia now and the room was too dark to see anything. She sat back and closed her eyes and thought about the excavated convict colony and wondered again about the pregnant woman and what she'd had to endure. And she told herself that whatever problems she herself had and however frustrated she felt back in Ireland, they were nothing compared to whatever that poor girl had gone through.

She opened her email application again and addressed a message to Keith. She told him that she still missed everyone, that she was getting cabin fever from being at home and that her contribution to Irish society so far was shopping. Supermarket shopping. He'd laugh at that. He knew how much she hated it. It was a chatty, light-hearted message with no possible reason for him to think that she was harbouring lustful or romantic thoughts about him. It was the kind of message she'd sent to him in the past. Just because he'd gone to Perth, she told herself, didn't mean that he wouldn't like to hear from her. Just because he'd been a bit dismissive in his phone call didn't mean that he was trying to push her out of his life. She'd read too much into that. He's my friend, she reminded herself. It's perfectly OK to keep in touch with him. She re-read the message to make sure that it was as cheerfully friendly as she'd intended and then added a little smiley beside her name before clicking on the send button. There was a comfort in the swooshing sound as it went – in her head she imagined her words being grabbed by an invisible hand and being hurtled around the world to land on Keith's computer.

You know that you're now officially cracked, she told herself as she closed the computer again. You're starting to hallucinate, which surely isn't a good thing.

Chapter 12

Darragh sat in his office with Alex and Stephen, his finance officer and company secretary, and brought them up to speed on his trip to Geneva. Darragh had enjoyed Geneva very much, staying in the luxurious Hotel d'Angleterre with its clubby, business feel and its excellent views of the lake. He'd eaten in the hotel restaurant every evening (red meat in rich sauces and no steamed vegetables!); he'd had a relaxing massage in the spa on his last day and uninterrupted sleep in his elegant bedroom every night. When he woke up each morning he'd felt pampered and refreshed. It helped, he supposed, that he wasn't disturbed in the middle of the night by Mimi coming into the bed as she so often did at home, squirming down between him and Giselle and falling happily asleep while he struggled to drop off again. There was a lot to be said, Darragh reckoned, for sleeping on your own. There was also a lot to be said for having some time to himself, away from his family. He loved Giselle and Mimi. But sometimes he felt surrounded by femininity and it was nice to get away from girlie things for a few days. Every morning as he'd gone down to breakfast he'd felt proud of himself, a businessman abroad. He read the *Financial Times* over coffee; he never bothered with it at home, but he felt that the pink paper lent him a certain gravitas in the hotel dining room. He had to admit that although he was disappointed about not being able to do the Barbados trip with

Giselle there was a definite satisfaction in being away by himself.

He'd seen a number of prospective companies which he decided might be possible takeover targets during his three-day trip and he wrote up notes on them each evening so that he could explore the issue in more depth back in Dublin. He'd circulated his findings to Stephen and Alex and had called the meeting to discuss them further.

Stephen, although he usually backed Darragh up whenever he talked about Swiss engineering, had a completely different agenda. He had, he told Darragh, been approached by a German company, Hemmerling, who were interested in a partnership deal.

'What sort of deal?' asked Darragh.

'They're looking to expand into Ireland,' explained Alex. 'They want to get involved in projects here.'

'And how do they think we can help?' asked Darragh.

'Synergies.'

'What sort?'

Alex shrugged.

'They must have put something definite to you,' said Darragh, irritated by the other man's reticence.

'Nothing concrete,' said Alex. 'Just that there are things we could do together. They have a lot of expertise in areas that we don't. It might be a good fit.'

'Do you want to get them over to talk?' asked Darragh.

'I suggested it.'

'OK then. In the meantime, what do you think about the energy company proposal?' Darragh had met with the company in Switzerland. Its business was very different from Dolan's but he couldn't help thinking that in the changing world environment, it had prospects.

'Not really our thing,' said Stephen. 'The synergies wouldn't work.'

They both loved that word, thought Darragh. He wondered if they actually knew what it meant.

'I know it's a different sort of business,' he said. 'But it could have some real long-term benefits.'

Alex and Stephen exchanged glances.

'But here and now,' said Alex, 'the German deal looks more interesting.'

'Leave the paperwork with me,' said Darragh. 'I'll go through it all. But I don't like to think that I went to Switzerland and returned to find a German deal on my desk.'

'These things happen,' said Stephen. 'Besides, this deal could be really good for the company.'

'And the energy one wouldn't?'

Both Alex and Stephen looked unimpressed. Darragh shrugged. 'OK. We'll talk again after I've gone through this stuff.'

The two men nodded and left the office.

Darragh leaned back in his black leather swivel chair. He wasn't sure about Stephen and Alex. On the one hand they were very experienced. Nevertheless, he often wondered how much they cared about the company. They'd been with Dolan's a long time and he trusted them completely but he couldn't help feeling that they were getting complacent. They'd lost the competitive edge. They didn't care enough about the business they'd lost. They wanted easy answers to the challenges Darragh knew the company faced. Maybe, he thought, they were too well paid and too comfortable these days. Perhaps he hadn't tied their pay into their performance enough (something Kathryn banged on about all the time and the only thing that he reluctantly agreed she might be right about, even though he never said that to her). But sometimes he felt that neither Alex nor Stephen had the long-term interests of Dolan's at heart because it didn't matter enough to them.

He had to have those interests at heart himself. It was the legacy. It was important. Losing Jim Cahill's business had proved to him that they were getting left behind, even if Jim had been poached by predatory pricing. Dolan's couldn't afford to be left behind. It was just that he wasn't entirely sure about the right way forward. And he had a sinking feeling that neither Stephen nor Alex was going to be any great help with that.

Kathryn sat at her desk and stared unseeingly at the computer screen in front of her. She was supposed to be tracing a series of receipts and payments for a client company but the accounting trail, normally an open book into a business as far as she was concerned, was eluding her right now. She knew that there were questions she needed to ask and avenues to pursue but she couldn't decide what they were.

Her head was pounding and the narrow shaft of sunlight that barely made it through the office window (not a corner office despite what Romy thought) was glinting off the screen, making it difficult to read.

She got up and took a bottle of water from her mini-fridge. Then she popped a couple of Advil from a packet in her desk and swallowed them. They were good tablets, she thought. They'd get to work on the ache in her head. The only problem, she told herself miserably, was that they wouldn't be able to do anything for the ache in her heart. It's only one part of my life, she muttered, angry at her self-pity. The bad part. There are lots of good parts but this is overshadowing them at the moment. What I have to remember is that the good things will come through in the end. The investigation on my desk is an interesting one. It will bring in a lot of money for the company once I work it all out. I'm kicking ass in the hardest city in the world for ass-kicking. I'm a success. I really am. A money-making success.

She closed her eyes. The current investigation would bring in money if she worked it all out, that was the thing. But right now, despite telling herself that she was a success, she didn't know how to work anything out. Her confidence was at rock bottom and she didn't know how to deal with that because she knew that she only worked well when she was confident. Usually she was very confident. But right now she had no confidence in herself at all.

It was like when she was younger, when she would try so desperately to please Veronica though her mother never seemed to see it, so that everything she did was wrong. It was as though the two of them were on completely different planets – Kathryn would bring home the results of her school tests and Veronica would look at her good grades and tell her that she was really proud of her and then suggest that perhaps it would be a great idea if they went and got Kathryn's hair cut. Or, she'd say, maybe as a treat they could go shopping and buy themselves something really nice. Kathryn knew that hair-cuts and shopping were meant to be a reward but they weren't the reward she wanted. She wanted Veronica to believe in her, to recognise that she was smarter and cleverer than Darragh and to stop thinking of him as the brains in the family. Because he wasn't. Darragh was a plodder. But Veronica didn't see that. And so Kathryn would always get upset whenever Veronica suggested new clothes or new hairstyles and she decided that she didn't want anything to do with fashion or style because she knew that it broke Veronica's heart to see her slope around all day in baggy jeans and worn T-shirts with her long dark hair hiding her face. When Veronica begged her to get it cut or suggested that wearing a nice skirt would be an improve-ment, Kathryn, rather primly, would retort that her future career was far more important than how she looked or what she wore and Veronica would tell her that models carved careers out of wearing nice things, which made Kathryn snort with disapproval.

Kathryn sometimes wondered how many teenage girls rebelled by being the perfect student. A few years later she saw Romy's rebellion as a more normal one – choosing to do something different with her life, breaking free of the notion that work meant being in an office and behind a desk. She remembered Veronica telling Romy that Tom had worked hard so that none of his children would have to get dirty for a living and Romy had, naturally, remarked that Tom's desires had nothing to do with her and that she liked the idea of dirt under her fingernails although (and Kathryn remembered the sarcasm in Romy's voice at the time) obviously when a person had long and totally impractical nails like Veronica there was a lot more room for dirt.

We weren't nice children, she thought. And I don't know why, because despite everything, Mum did her best for us. We never wanted for anything and yet we never seemed to have what we really wanted. But then we never knew what we really wanted. Maybe we still don't. I certainly don't.

I thought this time that I wanted to be married.

Kathryn leaned against the window.

First I thought I wanted to have the great exam results and the glamorous career; after that I thought I wanted to have the successful husband. I know I definitely wanted to have the Upper East Side address. Now I have those things. But none of them are like I expected.

But then, wondered Kathryn bleakly, was anything in life what you expected? What she'd really wanted from her successful career was her own company but she hadn't achieved that because she'd got sidetracked into forensic accountancy and she was good at it. But the plan had been to set up a company that would one day buy into Dolan Manufacturing Components, shocking Darragh, and take it in a new direction while he ranted and raved and admitted that she was a better managing director after all. Perhaps, she acknowledged, that wasn't a serious plan. But it was a great daydream. Of course it might have had more chance of becoming reality if she hadn't indulged in the successful husband daydream instead.

And that was such a stupid thing, she muttered under her breath. Marrying him because, deep down, I wanted to shock Veronica. To make her see that I could do it, despite everything.

Marrying Alan had justified her lack of interest in being part of the in-crowd of girls who always had a boyfriend waiting for them when they came out of the school gates and who wore cropped tops and low-slung jeans to show off their flat stomachs and lacy thongs. Kathryn thought that girls showing off their lacy thongs looked trashy. She wanted people to look at her and know that she was successful. Not to look at her and wonder where she bought her knickers.

When she married Alan it was like all of the parts of the plan had come together. She'd got the career and she'd got the husband and she hadn't had to flash a lacy thong to do it.

And now (despite the fact that she still hadn't become the CEO or the MD of a company that would take over Dolan's) she was doing better than Darragh. She was part of a power couple. She'd heard someone say that once and it had sent a thrill of excitement up her spine. A power couple. It sounded good. Better than an upwardly mobile couple or whatever it was that dopey Darragh and goofy Giselle were called. Alan Palmer was the first man Kathryn had dated whose own success didn't make her feel inadequate. She didn't quite know why this was, but there was something about his assumption that she was smart and ambitious that disarmed her. And then when she eventually realised that she had fallen in love with him, she understood that she'd done so precisely because he was so successful himself. She loved him because he was stronger and more determined than her. Cleverer by a mile too. And because he was so confident in his own success. She was pretty certain that she needed to be married to someone much more successful than her because other-wise the balance of power in the relationship would be tilted in her favour and she didn't think that was a good idea. The reason she thought that way was because she knew that when she was in charge of things, in control, she was relentless and determined and she knew that men didn't really like women like that.

Darragh had always complained about bossy women when they were younger. Kathryn had suggested to him that most men actually liked being bossed around and that they needed women to look after them and that he was a case in point, wasn't he, lazy as sin until he was made to do something? And although her brother would laugh at her and tell her that she didn't have a clue, she knew that she was right. He'd broken up with Myrna Connolly, hadn't he, smart and pretty and a girl that Kathryn herself had liked very much. But Darragh had complained that she was always on at him over something or other and when Myrna had graduated with a much better degree than Darragh, he'd dumped her. He'd also dumped Alison O'Neill, the girl he'd gone out with after Myrna, and who was equally smart.

It wasn't that Darragh wanted silly women, Kathryn thought now as she gazed down at the clogged New York streets beneath her; it was that he didn't want to be put into second place. And Kathryn could understand that, because no one really liked being in second place. She didn't either.

In the end, Darragh hadn't compromised. He'd married the lovely Giselle, who didn't threaten him in the brains department although she was, Kathryn reckoned, very shrewd indeed. Giselle was smart in a way that Kathryn wasn't. Kathryn knew that she was just clever, whereas Giselle knew more about life. It was a silly distinction but it was true nonetheless.

What would Giselle do, Kathryn wondered, in a situation like hers? If Darragh was the problem. Would she stay or would she go?

Kathryn knew that there was no real choice in the answers. Giselle would go. She'd lose all of her airy-fairy prettiness and she'd fight like a tigress for everything she deserved. Why, Kathryn wondered, was it always easier to know what other people would do than what you should do yourself? If someone else had come to her and laid it all out in front of her, she wouldn't have thought twice, she would have said to them that they should throw him out and change the locks.

So why the hell couldn't she do that? What was wrong with her that she was totally unable to take her own advice? What was wrong with her that she was allowing her life to become a train wreck? Was she somehow thinking that being married to someone, even someone like Alan, was better than not being married at all? She didn't really think that. She knew she didn't. But not doing anything about it, being afraid to do something about it . . . well, didn't that just prove how dumb she was herself? And all of the times that she'd looked down on Darragh for being thick and Romy for not really having a clue, well, she'd been the one who was making the mistakes, hadn't she? Darragh was happy as a clam with the lovely Giselle and Romy was equally happy with her mucky bones. While she, Kathryn, the clever one, the one who knew more than the other two put together, was now utterly, utterly miserable. And very, very scared.

Her phone buzzed and startled her so much that she actually banged her head against the glass.

'Fuck,' she said loudly into the empty room as she rubbed her temple. 'Fuck, fuck, fuck.'

Romy was watching afternoon TV with Veronica. Normally she wouldn't have dreamed of watching TV in the afternoon but it was chucking down rain and Veronica had pointed out that there was a repeat of one of the *Time Detective*-type programmes on which she reckoned Romy would enjoy watching.

'It's about them finding a twelfth-century monastery in a school field,' said Veronica. 'Your sort of thing, surely.'

So Romy had agreed to watch, and being honest with herself, she was enjoying following the site excavation and the discovery of a burial ground. And she was (sort of) enjoying sitting beside her mother and sharing the moment, even though Veronica would scrunch up her nose and say 'yeuch' every time the team carefully brushed away the earth to reveal human remains beneath the soil.

'You do this?' demanded Veronica as one of the team excitedly beckoned to the others that she'd found a hand.

Romy nodded. 'But often you don't find them like that, all together,' she told her mother. 'Most times it's just bits of bones and stuff and they're quite difficult to identify unless you know what you're looking for, of course.'

'It's quite technical, isn't it?'

'Well you need to know what you're doing,' agreed Romy.

'So I guess you didn't waste your smarts after all.'

Romy looked surprised. 'I didn't realise that you thought I was smart.'

'Of course you are.'

'You never say so.'

'I don't need to say so.'

Romy said nothing.

'I suppose I had the wrong idea about it,' said Veronica. 'I always thought that being smart meant going into business.'

'That's just because there's a family business,' said Romy. 'Tom's children have business blood in them. I have Dermot's blood and it's quite, quite different.'

'You're obsessed about that,' said Veronica. 'You're not different at all.'

'Mum, I'm completely different,' Romy told her. 'I don't look like them and I don't think like them and I never will.'

'You're not unalike to look at,' Veronica said. 'You and Kathryn both have the same dark hair. So has Darragh actually.'

Romy laughed suddenly. 'None of us gets our hair colour from you,' she said. 'Even allowing for your flirtations with different shades of blond, their dark hair comes from Tom and mine comes from Dermot. Darragh's is a little bit wavy, which is how yours is when you don't attack it with that hair straightener thing you use. Kathryn's is straight but that's because Tom's was straight. Mine is dark and straight because of Dermot. Genetics.'

'You don't know that,' said Veronica. 'Yours and Kathryn's could be from exactly the same gene, which would be from me.'

'Nope,' said Romy firmly. 'Kathryn's hair is lovely – fine and silky, like yours. Mine is strong and coarse like Dermot's. Very, very different.'

'Did you spend hours thinking about it?' asked Veronica. 'Checking everyone's hair?'

'Of course not,' said Romy impatiently. 'It's obvious, that's all.'

'Why do you want to be different?' asked Veronica. 'Why is it such a big deal for you?'

'I don't want to be different.' Romy hesitated before replying. 'I never specially wanted to be different, why would anyone? But there always was something, wasn't there? The shadow of Tom over everything.'

'Don't be daft.'

'I'm not,' said Romy. 'Darragh and Kathryn felt it too. Their legacy. The damn company, always there in the background and nothing to do with me or with Dermot. We were outsiders because of that company and we always will be.'

'Oh, Romy.' Veronica's tone was heartfelt. 'Dermot used that as an excuse. He had plenty of opportunities to get involved. I thought once . . . well, I tried to make him take an interest, but he walked away from it. He didn't want to be involved in it, didn't want to be part of the family.'

'How can you say that!' Romy pointed the remote control at the TV and muted the sound. 'He married you! He was part of the family. Just like I am. But in your head Tom is still more important to you than Dad, just as Darragh and Kathryn are more important than me.'

'That's so untrue!' Veronica was shocked. 'I don't favour any of my children over the others.'

Romy didn't want to argue with her. But she knew that Veronica was wrong.

Chapter 13

The following morning Romy did a jig of delight when she received a text from her friend Colleen to say that she was coming up to Dublin for the day. She'd been beginning to think that all her Irish friends had deserted her and that she'd been totally airbrushed out of their minds. She had contacted Colleen before she'd left Australia, telling her that she was on her way back to Ireland and that she was looking forward to meeting up with her again. Colleen was excited at the thought of getting together but, she warned Romy, her time was totally not her own right now and she'd have to make some strategic plans before she'd be able to get to town.

Colleen Rafferty had been Romy's friend since school and they'd stayed in touch by text and email. The two of them had once made plans to volunteer on digs around the world together to get as much experience as possible, but things hadn't worked out like that because just before graduation Colleen discovered that she was pregnant.

'It's not the worst that could happen,' she'd told Romy as they sat together in the college cafeteria. 'After all, Gil and I are for ever. But it's so not what we wanted right now.'

Gil Gleeson and Colleen had been an item since secondary school and everyone knew that one day they'd get married. But both of them had wanted some freedom first. They'd married after baby Shaun was born, though, and had moved to a housing estate near Avoca, about fifty kilometres from the city, where Gil worked as a physiotherapist specialising in sports injuries and Colleen was a full-time mother.

'It took a while but it's all working out now,' she told Romy in the café at Rathfarnham Castle where they'd met for coffee. The sun was slanting through the windows and reflecting off the polished wood floor, the air was warm and sweet-smelling and the two girls were feeling light-hearted and gossipy. 'I struggled with the whole motherhood thing for a while but it's not so bad. All the same, it's a real freedom thing being out as an adult without having to worry about a kid too.'

Romy carried her tray with its sinful slab of banoffi pie to a table near the window which overlooked the green lawn behind the castle and settled down to chat. She asked Colleen if she ever thought about getting back into archaeology again.

'Not right now,' Colleen replied, shaking her head vigorously so that her strawberry-blond hair bobbed around her face.

'Why not?' asked Romy. 'You'd have plenty of opportunity to be out as an adult! And it would be good to do something, wouldn't it?'

'Like I'm not now?' Colleen's tone was dry.

'Oh, you know what I mean!' cried Romy. 'Don't come over all "my work in the home" crap with me. Something different is what I meant. Something for you.'

'Yeah, well, maybe I would've thought of it,' agreed Colleen as she licked carrot cake crumbs from her fingers. 'But it's on hold for the moment.'

'Why?'

'You young, free and single girls are so thick,' said Colleen. 'I'm pregnant again, that's why.'

'Oh!' Romy looked at her in surprise.

'Only just,' admitted Colleen. 'You're the first person besides Gil who knows.'

'Planned?' asked Romy.

'Not unplanned,' replied Colleen. 'Unexpectedly quickly, though. So I'm afraid it'll be a bit longer before I can "do things for me" as you put it.'

'I'm sorry,' said Romy. 'I know that sounded patronising. I guess I'm just in shock at the idea of you being a sensible married woman with a family when I know deep down you're a flighty soul!'

Colleen chuckled. 'Ah, you didn't mean to be patronising. You're just coming from a completely different place. Being married with a family *is* different. Priorities are different. What matters is different. I don't just do things for myself. I have to think of Gil and Shaun too. And then there'll be the new baby to consider. But that doesn't make it a terrible life. It's not a chore.'

'You make me feel very selfish,' said Romy.

'Selfish! Romy, you came home to look after your mum. You're not selfish.'

'I'm not doing it with a good heart,' said Romy. 'So I think I am selfish really.'

Colleen looked at her sympathetically. 'How is your mum? On the mend?'

'Getting better,' agreed Romy. 'But driving me round the bend.'

'You're probably both driving each other round the bend,' said Colleen sympathetically.

'Oh no,' said Romy. 'I think I'm closer to it than her.' She sighed deeply and massaged the back of her neck.

Colleen laughed. 'It's probably not that bad.'

Romy sighed again. 'Even if . . . even if . . .' She stopped and started again. 'We're just not compatible people,' she said finally. 'We look at things from a completely different view-point.

'I'm sure you can cope.'

'Theoretically, yes,' said Romy gloomily. 'But although I tell myself every day not to get into an argument with her,

197

somehow I always do. I want to make allowances because she's gone through the mill and she hasn't been able to wear her high-heeled shoes but it's hard!'

Colleen laughed. 'I think it's great she still wears killer heels. And Romy, you were always far too conservative about what she should wear. I remember you complaining once that her top was too low-cut. You sounded like a right old granny.'

'Her tops *were* shocking,' said Romy defensively. 'And she was supposed to be going out with her girlfriends that night.'

She remembered it clearly. Veronica wearing an electric-blue top with a ruffle around its incredibly revealing V-neck. Romy could see the pushed-up Wonderbra roundness of Veronica's boobs beneath the top and she'd been horrified that her mother could even contemplate wearing it.

'I know you don't agree, but I admire your mum,' said Colleen. 'Sure, she's a bit OTT sometimes but she loves her partying and dressing up and all that sort of stuff, and if you're not really that keen – so what! Let her get dolled up if that's what she wants. It's not harming anyone and it makes her happy.'

'Huh.'

'You can't blame her for ever,' said Colleen.

Romy looked up from the remnants of her pie.

'You do,' said Colleen. 'As far as you're concerned it's her fault that the marriage broke down. But it takes two, Romy. You know it does.'

Romy stirred her coffee slowly. 'I don't blame her for their marriage failing,' she said. 'I did, I admit, at the start. But then afterwards, when they got divorced and I spent time living with Dad, well – I could sort of see her point. I love him to bits, of course, but he was always so caught up in his work. It must have driven her nuts.' She grinned suddenly. 'Veronica once said that she thought Dad was dashing and handsome. Unfortunately he always seemed to be dashing somewhere else.'

'Just like you,' said Colleen, and Romy smiled.

'How's Keith?' Colleen, who had met him in Ireland and who knew that he and Romy had shared the house in Sydney, decided that it was time to change the subject.

'Oh, Keith.' Romy looked rueful.

'Well?' Colleen looked at her expectantly.

'I made a complete hash of it with Keith,' said Romy.

Colleen frowned. 'How? I always thought you two might get it together some day.'

'We were friends,' Romy explained. 'That's all.'

'Yeah, yeah, I know all that sort of "just friends" stuff. Everyone has to say that! But wasn't there something more? I mean, you were really close when he was here and then you moved in with him in Oz.'

'As friends,' Romy reminded her.

'And? How did you mess it up?'

'I kissed him.'

'Aha!' Colleen looked at her friend in amusement. 'And that's a problem because . . . ?'

'Because he didn't want me to.' And Romy explained about practically turning into a koala bear at Sydney airport by hanging on to him and not wanting to let go and how Keith had been shocked and distant ever since and how he'd now run off to Perth.

Colleen giggled.

'It's not funny,' hissed Romy. 'I used to be able to talk to him about anything but I hardly ever hear from him now. I bet he moved from Sydney to Perth to make it harder for me to track him down. He probably thinks that I've been harbouring this secret lust for him for years! Which is so not true.'

Colleen looked at her sceptically.

'Honestly,' said Romy. 'We were comfortable together. Not the same thing at all. And now it doesn't much matter because it's all gone pear-shaped. Why is it that men are so hopeless? Or,' she added glumly, 'why is it that I'm so hopeless?'

'You're not hopeless,' said Colleen. 'Just a bit distracted at the moment, what with your mum and everything.'

'I guess.'

'No point in pining away.' Colleen grinned at her. 'Certainly not over a man who was supposed to be a friend but who bolts at a sympathy kiss!'

Romy smiled in return. 'Maybe I only miss him to bounce things off. To have a laugh with. Which has had the effect of turning me from the normally chirpy, cheerful Romy you know and love into some mad malicious bitch who hasn't a good word to say about anyone and who wakes up every day just waiting for her personal cloud to piss down on top of her.'

Colleen burst out laughing and Romy reluctantly joined in.

'You're a hoot,' said Colleen when she'd calmed down. 'Drama queen isn't even enough for you.'

'I know, I know.' Romy looked shamefaced. 'But I can't help it right now. I feel like . . . oh, a boiling pot with a lid on. And sooner or later I know I'm going to explode.'

'But why?' demanded Colleen. 'What's so bloody awful that has you feeling this way? It can't just be living with your mum again.'

'It can,' said Romy darkly.

'My mum did some pretty shitty things to me when I was growing up,' Colleen said. 'Mothers do. It's a kind of duty, I think. But I never harboured a grudge. Now she's great at helping me out, looking after Shaun; we get on really well . . . I wouldn't be able to cope without her. You've got to get over it, Ro.'

'I know,' said Romy. 'And I've got over loads of things. But . . .' She looked down at her plate and up at her friend again. Colleen was watching her sympathetically.

'What?' asked her friend. 'I've always known there was something more to it than you and Veronica just not getting on. What awful thing did she do?'

Romy said nothing.

'Look, don't tell me if you don't want to,' said Colleen. 'Hey, whatever it was it was years ago and who cares? But if it helps . . .'

'It *is* kind of awful,' Romy said edgily. 'Typical Veronica, totally tacky, but still crap.'

'What then?' This time Colleen looked at her expectantly. 'If you tell me maybe you'll get over it.'

'I don't know about that,' Romy replied. 'It's not all that easy to get over the fact that your mother tried to shag your boyfriend.'

Giselle was fed up with her pregnancy. Everyone said that she looked neat and gorgeous but today she was feeling fat and nauseous. She wished she hadn't decided to call on Veronica but it had seemed like a good idea earlier in the day. She'd been harbouring some residual guilt from the previous night when Darragh had gone to see her and she'd had to admit that she hadn't called over in a while. In some ways it had been a relief knowing that Romy was there and that there was no need to check on her mother-in-law, but Giselle also thought that it might not necessarily be a good idea for her to stay away too much. So, regardless of the fact that Darragh had done his duty the night before, she decided that she'd do hers that day. Magda was bringing Mimi to a birthday party for one of her ballet class friends and it would be a worthwhile way for her to put in a few hours. Besides, she genuinely enjoyed spending time (though not too much time) with Veronica. Giselle hoped that she would age as gracefully as the older woman, who was an absolute credit to pro-retinol creams, botox injections and microdermabrasion.

Veronica was probably looking a damn sight better than her these days, she thought, as she pressed the bell and glanced down at her increasing belly. Right now, despite her pretty new dress and her elegant matching sandals she felt like a frump.

She waited impatiently for Veronica to open the door. She had to steel herself not to ring a second time because she knew how annoying it would be to someone who couldn't walk quickly to hear an impatient buzz. But, she thought, it was a pity that there wasn't any access to the back of the house where Veronica had undoubtedly been sitting in the afternoon sun, because then she could have called without dragging Veronica all the way to the front door. Darragh, however, had closed off the direct entrance to the back garden a number of years earlier when there had been a spate of burglaries in the area. Despite the expensive alarm system, he hadn't wanted Veronica to feel vulnerable alone in the house.

The door finally opened and Giselle stepped inside. She kissed her mother-in-law on the cheek, conscious that despite the fact that Veronica was well dressed in loose cotton trousers and a simple silk blouse, her face still looked drawn and the shadows under her eyes were artfully concealed by Touche Éclat.

'I was making some tea,' said Veronica. 'Fancy a cup?'

'Love one,' Giselle replied. 'Though quite frankly, the sooner I can have a glass of wine again the better.'

She followed Veronica through the house and into the kitchen. Veronica had opened the sliding doors to the decking outside.

'It's warm,' she said. 'We might as well get some fresh air.'

Giselle agreed with her but opened the parasol so that the wrought-iron table was in the shade.

'I'll get the tea,' she told Veronica. 'You sit down.'

'Oh, let me.' Veronica shook her head. 'I'm fed up with people doing things for me.'

'If you're sure . . .' Giselle looked at her doubtfully.

'Please don't give me that look,' begged Veronica.

'What look?'

'The "hope the old dear doesn't do anything stupid" look,' Veronica told her. 'The look that Romy gives me every bloody day.'

Giselle smiled sympathetically. 'I suppose it must get a bit wearing.'

Veronica said nothing while she went into the kitchen and brought out the tea things. Then she eased herself into the seat opposite Giselle.

'How are you doing?' asked her daughter-in-law.

'Not too bad,' replied Veronica. 'I was feeling great the last couple of days but today for some reason I'm not as perky. My back is aching more than usual and I just feel a little off.'

'I suppose it takes time,' said Giselle.

'It all seemed to be going so well,' said Veronica irritably. 'But I suppose I have to accept some days will be better than others. Still, at least you're here to cheer me up.'

'Isn't that Romy's job?' Giselle grinned and Veronica threw her eyes to heaven.

'As bloody if! I know I need her here but it's a trial for both of us.'

'You know that we would have had you to stay with us but—'

'That would've been far too much trouble for you,' said Veronica quickly. 'Romy and I will cope. It's just nice to talk to someone else.'

'Have you heard from Kathryn lately?'

'Oh, Kathryn!' Veronica poured some tea. 'You know, Giselle, I try really hard but I don't understand my own daughters. They're my children and I love them but sometimes I could kill them. Kathryn because she's so far up her own backside that she can't see the light – I've never known anyone to take life as seriously as her; and Romy because she carries more chips on her shoulder than a Big Mac Meal.'

Giselle said nothing for a moment. It was a great opening

to have a go at Romy and she loved the idea of dissing her sister-in-law, but deep down she didn't think that it was the right time. After all, she didn't want Veronica to suddenly decide she'd be better off staying with her and Darragh after all. 'I agree with you about Kathryn,' she said eventually. 'I can't understand how a great woman like you managed to have a daughter like her! She drives Darragh demented.'

'Still?' Veronica proffered a plate of foil-wrapped chocolate biscuits but Giselle shook her head and pushed it to one side.

'Oh yes. She's forever ringing up offering advice,' Giselle told her mother-in-law. 'Unwanted advice. Unasked-for advice.'

'Advice on what?'

'The company,' said Giselle. 'Kathryn thinks that Darragh doesn't know what he's doing.'

Veronica nodded. 'She always felt like that. She wanted to be involved. But – industrial components! I ask you! She's better off doing what she's doing. Besides, she'd need to know a bit about engineering and she doesn't.'

'She was banging on a few months ago about expanding overseas,' said Giselle. 'And of course that meant that Darragh got into a flap about it.'

'Is he thinking about it?' asked Veronica. 'He didn't say anything to me.'

'That's why he was in Switzerland,' Giselle reminded her.

'Oh yes.' Veronica nodded. 'Sorry, my head is still a bit soupy. I forget things.' She made a face of frustration. 'Senior moments. I'm putting it down to the anaesthetic. I was never forgetful before. I still feel sick from it too.'

'You poor thing.' Giselle was consoling and Veronica warmed to the understanding in her voice. Romy never sounded as sympathetic as she would have liked. And Kathryn, on the rare occasions she did call, was simply brisk and practical. 'I'm sure you'll get over that soon. And as for the forgetfulness – well, I spend half my life walking into rooms and wondering why I did it. I think it's pregnancy hormones. I'm hoping, anyhow.'

'Being pregnant messes up your head as well as your body,' agreed Veronica, glancing down at her own trim stomach. 'Men are so damn lucky not to have to go through it.'

'So I keep telling Darragh,' Giselle said. 'And his retort is that men can't afford to get pregnant because they're too busy providing for us.'

Veronica laughed. 'He wouldn't cope with childbirth. He's no good with pain. So is he going to do something in Switzerland?'

'I don't really know,' Giselle replied. 'He's looking at two deals and he likes one but not the other. Alex and Stephen fancy the one he doesn't. So I don't know where it'll all end up.'

'Darragh knows what he's doing,' said Veronica.

'Of course he does. But he gets frustrated when Kathryn calls and asks him about it.'

'She always wants to be involved.'

'Yes, but she has her own career now,' said Giselle. 'She should butt out.'

'Oh, Kathryn isn't the butting-out sort. She's the kind of person who'd put her hand in the fire because you told her not to. Stubborn.' Veronica shook her head. 'It doesn't do her any good. I'm utterly convinced she'd do better if she listened to other people from time to time. But no, she always has to be right, even when she's wrong. She gets her drive from Tom but I don't know where on earth the stubborn streak comes from.' This time Veronica laughed shortly. 'I find it harder to understand my girls than Darragh.'

'Romy?' Giselle thought it was worth a little bit of gossip about her now. 'Is she stubborn too?'

'I guess she is, although not as bad as Kathryn. She's really her daddy's girl and always will be. It doesn't matter how hard I try, she'll never be anything else. And her damn daddy isn't such a great man, you know.'

'I know,' said Giselle.

'It gives me a headache just to think about them.' Veronica rubbed the back of her neck. 'Hopefully you'll do better with Mimi. And Junior.'

'I'll do my best.' Giselle leaned back in the chair. She would have liked to badmouth the two girls a bit more but she didn't want to push it. Veronica would bitch about them occasionally but there was a line she never knowingly crossed. Giselle changed the subject. 'Those hanging baskets look lovely.'

'They need to be thinned out a bit,' Veronica said. 'But I can't do it and although I mentioned it to Romy she obviously forgot.'

Giselle grinned. 'I'm surprised she let the opportunity to do a bit of digging go a-begging.'

Veronica smiled. 'Not quite her scale of things, I guess.'

'I'll do them for you in a while,' promised Giselle.

'Oh, no, don't. You'd have to get the stepladder out of the shed to reach them. Leave it for Romy.'

'I'd like to do it,' said Giselle.

'Well if you don't mind, that'd be great.'

'Oh, I almost forgot.' Giselle opened her big Birkin bag. 'Here's a couple of *House and Home*s for you. And . . .' she dug deeper, 'last month's *Tatler* with the picture of me and Darragh at the Expo Awards night.' She opened the magazine and pointed to the photograph of herself and her husband. He was wearing a tux and she was dressed in a full-length dress in soft grey satin.

'Fabulous,' said Veronica. 'You look stunning.'

Giselle smiled. 'See what they say? Entrepreneur and businessman Darragh Dolan, and his wife, style icon Giselle Dolan.' She giggled. 'It's good to be recognised as a style icon.'

'Yes, it is,' said Veronica warmly. 'That dress is fabulous.'

'Prada,' said Giselle. 'Cost a packet but don't tell Darragh. I paid for it out of my own money.'

'You're entitled,' said Veronica.

'It was the biggest night of the year,' Giselle said, 'and I had to look good. Still, I was reeling at the price myself!'

The two women smiled complicitly at each other and sat back in the chairs. The sun's rays were shafting beneath the parasol but neither of them moved. It was warm and it was pleasant and the scent of the garden flowers hung in the still air.

If only she could sit here like this with Romy, Veronica thought, how much simpler life would be.

'Which boyfriend? When?' Colleen was still astounded by Romy's statement. 'I can't believe your mother would . . . oh, yeuch, Ro, that's revolting.'

'Perry Fitzpatrick,' said Romy. 'At Kathryn's twenty-first.'

'Oh, wow.' Colleen's eyes were wide. 'That's so gross. You never said.'

'What the hell was I going to say?' asked Romy. 'I couldn't believe it. And I was too ashamed to tell anyhow. My boyfriend. And my mother!'

'He was a good bit older than you, wasn't he?' Colleen remembered.

'Old enough not to be such a shithead,' said Romy.

She'd met him at a different birthday party – the eighteenth birthday of Sarah Ryan's sister. Sarah had been in the same class as Romy and Colleen in school. Perry was a friend of Sarah's older brother, Michael, who'd also been invited.

Romy had gone out once or twice with a number of boys, but they'd all been around the same age as her and had all gone to the local school. Perry Fitzpatrick was from Wicklow and studying at UCD. From the first moment she'd seen him Romy had been attracted to him. He was tall, fair and very, very attractive. His body was lean and hard and she could see six-pack abs beneath his casual cotton shirt. She had never fancied a guy as much in her whole life.

Astonishingly, he'd seemed attracted to her too. He'd spoken to her in the kitchen when she was fixing drinks for herself and Colleen and she'd stuttered and stammered and been totally inarticulate and so reckoned she'd blown her chances completely. Colleen, in whom she'd confided, had told her not to worry, that it was all practice and sure weren't there loads of other guys around although, she conceded, Perry Fitzpatrick was way up there with the best.

Later in the night when Romy had been sitting in a corner a little the worse for wear thanks to the Bacardi Breezers she'd been knocking back (Veronica had told her that she could drink three, an allowance which Romy had automatically doubled), Perry came over to her and started to chat and Romy had been completely smitten. Perry was, without a doubt, her first serious boyfriend. She'd never gone out with anyone who'd finished school before and she was a little embarrassed to still be categorised as a schoolgirl even though she was nearly seventeen and would be doing her leaving exams the following year. Perry didn't seem to be worried about that and they'd gone on a couple of dates – the cinema and a local restaurant and even the theatre (with the exception of school trips and going to pantomimes as a child, Romy had never been to a live play before) – all of which made her feel remarkably grown-up.

And so when Kathryn's twenty-first came along, she asked Perry if he'd like to come to the family and friends party in the Glenview Hotel near Delgany and he'd said that he'd be delighted, and she'd been delighted too because she knew that she'd be turning up with a gorgeous bloke in tow and that would put a stop to Veronica's incessant whingeing about the fact that she didn't make the most of her appearance or anything, because clearly she'd done enough to nab Perry Fitzpatrick.

Veronica had been gobsmacked when Perry arrived looking devastatingly handsome in a casual suit and open-necked shirt.

So had Kathryn – Romy remembered her pulling her to one side and asking her where on earth she'd found such a hunky guy, and Romy had felt a flush of pleasure that the two other women in the family had found her new boyfriend so attractive.

Other members of the family (the Dolan family, of course, because at that point Dermot and Veronica had been separated for nearly six years) had commented to Romy about her gorgeous boyfriend too – including Veronica's sister Angela, who remarked that if only she was a few years younger she'd go for him herself. But Angela had said it in a friendly, teasing way and Romy had joked with her about him. Romy liked Angela, who wasn't as high maintenance as Veronica. She had married a farmer from Donegal and now lived in the wilds of the country.

There had been lots of dancing at the party; the band was great and almost everyone was up on the floor letting themselves go and having a good time. Romy and Perry danced nonstop until eventually Romy said that she had to sit down and rest for a while because her feet were on fire. Then Veronica had asked Perry up to dance with her and people had stopped to watch them because, unlike Romy, Veronica was a really good dancer. And she looked utterly fabulous that night, her honey-blond hair in its huge curls falling lazily into her blue eyes, her cheekbones accentuated by her perfect blusher and her lips glossy and pink. She was wearing a black and white dress with a full skirt and plunging neckline, and although it should have looked too young for her somehow Veronica managed to pull it off. Romy watched them for a while and then went to reclaim her boyfriend but Perry told her that he was going outside for a cigarette and he'd be back in a few minutes.

Afterwards she wondered whether it had always been arranged. She didn't really think so and yet she couldn't be sure. It had been so convenient, so easily done it was hard to believe that it was all down to chance. And yet they both insisted it had been. She should have gone with him, of course. But it simply never occurred to her. So she stayed sipping her drink while he went outside and never for a second did she think that the next few minutes would change her relationship with her mother for ever.

She wished now that she hadn't eaten the banoffi pie. She felt sick to her stomach remembering.

'Are you OK, Ro?' asked Colleen gently.

'I guess so,' said Romy. 'I mean, yes, I am actually over it really but the whole thing is disgusting.'

'Did they really . . . you know? I can't believe it of your mum.'

'She's a slapper,' said Romy dismissively. 'You could believe anything of her.'

'Oh Ro, not really,' protested Colleen. 'She's a party animal, but—'

'But nothing,' said Romy. 'She was quite happy to do the dirty with my bloody boyfriend in the grounds of the hotel.'

Romy had strolled out into the garden when she'd finished her drink, partly looking for Perry and partly enjoying the warmth of the summer's evening and the scent of woodstock in the air. She'd taken off the unaccustomed high-heeled sandals which were killing her and was walking barefoot in the dewy grass when she heard the giggle coming from behind a clump of bushes. And she'd grinned to herself at the thought of whoever was making out behind them.

She'd tried not to look towards them as she walked by but she'd caught a glimpse of white silk and hadn't been able to look away completely. And then she'd realised that the white was the skirt of the black and white dress that Veronica had been wearing that night and she'd stopped in her tracks, quite unable to move.

She couldn't believe that her mother (her mother, for God's sake; the woman was in her fifties, had she no shame?) was fumbling in the bushes with some other wrinkly like a teenager.

She, Romy, was the teenager here and she wouldn't have slipped out for a quickie knowing that anyone could have spotted her!

And then Veronica walked out from behind the shrubbery, followed by Perry, and Romy's heart nearly stopped. She stared at them. It was the only time in her life she'd ever seen her mother look truly shocked.

'Shit,' said Veronica.

'Oh crap,' muttered Perry.

And Romy was unable to say anything at all.

'Afterwards?' asked Colleen, who'd listened wide-eyed to Romy's account of events.

'Afterwards she tried to tell me that it wasn't anything – that she'd had too much to drink and that he'd offered her . . .' Romy sighed. 'They'd been smoking joints – can you believe it? She's supposed to be setting me a good example but she's puffing away at her daughter's twenty-first. I know she was a child of the sixties but you'd think she'd have taken it then if she wanted the experience.'

'I very much doubt you'd have got your hands on any dope in Ireland in the sixties,' Colleen told her.

'It doesn't mean she had to go for it the first time she was offered it,' said Romy. She looked disgusted. 'She said it made her feel . . . feel . . . sexy.'

Colleen grimaced.

'Exactly. You don't want your mother feeling sexy! And if she is, you want her to be feeling sexy with someone her own damn age.'

'Poor Romy.' Colleen grabbed her by the hand and squeezed it. 'But it was ages ago. It doesn't matter any more.'

'Y'see, it's really easy to say that. And on a kind of day-to-day level I know that. But the point is that my mother thought it was perfectly acceptable to grab my boyfriend and drag him into the bushes at a family gathering. Now in all honesty, Col, is that the behaviour of a normal woman?'

'Maybe of a normal woman,' Colleen said, 'faced with someone like Perry Fitz. He was incredibly attractive, you know. I would've shagged him myself. But it's not what you'd expect of your mother, I agree.'

'See, Veronica doesn't want to be a mother,' Romy said. 'In her head she's still twenty and terrific. She looks in the mirror and she still sees the woman she was, not the woman she is. No other woman her age would flirt with young guys at a party.'

'They might,' said Colleen, 'if they were as hot as Veronica. Think of all those actresses who've latched on to toyboys.'

'Are you on her side or something?' demanded Romy. 'Only it seems to me that you're making loads of excuses for her.'

'Not at all!' cried Colleen. 'I'm just thinking that older women might not see themselves as older. You and me – we can spot it straight away. But they don't want to admit it. And your mother is a prime example.'

'They all said that she was baby-snatching when she married Dad,' said Romy mournfully. 'Little did they know.'

'It was a bit rich going after your boyfriend all right,' said Colleen. 'I don't blame you for losing it. And I'm shocked at Perry. I thought he was a nice guy.'

'Yeah, well maybe he had a thing for older women,' said Romy. 'Although loads of Kathryn's college friends apparently thought Veronica was her older, sexier sister. Well, you know what she's like – from a distance anyone would think that. I'm just surprised they kept going when they got closer, that's all.'

Colleen giggled. 'Not quite the same thing grabbing saggy boobs, I guess.'

'Oh, don't!' Romy groaned. 'They're the kind of images I kept having to blank out of my mind. And the thing is – she knew he was with me. But she was so utterly shameless about it.'

'I can see it must have been a bit of a trauma,' agreed

Colleen. 'And I don't blame you for bearing a grudge. What she did was totally unacceptable even if she was going through a mid-life crisis.'

'Veronica's been going through a mid-life crisis ever since she hit thirty,' said Romy gloomily.

Colleen laughed. 'What did Perry say about it all?'

'He was out of his head,' said Romy. 'He didn't say much, just kept muttering shit, shit, shit under his breath and then he legged it and I didn't see him again.' She giggled suddenly. 'And Veronica kept on saying over and over that she was sorry and that she never meant for that to happen and that she wouldn't have hurt me for the world. Lying cow! I told her that I hoped she'd been sensible and taken precautions and she just stared and kept mumbling about it not being that sort of thing at all and it just being a bit of fun and that there was no way, absolutely no way . . . and I said oh, it didn't matter because she was going through the menopause so she was too old and withered to get pregnant anyhow.'

Colleen guffawed.

'She was raging with me,' said Romy. 'I knew I'd really gotten to her then. But she deserved it.'

'Yes, she did,' agreed Colleen. 'So what then?'

'Well, you know, it's not like I could make mad gestures,' said Romy. 'I was at school. I thought about asking my dad if I could move in with him but there wasn't really room for me to live full-time in his apartment. So it was a bloody nightmare. I stayed at home.'

'And said nothing to anyone.' Colleen looked at her accusingly.

'I couldn't,' said Romy. 'It was too awful.'

Colleen nodded her agreement.

'Anyway, every day afterwards Veronica came to me and apologised again and she repeated that it was just a silly thing not worth making a fuss over; that they'd got a bit carried away and that Perry was a lovely boy and everything but clearly not for me and not for her either!'

'Yeew.'

'I didn't – still don't – entirely believe her. One day I told her that whether something happened or not – and the idea still makes me want to puke – the intention was there. She would have shagged my boyfriend in the garden of a hotel with all our family around the place. Ugh! I told her that she'd betrayed me and that was the worst thing a mother could do and she laughed and said that there were plenty worse and I asked her what and she couldn't actually answer.' Romy's words were tumbling out now. 'And she told me that I was only a kid and I knew nothing and that sometimes people did things they regretted but that it didn't make them bad people and I told her that she was a fucking cow and a totally bad person and that the sooner I could get out of the house and away from her for good the happier I'd be.'

'Understandable,' said Colleen. 'I'm surprised that you came home at all.'

'Oh, eventually we had a forgiveness moment,' said Romy in resignation. 'After a few weeks when the atmosphere at home was like a slab of ice she insisted on having another talk about it and she swore again that she never would have done it if she hadn't had the pot – her first experience of recreational drugs, she said – and that she truly, truly was sorry. And mortified, she said. And she wanted me to know that she loved me and cared about me and that she'd never hurt me. She told me that it had just been . . .' Romy's voice quivered, 'a bit of a grope! And I wanted to believe her only I couldn't really because, of course, later on I heard that bastard Fitzpatrick had told all his mates that my mother was a great lay!'

'No he didn't,' said Colleen quickly. 'For heaven's sake, Ro, even I didn't know anything about it! I would've heard.'

Romy shrugged. 'Maybe he didn't tell everyone. But I'm sure there was gossip. I was utterly humiliated by him.'

'He didn't blab. Honestly. Everyone would have known and I would've said something to you before now.'

'Either way,' said Romy, 'I knew what she'd done and it was bloody difficult. Anyway in the end I told her that it was OK and that it was probably all his fault, and we tried to get on with each other, but I never felt the same again. And so when I went to college it was handy to move out and the truth is that once I moved out I was quite happy not to come back.'

'Poor you.' Colleen squeezed her friend's hand again.

Romy was embarrassed to realise that she wanted to cry.

'The thing is,' she said, after she'd composed herself once more, 'even though I know it's all in the past and it's not that important in the whole scheme of things; and even though I try to behave normally when I'm in the house with her, I still can't help remembering. And I know that she knows that I know . . . well, you get the drift.'

'It must be a bit of a nightmare all right,' agreed Colleen. 'Did Darragh and Kathryn ever find out?'

'Oh God, no!' Romy looked horrified. 'Darragh would flip his lid altogether because as far as he's concerned the sun shines out of Veronica's arse . . .' She grinned shakily. 'Maybe not the best metaphor given the circumstances, but still! And Kathryn – well, Kathryn has always been in her own world. Actually, if she had found out she probably would've just told me to get over it. She's madly unemotional, is Kathryn.'

'It's just that it was her party,' said Colleen. 'You'd think she'd have heard.'

'Maybe she does know something.' Romy shrugged. 'But she's never said a word, which is typical of her.'

'I always liked Kathryn,' said Colleen thoughtfully. 'She's so . . . together.'

'I know.' Romy nodded. 'I envy her, really. She did all the sort of stuff that I wanted to do only much better.'

'You never wanted to go to Wall Street!' Colleen laughed.

'No. But Kathryn is such a . . . a competent person,' said Romy. 'I always wanted to be competent, but to tell you the truth I'm still just as much of a mess as I was when I was sixteen.'

'Ah, you're not,' said Colleen. 'Lookit – you've come home and you're looking after your mum and you're dealing with it really well.'

'That's the thing,' said Romy. 'I'm not dealing with it that well at all.'

'You're being hard on yourself,' Colleen told her. 'Anyway, I'm only a phone call away, so if you feel like you're going to crack up, just ring.'

Romy smiled. 'I'd forgotten how good it was to be friends with you.'

'Thanks.' Colleen smiled in return. 'Now how about we—'

Her words were lost in the sudden shrill of Romy's mobile phone. She grabbed it and hit the answer button, registering that the call was from Veronica and wondering what on earth it was her mother wanted now.

'Come home, quickly,' said Veronica when Romy answered. 'It's Giselle. She's had a bit of a tumble and she's spraying blood all over the place. I need you here. I feel really sick and I think I'm going to faint.'

Romy had walked to the castle but Colleen gave her a lift back to the house in her ancient red Toyota. Romy jumped out of the passenger seat and slammed the door, telling Colleen that she'd be in touch. Her friend waved, revved the spluttering engine and disappeared down the road while Romy hurried up the driveway and into the house.

'Is that you?' Veronica's anxious voice carried into the hallway.

'Of course it's me – I'm glad you haven't keeled over. Oh!' Romy walked into the living room. Giselle was sitting on

216

the sofa, her face chalk white with a purple bump in the middle of her forehead and a streak of blood across her face.

'What happened?' Romy asked Veronica.

'I can't . . .' Veronica looked at her and Romy had to hurry to catch her mother by the arm. 'I'm sorry,' said Veronica as Romy helped her to a chair. 'I thought Giselle had been killed. And then her nose started to pump blood and I thought she had a brain injury.'

'What happened?' repeated Romy.

'I fell off the stepladder,' said Giselle. 'I hit my nose as I landed. And the bump on my head is from the scissors falling and hitting me.'

'The handles of the scissors,' said Veronica. 'She was lucky. She could've been stabbed in the eye.' She swallowed. 'I feel sick. I have a terrible pain in my stomach. And my back hurts more than ever.'

'You're fine, Mum,' said Romy briskly. 'You got a fright, that's all. Sit back and take a few deep breaths while I get you a drink of water.'

This was so typical of Veronica, she thought as she filled a glass. In the middle of someone else's drama she was still the one who demanded attention. Just as she always did. Just as she had at Kathryn's twenty-first.

'I'm not well.' Veronica's lip trembled. 'I know the difference between shock and something else. I got a shock, sure. That's not what's making me sick.'

Romy ignored her and went to get the water, which she then handed to her telling her to sip it slowly.

'What were you doing on the steps in the first place, Giselle?' Romy turned away from her mother.

'Tidying the hanging baskets,' Giselle told her. 'I was only on the third step and I suddenly felt a bit dizzy and I slipped. It wasn't a bad fall, really it wasn't. But I got an awful fright and my nose started gushing blood.'

'Why on earth were you . . .' Romy looked at both her and

Veronica. 'I said I'd do them at the weekend! There was no need . . .' She sighed. 'Giselle, how about the baby? D'you think you should go to Casualty? Get everything checked?'

'You must be joking!' The colour was coming back into Giselle's cheeks. 'If I went to Casualty I'd probably be waiting till midnight for some junior intern just to tell me I'm pregnant! The baby's fine. Honestly. It truly wasn't much of a fall at all. It was the shock more than anything.'

'And the blood,' said Veronica faintly.

'All the same, that bump looks a bit nasty,' said Romy. 'And I really think—'

'Can I see?' Giselle went to stand up but Romy stopped her.

'I'll get you a mirror. Stay sitting for a bit longer.'

She returned with the magnifying mirror from Veronica's downstairs bedroom.

'Oh shit!' Giselle looked at her reflection. 'I'm a fright, I really am. And I'm supposed to be going to a charity lunch on Friday. I so can't, looking like this.'

'Maybe it'll have gone down by then,' said Romy comfortingly.

'I look like I've an ostrich egg on my forehead!' she wailed.

'If that's the worst of it, you should consider yourself lucky.'

'Well I do, of course, but . . .' Giselle continued to peer at her reflection and dab at the dried blood streak with a paper tissue.

'I really do think you should get yourself checked out,' Romy told her. 'I know you're probably only shaken, but under the circumstances . . .'

'I suppose you're right.' Giselle looked at her watch. 'My doctor isn't so far away and if I get there now I might beat the hordes calling in on their way home from work.' She snorted. 'It always amazes me how many people are in the surgery on any given day. What the hell can be wrong with us all?'

She stood up and wobbled.

'I'll drive you,' said Romy. 'You're still shaky.'

'Well . . . thanks.' Giselle looked doubtful. 'What about Veronica?'

'Mum?' Romy looked at her. She was still annoyed at Veronica's attempts to hog the limelight.

'I'll be all right,' said Veronica. 'I'll just sit here quietly till you come back. I still feel shaky but I should be OK if I take it easy.'

'It might be a couple of hours,' warned Romy, who knew what Giselle was talking about when it came to crowded surgeries.

'I can manage.' Veronica's voice was firmer. 'I'm not entirely useless.'

'Good,' said Romy. 'You don't feel as though you're going to keel over or anything?'

'Of course not.'

'OK then.' Romy picked up her bag. 'C'mon, Giselle. Let's go.'

Chapter 14

Giselle had been right about the queues at the doctor's surgery but they didn't do too badly, only having to wait an hour before she got to see him. Romy sat and gorged herself on back issues of *Hello!* and *OK!* while Giselle (who bought them every week and so had read them before) had to make do with a copy of that day's newspaper to keep her occupied. By the time it was her sister-in-law's turn to see the doctor, Romy was almost up to date on celebrity gossip. She was looking enviously at a photo of Angelina Jolie standing on the beach when Giselle returned.

'She's lovely,' said Giselle, glancing down at the photo, 'but quite honestly I prefer Jennifer Aniston. I don't know what Brad Pitt was thinking!'

'It was probably the whole motherhood thing. Some men fall for it, don't they?' said Romy cynically as she closed the magazine. 'So how are you?'

'I'm fine and the baby's fine,' said Giselle. 'Honestly, Romy, it was more of a gentle topple off the stepladder than anything else, but you know what Veronica's like, she panicked completely and she made me feel panicky too. I have an appointment with the pre-natal clinic the day after tomorrow so I'll talk to them about it too.'

'You said you were light-headed,' Romy recalled. 'What caused it?'

'Um. Hello. Pregnant.' Giselle pointed at her stomach.

Romy grinned. 'I know, but I thought it might have been something else.'

'Pregnancy sucks,' said Giselle. 'Just so's you know.'

Romy raised an eyebrow, surprised at the sudden vehemence in Giselle's voice.

'Right,' she said. 'I'll keep that in mind.'

'Oh, do,' said Giselle. 'I'm sure you don't have any plans to disrupt your lifestyle with kids.'

'Nobody I want to disrupt it for,' said Romy. 'Are you ready to leave?'

They walked out of the surgery and Romy looked at Giselle and then at the car. They'd taken Giselle's SUV rather than Veronica's Golf. 'Will I drive again or do you want to?'

'Oh, you go ahead,' said Giselle. 'The traffic is shit now and I need to relax.'

Romy got into the driver's seat. She liked driving the SUV although she was passionately opposed to them as some kind of city fashion statement. But on digs she often drove trucks or utility vehicles because of having to transport samples, and the truth was that she enjoyed being higher than the traffic around her.

It was nearly six by the time they pulled into the driveway of Giselle and Darragh's house. Romy had never visited them there before and she couldn't help being impressed by the redbrick double façade, the immaculately landscaped front lawn and cobble-locked driveway, and the general air of quiet wealth that the house conveyed.

'Come in and have coffee,' said Giselle, unlocking the front door.

Romy followed her into the house. The signs of money were everywhere – real paintings on the wall and expensive furniture in rooms which had definitely benefited from the advice of an interior designer.

'Mummy!' Mimi beamed at them as they walked into the playroom.

'Hello, Mrs Dolan.' Magda, the nanny, greeted her formally, her eyes widening as she saw the lump on Giselle's forehead. Giselle explained about it and told Magda that she was fine and that she was sorry if she was a little bit late home. She asked if Mimi had been fed yet.

'Of course,' said Magda. 'We are just having some fun together.'

'Do you think you could cook something for Mr Dolan tonight?' asked Giselle. 'I don't feel up to it myself. I'll keep an eye on Mimi. In the meantime, though, coffee for me and Romy – my sister-in-law – would be nice.'

'Certainly,' said Magda and headed towards the kitchen.

'I can make us coffee.' Romy felt uncomfortable with the idea of someone doing it for her.

'It's her job.' Giselle shrugged. 'She's a nanny but she also does light domestic work for us. I have another girl, Jelena, who does a major clean every week but Magda is fine for the day-to-day stuff.'

Romy nodded but she still didn't like it. She knew that lots of people had domestic help these days because it was impossible to do everything yourself, but the idea of someone making her a cup of coffee in the house was outside her experience. If Giselle and Darragh were used to it, she thought, why should he have been so against her suggestion of hired help to look after Veronica? It wasn't much different, after all!

She sat on one of the plumped-up sofas and drank her coffee while Giselle, having kicked off the dainty high-heeled sandals she'd been wearing, eased herself into an armchair and cuddled Mimi indulgently. Romy wondered what it would be like to live the Dolan lifestyle. When they'd been younger and living with Veronica they'd never actually wanted for very much, but there hadn't been this level of comfort. And, of course, Dermot wasn't a luxury sort of man and so he wouldn't have cared about the latest in interior designs. But times had changed and so had ways of living. Everyone seemed to have designer homes filled with the kinds of accessories that were once only the preserve of glossy magazines but were now taken for granted as being available for all. I'm his sister, she thought, his half-sister anyway, and yet I don't have any of this stuff and I'm never likely to. Is it me? Or is it them? Am I genetically disposed to being a slob? Is it because of Dad? Dermot and Larissa's house wasn't like this, Romy reminded herself. It was bright and cheery and comfortable, but not luxurious. She had to admit, reluctantly, that the luxury was actually very, very nice even though she didn't feel at all at home with it.

She'd just finished her coffee when the door opened and Darragh walked into the room. Romy was startled because she hadn't heard his key in the front door but Giselle just looked up at him and smiled.

'What on earth happened to you?' he asked.

Giselle explained while Darragh listened with concern.

'But why should you have been doing that?' he demanded. 'Romy is supposed to be looking after Mum. That's what she's here for.'

'Yes, but Romy was out and—'

'But nothing.' He turned to Romy. 'Is it too much to ask that you do a few things around the house to help Mum?' he asked. 'And why were you out anyway? If you're here to help then you should have been there.'

'Get real, Darragh,' said Romy. 'I'm not a slave! I was meeting an old friend and I didn't know that Giselle would be there. I'd already told Veronica that I'd do the hanging baskets later this week.'

'I'm not saying you can't meet people,' Darragh told her. 'I'm just saying that you should make sure that everything in the house is done first.'

'For crying out loud!' exclaimed Romy. 'I can't be in the house every minute of the day and it wasn't my fault that Giselle fell off the ladder – though if she hadn't been wearing those ridiculous shoes it mightn't have happened.'

Giselle, who'd been silent during the exchange, looked at Romy with irritation.

'There's nothing wrong with my sandals,' she said as she glanced down at them, upturned on the floor. 'Romy, thank you for all you did for me this afternoon. I think it's time you went home.'

Romy shrugged. 'I was your best friend when I was bringing you to the doctor and waiting for you and driving you home, but now Darragh's back I'm the villain of the piece.'

'Oh, Romy, it's not like that,' said Giselle. 'And I do appreciate what you—'

'Just forget it,' Romy said dismissively. 'I don't care whether you appreciate me or not.'

'Romy, you're being ridiculous,' said Darragh. 'But then that's not a surprise, because you were always carting that chip around on your shoulder.'

'I don't have a chip on my shoulder,' she told him. 'You keep saying that just so's you don't have to think about things yourself. Blame everything on me having a chip on my shoulder. That means you don't have to blame yourself for being an insensitive shit.'

'I'm right to blame you in this instance,' said Darragh. 'You should have been there. And by the way, if you'd done the decent thing like we asked before and taken Mimi for a few days while we went away, then this probably wouldn't have happened in the first place.'

'I don't fucking believe you!'

Dermot had always told Romy that when you were reduced to swearing you'd lost control of the situation, and she normally agreed with him, but right now she didn't care. Her frustrations of the last few weeks suddenly bubbled over and she couldn't help herself.

'You're blaming my refusal to spend my time looking after your daughter for the fact that your stupid wife fell off a stepladder that she didn't need to be on in the first place. You're unbelievable. You really are, you arrogant arse!'

'There really is no need for all this.' Giselle lifted Mimi, who had begun to cry, into her arms.

'No, there isn't.' Romy shook her head. 'I'm off. Back to look after Mum. Your mum too,' she called to Darragh as she stalked out of the room. 'But, oh, I forgot, she's only your mum when she's in the fullness of health or it's convenient for you or when she's being all matriarchal over the family business. Oh yeah, forgot that too – your family business, not my family business. Tosser!' And she slammed the door behind her.

Darragh and Giselle looked at each other.

'She's impossible,' he said angrily. 'She's so damn childish. She's always been childish.'

'She gets into a state over things, doesn't she?' Giselle set Mimi, who had quietened down and was sucking her thumb, on to the sofa. 'And you seem to bring out the worst in her.'

Darragh looked at Giselle in surprise. His wife shrugged. 'It's true,' she said.

'She has this thing about the company,' said Darragh. 'And being left out somehow. But why? She was never interested in it and it had nothing to do with her. It might have been different if her father had had the decency to take the very generous job offer the board made him, but no, he was too pig-headed.'

'She's like him in that case,' said Giselle.

'She needs taking down a peg or two,' Darragh told her. 'Honestly, I've never heard anyone rant like her. And I'm in the right. She's home to look after Veronica, not to swan around having cups of coffee in the afternoon.'

'To be fair,' Giselle looked uncomfortable, 'she can't be with her every minute of the day.'

Darragh pinched the bridge of his nose between his fingers. 'She's given me a bloody headache,' he said, and Giselle got up from the sofa to rub his shoulders and calm him down.

'You're a pet,' he told her after a minute. 'You really are.

I should be doing that for you. You're sure that you're all right?'

'Absolutely,' she assured him. 'To be honest, I think Veronica came off worse than me. She got such a fright, and then when my nose started to bleed . . . Well, you know what she's like.'

'All the same, I'll give her a call later. See that she's OK.'

'Meantime . . .' Giselle smiled at him. 'I asked Magda to cook tonight. Why don't we sit in front of the TV and have a relaxing evening? I could do with some down time after the day I've had.'

Romy was outside the house and trembling with rage. It seemed to her that ever since Darragh's initial phone call she'd spent a lot of time in a rage – at him, at Veronica, even at her father, who she couldn't help blaming for part of it all. Because if he'd done what Veronica had asked, if he'd spent less time away from her, then maybe they'd still be married and maybe she wouldn't feel like the spare part in the family. But Dermot had done his own thing and was still doing his own thing. He always would, thought Romy. That was the kind of person he was. And in many ways the kind of person she was too. Which was why looking after Veronica was turning into such a nightmare. Romy knew that she was hopeless at family stuff. She didn't know how to behave properly at all.

But still. She wiped an angry tear from her eye. Darragh had no right to talk to her like that, and as for Giselle – well, she'd have thought that Giselle would have stood up for her a bit more. Silly thought. Her shallow sister-in-law had sided with Darragh as she always would because, Romy told herself, she knew which side her expensive bread was buttered.

God, but her family were all such pains! Darragh was an arrogant shit, and now that she thought about it, he got it from Veronica. She was arrogant too in her own way.

Demanding attention all the time. Wanting people at her beck and call. Wanting things she couldn't have.

Sod them. She stood on the pavement outside Darragh and Giselle's house and looked back at it. Sod them and their luxury lifestyle and their nannies and their holidays in Barbados which, hah! thanks to her they hadn't had. She didn't give a toss about them and she never would. And sod Veronica too. She'd danced enough attendance on her. She was going to go back to Oz and be with people who really cared about her, and the Dolans could do whatever they liked!

She wallowed in self-righteous indignation and anger as she walked down the quiet road. And then she realised that she was three miles from Veronica's house and that she didn't have a cent in her pocket because she'd forgotten to bring her handbag in the whole rush of getting Giselle into the SUV and that she was going to have to walk all the way back. And it wasn't as though three miles was such a big deal, but it was mainly uphill and she was tired and angry and . . . She gritted her teeth – she hated them all, she really and truly did. She was going to pack as soon as she got home!

Forty-five minutes later she was back at Veronica's and sliding her shoes from her feet, cursing the fact that although her shoes were flat, unlike either Giselle or Veronica's shoes of choice, they still weren't walking shoes and for the last twenty minutes she'd been nursing a blister on the little toe of each foot.

'Is that you?' Veronica walked slowly into the kitchen where Romy was grimacing as she allowed the cold marble tiles to soothe her raging feet. 'What's the matter with you?'

'My feet hurt,' said Romy. 'I walked home.'

'Why on earth did you do that?' demanded Veronica. 'You should've got a taxi. Or waited for Darragh to come home and give you a lift.'

'I couldn't get a taxi because I had no money with me,' said Romy. 'And I don't think there's a chance in hell of Darragh ever giving me a lift anywhere again.'

'Why?'

Romy gave Veronica an edited version of her row with her brother and Veronica groaned.

'Why can't you all get on?' she asked in despair. 'What is it about my children that makes them spit at each other like wildcats all the time? Other people have perfectly happy families where everyone gets on. Why can't we be like that?'

'Because Darragh thinks the sun shines out of his arse and he expects to be treated like the golden child all the time.'

'I treat you all exactly the same,' said Veronica. 'I always have.'

'Oh Mum, you don't! You never did,' cried Romy. 'Darragh was made MD of the company but neither me nor Kathryn was ever offered a job! OK, I know I'd never be management material, but Kathryn? She's the really smart one, yet you never listened to her. You kept on and on at her about clothes and haircuts when all she wanted was to get on in the company. You just don't understand!'

And Romy stalked out, slamming a door behind her for the second time that day.

Veronica sat down gingerly in the high-seated recliner chair. She didn't recline it but sat upright and stared unseeingly ahead of her. She'd never before realised how Romy was thinking. In Veronica's mind all her problems with her younger daughter had stemmed from that embarrassing incident at Kathryn's twenty-first birthday party when she'd fooled around with Perry Fitzpatrick in the grounds of the hotel. She knew, of course, that she and Romy were complete opposites at the best of times but she had always been sure that if the incident with Perry hadn't happened her relationship with her youngest child would never have become as difficult as it was now.

She felt herself grow hot with shame at the memory. It had been a terrible thing to do, she knew it then and she knew it now. She'd never quite forgiven herself for it because she also knew that it had opened a fault line in her relationship with Romy that could never truly be repaired. She'd tried to make light of it, telling her that nothing had happened and that she'd been under the influence of a couple of joints, but Romy wasn't having any of it. Yet the joints, while they mightn't have excused her behaviour, had certainly contributed to it. She never would have followed Perry into the gardens if she hadn't been high and she wouldn't have been high if she hadn't accepted the joint from one of Kathryn's friends. Smoking it had made her feel part of the younger set, made her feel accepted by them. She liked to think that she still had what it took to be part of a young crowd. And when Perry – also spaced out – had asked her to walk outside with him because it was stuffy inside the hotel she'd agreed straight away. It would do her street cred no harm at all, she thought, to be seen chatting to the handsome nineteen year old who was far too attractive for her lumpen daughter.

They'd talked for a while, Perry telling her about his college choices and how difficult life could be, and she'd sympathised with him, never once falling into the trap of telling him how things were in her day (she hadn't gone to college – it would have been unheard of in the sixties for someone like her) but talking to him seriously, one-to-one, as though they were friends.

And eventually he told her that she was great, that she understood him like nobody else and that there was a lot to be said for maturity and being a bit older – not, he'd added hastily, that she looked in any way old; she was absolutely fabulous and by far the most attractive woman there that evening.

She'd been flattered. Why wouldn't she be when she was with a hunk of a guy who had suddenly moved her away from the lights of the garden and into the shadow of a low-hanging tree and who had put his arm around her (still trim) waist and was holding her close to him. And for a moment Veronica didn't think of the fact that Perry had come to Kathryn's party with Romy or, indeed, that this was her elder daughter's birthday party at all; she'd just lost herself in the feeling of a man's arms around her and a man's lips on hers and it had been such a long time since that had happened to her that she wasn't going to give it up for anyone.

She didn't know exactly what it was that had brought her to her senses. But as he fumbled at the zipper of her dress, she remembered that he was nineteen and she was the mother of the party girl and that he was also Romy's boyfriend. She could have ignored his age (in fact she'd have ignored his age quite happily) but she couldn't ignore the rest. And so she'd pulled away from him and told him that she was sorry but that this was getting a bit out of hand and she'd laughed a little to defuse the potential embarrassment of the situation. Which was when she'd looked around and seen Romy staring at her, an expression of disgust and betrayal on her face.

It wasn't my fault, thought Veronica miserably. I did nothing wrong, after all. I pushed him away. I wouldn't hurt her deliberately. She knows that but she always chooses to ignore it. Just as she's always chosen to ignore the realities of the family situation and the fact that the break-up of my marriage to Dermot was just as much his fault as mine and that I was gutted at how she had to shuttle between us but I agreed to it because I thought it was best. And she chose to ignore the fact that Tom was so very, very definite about passing on the business to Darragh and that it never made sense for either her or Kathryn to be involved. Of course, Veronica thought, Tom had left shares to Kathryn but he'd never anticipated that she'd want to have anything to do with the running of the company. At that point she'd been just a baby and Tom couldn't have seen any further than her chubby talcum-scented body nestling in a bundle of blankets. He'd changed his will to leave her the shares a week after she'd been born. He'd never got to know her, but even if he had, Veronica felt sure that he would still have wanted Darragh, his son, to be the person who took over the family firm. Why would either Kathryn or Romy want to be involved anyhow? Didn't Kathryn have her own life in New York? Wasn't she too damn busy ever to come home? Didn't she only communicate through irregular, terse emails? And wasn't Romy herself only chomping at the bit to get back to her dig in Australia? So what was the big deal about Dolan Component Manufacturers? Why did Romy care one way or the other?

Veronica gasped as a spasm went through her stomach. She didn't know whether it was the after-effects of the anaesthetic or the tension of living in the same house as her younger daughter that was making her feel so ill. The sooner her back healed, the better for all of them.

Chapter 15

Romy took her bag from the wardrobe and began stuffing clothes into it. She was totally pissed off. At her brother, at her mother, at everything to do with the Dolan family and her part in it. Her walk-on part in it, she reminded herself as she tugged at the zip to close it, because she was a Kilkenny after all.

She opened her laptop and logged on to the internet. There was a variety of flight options to Australia out of London although they meant upgrading her ticket. She didn't really have the money for that but she was prepared to let her credit card bail her out. Her best bet would be to head off as early as possible in the morning and see what she could get. And she didn't care if she had to overnight at Heathrow, it would be preferable to spending another night at home.

She logged on to Skype and looked at her contact list. Keith was offline, which was probably a good thing. She wanted to rant and rage at somebody but it wouldn't be a good idea to rant and rage at Keith even though she felt she could do with some of his matter-of-fact common sense. She was feeling utterly overwhelmed by everything to do with Veronica and the Dolans and she longed to let off steam to someone. She couldn't go through it all again with Colleen (who, Romy thought, hadn't really appreciated how truly awful Veronica's behaviour had been), but Keith would understand. And maybe put her up in Perth . . . Of course, she realised suddenly, she shouldn't really have been looking for flights to Perth at all. She should have been looking at Sydney or Melbourne where there was more likelihood of work. But she'd chosen Perth because he was there. She frowned. Hadn't she suspected that he'd gone to Perth to distance himself from her? So he'd hardly welcome her flying there to throw herself on him and sob! She groaned softly as she looked at the screen doubtfully. Then, telling herself that she was acting against her better judgement, she dialled his mobile. She thought she felt relieved when it went straight to voicemail. She didn't leave a message. Instead she opened her email and started to type. She told Keith that she was totally fed up and that it had been a mistake to come home and think that she could look after Veronica and get on with Darragh and Giselle. She said that they were all even worse than she remembered and that her father was too caught up in his own life to care about her. And she told him that Tanya was going to be a supervisor in Melbourne and that as far as everyone in Australia was concerned she might as well never be coming back for all the contact she got from them. And then she said that she missed him more than anyone in her life before and that she wished she was with him and that she loved him.

She hadn't meant to say that she loved him. And she wished, as she listened once again to the swoosh of the email being delivered, that she hadn't said it at all.

It was dark when she came downstairs again. She wanted to tell Veronica that it wasn't working out, that she was more of a hindrance than a help and that she was going. But there was no sign of her mother. Romy frowned. She couldn't have gone out, could she? She dismissed the thought. Veronica was prob- ably sulking in her room.

There was a stain on the carpet from Giselle's nose bleed. Romy took some spray-cleaner from the utility room and rubbed at it until it had faded into a dull brown patch. Better, she thought. Less like a crime scene. But still in need of professional attention. Well it wasn't her problem. None of it would be her problem after tomorrow. Darragh and Kathryn could look after their mother. It was their turn to do something useful.

She turned on the TV and idly flicked through the channels. Then she switched it off again. She would go to bed, she thought. Get an early night so that she could get up early in the morning and head off to the airport. She'd ring her father from there. Her heart constricted as she thought of leaving without seeing her father again. He'd always been special to her but now, with his new family, she wasn't special to him. So what. She was her own person. She didn't need him. She didn't need any of them.

She heard the noise as she walked past the guest bedroom. She stopped outside the door and listened.

Her mother was crying, soft, muffled sobs. Romy hesitated at the door. The last time she'd heard Veronica cry was the night that Dermot had left. She'd gone into the bedroom then and told her mother to stop, that all she had to do was ask Dermot to come home and he probably would because he loved them all really; but Veronica had looked at her from puffy red eyes and told her to leave her alone, that she didn't want Dermot to come back and that he'd never loved them. Romy had closed the door and walked away, knowing that her mother was angry but sick at the thought that Dermot might never have loved either of them. This time she didn't open it at all.

She found it difficult to sleep. She couldn't hear any more sobs coming from Veronica's room but she'd pulled the pillow around her head to block them out anyway.

When she eventually dropped off she dreamed of Australia,

of sitting on the deck of an unknown house beside Keith, watching the sun slide behind the ocean in a palette of reds and golds. Her head was resting on his shoulder and she felt utterly content. And then, just as he turned to her and she knew that he was about to kiss her, Veronica arrived, dressed in the skimpiest of bikinis and looking like a million dollars. And she walked up to them and looked at Romy and laughed and told her that Keith would never kiss her because she wasn't the sort of girl that men wanted to kiss. She didn't know how to seduce a man. Look at you, Veronica said, in your sackcloth and ashes. And when Romy looked down she realised that she was wearing a black plastic bin-liner and Keith was suddenly staring at her and asking her if she had no dress sense whatsoever. Then Veronica put her arms around Keith and Romy knew that she was going to make love to him and the thought revolted her so much that she got up and ran towards the sea. She could hear her mother's voice calling to her, mocking her, her feet stamping on the wooden deck . . .

'Romy!'

Her eyes snapped open.

'Romy!' It was Veronica's voice and she was tapping at the door.

Romy looked at her bedside clock. It was six thirty. She pushed the covers from the bed and walked across the room.

'What?' she asked as she opened the door. 'What's the matter?'

Veronica stood there in a white silk nightdress. Her face was pale and her hair hung limply around her shoulders. There were beads of perspiration on her forehead.

'I don't feel well,' she said.

'In what way?' Romy wasn't entirely convinced about another illness.

Veronica winced and squeezed her eyes closed.

'The pain from earlier,' she told her. 'It's really bad. It's like a poker in my back and my side. It's been getting worse all night.'

'Did you eat anything odd yesterday?' Romy asked. 'When Giselle was here?'

'No,' said Veronica. 'Well, we had a couple of biscuits, but that's all.'

'How bad is it?'

'Excruciating,' said Veronica simply. 'I think I'm going to die.'

'You're not going to die,' said Romy firmly.

Veronica's eyes glistened with tears. 'How do you know that? How do you know that I haven't got some fatal disease?'

'Because you probably have indigestion,' Romy told her. 'Oh Mum, you don't have a fatal disease. You know you don't. You're being melodramatic.'

Veronica cried out again and doubled over in pain.

'OK, OK.' This time Romy put her arm around her mother's shoulders. 'Come in and sit down for a moment.' She led Veronica into the room and sat her in the small armchair at the end of the bed. 'D'you think it could be your appendix?'

'No,' said Veronica simply. 'I had that out after Kathryn was born.'

'Oh. I didn't know that. OK, then maybe it's just some sort of spasm.'

'Yes, but honestly, Romy, it's just getting worse and worse.'

'You're supposed to be seeing Dr Jacobs today.' Romy realised that she'd forgotten about Veronica's appointment at the hospital when she'd been planning her escape back to Australia.

'He's a back doctor,' snapped her mother tersely. 'He won't be able to diagnose this.'

Romy glanced at her packed bag and then at her mother. Psychosomatic or not, Veronica did seem to be in genuine pain. She couldn't walk out if there was something really wrong with her.

'Give me a few minutes to get dressed,' she told her. 'Then we'll go to Accident and Emergency.'

'Thank you,' said Veronica weakly. 'Thank you very much.'

They sent Veronica for a scan. Romy sat in the waiting area and wondered if there truly was anything wrong with her or whether, somehow, her mother had guessed that she was thinking of going and had managed to fake an illness to stop her. It wasn't as though Veronica hadn't done it in the past. There had been the time when Dermot was due to go to Kuwait and two days before his departure date Veronica had fainted. Three times. Dermot had been overcome with worry and had brought her to the doctor, but in the end they'd been told that there was nothing physically wrong with her and that it might be stress.

'Stress!' Dermot had looked at her in astonishment. 'What have you to be stressed about? You're not going to a war zone.'

And Veronica – Romy had completely forgotten about this until now – Veronica had snapped back at him that their house was a war zone and probably a much more dangerous one than bloody Kuwait!

'We've admitted your mother.' A nurse eventually came to Romy with information. 'The doctors want to run some tests on her.'

'Tests?' asked Romy fearfully. 'What sort of tests?'

The nurse shrugged. 'Tests to find out what's wrong with her, obviously.'

'Can I see her?'

'Sure.' The nurse gave her directions to the ward where Veronica was already in bed. It was a semi-private room, but for the moment, at least, the other beds were unoccupied.

'You see,' Veronica said softly to Romy, 'they're taking me seriously.'

'I took you seriously too,' Romy lied.

'OK then.' A junior doctor walked into the ward and picked up Veronica's chart. 'Let's get this show on the road.'

'When will I come back?' asked Romy.

'You could give us a call later this afternoon,' said the doctor cheerily. 'I'm sure we'll have finished with your mother before then. Though, goodness knows, the two of you could be sisters.'

Veronica flashed a sudden beaming smile at the doctor and Romy sighed. It didn't seem to matter when or where as far as Veronica was concerned. Once there was a man involved she seemed to turn on some inner charm.

When she got home from the hospital, Romy phoned Darragh's office to tell him about Veronica's latest episode. But Darragh wasn't available to take the call. His PA told her that he was in a meeting and couldn't be disturbed.

'Why?' asked Romy.

'It's a business meeting,' said the PA impatiently. 'He left instructions not to be interrupted. Can I take a message?'

'Yes,' said Romy. 'You can tell him I called. His sister.'

'Kathryn?' She sounded surprised.

'No. Romy.'

'Oh. OK.'

Romy hung up wondering how often Kathryn called the company. A lot, she supposed. She knew that Kathryn had always wanted to be involved in Dolan's.

Her mobile beeped and she took it out of her pocket. She'd half hoped that the text message would be from Keith, but it was from her father reminding her that she was supposed to meet him for dinner soon. She'd forgotten about that too in her escape plan.

Well, she wasn't going anywhere until she knew what was wrong with Veronica.

She went upstairs and took the clothes from her hastily packed bag. Then she hung them in the wardrobe again and wondered exactly when she would manage to leave. She'd got over her rage of the night before and now didn't feel the need to fling herself on to the first available flight out of the country. But as soon as Veronica is OK again, she promised herself. Then I'm definitely off.

She made herself a cup of coffee and flicked through one of her mother's magazines, then phoned her father to let him know the latest on Veronica's medical condition.

'That woman is such a hypochondriac!' exclaimed Dermot. 'She never just has a stomach ache like a normal person.'

'I know,' said Romy. 'I thought she was having me on at first. But she was in agony.'

'I'm sure she'll be fine,' said Dermot. 'She always bounces back.'

'That's true.' Romy giggled at a sudden image of a bouncing Veronica.

'Well, keep me in touch with how she's doing,' said Dermot. 'Look, honey, if she has to stay in hospital again, why don't you come over to us tomorrow night?'

'I don't want to be in the way,' said Romy.

'You won't be,' Dermot told her. 'Larissa has to go out for a while anyhow. Come over and spend some time with your old man.'

Romy felt a lump in her throat.

'Sweetheart?'

'OK,' she said.

'Lovely,' said Dermot. 'I'll do my special for you. And in the meantime, chin up. It's not that bad. If you're talking to Veronica, tell her I was asking for her.'

'Will do.' Romy agreed a time to drop over to the house and ended the call. She glanced at her watch and decided it might be worth ringing the hospital.

'Your mum is still having tests,' said the nurse. 'But we

240

think it's probably kidney stones. It would account for such a severe pain.'

Poor Veronica, thought Romy. One of the guys from Heritage Help had had kidney stones, and he'd been in absolute agony (although the girls had murmured about 'man sickness' because after he'd come back to work, he'd gone on and on about the pain he'd been in until they threatened him with much worse if he didn't shut up moaning about it. Nevertheless, it was universally agreed that kidney stones were excruciating).

The phone rang again almost as soon as she'd replaced the receiver and she recognised Darragh's number.

'Why didn't you call me sooner?' he demanded. 'I could have come over.'

'I didn't have time,' said Romy, who (despite the passing of her rage) was still pissed at him for his rudeness the previous day. 'It was an emergency and we went straight to A&E.'

'Have they finished the tests yet?'

'No, but I've just been speaking to one of the nurses and she thinks it's kidney stones.'

'Thank God, that's not too serious,' said Darragh.

'But very very painful.' Romy was feeling extremely guilty about having thought that Veronica was feigning illness in the first place.

'Ring me as soon as you hear for definite,' said Darragh. 'I've got to go now, I have another meeting.'

He hung up and she was left holding the receiver. She stuck out her tongue at it before replacing it in its cradle.

Darragh put his concerns out of his mind as his company secretary and financial officer walked into his office to discuss his proposals for diversification. He favoured an alliance with the environmental energy company he'd met in Switzerland.

'We put up some capital,' he said, 'become a partner with

them. They're aiming to penetrate the residential markets with new technology.'

'What new technology?' asked Alex.

'It's all in the report,' Darragh told him. 'Look, I know that this is something out of left field for us, but this crowd seem to know what they're doing and there are great opportunities—'

'Yes, but Darragh,' Stephen interrupted, 'it's not our area of expertise.'

'I know that.' Darragh looked at him impatiently. 'But we've got to stretch ourselves a little. Times have changed. Once everything was about plant and machinery and Dolan Component Manufacturers was right up there with the best of them. But nowadays more and more things have been taken over by some kind of technology with a computer chip and they don't need the stuff we produce. It seems to me that the only way of staying in the game is by diversifying.'

'I agree with you,' said Alex. 'But looking at other opportunities doesn't mean that we should ignore relevant ones. Which is why I think that the Hemmerling deal looks so good for us. After all, there's only so much a microchip can do. You still need machinery.'

'Hemmerling want to take us over!' cried Darragh. 'And if you remember, your first words to me about it were that they wanted to get a foothold in Ireland. We have our own business in Ireland and we don't want to facilitate someone else getting in.'

'You've misinterpreted it,' said Alex. 'They just want a partnership on some things.'

'Rubbish!' Darragh snorted. 'I could see where they were coming from right off. They'd have got access to some of our processes and clients and the next thing you know they're trying to take control.'

'I think you're being a touch paranoid,' said Stephen. 'We do need fresh markets and maybe some fresh capital ourselves. Hemmerling could provide the capital.'

'What d'you mean, fresh capital?' demanded Darragh. 'Weren't profits up last year?'

'Yes but if we invest in some new processes . . . with the help of another company . . .'

'We don't need anyone's help!'

Alex scratched his head. 'We need to formulate a strategic plan,' he said. 'We haven't a clear vision of what we're trying to achieve here.'

'Leave it with me,' said Darragh finally. 'I'll have something to put before you in the next week or so.'

'Fine,' said Alex, 'but in the meantime, that environmental thing? There are loads of those companies and a lot of their plans are totally pie in the sky. I really don't think it's where we need to be going.'

'Maybe you don't,' said Darragh, 'but you clearly haven't read about their industrial solar panel technology. I think it's got potential.'

Alex shrugged. 'You're the boss. But I wouldn't recommend it.'

'Perhaps I'll get involved on a personal level,' said Darragh pettishly. 'Leave the company out of it.'

'That's fine by me.'

'Right,' said Darragh. 'That'll do for today.'

After his company secretary and financial officer had left the room, Darragh leaned back in his chair and stared at the ceiling. He'd been very impressed by the environmental energy company. And all this alternative power stuff was good business. Difficult, he agreed. But potentially ground-breaking. Alex and Stephen were being narrow-minded about it. Too cautious by far. But in the end their opinions didn't really matter. They didn't have any influence over the future direction of Dolan's. It was all up to the board. Him and Veronica and Kathryn.

And eventually they'd agree with him. Kathryn would voice her ridiculous objections – probably the same objections as

Alex and Stephen – but since she always objected to whatever he wanted that wouldn't matter. She'd sent him an email about Hemmerling after he'd forwarded information to her, suggesting that having talks with them couldn't do any harm, but Darragh hadn't replied. He wasn't going to talk to another company about a way they could get a slice of Dolan business. He was surprised that Kathryn couldn't see through this deal for what it was. Anyway, she could vent her frustration at not being able to do things her way all she liked, but when it came to the vote, Veronica would back him as she always did. Nevertheless, he was looking forward to the day when Veronica finally signed over her shareholding to him completely. That would leave him with seventy-five per cent and control of the company, and Kathryn's voice would be irrelevant. At the moment, even though with Veronica's support he could bypass Kathryn's irritating suggestions, he still had to listen to her. He'd put something together for her and for Veronica to look at, outlining the potential of the energy deal and giving them some options on an overseas company to buy. There weren't very many suitable ones, that was the problem. But they were out there. He knew they were.

Romy and Dermot sat at the big dining table in his house the following evening. Larissa had gone to the movies with a friend and Erin was watching *The Invincibles* on DVD.

'So have they made a definitive diagnosis on Veronica?' Dermot asked Romy as he slid a plate of his speciality – one-pot spicy chicken with saffron rice – in front of her.

Romy swallowed a piece of chicken and took a gulp of water. 'Ow – ow – hot, but lovely!' She replaced the glass on the table and looked at her father. 'It's definitely a kidney stone. Or stones. They're keeping her in for another day at least but they're hoping she'll get rid of it naturally.' She wrinkled her nose in disgust at the thought.

'So not one of her hypochondriacal moments then.' Dermot looked a little shamefaced.

'And I wasn't very sympathetic either,' Romy admitted.

'Only because you know what she's like. There's always something with Veronica.'

'I know.' Romy looked at him glumly. 'It drives me crazy. All the same, it was worrying because she really was in pain.'

'Um. Her pain is always a drama. But I'm glad she's OK.'

'So am I,' said Romy. 'And hers wasn't the only family drama.' She recounted the story of Giselle's fall and her own row with Darragh.

'He's such a shit,' she told her father. 'He swaggers around as though he's lord of the manor and Veronica does nothing to keep him in check.'

'I'd flay him alive if he was here now,' said Dermot furiously. 'How dare he talk to you like that?'

'Dad, he always talked to me like that,' said Romy. 'That's how he is!'

'I didn't realise it was quite that bad.'

'Oh, it was,' Romy assured him. 'And Kathryn wasn't much better.'

'I can't agree with you there,' said Dermot. 'Kathryn is a good-hearted girl.'

'When she wants to be.'

'You're very bitter,' said Dermot.

'Not really,' Romy told him. 'Just realistic.'

'Maybe a bit harsh,' suggested Dermot. 'Oh well, perhaps Erin will turn out to be the sister you never felt you had.'

'Dad!' Romy laughed. 'Erin is like – like a niece to me. There's no way I'd ever think of her as a sister. Besides, I hardly know her.'

'You could get to know her,' said Dermot. 'She's a sweet little thing.' His eyes softened. 'I never realised what it was like before, being there for a baby. I'm sorry I missed it with you, Romy.'

Romy swallowed hard.

'But I've made a promise to Larissa to be around as much as possible.'

'Good for you,' she said drily.

'I was too young when I married Veronica,' Dermot said.

'You were only a few months older than I am now,' Romy reminded him.

'Well, you're hardly settling down, are you? And it was way too young for me.'

Romy nodded slowly.

'I'm sorry it didn't work out,' he said. 'But at least we ended it civilly.'

'Civilly!' Romy's fork clattered on to her plate. 'Civilly! Your rows were legendary. I used to hide in my bedroom when you got going with each other.'

'Don't be silly.'

'Excuse me. I'm not being silly. You said horrible things to each other and I hated every minute of it and none of it was one bit civil.'

'Romy, we shared custody of you and we never badmouthed each other in front of you.'

'You didn't need to at that point,' she said. 'I'd heard it all already.'

There was an awkward silence filled only by the sound of Erin chatting happily to the cartoon characters on the TV.

'I'm sorry,' said Romy eventually. 'I'm not trying to pick a fight with you. God knows, I've been picking fights with enough people in the family already! I don't need to row with you too. But you should know that it wasn't a bed of roses for me either when you were married to Veronica or afterwards; and if you think any different then you're just kidding yourself.'

'She always told me you were fine. And you always said you were too.'

'And what else was I supposed to say?' asked Romy. 'That

I was heartbroken because my father preferred to live on his own than with me and my mum?'

The silence between them grew again.

'I told you before,' Dermot said, 'that Veronica and I were wrong for each other.'

'And I told you before that you'd stuck it out for fourteen years, and it's not that I would've wanted you to stay together for my sake but it seems to me that you're doing all this stuff with Larissa and Erin that you wouldn't do for me and Mum and so it's a bit difficult for me to think that you're having all this happy family stuff now when it hasn't changed one bit for me!'

Dermot stared at her.

'Aren't you happy?' he asked eventually. 'I thought you liked what you do. I thought you wanted to travel. I thought you couldn't wait to get back to Australia.'

'Of course I like what I do; that's a completely separate issue.' Romy could feel the tears welling up in her eyes. 'But that's nothing to do with wishing that my mum and dad could've lived together the way that you and Larissa are. And that I'd had a sister or brother of my own – not a half-sister or a half-brother, because it's different no matter what you think. But none of that happened and, fine, I accept it, only don't go on and on about how damn wonderful your life is now. It was wonderful then too – but for you, not us.'

Dermot picked up the bottle of wine and refilled her glass.

'I didn't know you felt like that,' he said. 'I didn't know you resented me.'

'I don't resent you.' She blinked away the tears. 'I – I love you, of course I do, you're my dad. But I just think that it was so easy for you, doing what you wanted all the time, and it wasn't quite as easy for everyone else. And I'm sorry, but ever since this thing happened with Veronica's back, Darragh has been going on at me about my selfish nature and I can't help thinking that I got it from you.'

Dermot rubbed his forehead.

'You're not selfish,' he said. 'You gave up your job to come back and that wasn't selfish at all. And as for me . . . maybe I was selfish. Maybe I still am. But I still care deeply about what happens to you. You're my eldest daughter. I love you too. I always will.' He got up from the table and put his arm around her. 'Just because I have a new family doesn't mean I've forgotten my old one.'

'I know.' She sniffed. 'I'm being silly. I'm sorry.'

'And I'm sorry if all my arguments with Veronica impacted so badly on you. I wouldn't have wanted that to happen for the world. You know how much I love you, don't you?'

She'd always known. Even when Veronica had made her think, for an instant, that he hadn't.

'Of course,' said Romy. 'And I know that neither of you did things because you wanted to upset us. But it happens anyway. And I wouldn't really have wanted you to stay together and be miserable – it was obvious that everything wasn't right. It's just . . . I guess everyone wants the dream, to think that things will turn out perfectly for them.'

'Sometimes they do, in the end,' said Dermot.

She smiled at him. 'I'm glad they did for you.'

'And they will for you too,' he told her. 'I promise.'

Chapter 16

Why was she still here?

Kathryn sat in the limousine beside Alan and stared straight ahead of her, her fingers unconsciously rubbing the diamond bracelet on her arm. He'd given her the bracelet earlier in the week when he'd surprised her at home with flowers and champagne – stunning roses, expensive champagne and, of course, the fiery, glittering diamond bracelet which was so beautiful she hadn't been able to resist picking it up even though she knew, deep down, that it was as much a bribe as anything else. He'd apologised to her then, blaming himself for everything that had gone wrong. She didn't quite believe him. But she hadn't tried to talk to him. She hadn't wanted to. Instead, she'd carried on as usual and gone to work.

But she hadn't been able to concentrate on her work. It had always been something she could relax into before. Schoolwork, college, studying for professional exams – she'd always been able to lose herself in it so that things in the outside world simply didn't matter any more. But she couldn't block it out this time. She kept thinking of him, over and over, and wondering who was in the wrong. Him or her?

Both of them? Neither of them? But it couldn't be neither of them, because despite the fact that just before they'd come out that evening Alan had kissed her on the forehead and told her that she was a priceless jewel, things weren't right between them.

His words had been the opportunity to talk about it, but she hadn't taken it. Instead she'd smiled faintly at him and told him that she didn't need to be treated like a priceless jewel, that she was an ordinary person, not someone he had to keep in cotton wool, and then her voice had trailed off because, of course, he wasn't exactly keeping her in cotton wool any more either.

She hadn't minded how devoted he'd been when he'd first taken her out and made her feel so special. And every night after that as she'd lost her heart to him so completely, never realising that this could happen to her. She'd been thrilled at his attention, at the way he would unexpectedly call her and ask her how she was doing and tell her that he was thinking about her. She'd loved that because nobody had ever called her for no reason before. She could talk to him too, in a way that she hadn't been able to talk to any of her previous boyfriends, so that she considered him a confidant as well as a lover. Although he excelled as a lover. He was also great at making her talk, making her reveal things to him that she'd never revealed to anyone. Letting him in on her insecurities about her style and her looks and her fear of being found wanting against the armies of glamorous women that stalked the city.

'But of course you're not wanting.' He'd looked at her, a puzzled expression in his dark eyes. 'Why would I think that? You're beautiful, Kathryn.'

'Not really,' she'd replied. 'My eyes are too wide. My nose is too long. My lips aren't full enough. My eyebrows are too thick – and I know it's meant to be fashionable this season, but that's tamed and thick; mine are just like vegetable patches over my eyes unless I attack them every single day.'

'Katy, Katy.' He only ever called her Katy when he was amused. 'If I wanted a high-maintenance girl I'd call Camille Carson. Or, like, you know – whoever.' He'd grinned at her then and pulled her towards him and reminded her that she mightn't be high maintenance but she was, in fact, a stunning woman and that he'd been struck by her beauty the very first time they'd met. And she hadn't even been trying then, he said, she'd been wearing her black business suit and black shoes and white blouse . . . and then he'd laughed again and told her that actually he probably had a bit of a dominatrix thing going on because he'd found that entire outfit very, very sexy.

'More than this!' She looked at him in mock horror. 'I'm wearing Dolce and Gabbana!'

'Well, clearly not more than that,' he acknowledged. 'But I did like the business look.' He grinned at her. 'And so do you – you wore a suit the night we got engaged.'

He'd proposed three months after they met by bringing her to dinner in the Pool Room at the Four Seasons and placing a velvet Tiffany box containing an enormous diamond ring beside her plate. She hadn't known what to say. She hadn't been expecting his proposal. It had never occurred to her that he would want to marry her. The dinner, directly after work, hadn't had any significance for her at all until he produced the ring. And she'd nearly fallen off her chair with shock.

Probably, she'd thought, the only person who'd be more astonished than her at the news of the wedding proposal would be Veronica, who'd rated her chances so poorly. If only to hear the astonishment in Veronica's voice, Kathryn wanted to get engaged to Alan. In the end, of course, she did it because she loved him and because there was no way she ever wanted to leave him. But she was also grateful to him for giving her the means by which to shock her mother. She loved Veronica but she thought her a very silly woman. She didn't resent her in the same way that Romy seemed to (Romy, in her view, held on to a grudge for far too long), but she was dismissive of her. After all, she'd told herself night after night as she studied in her bedroom overlooking the garden, Veronica simply married well. She didn't do it for herself. Kathryn wanted to do it for herself. She didn't see the point in wanting a man to whisk her away, not that that happened any more, but so many girls of her age seemed to think that getting married would miraculously solve problems instead of simply creating more. Her closest friend, Sybil, was forever talking about getting married, finding a soulmate, having someone to call her own.

'You don't own a man,' said Kathryn one day. 'You live with them. And they have a habit of leaving.'

'Why are you so damn cynical?' demanded Sybil. 'Anyone would think that you were some worldly-wise old dear who's talking from a lifetime of experience.'

'My dad died,' Kathryn said. 'And my stepfather left. So father figures don't have a good track record for me.'

'That's a unique situation.'

'Not really,' said Kathryn. 'More and more people are in second or third or even fourth marriages these days. Finding a guy doesn't mean it's for ever.'

Sybil had snorted dismissively. But Kathryn knew she was right. And nothing that happened during her college years made her feel any different. Boyfriends came and went, but as far as she was concerned, men just weren't dependable. The only person you could truly trust was yourself.

She'd come to the States to do it on her own, as part of an exchange programme with the US branch of the company she worked for in Dublin. Kathryn got New York in a way that she'd never got anywhere else. She loved its buzzy, frantic pace and its feisty, optimistic inhabitants. And away from Veronica's constant desire to make her cut her hair or change her clothes, but in a city overflowing with big-name stores and designers, Kathryn dipped her toe into the world of fashion and found that she quite liked it.

One day she booked herself into the Elizabeth Arden Red Door Spa and emerged that evening a completely different woman. She'd had her hair cut and coloured, her nails manicured, her skin treated and had learned more about beauty and make-up than she ever had in all the time she'd watched Veronica sit at her dressing table putting on her war paint.

She might not approve of spending hours in front of the mirror, Kathryn acknowledged, but there was a case to be made for good grooming. A case that was strengthened by the fact that her own career took off shortly after she'd gone through the whole makeover experience.

Then she'd met Alan Palmer. She sometimes wondered whether he would have noticed her if she hadn't done the entire spa treatment thing, but, she told herself, all she'd done was change the packaging. Rebranded herself. The person inside was still the same.

And so she'd been taken aback to realise that a man like Alan – truly handsome, successful and charming – wanted to marry her. Somehow, in her head, she'd always carried the mental image of herself as the tree-hugging environmentalist that Veronica was so scathing about. (She wouldn't have minded marrying an environmentalist, they were hot property these days, but she'd never actually met one.)

Their wedding was at the Four Seasons too – it was one of Alan's favourite places in the city and she thought it was sweet that he wanted to have their wedding reception in the same place as he'd proposed to her. A small wedding, he'd said, but with everything exactly right. She'd been surprised at how keen he was to have everything exactly right and surprised too that he'd organised so much of the event – at least by being the one to hire the wedding planner – but it really had been the best day of Kathryn's life.

Veronica had been spellbound by the whole thing, with its New York glamour and haughty elegance, and spellbound too by Kathryn's new look and her snow-white Charo Peres wedding dress. 'I always knew you could look fabulous,' she'd said when she saw Kathryn in her gown. 'I always knew it and it broke my heart that you didn't see it yourself but you look fantastic now and I'm so, so proud of you.'

Darragh and Giselle had been awed too, Kathryn knew. For once Giselle hadn't said a word about how things could have been done better or made a barbed comment about Kathryn's appearance because there was nothing that she could say. Weeks later Kathryn, looking at a photograph of the two of them standing side by side, basked in a self-satisfied glow of knowing that for once she'd outshone her sister-in-law. And looking at a family photograph too she'd acknowledged that she outshone everybody else as well.

Romy hadn't been at the wedding. Nor had Dermot. Asking Dermot had been a difficult issue. Kathryn had wanted him to be there but when, tentatively, she'd suggested that he should be the one to give her away, she hadn't needed Veronica to say a word to know that her mother wasn't at all happy at the idea. Kathryn had the feeling that her wedding could turn into a complete disaster with the Dolan and Kilkenny factions lining up on either side and she didn't want that to happen. She'd phoned Dermot and told him that she was getting married and that it was in New York and that Veronica was coming over and she hadn't had to say anything because Dermot had laughed and said that he guessed he'd be *de trop*. She hadn't liked to say it out loud even then but he'd told her not to worry, it was only one day in her whole life and he was sure he'd see her next time she came to Ireland.

It wasn't a hugely likely prospect. She didn't have any plans to come home, and even if she had, the idea of calling on Dermot seemed far-fetched. She never really knew how she felt about Dermot, whom she'd loved as a little girl and who'd loved her in return. She hadn't stopped loving him when she'd discovered that he wasn't her biological father but she knew that something inside her had changed. Besides, Veronica had told her all about Tom then, and the Dolan Component Manufacturers legacy which was exclusive to her and Darragh and Kathryn, and that had shifted everything into a different perspective. Later, when it came to taking sides in the disintegration of his marriage to Veronica, Kathryn had found herself siding with her mother – even though she and Dermot had often ganged up against Veronica in the past, teasing her for spending so much time in front of the mirror or for sticking rigidly to her low-carb diet or for knowing nothing about the Middle East conflict (how can she not know about it, Kathryn had once wondered, when Dermot is in the thick of it?). She'd felt connected to Dermot those times and she'd never really connected with Veronica at all, but when it came down to it, Veronica was her mother and Dermot was just someone who was nice to her and cared about her but wasn't, actually, related to her.

It's so hard to know, Kathryn thought, as the limousine made its way through the busy streets, how you're supposed to be with your family. Especially when you're not even sure who's actually part of it any more. And she thought of Romy, who'd been really excited about the wedding when she'd first heard about it but who'd suddenly been unable to leave the dig where she was working when she'd learned that Dermot wasn't going. We take sides all the time, Kathryn mused, but sometimes we don't take the right one. And most times there shouldn't need to be a side at all.

There were sides in Alan's family too. In some ways that came as a relief to her, because she often felt that the Dolan-Kilkennys were completely screwed up. But Alan had been married before and had a daughter from that marriage – a ten year old named Talia who now lived with her mother in Dallas. Alan never spoke either to her or to his former wife. All their communication was done through their lawyers. Kathryn didn't know a lot about the break-up of Alan's first marriage. When she'd asked him about it he'd called it one of the biggest mistakes of his life. When Kathryn herself had started to wonder whether marrying Alan had been the biggest mistake of hers, she'd considered getting in touch with Naomi. But she had no address for the other woman and she found the thought of contacting her behind Alan's back difficult to contemplate anyway. She knew that if he found out he'd be furious with her, and that was the very last thing she wanted.

The limo pulled up outside the hotel. Alan turned to her and smiled the disarming smile which had so charmed her when he'd first used it on her. And she couldn't help wondering, as the car door was opened, whether somehow she wasn't overdramatising, creating a crisis where none really existed. Because maybe everything really was OK. Maybe it would be OK from here on in.

They got out of the car and were met by a barrage of popping flashlights. The awards dinner that they were attending that night (another corporate event; there were loads of them in the city) wasn't truly high-profile but the PR companies had been out in force and had made sure that the media would be there. They'd also managed to line up a smorgasbord of celebrities to attend the event to make it worth the photographers' time.

Kathryn and Alan walked up the red carpet and into the hotel, and as Kathryn tugged at her dress and hoped that it was wrinkle free and covering her in all the right places, she wondered what it would be like to be really and truly famous so that every second of your day was taken up by how you looked and how you would look to millions of people as they studied your picture in the papers or the magazines.

It's horribly superficial, she thought, following Alan into the banqueting room. But it's the way things are now. Veronica was very, very right when she told me that appearances might be deceiving but that they are, in fact, everything. The wrong look, the wrong gesture – they can be recorded and define you for ever.

Alan's invited guests for the evening were already at the table when they arrived. They sat down and everyone introduced themselves, immediately beginning to chat about the awards and who was likely to win. One of Alan's clients, an electronics company, had been nominated and had already prepared lots of material for the media in case they were successful. The CEO of the firm was at their table, trying not to look too hopeful.

It might be more sophisticated than spending an evening in a nightclub, Kathryn thought a couple of hours later as the ceremony still continued, but it was dreadfully boring. She didn't really know any of the people involved and Alan's client, who was seated beside her, had evidently calmed his nerves by snorting coke on one of his frequent trips to the bathroom. He wasn't now worried about winning or not winning but he was hyper-excited and kept grabbing Kathryn's wrist each time an award was announced so that she felt sure she'd be bruised by the end of the night.

Alan hadn't appeared to notice the CEO's behaviour which was probably a good thing because she knew that he'd get tense himself as a result. Rather fortunately, she thought, his attention was being almost completely distracted by the truly stunning woman sitting beside him, who'd been introduced to them all as Ayesha and who also worked in the electronics firm.

They didn't win the award. Kathryn saw the disappointment on the CEO's face, which was quickly replaced by an expression of indifference. Alan was disappointed too; she could see his eyes darken and a frown furrow his brow, but he immediately called for champagne to take the edge off it and soon they were all clinking glasses and rubbishing the entire awards system.

Kathryn was unsteady on her feet by the time she got up to go to the bathroom – she hadn't eaten a lot of food and the three glasses of champagne she'd drunk in quick succession had gone straight to her head. She locked herself into one of the cubicles and closed her eyes for a few minutes, wishing that she hadn't drunk the champagne at all. She had tried very hard to avoid alcohol this week, deciding that if her marriage was going to work it wasn't just Alan who was going to have to change (and he'd promised that he would) but she'd have to make an effort too. And it seemed to her that if she couldn't drink just one glass of whatever it was without wanting to drink more straight away, then she shouldn't drink at all.

She sometimes wondered if she was an alcoholic. She didn't think so but she did worry about the fact that alcohol was playing such a large part in her life right now. Had been playing, she reminded herself as she stood up and flushed the toilet. Had been. Perhaps that had been part of the problem too. But she'd promised herself that she wasn't going to use it as some kind of support mechanism any more. She'd let it slip a bit tonight but until now a drop hadn't passed her lips all week. And from now on she'd drink nothing but water.

It was late by the time they got back to the apartment. Kathryn had stuck to her decision not to have any more alcohol so she wasn't feeling half as tired as she normally would, although Alan was slightly the worse for wear; after the champagne he and the CEO had shared a bottle of Jim Beam to dull their disappointment. Kathryn was always surprised at how well Alan normally held his drink, but tonight he walked straight into the bedroom and flopped, fully clothed, on to the enormous bed. She hoped he'd fall asleep. His bitterness at his client not winning the award had finally surfaced and he'd been irritable during the car ride home. If he fell asleep now he'd have got over it by the morning.

She went into the kitchen and made herself a cup of coffee, which she knew probably wasn't a good idea at that hour of the night but which she took outside to the balcony and drank as she listened to the sounds of the city. She always felt more at home in New York at night than at any other time of the day. She liked the idea that at three a.m. there were still people walking, talking and living their lives, that there was a whole social scene going on despite the hour. She lit a cigarette and smoked it slowly. Another vice she'd promised to give up. Alan didn't like her cigarette breath. Not surprising; she didn't much like it herself, but these days she found smoking very therapeutic.

She drained her coffee cup, ground out the cigarette and returned indoors. She put the cup into the dishwasher and walked through the living room towards the bedroom. It was then that she saw the blinking light of the answering machine.

'Hi, Kathryn.' It was Romy's voice. 'A news update from the accident and emergency division of Rathfarnham. Mum will be in hospital again for a few days while they do tests to see if she has a kidney stone. It's always something! Call me when you can if you want any more information. Darragh said you might be thinking of coming over. Let me know if you're making plans. Thanks. Goodbye.'

Kathryn replaced the receiver slowly. She couldn't go to Ireland now. Alan would see it as some kind of challenge. Or maybe even a threat. Anyway, Veronica would be fine. She always was.

She pushed open the bedroom door. She'd expected him to be asleep but he was still awake. He hadn't even gone to bed.

'What kept you?' His eyes were a little unfocused but his voice was strong.

'Nothing. I had a coffee. I thought you'd gone to bed otherwise I'd've brought you one too.'

'Who was on the phone?'

'A message from Romy.'

'What about?'

'Mum's in hospital again.'

'The old bird going to croak?' he asked.

'Alan!'

He shrugged, then sniffed the air and frowned. 'Have you been smoking?'

She held her breath. She shouldn't have had that cigarette. He hated it when she smoked before bedtime.

'I've nearly finished the packet,' she said hesitantly. 'I won't buy any more.'

'Get it.'

She took the packet out of her bag. There were three cigarettes left.

Alan took them out of the carton and began tearing at them. When he had reduced them to shreds he sprinkled them over her side of the bed.

'I'm sorry,' she said. 'I should've binned them earlier.'

'It's a filthy, disgusting habit.'

'I know.'

'You said you'd given them up for good.'

'I have now.'

His eyes, still slightly unfocused, narrowed. 'Don't be smart with me.'

'I would never be smart with you,' she said sincerely.

'And you'd never betray me either, would you?'

She looked at him, concern in her eyes. 'Betray you?'

'With someone else?'

She moistened her lips. 'Of course not,' she said. 'You know that.'

'Only it seemed to me, darling, that you were paying a lot of attention to our guest this evening.'

'I – I wasn't,' she said.

'Holding his hand,' said Alan.

'Holding his hand?' She looked at him in genuine astonishment. 'I never held his hand. I didn't. He grabbed me once or twice when names were being announced but I swear to you I never held his hand.'

'I wish I could believe you.' He looked grim. And she knew for certain that she should have left him before now.

Chapter 17

Romy sat at the back of the house, a glass of red wine in her hand. The evening sun, filtering obliquely between soft pillows of cloud, was gently warming, and the only sound apart from the distant hum of traffic from the main road was the occasional rustle of leaves from the apple and plum trees in the garden.

It was peaceful. Romy could feel the stress of the last few days draining out of her body. She sipped the wine and leaned back in the comfortably padded garden chair. Then she closed her eyes and luxuriated in her solitude.

The doctors thought that Veronica might have passed the kidney stone but she was nevertheless scheduled for further scans. She wasn't in pain any longer and that was a relief, but she was still worried about her health and not entirely convinced that the excruciating pain could have been caused by something so tiny as a kidney stone. It didn't matter how often people told her that it *was* agonising, Veronica wanted to be worried.

'You won't leave me, will you?' she'd said to Romy that afternoon when she'd come to visit.

'What d'you mean?'

'I know that you're peppering to go back to Australia. I know you hate it with me. But you won't go, will you? Not yet. Not till I know I'm all right.'

Romy exhaled slowly.

'This has knocked me back,' continued Veronica. 'I know I was beginning to improve a bit but now I'm back to square one again.'

'You're not,' Romy told her. 'This is a completely different thing.'

'But I can't be on my own,' said Veronica. 'Not yet.' She looked tearfully at Romy. 'I know you were upset the other night. I know you think I'm a horrible person. But I need you.'

And when I needed you, thought Romy, where were you? Off shopping for make-up, getting your hair done, dragging my bloody boyfriend into the shrubbery . . .

'It's not all black and white,' continued Veronica. 'I know I did things that you didn't like. I know you were cut up about the divorce and about . . . about . . . Perry.' She stumbled over his name. 'But I didn't do those things to hurt you. I never would.'

'It doesn't matter,' said Romy tiredly.

'It does!' cried Veronica. 'I don't want you to think that I'm a terrible mother.'

Romy had spent all her life thinking that Veronica was a terrible mother.

'You're not a terrible mother,' she said.

'If I die . . .' Veronica looked at her fearfully. 'If I die, I don't want—'

'Mum, you had kidney stones. You're not going to die.'

'I might,' said Veronica anxiously. 'I might and then you'll always think that I was this horrible person.'

'I won't.'

'You will.'

'All right then.' Romy didn't have the strength to hold a supportive conversation with her. 'I will. If that makes you happier.'

Veronica's face crumpled.

Romy felt a stab of guilt. Her mother was sick and she was

262

behaving like a child. Perhaps Veronica was a terrible mother, but that didn't mean that Romy had to be a terrible daughter.

'I'm sorry, Mum.' Without realising what she was doing, she reached over and hugged her. 'Come on, you'll be fine.'

Veronica held tightly on to her. 'Promise me you won't leave.'

'I won't leave,' said Romy. 'Not yet. I promise.'

Eventually Veronica released her grip and Romy told her that she was going home but she'd be back the following day. And every day until she was better.

It was nice to be alone now, she thought, away from the drama that Veronica always seemed to generate. She liked being on her own. Usually, on her various digs, she'd have to share a house or apartment (or sometimes a tent) with a range of people, and although she was happily outgoing about it there was something restful about having her own space, knowing that nobody could walk in on her unexpectedly and disturb her.

She stopped thinking about her mother and allowed her mind to drift into the past. It was her defence mechanism, her way of escaping the pressures of the present. She didn't think about her personal past, but slipped into history, visualising the surrounding area over the centuries, thinking of all the people who might have sat in the exact same spot in the past, worrying about their own, very different, concerns.

She knew that the earliest written history of Rathfarnham dated back to 1199 but that a fort had existed there long before that. (The Irish word for a fort was, after all, *rath*.) As a child, Dermot had brought her on a tour of the castle and had thrilled her with stories of attacks on it by various clans all looking to take control.

'Back in 1649,' he'd told her as they stood in the rolling lands outside and looked back at it, 'the castle was stormed and taken by Royalists but the army later withdrew to Kilkenny.'

'We're Kilkennys,' she'd said, pleased that their name was part of the story.

'Yup.' Dermot had grinned and swung her in the air. 'You and me, Romy, we have a long history.'

But of course the history of Rathfarnham went back way before the battles of the seventeenth century, back to the fort and even earlier. And so it was a succession of people – from the Stone Age to the Bronze Age, from medieval times to the battles of the Rising and afterwards – that occupied Romy's thoughts. She pictured women sitting in the same place as her (and without the comfort of the padded chairs), worrying about finding food, worrying about their menfolk, worrying about the battles and wars that were raging around them, and she thought that she was, in fact, very lucky to be here now with her glass of wine and nothing to worry about at all.

Nothing of significance at any rate. The things that bothered her – her relationship with her mother and the rest of her family, her unhappiness at missing out on the job in Melbourne – were trivial things in the whole fabric of what had gone on before. Other women had to worry about staying alive; she only had to worry about living her life.

It's a pity, she thought as she opened her eyes and finished her wine, that I'm so damn bad at it.

The sun dipped beneath the horizon and the clouds began to build into darker columns. The breeze, though still warm, was whipping up so that the branches of the trees had started to sway. Romy moved inside but stood by the kitchen door, gazing out at the garden, her mind still on people who had long since died.

She suddenly realised that the weather was turning quickly for the worse and she went out again to put the chair cushions away. She locked the door when she returned to the kitchen, then poured herself another glass of wine before wandering through the house again. She did it as she had done the first night she'd been there on her own, starting with the living room, then the den and the upstairs bedrooms . . . Funny, she thought, I don't feel so much of a stranger here any more. It doesn't seem so alien and unfriendly. Yet it's still the same house.

She pushed open the door to the master bedroom. Veronica had intended moving back into it at the weekend because she'd been finding it easier to negotiate the stairs, but her kidney stone had put a temporary stop to that. Romy looked at the feminine décor, the fairy-princess furniture and the expensive bedclothes and she was struck by a sudden and unexpected sympathy for her mother, who was surrounded by such lovely things but didn't have anyone living with her. And who was so scared of being on her own now.

Romy enjoyed solitude but how would it feel for that to be the default setting on her life? To think that maybe she'd never share a home with anyone? She leaned her head against the door. She wouldn't like to think that there'd never be someone, that she'd spend the rest of her life roaming from dig to dig, sharing houses with strangers or finding places by herself. She loved it now but she wasn't sure that it was something she'd want for ever. She wanted to believe that there was a man out there for her; someone she could feel settled with. It wasn't wrong to want that, was it? In the end, everyone did. Veronica, Dermot, Darragh, Kathryn . . . none of them wanted to be alone.

She thought of Keith. Over the last few days she'd tried not to think about him and how, once again, she'd done something stupid. On top of the comfort kiss, pouring out her heart about her family and then saying that she loved him was incredibly daft. She hoped that he'd take the love part lightly, in the way she'd intended, as a throwaway comment like 'take care', words that people say without thinking about their true meaning. But she was worried that he'd actually think that she was really in love with him. She was almost certain that she'd signed off emails to him before with the word 'love'. But she hadn't noticed. She couldn't understand why it was that whenever she thought about him now, everything seemed to be in some kind of high-definition detail. And the problem was that it was becoming impossible to think of him in the easy way she'd done before. As a friend. So it was better not to think of him at all because, after all, he wasn't the one she imagined settling down with. He was a mate, not a soulmate.

Soulmate! She laughed cynically at the thought. How many marriages were really between soulmates? How many were just because people thought they were in love but were actually panicked about the idea of being on their own? She could see how it might happen.

And she wondered if that was what had happened between Veronica and Dermot, at least from her mother's point of view. Veronica wasn't good on her own. She liked people and partying and talking. So how on earth had she felt when, after Dermot had gone, her children had left one by one too. Had she feel lonely rattling around such a big house on her own? Was that why she'd married Larry? If so, she must have felt even lonelier when they divorced. Even though being alone didn't really bother her, Romy could still feel the weight of the empty house around her. How long before it became too much? A few years? A few months? A few weeks? Maybe even, for someone like Veronica, a few days. Her mother was such an outgoing, vivacious woman it was hard to imagine her sitting at home alone.

Maybe she didn't! Maybe she brought a myriad of men friends back to the fairy-princess bedroom and maybe she hadn't spent a single night by herself until her back started giving her trouble. Romy shuddered at the thought and took a gulp of wine from the glass she'd carried with her.

She didn't really think that Veronica kept a stable of men. She'd only met two of them herself, Will Blake from the bridge club and a guy named Noel Miller from the musical society.

'I didn't know you sang.' She'd looked at Veronica in surprise the day she'd come home from the post office and found Noel sitting in the living room surrounded by flyers for their next musical. Although she felt uncomfortable when Veronica had male callers, she was pleased at the idea of her feeling able to talk to people again.

'I don't,' said Veronica. 'I help out with getting sponsorship and doing the programmes and things like that.'

'Oh, right.' Romy was still surprised. She hadn't imagined Veronica as the sort of person who'd get involved with an amateur society at all.

'It gets me out of the house.' Veronica had changed the subject after that, as though admitting that she needed to get out of the house was in some way shameful. And yet, Romy thought, it appeared that when Veronica was in the fullness of health she was out of the house a lot. As well as the bridge club and the musical society, she also met a variety of friends for lunch or for dinner, she was in a book club and a film club – in fact there didn't seem to be anything she wasn't involved in.

'Yes,' she said when Romy had commented on it one day. 'I like to live life to the full.'

Romy now wondered whether Veronica actually did live life to the full or whether she spent so much time out and about because she didn't like being on her own. She remembered that after her parents split and she spent the weekends with Dermot, Veronica would talk about how she'd gone out with friends or gone to the movies, of how she'd been incredibly busy while Romy had been with her father. Did she miss me? wondered Romy now. I always thought she'd be glad to see the back of me, but perhaps . . . She rubbed the back of her neck. It was so hard to know with Veronica. She would never have considered her mother to be the lonely type. But perhaps she was. Sometimes.

And now, Romy knew, she was worried.

Romy had never seen Veronica worried before. She'd seen her angry and upset, mostly over Dermot (and, of course, angry with Romy herself on a regular basis), but whenever

Veronica was annoyed about something or feeling down she'd usually dressed up in her nicest clothes and adorned herself with her most expensive jewellery and gone out with friends, always returning in good spirits and telling any of her children who happened to be around that it was important to have fun in your life. Romy had resented her having fun because she wasn't having fun with Dermot. Kathryn had been dismissive of her – Kathryn's idea of fun was spending the night with an accountancy problem; only Darragh had encouraged her to have a good time and, of course, when he'd married Giselle the two women had sometimes gone for a night out together, something Veronica had never done with either Romy or Kathryn.

Veronica would regain her sense of fun, Romy was sure about that. But earlier in the day when she'd called in to see her, she'd realised that her mother – despite feeling better physically – was a shadow of her former self. She'd barely bothered with the merest hint of make-up and the only jewellery she wore was the half-hoop of emeralds on her wedding finger which she'd bought for herself after her divorce from Dermot. It had, of course, briefly been substituted by the white gold and diamond wedding band that Larry had given her. But she'd reverted to the emeralds again after her second divorce.

Beauty could be a curse as well as a blessing, thought Romy. Perhaps if Veronica hadn't been so beautiful when she was younger she wouldn't be so obsessed with how she looked now. For the life of her Romy couldn't see what was so wrong about a few wrinkles. But maybe it would be different if they were *her* wrinkles. Maybe you could only afford to be relaxed about it when you were young and clear-skinned and wrinkles were confined to some distant time in the future.

A rattle of rain against the window pane startled her. The balmy late spring evening had suddenly become wintry, the wind picking up force by the minute and the rain growing in intensity. Romy shivered and went back downstairs.

At eleven o'clock, having finished the bottle of wine (she hadn't actually drunk the whole bottle, she told herself virtuously; it had already been open), she went to bed. And by ten past eleven she was fast asleep.

It was the house alarm that woke her, its shrill tone blasting through her fug of sleep and alcohol. She blinked a couple of times while her heart raced as she identified the sound. And then, abruptly, it was silent again. Romy looked at the clock beside her bed. It was just past one. She could still hear the raging of the wind and the drumming of the rain against the bedroom window and she wondered whether it was the force of what was now a storm which had set off the alarm. But if that was the case, she thought worriedly, how come it had stopped?

She sat upright in the bed, the quilt cover pulled to beneath her chin as she considered the options. The most likely scenario was that the wind had set off the alarm. Maybe there was some kind of automatic cut-out device which switched it off. But why? That didn't really make sense. The whole point of an alarm was to make noise. So perhaps someone had switched it off.

The burglars, she thought shakily. The ones who are downstairs now robbing the house.

Veronica would flip altogether if she thought the house had been burgled. Added to her back and her kidneys, she'd now have the fact that some of her much-loved treasures had been stolen. If she was miserable now, she'd be twice as miserable after that news!

I have to call the police, thought Romy. I have to do something. She reached for the cordless phone but it wasn't there. Neither was her handbag. For one awful moment she thought that the burglars had already been in her room. But then she realised that she'd left the house phone and her bag containing her mobile phone on the kitchen counter where she'd put the empty wine bottle before she'd staggered up to bed.

You bloody fool, she told herself. That's what happens when you slug back the best part of a bottle of wine and tell yourself you didn't have that much. You idiot! She couldn't do nothing. Whoever had broken into the house could yet come upstairs and find her. And what would happen to her then? She felt her heart beat even faster and the tang of fear in her mouth.

There was another handset in the downstairs guest bedroom which Veronica was using. The bedroom was near the stairs and it was highly likely that the burglars were too occupied with the living room's goodies to worry about it yet. Romy took a deep breath and got out of bed, pulling her light towelling robe around her. She opened her wardrobe door. When she'd first arrived and unpacked she'd been astonished to see her old hockey stick at the bottom of the wardrobe. She hadn't been very good at hockey at school but it had been on the PE curriculum and she'd had to play it until one day she'd got into a fight with one of her team-mates and had come home dishevelled, with a split lip and a black eye. Veronica had forbidden her to play ever again. Romy had acted annoyed with Veronica, but actually had been quite grateful because she was fed up getting hacked down by more enthusiastically physical players than her. But being forbidden to play had given her another excuse to be bad-tempered around the house and blame Veronica for her mood. When she'd opened the door and seen the hockey stick in the wardrobe she'd wondered why Veronica hadn't thrown it out, but now she was glad.

She tiptoed across the landing, holding the stick in her hand and telling herself that everything would be OK.

The hall light was on. Romy felt a surge of anger at the audacity of people who broke into houses and switched on the lights. Maybe they were high on drugs, she thought anxiously. In which case she most definitely didn't want to be seen by them. She would just sneak quietly into the bedroom and call the guards.

She edged her way silently down the stairs. Halfway down she froze as she heard the sound of footsteps walking across the kitchen. She stayed motionless as the door opened. Her heart was tripping in her chest. Then, as she saw the outline of a person emerging from the room, she raised the hockey stick higher and let out a loud cry. As she moved forward she stepped on the trailing belt of her towelling robe, cried out again (involuntarily this time) as she realised what she'd done and then toppled forward, landing in a crumpled heap on the floor while the hockey stick thudded to the ground beside her.

I'm doomed, she thought, as she lay winded on the polished wood. I'll be beaten to death with my own hockey stick and Veronica will come home to find my battered and blood-soaked body lying here to greet her. She squeezed her eyes tightly closed and tried not to think about her impending ordeal.

'Romy! Oh my God! Are you all right?' The voice was scared.

It took a moment for it to register. And then she opened her eyes slowly and with relief.

'Kathryn?' She struggled to sit up. 'What the hell are you doing here?'

'Take it easy,' said her sister. 'You had a terrible fall. Are you OK?'

'I think so.' Romy flexed her body gingerly and realised thankfully that she hadn't been badly hurt. 'You scared the living daylights out of me! I thought you were a burglar. Or worse.'

'I'm sorry,' said Kathryn. 'I wasn't sure whether you'd be here or staying with Dermot while Mum was in hospital again. So I let myself in. And then my mind went blank and I just couldn't remember the alarm code for a minute. It's a different one at home. When you didn't come down straight away after it had gone off I assumed you'd stayed with Dermot.'

'No!' Romy retorted. 'I was cowering with terror in my

bedroom imagining the rampaging hordes of burglars downstairs!'

'I'm sorry,' repeated Kathryn.

'Why didn't you tell me you were coming?' demanded Romy. 'And what sort of an hour is this to be getting here anyhow?'

'I didn't call because I wasn't sure about coming, although I did text you when I arrived in Shannon but you didn't reply. The flight was delayed,' explained Kathryn as they both walked back into the kitchen. 'We were diverted to Shannon because of high winds. It's pretty wild out there, you know. I was going to stay there overnight but they'd organised a bus up to Dublin and so I thought I might as well take it.'

Romy's heartbeat was beginning to return to normal. 'You should've rung the doorbell,' she said accusingly. 'I would've preferred to be woken up by the doorbell than that bloody alarm. And when it did go off you could've called to let me know it was only you.'

'I'm sorry,' said Kathryn for the third time. 'I was sure that you were out. Force of habit, I guess. When you lived here, you were hardly ever in.'

'I suppose.' Romy shrugged. 'I'm not the better of it, though. My heart is still going like the clappers.'

'I was in the middle of making a cuppa,' said Kathryn. 'Want some?' She grinned at Romy. 'I'll dump loads of sugar in for the shock if you like.'

'I'm not that shocked,' Romy retorted and then exhaled with relief. 'But tea would be nice, thanks.'

Kathryn poured a cup and handed it to her.

'So I guess it's good to see you,' Romy said after she'd taken a sip.

'Wow. Thanks for your enthusiasm.'

'I might have been more enthusiastic in the light of day when I wouldn't have thought you were breaking in,' said Romy with spirit, and Kathryn laughed.

'I'm just grateful you didn't clobber me with the hockey stick.'

'I was always useless at it,' Romy reminded her. 'Just as well really.'

'I wasn't much good at it myself,' Kathryn mused. 'Hated the gear as well. I looked crap in it.'

'You look great now,' Romy told her, although even as she said the words she wasn't sure how accurate they were. Kathryn did look great in an ultra-thin, New York kind of way. She was wearing a black trouser suit, a white blouse with a high collar and black stiletto shoes. Her fine dark hair was cut into a sleek bob just above her shoulders and framed her slightly long face. She looked cool and sophisticated but she didn't actually look well. Her face was very pale, there were dark circles under her eyes and her slenderness verged on being gaunt.

'You look great too,' said Kathryn. 'Sort of rosy-cheeked and healthy.'

'Is that a good thing?' asked Romy.

'Definitely.'

Maybe it was, thought Romy, in the eyes of someone who looked positively skeletal.

'So are you here for long?' she asked.

Kathryn shrugged. 'I'm not certain. I was concerned when I got your message, wanted to see how Mum was doing.'

Romy brought her up to speed on Veronica's condition. 'I'm still surprised you showed up. I thought you were far too busy to take the time,' she added.

'Not now,' said Kathryn. 'I've just finished work on a particular project. I'm due some time off.'

Romy wondered whether she could take enough time off to take over Veronica's care. But it wasn't a question she was going to ask now.

'How's Alan?' she asked instead.

Kathryn's lips tightened slightly. 'He's fine.'

'Any sign of a little Palmer?' Romy grinned at her.

'Honestly, Romy, what a daft question to ask.' Kathryn put her cup down on the kitchen counter. 'Why is it that people think it's perfectly acceptable to ask married women if they're planning to have a baby? What business is it of anyone?'

'Hey, sorry.' Romy looked at her in surprise. 'I didn't realise it was a touchy subject.'

'It's not,' said Kathryn. 'It's just . . . none of your business, that's all.'

'Hey, fine, no problem,' said Romy who really didn't care whether Kathryn was planning a family or not. 'I was just trying to make conversation.'

'There's enough to talk about,' Kathryn told her. 'What's the situation with Mum? How's she coping with being unwell?'

Romy related her most recent conversation with Veronica.

'That's not like her,' agreed Kathryn.

'Never mind,' said Romy. 'Maybe she'll perk up when she sees you here. She'll probably be delighted to have someone besides me around the place.'

'She told me that you were being fantastic,' said Kathryn.

'She did?' asked Romy in astonishment. 'When?'

'One evening when I phoned.'

'She never says it to me.'

'Maybe she doesn't think she has to.'

Romy grunted.

'Well, look, if you don't mind I'm going to head off to bed,' said Kathryn. 'I'm really tired what with the diversions and the drive up from Shannon and I know that I'm going to pass out any minute.'

'Sure,' said Romy. 'D'you want a hand with your stuff?'

'I don't have much,' said Kathryn. 'Just one bag. It's in the hall. I'm surprised you didn't see it. That would've stopped you thinking that I was a marauding killer.'

'I didn't notice, but even if I had I'd've probably thought it was for the swag,' said Romy.

Kathryn laughed. 'And you probably would've hit me over the head as I went to get it.'

'Possibly,' admitted Romy. 'I was in act-first-think-afterwards mode.'

The two of them walked out of the kitchen. Romy switched off the light and then followed Kathryn upstairs.

'Oh,' said Kathryn as she opened the door to her bedroom. 'It's all changed.'

'Mine too,' said Romy.

'Typical Mum! It's nice, though.'

'Um, apologies for the stain on the carpet. That was me early on. Spilled some tea. Or coffee.'

Kathryn grinned at her. 'Still as graceful as ever.'

'Sod off.' But Romy smiled too. 'Anyway, it won't affect your sleep, I'm sure.'

'I could sleep on a log,' admitted Kathryn. 'Good night, Romy. See you in the morning.'

'Good night,' said Romy and went along the landing to her own room.

She climbed into bed again but she couldn't sleep. She was still running on adrenalin and the tea she'd drunk with Kathryn was keeping her awake too. At a quarter to three she got out of bed and switched on her laptop.

It wouldn't have been any use for making panicked 999 calls about intruders but maybe there'd been an email from Keith. She didn't really want to get excited about possible emails from Keith. They'd never been important before. They'd arrive and she'd be happy to see them but that was as far as it went. Now the idea of an email from him was making her heart beat faster. They'd somehow taken on a significance they didn't deserve.

She saw his name in her in-box. Her fingers hovered over it for a moment before she double-clicked on the mail.

'Poor Romy,' he'd said. 'Cheer up. Things aren't that bad, I promise. Here's a pic to lighten your day up.' The attachment was an underwater photo of a shoal of yellow and black striped tiger fish near the wreckage of a boat. She often used underwater photos as screensavers, finding the blue background restful. She felt a lump in her throat.

She opened Skype and saw that he was online so she double-clicked on his icon.

'Hey!' His face, out of sync with the sound again, smiled at her.

'Hey.' She smiled back.

'How're you doing?' he asked. 'Isn't it the middle of the night there?'

'Yes. But it's been an eventful night.' She described her descent downstairs with the hockey stick.

'I'd have liked to see you like that!' Keith chuckled.

'I was an awful eejit,' she told him. 'If Kathryn had been a burglar I'd have been in big trouble. And if I'd been better at what I was doing I'd've murdered her, which would've been even more trouble!'

'I'm glad that you're feeling feisty again,' said Keith. 'You sounded a bit miserable in your last email.'

'Yeah, I know. I'm sorry. I . . . I said stupid stuff which of course I didn't really mean . . . It was just that I was in dumping mood and I dumped on you.'

'I tried to ring you earlier,' Keith told her. 'But your phone was switched off.'

So that was why she hadn't got Kathryn's message. The battery must have run out.

'I kinda lost it a bit with that email,' Romy continued. 'I mean, you know, I . . . well, I hope you don't think I'm being all needy and pathetic 'cos I'm not. Everything's fine again really and—'

'It's cool,' said Keith. 'No worries.'

'You keep saying that to me.' She smiled at him.

'Because it's true.'

'You're a good friend,' she told him sincerely. 'A real friend. It means a lot.'

'Hey, we've always been friends, haven't we?' he asked. 'We have a connection.'

'Yes,' she said quickly. 'We hit it off. In a good kind of way.'

She hoped that she was saying enough to make him understand that 'love you' didn't mean 'I love you'. Stressing the friendship aspect was important.

'What's happening with your mum?' he asked, after a moment where neither of them spoke.

She brought him up to date.

'So you won't be coming back any time soon?'

'I . . . don't think so,' she said carefully. 'I think I need to wait till she's a bit better. I don't want to, but I think I should.'

'I think you should too,' he told her.

Maybe he thought that because he wasn't convinced that she was anything other than a desperate, needy, pathetic sort of person. But hopefully not.

'Yeah, well, it's family, isn't it?' she said wryly.

'Don't sound so enthusiastic.'

'You don't know how lucky you are with yours,' she said.

'Actually, I do.'

She grinned at him. 'I guess so.'

'Keep in touch,' Keith said. 'Let me know when you're coming.'

'Sure I will,' she told him.

He smiled. She liked his smile.

'You should go to bed,' he told her. 'You look tired out.'

'Do I?'

'Either that or this connection is getting worse.' He chuckled.

'I *am* a bit tired,' she admitted.

She said good night, signed off and closed the computer. Then she crawled into bed. She was suddenly exhausted. He'd said that she looked tired out. Should she have Skyped him looking wretched? Friends were OK about seeing each other tired out, weren't they? All the same, she didn't like the idea of him seeing her looking knackered! She thumped the pillow in frustration. If she didn't care, then what the hell did she want? Right now, she didn't know. What she did know, though, what she was absolutely sure about was that if it had been Veronica calling someone, friend or not, she wouldn't have done it without putting on her make-up first.

Chapter 18

Kathryn didn't know where she was when she woke up the following morning. She rolled over, eyes half open, and turned anxiously to look for Alan, but when she saw the empty bed beside her she remembered that she was in Ireland and that Alan wasn't here and that she was on her own. Her heart, which had begun to race, slowed down again. She opened her eyes fully and gazed around the bedroom.

Even though it had changed completely, it still felt like her room. The sun was streaming through the voile-curtained windows and flooding it with morning light. Last night's storm had blown itself out and the weather was glorious again. She looked at the silver watch on her wrist and realised that it was almost eleven. Eleven in the morning! She couldn't remember the last time she'd slept so late. Usually she had a mound of work done by that hour and, at the weekends, as Alan wasn't someone who enjoyed sleeping in, she was always up early too. He usually went for an early-morning jog around Central Park on Saturdays and Sundays and liked to come home to his breakfast at eight thirty. Eggs and bacon. It revolted her, but she always had it ready for him.

Eleven in the morning! It was unbelievable.

She got out of bed, gingerly stretching her aching arms over her head before going downstairs. The kitchen door was open and she could see the top of Romy's head over the back of one of Veronica's garden chairs.

'Well hello there,' said Romy as Kathryn came out on to the deck. 'Glad to see you've finally rejoined the land of the living.'

'I was obviously more tired than I thought.' Kathryn pulled the collar of her rose cotton pyjamas closer around her neck.

'Like the PJs,' remarked Romy.

'Thanks.'

'Even your sleepwear is nice,' said Romy. 'You've changed so much.'

Kathryn shrugged. 'Not really.'

'Yes really,' said Romy. 'I can't believe how amazing you look! Mum showed me a photo of you from a newspaper clipping and I thought you looked fabulous, but – and I know we didn't have time to talk about it last night what with me being about to brain you with a hockey stick – but . . . you look like Mum.'

'I do not!' Kathryn was taken aback.

'In a good way,' said Romy hastily. 'You know, when she gets it totally right and everything matches and she's not trying to look like some teenager out for the night or Dolly Parton on speed . . . more like when she does her Board Member of Dolan's look.'

'I hardly think I'd be going to board meetings like this.'

'You know what I mean,' said Romy testily. 'You've got the look, Kathryn, that's what I'm saying. The Veronica look.'

'You're talking utter rubbish, but whatever.' Kathryn was dismissive.

'*And* you're model thin,' said Romy. 'You must be on some mad New York Fifth Avenue Princess diet.'

'For heaven's sake, Ro, New York isn't another world,' said Kathryn. 'I live a normal life there.'

'You couldn't possibly,' said Romy. 'You look like someone who lives a . . . an exclusive life. Which I guess you do, being married to the mogul and everything.'

'You're being silly,' Kathryn told her.

Romy shrugged. 'So what d'you want to do today?'

'I was rather expecting to see Mum. Will she be still in hospital or is she coming home?'

'I rang earlier,' Romy told her. 'She'll be there for one more night. She's got rid of the kidney stone . . .' she scrunched up her face, 'but she was in panic mode yesterday and reckoned that her days were numbered so she's probably trying to persuade them that she's actually suffering from some fatal disease and to do a test for Ebola or something.'

Kathryn laughed. 'That's harsh.'

'Actually I think she's probably just staying there to get away from me for another night,' said Romy ruefully.

'Haven't you two been getting along?'

'Um. Well, I'm trying my best but I get the feeling that every time she looks at me she's wondering where the hell she went wrong, and every time I look at her I'm thinking "Is she really my mum?" and so it can be a bit . . . testy.'

'You don't make allowances,' said Kathryn.

'Allowances!' Romy laughed. 'What allowances do I need to make, for heaven's sake?'

'She's living on her own,' said Kathryn. 'She has her own way of doing things. It's probably just as hard for her to have you here.'

'I know, I know. I think the problem is that she needs me around the place but I'm actually going demented with boredom.'

'So get a job.'

'People keep telling me that,' said Romy irritably. 'I'm not expecting to stay here long enough to need a job.'

'Oh, I forgot. Running away again.'

Romy looked at her in astonishment. 'I don't run away.'

'Whatever.'

'I *don't*.'

'OK, OK.'

'I have a job that means I travel,' said Romy. 'That's not

running away. Anyway, you can talk! Living in the States. At least I can come home whenever I want. You've moved lock, stock and barrel.'

'I got married,' said Kathryn.

'And you didn't invite Dad.' Romy couldn't resist the jibe.

Kathryn sighed. 'I'm not going to go through all this with you, Romy. You know why.'

Romy looked impassive.

'I wanted him to come. I would've loved him to be there. But what was the point? I didn't want a bust-up and there would've been one. You know that. So did Dad. I was sorry you didn't come but I realised that you were too busy.'

Romy blushed. 'I'm sorry I didn't come either,' she said finally. 'I should've.'

'I'll make us some coffee.' Kathryn smiled at Romy, then went inside and poured water into the filter machine. While she waited for it to brew she hurried upstairs and took her phone and her cigarettes out of her bag. She'd bought more at the airport. Right now, she hadn't managed to give them up. She shook a cigarette out of the pack and lit it, then walked back out to the deck and took a deep drag of smoke.

There were no messages on her phone. She didn't know whether she was surprised or not. Part of her had expected him to call. But another part of her wondered whether he'd change his mind about her now that she'd gone. In the note she'd said that she was going to her mum's for a week or so, just to see how she was. She'd said that she'd call him. But she hadn't quite believed that he wouldn't try to reach her first.

'I thought I'd go over to the hospital around two.' Romy's voice floated across to her. 'Darragh – and Giselle if she's coming – normally get there about three. I don't usually hang around while they're there but of course you're welcome to.'

'Two is fine,' said Kathryn. 'And after that . . . we'll see.'

'You can do whatever you like till then,' said Romy.

'I know I can,' said Kathryn. 'This is my home too after all.' She winced as she said the words, thinking that they would be like a red rag to Romy. But her sister just shrugged and then looked at her in sudden surprise.

'You're smoking!' Romy had smelt the cigarette smoke but it hadn't registered with her till now. 'You! Miss Organic Food 1995.'

Kathryn had done a school project about the potential for the organic food industry to be big business long before it had caught the public imagination. Her project had received the school prize for best work of the year. Kathryn had insisted on eating only organic produce all the time she'd been researching it, which had driven Veronica (going through the separation from Dermot at the time) utterly distracted.

'A minor vice,' said Kathryn.

'But . . . smoking!' Romy was truly astonished. 'It's so not you.'

'People change,' she said.

'Obviously.'

'But you haven't.' Kathryn inhaled deeply and then ground out the cigarette. 'No, you have your principles and you'll stick to them for ever, no matter what else changes in the meantime.'

Romy watched her as she walked back inside the house. Her back was ramrod straight. And her body seemed thinner than ever beneath her elegant pyjamas.

They set out for the hospital at half past one. They hadn't spoken much for the rest of the morning – Romy had pottered around the house doing various unnecessary chores and Kathryn had spent most of the time in the bathroom, luxuriating in a long, hot bath and giving herself a face mask and other beauty treatments.

She looked refreshed and elegant as she stepped out of the

car and Romy felt like an awkward schoolgirl beside her. She was annoyed with Kathryn for having betrayed everything she'd ever stood for – for her expertly plucked eyebrows and her almost translucent, polished skin; for her elegant new wardrobe and her gleaming, serum-enriched hair. Romy might not always have got on with Kathryn in the past (although their differences were only of personality, not of actively disliking each other) but at least they'd been two of a kind as far as beauty was concerned. Romy wished that she'd changed out of her usual jeans and T-shirt and into something classier before leaving the house. And then she wondered when she'd ever learn her lesson about clothes, because she always felt underdressed whenever she was with the female members of the family.

Veronica had been moved to a private room and had almost completely recovered from her misery of the previous day. She was propped up in bed, surrounded by gossip magazines and, once again, perfectly made up. Her eyes brightened at the sight of Kathryn and she cooed in delight at her tailored trouser suit – deep red this time, which enhanced Kathryn's creamy skin and dark hair.

'Come and tell me everything,' she cried. 'All about New York and all about Alan and all about your life!'

Romy perched on the window ledge while Veronica and Kathryn talked (or at least while Veronica fired rapid questions at Kathryn and she answered them) and daydreamed about returning to Australia. Maybe things with Keith would be back to normal in Australia and she'd stop feeling like some lovesick teenager and thinking of him in this weird boyfriend way that was all wrong.

'I'll go out for a bit of air,' she said eventually. 'Kathryn, you can meet me in the garden outside when you're finished.'

'Why are you going?' demanded Veronica. 'Stay and talk with us.'

But Romy shrugged and left the room.

Veronica stared after her.

'I guess she's feeling a bit left out,' said Kathryn.

'Oh, you know Romy. It's her way or no way,' Veronica told her. 'I try my hardest and sometimes I feel we connect, but mostly . . .' She shrugged helplessly.

'She sees things differently,' said Kathryn. 'Like I do. Only differently again.'

'That's true,' Veronica said. 'So what are your future plans? Children?'

Kathryn wanted to snap at Veronica in the same way as she'd snapped at Romy but she didn't. She just said that right now children weren't on the agenda. It was funny how easy that was to say, as though they might be on the agenda at some time in the future. Well, they might, she supposed. But not in their joint future. Never in a joint future. She wanted to say this to Veronica too but she couldn't. Not now. She was amazed at how little she was telling anyone. Amazed at how she was managing to compartmentalise her life.

'You've done a lot of work to the house.' It was easier to change the subject altogether. 'My room is lovely.'

Veronica smiled with pleasure. 'I'm glad you like it. Romy didn't say a thing about the décor! But I got people in last year and did everything. Made it all so much lighter and brighter. I was feeling as though I was rattling around in a mausoleum.'

'You still don't want to sell it?'

'It's my home!' cried Veronica. 'Our home! Where I've always lived. I can't sell it. It's . . . well, your father's memories are all there.'

Kathryn nodded although she couldn't help thinking that Veronica was holding on to an awful lot of memories when it might be better to let some of them go.

There was a tap at the door and Darragh and Giselle entered. They exclaimed in surprise to see Kathryn there and then hugged her while Veronica smiled happily from her bed.

'We should get together for dinner,' said Giselle. 'When you're out of hospital, Veronica. At our house.'

'Great idea!' exclaimed Darragh.

'Dinner would be lovely,' agreed Veronica. 'But let me organise it. It would be nice to have all of us together again, in the family home.'

'You can't possibly,' said Darragh quickly. 'It would be far too much work.'

'Kathryn and Romy can help,' said Veronica enthusiastically. 'It'll be fun.'

'You could do without the pressure,' said Darragh doubtfully.

'It won't be any pressure.' Veronica was really cheerful now. 'We can have a traditional dinner and talk to each other, catch up as a family . . . It'll be wonderful.'

Kathryn said nothing. As far as she remembered, their traditional family dinners had generally been eaten in silence because someone was usually fighting with someone else. But she didn't want to burst her mother's bubble of excitement.

'Am I invited?' asked Giselle.

'Of course you are,' said Veronica. 'What are you thinking, Giselle? You're family.'

'Not part of your traditional family,' she reminded Veronica.

'You're probably one of the most important parts,' her mother-in-law said warmly. 'And we couldn't possibly get together without you.'

'Easier to get together without Romy,' said Darragh.

'Darragh Dolan!' Two pink spots appeared on Veronica's cheeks. 'You're not to talk like that about your sister. She's doing her best.'

There was an awkward silence and then Darragh shrugged apologetically. 'Sorry.' He looked around. 'Where is she anyway?'

'She went out to give me and Mum some time alone,' said Kathryn. She looked at her narrow watch on its silver bracelet.

'I guess I'd probably better go look for her. I don't think she planned to come back to the room.'

'I'll drop you home if you like,' said Darragh. 'In fact, Katy, if you want to stay with us instead of at Mum's . . .'

'I'll be home tomorrow,' said Veronica. 'She can't leave!'

'It's fine,' said Kathryn. 'I'm happy to stay with Mum.'

Veronica smiled again.

'Fair enough,' said Darragh. 'We'll see you soon.'

Kathryn stood up, hugged everyone (wincing at the strength of Darragh's arms around her shoulders; she didn't think he cared that much about her) and then walked out of the room.

It was weird being back. She hadn't come home since her marriage and she'd expected it to be different when she did. But somehow she felt as though she were slotting right back into her life again. It was easy to be home. Easy to be with Veronica and Darragh and Romy – even though she'd hated it (and them) so much before she'd gone to the States. But, she wondered, had her feelings changed or was it just that home had suddenly become a refuge when it had always been a place to escape from before?

Romy was sitting on one of the benches in the grounds of the hospital. She knew that she'd been right to leave Kathryn on her own with Veronica so that they could have time together but then while she was getting a coffee in the cafeteria near the hospital lobby she'd seen Darragh and Giselle sweep upstairs; Darragh looking every inch the businessman in his Louis Copeland suit and Giselle, striking as ever, wearing a loose dress in pearl pink. And suddenly she was wishing that she'd stayed in the room so that they weren't all together without her. The feelings of isolation which were never far away threatened to overwhelm her and she'd taken the waxed cup outside and sat on the bench beneath a cherry blossom tree.

Did other people feel like this? she wondered. Did other

adult children still feel like the odd one out? So many marriages were second, third or even fourth attempts these days that there must be plenty of offspring who didn't connect with each other, and yet nobody ever talked about it. From what she could see, everyone seemed to get on just fine. And maybe they did. Maybe it was just her.

What did it matter, in the end? She was happy doing her own thing, wasn't she? She didn't need to be part of a story-book family to be happy herself. Her life was fine the way it was. There was nothing that being closer to Darragh or Kathryn or Veronica would do to make it any better.

'Hi, Romy!' Kathryn's voice carried across the air and she looked up. Her half-sister waved at her. 'Ready to go?'

Romy stood up. 'I thought you'd have been there for much longer what with the big family reunion going on.'

Kathryn laughed. 'You saw Darragh and Giselle arrive? And you didn't come up?'

'Are you off your rocker?' Romy grinned at her. 'Me and Darragh have already had as much of each other as we can take, and Giselle . . .' She shrugged expressively. 'Giselle does whatever Darragh wants.'

'She looks fantastic, doesn't she?' said Kathryn. 'She has that pregnant glow about her even though I've never seen anyone with a smaller bump in my life. And so glamorous with it!'

'I know,' said Romy glumly. 'Every time she calls over to the house I can see Mum looking at her and looking at me and wondering where in God's name she went wrong.'

Kathryn laughed. 'Not really.'

'Oh yes,' said Romy. 'And now that you've betrayed me . . .'

'Betrayed you?'

'Like I said before, you've gone all glam too!' Romy laughed suddenly. 'I'm left as the only one in the family who doesn't get all her body hair waxed on a regular basis.'

'I don't get all my body hair waxed,' Kathryn assured her.

'No? I thought everyone in New York did.'

'You've got some mad notions,' Kathryn said. 'And Darragh's right, you know. You haul an awful lot of chips around on that shoulder with you.'

'Give me a break.' Romy's smile faded and she started to walk towards the car park.

'Slow down.' Kathryn fell into step beside her. 'All I'm saying, Ro, is that you don't have to think the worst all the time. And it doesn't all revolve around you.'

Romy turned to her. 'What d'you mean?'

'It's always been about how hard-done-by you feel,' said Kathryn. 'Don't you think that me and Darragh have issues too?'

'Darragh? Issues!' Romy looked at her incredulously. 'That bloke doesn't know what an issue is.'

'You're wrong about that,' said Kathryn. 'We all have our own problems.'

'Yeah, well, perhaps yours are more easily solved than mine.' Romy shoved the parking ticket into the machine to validate it.

'I really wouldn't be so sure about that,' Kathryn told her, but Romy was collecting her change and wasn't really listening.

Romy had previously arranged to meet Colleen that evening, and despite her telling Kathryn that she'd cancel, Kathryn insisted that she wanted to be on her own for a while. Like Romy had when she'd first arrived, she wandered from room to room as memories flooded back to her. In the den she remembered the times when she'd sat with Dermot as he kept files and folders up to date. He used to sing while he worked and sometimes she'd sing along with him. She'd enjoyed those times even after Darragh had told her that Dermot wasn't her real father. That had been a shock. It had never occurred to her that the man who'd been there all her life and who she automatically called Dad wasn't actually her father. She couldn't remember how old she was at the time but she knew that she'd been quite young and she'd been telling Darragh about a toy that Dermot was going to buy her. And Darragh had looked angrily at her and told her that Dermot was trying to buy her affection because he wasn't her dad. She remembered crying and running to Veronica, who had sat her down and told her that even though Dermot wasn't her natural father he was a really nice man who loved her just as much.

Darragh disagreed. Dermot wasn't a really nice man, he said. And he didn't love them. He didn't love Veronica either. He only pretended. The only one he really loved was Romy.

Kathryn had spent a lot of time checking to see if Dermot was pretending. She would deliberately disobey him to see whether he reacted differently to her disobedience than to Romy's. It was hard to tell. He would scold her, of course, and say that she should have more sense. And he'd sometimes tell her that she was bigger than Romy and should know better. But he never sounded any angrier with her than he did with Romy; in fact Kathryn thought he could be very cross with his natural daughter (like the time she tore up a selection of his photos and stuck them back together again with Sellotape – she'd said that she was making a jigsaw) and would snap at her and tell her that she should be more like her older sister. Kathryn liked Dermot saying things like that. It meant that he approved of her and saw her as Romy's older sister and not just another kid in the house.

But whenever she tried to say all these things to Darragh he would dismiss them and tell her that she was being trapped by Dermot's charm and that she had to stand firm because they were Dolans, not Kilkennys, and they always would be. She knew that being a Dolan was important. She knew that it set her apart from Romy even though she didn't really want to be set apart from Romy because she liked the idea of having a sister. Especially one who, like her, wasn't in the slightest bit interested in clothes!

Well, she thought grimly, I'm a Palmer now. Neither a Dolan nor a Kilkenny. I have a new identity. And I am interested in clothes after all.

She looked at her mobile phone again but there were still no messages and still no missed calls. She supposed that she should feel relieved about that. But actually all she felt was worried.

Later that night, after she'd returned from a relaxed and gossipy evening with Colleen during which she hadn't given Veronica or any of the Dolans a moment's thought, Romy sat in front of her computer and read her email messages.

There were the usual group joke messages and one from Tanya saying that she was in Melbourne and it was great and that she hoped Romy wasn't too disappointed about missing out but that she was sure she'd be back soon. Romy gritted her teeth and told herself that – as everyone else said – there'd be plenty of other opportunities.

And then, as she scrolled through the messages, another one appeared in her in-box. It was from Keith again and he'd pasted a hyperlink to a site where jobs for a new dig in Ireland were being offered. She clicked on the link.

Seeking to appoint a number of archaeologists, including supervisors, for development project in Wicklow. Project will last approximately 3 months. Some team members may transfer to the post-excavation team thereafter. Successful applicants will need to be good team workers, flexible and motivated. Training provided to enable career development. Email CV to address below. Include references and contact details.

Keith had written that he thought it was near enough to her to interest her. And that a three-month project wouldn't be a bad thing to be involved in. And that the pay was better than usual. And that it might stop her moping.

She frowned as she flicked between his message and the job ad. Why had he sent it to her? Was it a hint? Don't come back to Australia. Don't come to Perth. Stay away from me, you possessive, needy loser. She could imagine him thinking like that despite him assuring her to her face that everything was 'cool' and that there were 'no worries'. After all, ever since she'd told him about having to come home all she'd done was be tearful and clingy. He'd never seen her like that before. She couldn't blame him if he didn't want her near him. He might be a friend, she realised, but he could just be a fair-weather friend. He was there for her when things were going well, when everything was fun and interesting. But he didn't really want to know when things were going badly. And she couldn't blame him for that.

She clicked on the Heritage Help site. There was a small story about the dig in Melbourne. Everything was on schedule. They didn't need her there. She'd only be in the way.

She felt tears pricking the back of her eyes. She didn't matter to them. She didn't matter to Keith either. But at the moment she mattered very much to Veronica.

She returned to the job ad. They were looking for supervisors and talked about training . . . She'd told everyone that she wanted to get on in her career and this was an opportunity to get on. So which was more important? Gaining the experience and training that was possible with this job? Or going back to Australia simply because she'd gone on and on about returning? (And because she'd spent nights imagining arriving back at the airport to find Keith waiting for her, telling her how devastated he'd been without her. But the point was that he wasn't devastated. Someone who was devastated without you didn't post links to jobs thousands of miles away!)

If she got this job, though, she'd be committing herself to at least another three months in Ireland. She wouldn't, of course, have to stay with Veronica. She could stay with her for a little longer, until she was more mobile and over her recent illness. A few weeks maybe. And then she could move to Wicklow, which wasn't very far away. It was coming into the summer, after all, and a nice time to be home.

If she wanted to be home.

She didn't know what to do. And she was still thinking about the job as she came downstairs again to join Kathryn in front of the TV.

Chapter 19

Romy collected Veronica from the hospital the following day. Her mother had been given a clean bill of health and it seemed to Romy that Veronica was even walking with more confidence now. She was standing in the lobby when Romy arrived and she looked a million times better than she had over the previous weeks. She was (having ordered Romy to bring them in the previous night) wearing another pair of her wide palazzo pants and another one of her vibrant kaftans Her hair was swept back and held by a mother-of-pearl comb and she'd spent time and effort on her make-up. Her eyes were outlined in smoky grey, her lashes were coated in dark brown mascara, her cheeks had been brushed with a shimmering powder and her lips were glossed with a soft pink colour.

'You look great,' Romy told her sincerely and Veronica looked at her in surprise. 'No, really,' Romy said. 'Until now t was clear that you were feeling rotten and in pain and miserble – it's good to see you back to your old self again.'

'Not quite my old self,' said Veronica. 'My back's still a bit odgy and I'm in flat shoes.'

'Perhaps,' agreed Romy. 'But you still look as good as you er did.'

'You're very cheerful all of a sudden,' Veronica remarked hey headed for the car park. 'And I didn't think you liked old self.'

'I don't know about being especially cheerful,' said Romy. 'But I'm pleased that you're OK.'

'Did you care?'

'Of course I cared.' Romy led the way to the car. 'I still do. So does Kathryn. And Darragh, of course. And so does Dad.'

Veronica stopped with her hand on the door handle of the car. 'Your father?'

'He asks after you whenever I talk to him.'

'Only in the hopes of hearing that I've fallen down the stairs and broken my neck,' said Veronica.

'Mum!' Romy shook her head. 'He was sorry to hear about your back and about your kidney stones too. I did tell you that. But you were probably too dazed to remember.'

'Goodness. Your father and you both concerned about me. That's a turn-up.'

'Dad was always concerned about you,' said Romy.

'Don't be silly,' said Veronica as they got into the car and Romy started the engine. 'He didn't give a damn.'

'You're being unfair on him,' Romy said evenly as she reversed out of the parking space.

'Look, I know he's the apple of your eye and can do no wrong,' said Veronica. 'But the truth of it is that the only thing he really cared about was that damn job of his.'

'It was important to him.'

'And we weren't?'

Romy said nothing. Veronica had a point; she'd said more or less the same thing to Dermot herself. But she didn't like conceding to Veronica that Dermot was less than perfect.

'It doesn't matter any more,' Veronica added. 'You shouldn't dwell on it.'

'I guess not.' Romy lowered the window and fed her parking ticket into the machine.

'I did love him.'

Romy turned towards her mother, startled by the comm

Veronica shrugged helplessly. 'Of course I did. He was gorgeous and handsome and why on earth *wouldn't* I love him?'

'You used to shout at him. You wanted him to give up his job.'

'That's true. We had a beautiful daughter to consider. And despite what he said, it was a dangerous job.'

Romy tightened her grip on the steering wheel.

'You'd better move,' Veronica told her. 'Otherwise that barrier might come down.'

Romy drove out of the car park, still without speaking.

'I didn't want the marriage to fail,' said Veronica. 'I really didn't.'

'You loved Tom more.' Romy was looking straight ahead, watching the traffic.

Veronica glanced at her. 'No I didn't.'

'You've gone back to calling yourself Veronica Dolan.'

'I know,' said Veronica. 'Well, after the divorce it seemed the right thing to do. And then after splitting up with Larry . . .' She sighed. 'I reckoned I should just stay Dolan. It was luckier for me.'

'Perhaps.'

'Don't judge me,' said Veronica.

'Hard not to sometimes.'

The two of them were silent and then Veronica spoke again.

'Did Kathryn say how long she was going to stay?'

Romy shook her head.

'I hope it'll be for a bit longer,' said Veronica. 'It's nice to have both my girls at home for a while.'

Romy raised her eyebrows.

'You haven't fought with her yet, have you?' asked Veronica.

'Nope.' Romy wasn't going to tell Veronica that she'd intended to brain Kathryn with a hockey stick.

'You were dreadful cat-fighters,' said her mother. 'I remember lumps of hair being pulled out of each other's heads. And yet there were times when you seemed to be good friends.'

'It was a volatile relationship,' Romy said. 'But we're supposed to be grown-ups now, so maybe that makes a difference.'

'Perhaps.' Veronica looked hopeful. 'Did she tell you about the dinner?'

'No.'

'I'm going to have a family get-together,' said Veronica. 'All of us for dinner.'

Romy's heart sank. It seemed to her that any occasion that involved all of them would only end in arguments. They couldn't help themselves. And she couldn't help asking who exactly came under the heading of family.

'My three children and me,' continued Veronica. 'All together for the first time in years. And Giselle too, of course.'

It would be a nightmare, thought Romy, but she could do it. If she had to. All she had to do – as Keith had told her before – was to say nothing. To rise above it. Ignore it completely.

'It'll be fun,' Veronica added. 'It's such a long time since we've been together as a family.'

Romy bit her tongue. She wanted to say that they'd never conformed to Veronica's idealised picture of how a family should be and that they were hardly likely to start now, but she didn't want to dampen her mother's enthusiasm. It was only now, seeing Veronica animated about something, that Romy realised just how depressed her mother had been.

'Perhaps it'd be better to go to a restaurant,' said Romy, who reckoned there was less chance of some kind of fight breaking out between them all if they were in public.

'Nonsense,' said Veronica firmly. 'I want to have everyone at home.'

'What about Alan?'

'Alan?'

'Kathryn's husband.'

Veronica looked thoughtful. 'I wonder if he could come

over.' She turned to Romy and smiled. 'Good idea. Wouldn't that be lovely?'

Lovely wasn't the word she'd use, admitted Romy to herself. It would still be a nightmare, perhaps even more so with Darragh and Kathryn flaunting their wonderful spouses while she was on her own. She wrinkled her nose. She didn't mind being on her own! On her own wasn't failure. She was perfectly happy to be young, free and single. She really was. Why was it, she wondered, that when you were quite happily single but you found yourself in a group with people who were married, you ended up feeling totally inadequate?

But not everyone in the group would be married, she reminded herself. Veronica was footloose and fancy-free too. Finally, she thought with a sliver of amusement, I have something in common with my mother!

Kathryn had organised a salad for lunch when they got home. She'd arranged everything on the table outside so the three of them sat on the sunny deck and ate, keeping their conversation light-hearted and trivial. Veronica reminded Kathryn about her plan for a family dinner and Romy saw the same look of foreboding pass across her sister's face as she knew had passed across her own. But Kathryn simply said that she planned to stay for a week or so and that if Veronica wanted to ask Darragh and Giselle over that was fine but there was no need to make a big deal out of it.

Veronica asked about Alan coming to Ireland but Kathryn very quickly said that she didn't think it would be possible, that Alan was extremely busy and it would hardly be worth the effort for him to come over for just a day or two.

'That's a shame,' said Veronica. 'It would have been nice to have everybody around me.'

Romy was thinking that at least if Alan wasn't there she

wouldn't be the one to stick out like a sore thumb as the unattached loser.

'I know I'm not having alcohol, but are you sure you girls don't want some wine?' asked Veronica as she dipped the last of the bread into some olive oil. 'It seems a shame not to have something crisp and cold with the food.'

'Not for me,' said Kathryn quickly. 'I'm off it for a while.'

'Me neither.' Romy shook her head. She didn't want to be the only one whose tongue might be loosened by the effect of a glass or two of Chardonnay.

'You're both being far too sensible,' said Veronica.

'Old age,' said Romy and then wished she hadn't.

Her mother raised her eyebrows.

'But you don't look a day over forty today,' said Romy. 'You really don't.'

'Do you think it matters so much to me that I can't take a joke?' demanded Veronica.

'Truthfully,' said Romy, 'yes.'

Veronica shook her head. 'You don't know me at all.'

Romy was glad that the ringing of the doorbell prevented her from answering. She'd been about to say that she knew Veronica only too well and she also knew that wouldn't have been the right comment to make. She got up to answer the door, telling Kathryn it was fine, she'd do it, yet pleased that suddenly she wasn't the only one having to rush around the place all the time.

A couple of minutes later she was escorting an attractive grey-haired woman out to the deck.

'Bernice.' Veronica smiled at her. 'How lovely to see you.'

Bernice kissed Veronica on the cheek. 'And you too. You poor thing, you've been through the mill a bit.'

'I'm over it now,' said Veronica. 'All I need is for my back to finally heal and I'll be as good as new.'

'Excellent,' said Bernice. 'And you'll be back to the bridge club?'

'Of course.' Veronica turned to Kathryn and Romy. 'Girls, this is Bernice McBride. She's the chairwoman of the bridge club. Bernice, these are my daughters. Romy, who let you in. And Kathryn.'

'I've heard all about you,' said Bernice as she sat down opposite them.

'Really?' Romy looked at her enquiringly. 'Good or bad?'

Bernice laughed. 'Only good,' she said.

'Would you like a glass of wine?' asked Veronica. 'My daughters are being madly abstemious and I can't at the moment, but there's some lovely Chardonnay in the fridge . . .'

'I'd love to but I'm driving,' said Bernice. 'And it doesn't take much to tip me over the limit, I'm afraid.'

'We've all become far too sensible,' said Veronica gloomily.

'Kathryn and I will leave you two to chat,' Romy told Veronica. 'I was thinking . . . would you like us to move your stuff upstairs again? Do you feel able to reclaim your own bedroom?'

'I think so,' said Veronica happily. 'That'd be nice, thanks.'

They brought some of the used crockery back to the house and stacked it in the dishwasher. Romy asked Kathryn if she'd like to help move Veronica's stuff upstairs. She told her how difficult she'd found it bringing everything down, seeing her mother's lingerie and shoe collection, peering, she told Kathryn, into Veronica's soul.

'Drama queen.' Kathryn laughed. 'So what if she likes nice underwear? So do we all.'

Romy remembered Kathryn's bras and knickers when they'd been younger – plain cotton M&S with nothing exotic or erotic about them. Maybe it's another Veronica gene that's missing in me, she thought. One that had eventually popped up in Kathryn. She shook her head briefly as though it would dislodge the sudden image of Kathryn and Veronica wandering around the house in basques and suspenders. I'm losing it, she muttered to herself. I truly am.

It only took a couple of trips to bring everything upstairs again. Kathryn brought the last of the bottles and jars into the en suite bathroom and then shrieked as a bottle of body lotion slipped from her grasp and thudded on to the floor. The bottle was hard plastic and split rather than broke, but there was mimosa-scented crème everywhere.

Romy came into the bathroom as Kathryn was cleaning up.

'It's nice to see someone other than me have a moment like this,' she said.

'I'd've thought you were super careful about stuff,' remarked Kathryn as she dumped another tissue into the rubbish bin. 'You can't afford to crush bones or things like that, can you?'

Romy shrugged. 'I am super careful when I have to be,' she agreed. 'At work. But at home I'm like Nellie the Elephant thumping around the place. Oh, you've got lotion on the back of your lovely blouse! How the hell did you manage that?' And she reached out to wipe it away.

'I'm fine!' Kathryn flinched and recoiled as Romy touched her shoulder.

'What's the matter with you?' Romy looked at her in astonishment.

'Sorry,' said Kathryn. 'You took me by surprise.'

'I was only trying to wipe the lotion away,' Romy told her. 'There's no need for you to leap around the place like a wounded gazelle.'

'Oh, relax.' Kathryn stood up and checked her collar in the bathroom mirror.

'I'm perfectly relaxed,' said Romy. 'It's you . . .'

'Yeah, yeah, I'm sorry,' Kathryn said as she tugged at the collar. 'Anyhow, it's fine. No harm done. Just a little mark and that'll come out in the wash.'

'It's silk, isn't it?' said Romy.

'Um. Yes.'

'So – dry-clean only.'

'You're right.' Kathryn threw the split bottle of moisturiser into the wastepaper bin and wiped her hands on a towel. 'D'you think Mum will flip over this stuff? It's very expensive.'

'Maybe she won't notice.'

'I'd notice! I think what I'll do is nip out and replace it.'

'Kathryn, she has loads of moisturisers. You don't have to rush off and get another one straight away. Besides, you might have to go into town for that. I doubt they sell it in the chemist down the road.'

'I'll check it out.' Kathryn wiped her hands and smiled at Romy. 'Or maybe I'll stroll into Rathfarnham village. I'm sure I can pick it up there. I'll be back soon.'

'Well . . . OK.' But Romy was talking to Kathryn's back. She had already walked out of the room.

Kathryn went straight to her bedroom and picked up her handbag. Then she left the house without saying anything to Bernice or Veronica, who were still sitting outside. The sound of her mother's laughter floated across the garden as she strode down the gravelled driveway. It was good to hear her mother laugh, thought Kathryn. At least it meant that some things in the family were getting back to normal.

The chemist in the village didn't sell Veronica's moisturiser. Kathryn hadn't really expected it to but she'd wanted to get out of the house and that had been her best excuse. Because she'd been horribly afraid that suddenly Romy would put two and two together and start asking questions, and she wasn't ready to answer them yet. If she ever would be. Her sister was so inquisitive! Kathryn supposed that was why she'd ended up doing what she was doing, that it was her nature to want to poke around and ask questions (even if everyone she was asking questions about was long dead). And she never let things go.

She was dogged. That was what Kathryn remembered most clearly about her.

She remembered the evenings when Romy was doing her homework and she'd look up and ask Veronica questions like 'Why is the earth round?' and Veronica would answer and then Romy would come back with another question like 'Why is the sun exactly far enough away?' and Veronica would try to answer that too but would eventually be stumped by yet another 'why' question from Romy so that she'd end up snapping at her to just do her bloody homework and stop getting diverted into other things. And then Kathryn would usually end up having a discussion with her younger sister (even after Darragh told her about them having different fathers she found it impossible to think of Romy as anything other than her younger sister) about the universe or biology or whatever it was that Romy was most curious about at that moment.

But there was a time for satisfying Romy's curiosity and a time for keeping things to herself.

She was standing outside the pub when she started to shake. It had only happened to her once before, this sudden inability to stop herself from trembling. She tried to breathe evenly and slowly but she knew that she was hyperventilating. She pushed open the door of the pub and went inside. It was almost deserted. A young couple were having a drink at one end of the bar and two older men were chatting over pints at the other.

She sat down abruptly in one of the seats and took her cigarettes out of her bag. She shook one out of the carton, aware that her fingers were trembling, and lit it.

'I'm afraid I'll have to ask you to put that out,' said the barman.

Kathryn looked at him uncomprehendingly.

'The cigarette,' he said. 'No smoking. It's the law.'

'Oh. Yes. Sorry.' She pinched it to extinguish it. 'I didn't realise what I was doing.'

'Can I get you a drink instead?'

She was supposed to have given up drinking too. But if she couldn't smoke, maybe alcohol would help instead.

'Vodka and tonic.'

He poured the measure. She handed him some money and took the drink to a corner seat. She swallowed it in three gulps.

I didn't want to do that, she thought. I'm supposed to have taken control of my life. But she'd needed the drink. She really had. Because she'd been so afraid . . . She pushed the glass away from her. Drinking wouldn't stop her from being afraid. Drinking didn't even help her to forget that she *was* afraid. She stared into the distance.

'Can I get you another?' asked the barman.

She didn't want another. But she didn't want to go home either. Not yet.

She pushed her glass towards him and he poured another measure.

She didn't care if it didn't help. Right now, it was a comfort.

Romy finished putting away Veronica's things and went to join her mother and Bernice outside. As she'd been tidying up it had occurred to her that Bernice was the first female who'd called to see Veronica since her operation. Until now her visitors had been mainly men, like Will Blake, who'd dropped by a couple of times, or Noel from the musical society, and another man whose name Romy had forgotten – something to do with a charity auction . . . It had been men who'd phoned to enquire how she was too. Romy wondered whether Veronica just got on better with men than women. It was quite possible, she thought. Perhaps other women saw Veronica and decided that she was a threat.

Maybe Bernice was confident enough not to think that way.

She was immaculately groomed and stylishly dressed herself, although, thought Romy with a sudden flash of realisation, she wasn't attractive in the same way as Veronica. There was something about her mother . . . not that she wanted to admit it . . . but something about Veronica that was slightly mischievous, something definitely sexy, something which made you think she'd be fun to know. Bernice didn't seem as though she'd be fun to know.

'I'm trying to persuade Veronica to come on our bridge trip to Cork,' said Bernice. 'A long weekend with the option of staying on a few more days if we want.'

'Why do you need persuading?' asked Romy.

'I'm not sure I want to sit in a car for four hours,' said Veronica. 'I'm not sure if I can, to tell you the truth.'

'Get the train,' said Romy. 'Then you can walk around.'

'That's what I suggested,' said Bernice. 'A few of us plan to travel by train.'

'So that's perfect,' said Romy. 'And by then you'll be even better – you know how quickly you were improving before you got sidetracked by the kidney stones.'

'Well . . .'

'You should definitely go.' Romy's voice was firm.

'You just want me out of the house.'

Romy looked at Veronica. 'Not really,' she said. 'I just think it would be good for you. And it's not for long.'

'I still can't get around so well.' She shook her head. 'I'm slow and creaky.'

'One thing you'll never be is slow and creaky,' said Romy.

Veronica looked at her in surprise.

'She's right,' said Bernice. 'Besides, think of the rest of the group.'

The two women looked at each other and chuckled.

'Marty Murphy,' said Veronica.

'Nora Gallagher.'

'Theresa Lynch.'

'Gordon Hayes.' Bernice's eyes twinkled. 'See, Veronica. You make that lot look sprightly.'

Veronica laughed. 'I'll think about it,' she promised.

'Excellent,' said Bernice. She stood up. 'I'd better get going. I'm glad you're feeling better.'

'I'll call you,' Veronica told her.

Romy let Bernice out of the house and then came back to join her mother.

'You should think seriously about this trip,' she said.

'It'd get me out of your hair,' said Veronica.

'Yes, it would. But that's not the point.'

'When are you thinking about going back to Australia?'

The question came out of the blue and Romy looked at her mother in confusion.

'I know you can hardly wait,' said Veronica drily. 'I know you were all set to rush off before I fell ill.'

'Well, actually . . .' Romy shrugged, 'I've applied for a job in Wicklow. Just for three months,' she added quickly. 'Nothing long-term.'

'What!' Veronica was astonished. 'What kind of job?'

'Supervising a dig, hopefully.'

'So you'd be staying here?'

'For a while anyway, unless you want me to go. I might not get this job. I haven't been interviewed yet.'

Veronica stared at her. 'You're thinking of staying in Ireland? For another three months? What about the boyfriend in Australia? What about the job there?'

'He's not an issue at the moment,' said Romy quickly. 'And one of the other girls in the place I worked has gone to Melbourne. So that's not available any more. I reckoned that a three-month job would give me time to think about my next career move.'

'I'm stunned,' said Veronica. 'I thought you couldn't get away from me fast enough.'

'I like to travel,' said Romy. 'But I don't mind a few weeks at home.'

'Well, well.' Veronica's tone was surprised. 'That's not something I ever imagined I'd hear you say.'

'A few weeks, that's all,' said Romy firmly. 'And then I'm off again.'

The two drinks hadn't had any effect and she didn't know whether that was a good or a bad thing. But the really good thing was that she hadn't had a third. A third would have been giving in completely and she wasn't going to do that. She wasn't going to give in to anything any more. She'd already made her decisions and she was going to stick with them no matter how hard they were. She'd never been afraid of hard decisions. Only this time it was so different.

She supposed she'd have to tell them. That was part of it, after all. But not yet. She was still dealing with it herself.

Soon, though.

Very soon.

Chapter 20

Veronica had gone inside to watch TV but Romy was sitting in the garden reading when Kathryn arrived home. She looked up and closed the paperback, memorising the page number and not turning down the corner of the page as Veronica did, which Dermot had always insisted was a horrible thing to do.

'Everything all right?' she asked.

'Of course.' Kathryn hesitated and then sat down beside Romy. She poured herself a glass of sparkling water from the bottle of Ballygowan on the table.

'Did you get the moisturiser?'

'Huh?' Kathryn looked at her in confusion.

'That's why you went out. To get moisturiser for Mum.'

'Oh. Yes. Well no, I didn't.'

Romy frowned. 'So where were you?'

'For heaven's sake!' Kathryn gulped back half of the water and replaced the glass on the table. 'What's this? The Inquisition?'

'I just asked,' said Romy mildly.

'There's no need to ask. You're not . . .' She broke off and gave her sister a half-smile. 'I was going to say you're not my mother, but that's a kind of ridiculous comment, isn't it?'

'Kind of,' agreed Romy.

'Anyway.' Kathryn shrugged and topped up her glass of water. 'How's Mum?'

'Kathryn, we don't need to talk about Mum. We need to talk about you.'

'No we don't,' said Kathryn.

Romy's expression was worried. 'I can't help feeling that there's something wrong. You—'

'There's nothing wrong,' said Kathryn. She stood up. 'Nothing that you need worry about. Really.' And she walked back into the house leaving Romy staring after her.

Veronica decided to have her family dinner on the following Friday. Giselle rang a couple of days beforehand, bubbling with enthusiasm, saying that she'd got a lovely new dress to wear and that both she and Darragh were looking forward to the evening tremendously. It was a wonderful idea, she said, because family was very important. She was, she said, delighted to be part of the Dolan family.

Of course you are, muttered Veronica as she put the phone down. Without us you'd never be living in the style you are now and able to buy new dresses for family dinners! She was shocked at the uncharitable thought, but something in Giselle's tone, something in the way she'd almost sucked up to her, had annoyed her.

Giselle has it easy, Veronica mused. She can loll around at home all day, pretending to work but not really doing anything at all. Playing at it. Calling herself a consultant when what she does is really a hobby and not a career. All it is in reality is giving advice to some friends. It's hardly working. Not like my own girls. And then she was annoyed at herself because the circumstances were very, very different. Giselle was the mother of her only grandchild, she was pregnant again and she couldn't be expected to hold down a high-flying job like Kathryn or a less high-flying but obviously demanding career like Romy.

She looked at her watch. It was early afternoon and Romy had gone to her Wicklow interview. Veronica had been both surprised and pleased by Romy's decision to look for a job in Ireland. She liked to think that her daughter would be around for another few months, which was odd really, because when Romy had first come into the house Veronica's only wish had been that she'd be out of it again as soon as possible. Yet Romy had been good to her even though they sparked off each other so much. She'd made her do her physiotherapy exercises, helped her to get around, taken her shopping (even though she always sighed in an exaggerated fashion at the amount of time Veronica spent comparing various clothes) and generally been much more supportive than Veronica had ever anticipated.

And although Veronica had expected her to stalk off in a rage the day that Giselle had fallen and they'd had such a momentous row, Romy had stuck around. Perhaps she hadn't had any choice because of the whole kidney stone incident but she could have gone as soon as she'd got her into the hospital. Yet she hadn't. She'd stayed.

I think I'm better at being a mother-in-law than a mother, thought Veronica as she walked through the house and into the living room, where Kathryn was curled up on the sofa. I seem to be able to accept the flaws in my daughter-in-law more than those in my daughters. Which is not generally the way of the Irish mammy!

She sat down opposite Kathryn, who lowered the copy of *Vanity Fair* that she'd been reading.

'Everything's sorted for Friday,' she told her daughter.

'Fine,' said Kathryn.

'You don't sound terribly enthusiastic,' complained Veronica.

'It's just dinner,' Kathryn told her. 'There's no big thing about it. We eat dinner every day.'

'I know, but it's special,' said Veronica. 'All of us together for the first time in years.'

'Hum.' Kathryn looked warily at her mother. 'I'm not sure that's something to get so excited about.'

'It is,' said Veronica. 'I like having my family around me.'

Kathryn laughed shortly. 'You don't get much of that, what with Romy globetrotting and me in New York.'

'Exactly,' said Veronica. 'Which is why it'll be so great. It's a pity Alan can't come.'

'Yeah, well.' Kathryn shrugged. 'Can't have everything.'

'I'm sure he's missing you like crazy,' said Veronica. 'It's lovely that you were able to take the time off, but have you made up your mind when you're going back?'

'I was due a lot of time,' Kathryn told her. 'I've worked very hard over the last couple of years. I guess I'll go back next week – maybe after you head off to Cork.'

'I'm still not sure about that trip,' Veronica said. 'I don't know why I let them persuade me.'

'It'll be good for you,' Kathryn assured her.

'If it had been in a few weeks' time perhaps,' agreed Veronica. 'But next week . . .'

'You need the break.' Suddenly Kathryn's voice was warm. 'You do, really. It's been a difficult couple of months for you.'

'I guess,' said Veronica. 'But you know, the good thing that came out of it is that you and Romy came home.' Her eyes suddenly filled with tears. 'I'm on my own,' she said. 'All the time. It's hard.'

'Oh, come on,' said Kathryn. 'You have Darragh and Giselle nearby.'

'It's not the same,' said Veronica. 'Having Romy in the house – well, I know it's Romy and I know she and I . . . but still, having her around . . .'

'I don't think she'll stay, if that's what you're angling at,' said Kathryn.

'She's gone for the interview,' Veronica said.

'I know. But . . .' Kathryn looked at her mother sceptically. 'She's not a stay-at-home person.'

'She might be,' said Veronica. 'There were reasons why she went. I think she's got over them.'

'Oh, Mum, I know all about Romy's reasons,' said Kathryn dismissively. 'It was my party after all.'

Veronica looked uncomfortable. She hadn't realised that Kathryn knew about it too, although she knew she shouldn't have been surprised. Kathryn always seemed to know everything! 'There's no need to rake over it now. But the point is that she's here and she's looking for a job and why shouldn't she stay? Isn't this a lovely home for her? Isn't it a million times better than a tent in Egypt or some dilapidated clapboard house in Australia? Why wouldn't she want to stay?'

'She'd cramp your style,' said Kathryn. 'You're only thinking like that because you've been stuck at home for the last couple of months. But when you're better and out and about again – what then?'

'Things have changed,' Veronica told her. 'I'm not the same. People know I've been sick. They see me differently.'

'Don't be silly,' said Kathryn.

'They do!' protested Veronica. 'Instead of looking on me as a feisty kind of woman they're thinking of me as a bit of a crock. Someone who grunts every time she bends down!'

Kathryn stifled a giggle.

'It's true,' said Veronica. 'Just you wait, missy, and you'll find out for yourself!'

'True or not,' said Kathryn, 'the only reason you want Romy to stay is because you've got used to her company. You and her might have called a truce and resolved whatever differences you have between you, but in the end she's like Dermot. She has wanderlust. And you won't be able to make her do whatever you want. When you're fit again she's not likely to be hanging around the house.'

'It's just a thought,' said Veronica. 'That's all.'

'It's a thought that you should probably get out of your head,' Kathryn told her bluntly. 'Romy won't come home for good and you shouldn't expect her to. Because if she did, the two of you would start to hate each other all over again.'

Romy was thinking about home as she waited in the Portakabin office to be called for her interview. It was festooned with detailed charts of the site as well as photos from the initial stages of the excavation, and seeing them made her heart beat faster with nervous anticipation.

Three months, she reminded herself as she gazed at a photo of the site prior to work having started. Three months wasn't very long. Afterwards she could head back to Australia, hopefully with some supervisory experience behind her, and no one in her family could ever again call her selfish and thoughtless and make snide comments about her gallivanting around the world and ignoring her responsibilities. And maybe by the time three months was up Keith would have forgotten that she'd said she loved him and they'd manage to resume their easy friendship. She hoped so. She really did.

'Romy Kilkenny?' The door to the small inner office opened and a tall, rangy man poked his head outside.

'Yes.'

'I'm Taig. I'm in charge of the dig. Let's have a chat.'

She liked Taig. He reminded her of Keith. Not Keith the way he was now, with his tidy hair and his new wardrobe, but the Keith she'd known before. Taig was wearing an old T-shirt and jeans, his shoulder-length dark hair tied back. His eyes were grey and thoughtful and his smile was open and friendly. They talked about her experience and she told him why she wanted the job. He asked if she'd be prepared to stay on after the dig and do some post-ex work and she said that it would depend on circumstances. He replied that he was OK with that and then he told her that they would be starting work the following week and she should turn up bright and early.

'I've got the job!' She looked at him in pleased astonishment.

'For sure,' he told her. 'You've got great experience. We're delighted to have you.'

'Excellent!' She grinned at him and told him that she was looking forward to it and then she got into Veronica's silver Golf and drove off site.

She checked the time. It would be about a quarter to one in the morning in Perth. But Keith was a late-night person. He'd surely still be up by now.

She pulled in to the side of the road and dialled his number on her mobile, waiting impatiently for the connection to be made.

'Hello?'

'I got the job,' she said.

'Huh? Who . . . Romy?'

'Yes, it's me. Who did you think it was?'

'I didn't,' said Keith. 'I'm sitting on the step of the house here, looking out at the ocean, and I didn't think.'

Romy closed her eyes and thought about the Indian Ocean lapping on the shore.

'You still there?' asked Keith.

'Sure,' she said, opening her eyes and finding herself back in Wicklow again. 'Anyway I was ringing to say . . .'

'. . . you got the job,' finished Keith. 'You said that, it just took a minute for it to register. Excellent. I knew you would.'

'And so I'm here for a while longer.' Suddenly her mouth was dry.

'Yeah, well, nothing much going on here,' he said. 'You might as well put in some quality time at home.'

'Are you keeping in touch with everyone?' she asked.

'Sure. But they're all doing their thing and I'm over here in Western Australia. So not quite the same,' he told her.

Say you miss me. The thought went through her head. Say you miss me and that you wish I was there.

'Busy, though,' he continued. 'Most evenings I just flake out.'

'No mad social life?'

315

'Naw, not really. A few tinnies at the weekends, a bit of messing about on boats. You know how it is.'

'Mm.'

'I miss everyone,' he admitted. 'Normally I like being away on my own, but this time it's different.'

'I miss everyone too,' said Romy. 'And you.'

She kicked herself as she said the words. I wanted him to say it, she told herself. Not me.

'I miss you too,' said Keith. 'Most of all.'

'Oh.' She felt her cheeks tinge pink. 'That's . . . well, that's nice,' she told him. 'It's always hard when your friends are miles away. And I'm the furthest away. So no surprise that you miss me the most.' I'm jabbering, she thought. It's like the comfort kiss all over again!

'Right.'

'Anyway . . . oh!'

'What?'

'I'm parked at the side of the road,' she told him. 'A big truck hurtled around the corner and I thought he was going to hit me.'

'You'd better move on,' said Keith. 'Wouldn't want to be responsible for getting you killed.'

'I'll Skype you again soon,' she said.

'Yeah. Take care.'

'You too.'

She closed her phone gently and then sat staring in front of her, imagining the Indian Ocean again, before another truck came around the corner and she decided that she'd better move on.

Darragh looked at the paperwork in front of him. He had all the information about the energy deal that he wanted the company to get involved in and he wanted to do a summary sheet so that he could give it to Kathryn and Veronica to look over. He thought it was a great deal and that it would do well for Dolan's. He knew that Kathryn would have issues about the fact that they were getting involved in a business that they knew nothing about, but then Kathryn wasn't really a forward thinker, like him. The reason she'd done so well in forensic accounting was that she was always looking for ways things could go wrong, never for ways that they could go right. Despite what she tried to pretend, she wasn't really an entrepreneurial sort of person at all. In fact, thought Darragh grimly, if she'd been the one in control of Dolan Component Manufacturers the company would still be operating on the lines laid down by Tom. And not that his father hadn't been a great man, but he'd never have hacked it in the age of technology and the internet. Tom was a nuts-and-bolts sort of person and that was what Kathryn had inherited from him – a nuts-and-bolts mentality.

Darragh smiled to himself at the analogy. Fortunately, he thought, I'm completely different. And she's going to thank me in a few years when this investment pays off big time and Dolan Component Manufacturers expands beyond her wildest dreams.

Later that evening while Romy was in the living room watching a celebrity edition of *The Weakest Link* with Veronica, Kathryn went up to her room and phoned home. This time she heard the interruption of the ring tone and she took a deep breath. But the answering machine cut in ahead of her – her own voice saying that neither she nor Alan were available at the moment but that if the caller left a message they'd get back to them.

'Alan,' she said. 'It's me. We have to talk about things. Call me on my mobile.'

She slid the cover closed on her phone and stared at the wall in front of her. Part of her was relieved that he hadn't answered her, that she didn't have to deal with everything yet. And another part of her felt deflated, knowing that at some point she was going to have to face up to the fact that there was only one solution to her situation and that it was to divorce

Alan. Normally she didn't flinch when it came to difficult solutions. But she didn't want to have to talk to Alan about a divorce. She didn't really want to have to talk to him at all.

Giselle was suddenly feeling very pregnant indeed. It had happened the last time too – she'd gone for months and months knowing that she was pregnant and not liking it very much but managing to cope with it. And then one day she'd suddenly looked down at herself and realised that no matter which way you rationalised it, she was fat again. Of course nobody called it fat and, fair enough, the bump of the baby wasn't fat. But it wasn't just the bump; it was her arms and legs too, which had, seemingly overnight, grown chubby and wobbly. She didn't think they'd been as chubby and wobbly with Mimi although she couldn't be sure about that. She'd spent the last few months of her pregnancy at home, telling everyone that the baby was at a weird angle and that she was too uncomfortable to go out. It was annoying beyond belief that models and actresses flaunted their pregnancies these days, wandering around with perfect bumps beneath their designer outfits. It made it so much harder for normal people to look good.

Why did it have to go wrong like this? Why couldn't she look as gorgeous and fabulous as she'd looked for the last six months? She rubbed her hand fleetingly across the top of her bump. Why was it that nature hadn't come up with a better way?

The desk diary was open in front of her and she flicked over the pages until she came to her due date, circled in red. She'd spoken to her gynae about inducing the baby on the day if it hadn't done the decent thing and arrived before then. She didn't want to be pregnant a single moment more than she had to. It was so hard to put up the façade of someone who was still leading an active life when actually all she wanted to do was slob in an armchair and not move. Maybe eat a few

choccies too, she thought miserably. She'd kill for a straw-
berry cream right now!

I forgot about this part of it, she thought. I forgot how
much I hated it.

And now there was Veronica's dinner party to get through.
She'd been looking forward to that until she'd started to feel
fat, but now she was dreading it. She didn't want to have to
sit at the table with the ultra-thin Kathryn (how did the girl
do it?), who would probably keep on coming out with questions about the company (which she always seemed to do
whenever Darragh was around; it was as though she actually
enjoyed making him uncomfortable). Nor did she want to
have to put up with Romy, who still hadn't apologised to
Darragh for the row the day she'd fallen from the stepladder.
Romy was so rude and so ungracious that she set Giselle's
teeth on edge. If it wasn't that it was so important to Veronica
she wouldn't go at all, but of course she couldn't let her
mother-in-law down. And besides . . . Giselle picked at the
fringe of one of her cushion covers . . . besides, it was important to remain close to Veronica while those two girls were
living in the house. Giselle could see them worming their way
into her affections and she'd warned Darragh about it but
he'd just laughed at her.

'I'm serious,' she'd said the previous night. 'They're both
in the house being dutiful and daughterly and I bet you
anything they're thinking all of a sudden that when Veronica
eventually . . . well, when Veronica dies, there's money in the
family and they want a bigger slice of it.'

'Sweetie, that's never going to happen,' said Darragh firmly.
'Besides, Mum is going to be around for a long time yet. She's
totally recovered. In fact, she hasn't looked better in months.
However, I was thinking of asking her about signing over the
shares sooner rather than later. That way I can get the big
deals through for the company without having to listen to
Kathryn banging on and on about prudence and risk-reward

and stuff like that. And . . .' he grinned conspiratorially at her, 'if we ever did sell, it would mean a bigger slice of the cake for us. Which we're entitled to seeing as we're the ones with the family.'

'Kathryn might have a baby,' said Giselle morosely. 'With her millionaire husband.'

'Can you imagine her with kids?' demanded Darragh. 'That's an even harder thing to picture than Romy as a parent! Nope, we're the future of the Dolan dynasty and Mum knows that, and there's nothing she's going to do to endanger it. Besides, when you have this baby he'll be our son and heir. A Dolan to carry on the family name. Kathryn's won't.'

It was all very well for Darragh to think like that, thought Giselle, but she knew what women were like. If it was her, she wouldn't stand for shares being handed over to an older brother. If she was Romy she'd be getting legal advice about it because Giselle knew that Romy didn't have any shares at all. And although it was perfectly fair and how Tom had wanted it, she knew that people didn't always look at things that way when there was money involved.

Kathryn didn't need it, of course. But Romy was very different. And Romy might pretend that money wasn't important but everyone knew that, in the end, it was.

Giselle held her arm out in front of her and jiggled the extra flesh. She wasn't going to eat a thing at the dinner. In fact from now on she was cutting back. She'd take some supplements for the baby but she couldn't let herself get any fatter. She really couldn't.

That would be the biggest disaster of all.

Chapter 21

Veronica was pleased that the weather had turned yet again and that driving rain was sweeping across the country, forcing people to abandon their sunny gardens and return to indoor living for a while. It wasn't that she didn't like good weather, but she'd decided to do her beef and Guinness pie for the family dinner and it was a dish more suited to chill winds and torrential rain than to the balmy pre-summer weather that they'd enjoyed for the past couple of weeks. Veronica felt that there was something very comforting about having a dinner party indoors when it was bucketing rain outside, and she wanted her family to feel comforted.

Romy had driven her to the village so that she could pick up ingredients for the meal. Her daughter had planned to accompany her around the shops but Veronica told her that she was perfectly capable of picking up the shopping herself and that Romy should head off and do something else. She'd get a taxi back, Veronica said, no problem. Romy, surprised, had pointed out that the shopping would be heavy and that Veronica wouldn't be able to manage it on her own, but Veronica had produced, from under the stairs, a long-handled wicker basket on wheels which she would be able to push around.

'It's my apple-cheeked-grandma trolley,' she told Romy with a grin. Romy laughed and told her to take it easy around the shops and not to tire herself out or to think that she had to have everything absolutely perfect – keep it trouble free, she'd said, as though she was actually expecting trouble.

There won't be trouble, thought Veronica half an hour before Darragh and Giselle were due to arrive. She sniffed appreciatively at the mingled aromas of her cooking. How can there be trouble when everyone will be relaxed and happy after a good meal?

Admittedly relations between her only son and her younger daughter were still strained at the moment, but that could be overcome. And it was true that relations between Darragh and Kathryn were somewhat strained too – Darragh had dropped by with information on his energy deal a couple of days earlier and Kathryn had picked holes in it (as she always did) – but Veronica knew that those issues could be overcome too.

She frowned slightly. They needed to learn to live together, to appreciate each other's point of view. Maybe she hadn't been good at making them do that in the past, but she wanted them to do it in the future.

The aroma of beef and Guinness bubbling away in the oven had wafted up the stairs and made Romy feel very hungry. She hadn't been eating particularly well since she'd come to Ireland – possibly, she thought, because she always felt on edge whenever she sat down to a meal with her mother – but there was no doubt that she was looking forward to tonight's food if not tonight's company. Cooking was one of the few domesticated things that her mother did well. In fact Veronica was really good in the kitchen, although she liked eating out as much as possible and hardly ever put her talent to use. Romy remembered the evening of a particularly frazzled day when Dermot had come home late and asked what was for dinner, hoping that it would be something hot and filling (Dermot, despite his lean frame, had a voracious appetite). But Veronica had just smiled sweetly at him and said,

'Reservations.' Then she'd ushered him out of the house again, telling him that they were eating in one of the small restaurants in Rathfarnham village and dashing his hopes of a home-cooked meal in front of the TV.

'Just because you're good at something doesn't mean that you have to become a slave to it,' she'd remarked when Romy asked her why she liked going out to eat when her own food was so good. It was something that Romy had taken to heart and so, even though she wasn't bad in the kitchen herself, she liked to cultivate an aura of being fairly hopeless. She was, she admitted, fairly hopeless at general domesticity. But she too could cook a mean beef and Guinness pie.

Kathryn wasn't hungry at all, although she had to admit that the aroma of the food was potentially mouthwatering. It was a long time since she'd eaten anything as hearty – in New York she existed on a diet of coffee and cigarettes, supplemented by bird-sized portions of low-fat, low-cholesterol, low-carb, low-salt and low-calorie food. She rarely ate an evening meal at home with Alan – most days he ate out with colleagues or clients – but when they did, it was usually a takeaway from the local sushi restaurant. And in the last few weeks she'd been on edge when they had eaten at home – terrified of saying or doing the wrong thing and setting off a chain of events over which she knew she'd have no control.

When they'd first married, Kathryn had looked forward to cooking meals for Alan. It seemed a loving thing to do even though she knew that she wasn't a very accomplished cook. However, she wanted to learn. She'd spent a happy afternoon in Borders Park Avenue loading up with Jamie Oliver, Nigella Lawson and a whole heap of other food-porn recipe books and she'd anticipated trying out some of the easier ones on Alan. But he'd said that he didn't want her getting dishwasher hands and that there wasn't any need for her to slave over a hot oven.

She sat down abruptly on the edge of her bed. Back then she'd thought that he loved her. Back then she'd thought it was going to be wonderful.

Darragh was sitting in the living room waiting for Giselle. He was looking forward to the food tonight but he wasn't looking forward to a potential spat with Kathryn about the energy deal. She'd been scathing when he'd mentioned it, telling him that Dolan Component Manufacturers knew nothing about the energy business and that just because he'd bought the DVD of *The Smartest Guys in the Room* (the movie about the collapse of the giant energy company Enron) it didn't make him an expert. He'd pulled her up pretty sharply then, and told her to quit patronising him. He'd reminded her that the business had changed dramatically over the past five years and that she hadn't been there for most of it, so who did she think she was, exactly, telling him what was and what wasn't appropriate for Dolan's?

She'd responded by saying that she didn't need to be around to recognise a stinking pile of crap when she saw it and that Veronica might have been ill lately but she wasn't stupid and surely she'd be able to see through this too. Veronica had been out shopping when they'd had the argument, hissing and spitting at each other like angry cats.

'Why is it you try to find fault with every single thing I do?' demanded Darragh furiously.

'Why is it that every single thing you do is such a mountain of shit?' she retorted.

He quickly pointed out to her that the company's turnover had increased the previous year and that she wasn't exactly talking from a position of strength. She'd backed down slightly then, admitting that the core business was doing well before going on the attack about the loss of Jim Cahill's business (he'd been hoping that she wouldn't notice it in the masses of information he'd given her, but of course it wasn't something she'd overlook) and the fact that other companies seemed to be undercutting theirs. And then she'd asked him why he hadn't had talks with Hemmerling, the German firm who were interested in investing in the business and who had a plan which was infinitely more measurable and sensible. He'd retorted that their plan was to buy the company and she'd asked whether that was such a bad thing, stopping him dead in his tracks because he'd never seriously thought that Kathryn would ever consider selling. He sometimes talked about the value of the shares if the company was bought out but he knew that he'd never sell. Why would he? The company was his life. He suspected that Kathryn was just riling him. But there was no arguing with her, no thrashing it through. She couldn't for a moment admit that she was wrong. Darragh wondered what on earth it was like in her home and he felt a stab of sympathy for her husband. Being married to Kathryn, he thought, would be only marginally less awful than being married to Romy. He was surprised, in fact, that anyone had married his sister at all.

Giselle looked at her silhouette in the mirror and frowned. The shimmering grey and silver dress which she'd bought for the night didn't look half as good as it had when she'd first tried it on in the shop, but with her bump expanding daily (or maybe even hourly, she thought miserably) there was nothing in her wardrobe that would look any better.

She knew that her baby was a girl (information she hadn't yet shared with Darragh, who was hoping for a son) but she didn't want to believe that she might have a daughter who was shaping up to be a big fat lump! There was no way, looking at her reflection now, that the child could be anything but huge. People said that the size of your bump had nothing to do with the size of the baby, but she wasn't convinced.

Giselle hating feeling fat and unattractive. She hated the idea that Darragh would look at her and wonder how the woman he'd married had turned into an elephant.

She turned around in front of the mirror again. Her face was rounder and her arms wobbled far too much. But the real problem was her baby.

Giselle didn't want her child to be fat. She didn't want to have to go down the road of diets and disciplined eating with her. It had been hard enough herself. Girls couldn't be fat in today's world, which was why she'd been so assiduous in sticking to salads and lean meats, but this baby clearly had different ideas. She'd obviously got her appetite from Darragh. And her fat from Giselle herself. When Darragh saw his daughter he'd wonder how they'd produced something that size and then he'd find out that she herself had once been a little fat barrel. She'd never shown him any photos of her during her tubby stage. She'd only ever shown him kiddy ones which didn't matter too much and then ones from after her dramatic weight loss. There was no way she wanted him to imagine her anything other than as slim as she was now. And no way she wanted him to have to put up with a daughter who wasn't gorgeous.

I won't eat much tonight, she told herself virtuously. That'll keep things under control. I'll train Miss Muffet in there to realise that she can't gorge herself every single day! Darragh said that Veronica is doing that awful beef and Guinness pie, so it's not the sort of food I would eat anyway. How much stodgier can a meal be? Darragh called it comfort food and he was really looking forward to it, but Giselle wondered if she couldn't ask Veronica for a green leaf salad instead.

Maybe not, though. Maybe she'd have to eat it because she wanted to create a good impression tonight. Which would give Muffie (as she'd taken to calling her) even more opportunity to pile on the pounds! Nevertheless, eating Veronica's meal might be more important, just this once. She knew that Veronica was fond of her but she had to ensure that she was more fond of her than she was of Kathryn or of Romy. She'd underestimated the guilt factor as far as her mother-in-law was concerned. She'd thought, at first, that having Romy stay would be a good thing because it got her off the 'looking after Veronica' hook while having the potential to increase the antagonism between her mother-in-law and her younger daughter. But it hadn't worked out like that at all and Kathryn's arrival had turned the whole thing into some kind of happy family scenario which filled Giselle with anxiety. Veronica wasn't supposed to get on with her daughters. She hadn't for a second thought it would happen.

It was important to Giselle that the two girls were always an afterthought in Veronica's mind, in a distant second place to Darragh, and by extension, to herself. Being the mother of her granddaughter helped. So did being pregnant. But it might not be enough. As far as Giselle was concerned, Veronica's support should always be for Darragh. She didn't want that irritatingly smug Kathryn or that annoyingly loopy Romy coming between her mother-in-law and her husband. And she was going to make sure it would never happen.

By seven o'clock Veronica, Romy and Kathryn were sitting in the living room. The heavy clouds and slanting rain had darkened the sky and so the room was lit by an assortment of mellow table lamps and scented candles. It was warm and welcoming and very cosy. Veronica had opened a bottle of Rioja and they were sitting in the comfortable chairs, glasses in their hands. Kathryn had hardly touched hers, although Romy was enjoying the full-bodied wine.

'Isn't this nice?' Veronica said brightly, waving her hand in a jangle of charm bracelets even though she couldn't help feeling that despite the cosiness none of them were truly relaxed. 'All girls together.'

Romy spluttered into her drink. In the last few days Veronica had seemed less like a flighty twenty year old than she normally did and more like a mature woman. (Although mature still probably wasn't the right word for her. Romy had tried a few before she'd settled on it – words like sensible or older – but none of them seemed appropriate either.)

'It's certainly strange being together,' Kathryn said.

Romy glanced at her half-sister. Kathryn was wearing another high-collared outfit, this time a figure-hugging dress in deep red which looked sensational on her. For the first time in her life Romy could clearly see the very obvious similarities between Veronica and Kathryn – both slim, fine-boned and with long, shapely legs. It was no wonder, now she came to think of it, that Veronica used to get mad at Kathryn for not making the most of her looks. She'd always known that Kathryn, behind her fringe and glasses, was attractive. But now the genes she shared with her mother were unmistakable. Nevertheless, Veronica was still the one with that extra quality that made her sexy as well as gorgeous. Kathryn was cool and stylish. But Veronica . . . it didn't matter how old she was, it really didn't. She just looked fabulous. Always too glitzy, Romy thought, but nonetheless amazing in a sky-blue cocktail dress with her hair coaxed from its poker-straight look into soft, gentle curls and held back from her face by silver clips with glittering blue stones. A gleaming sapphire hung from the silver chain around her neck.

Romy herself was wearing the black dress she'd worn on her last night in Sydney. It was the only dress (apart from some totally unsuitable strappy sun-dresses) she possessed and she'd had to scrape off a splodge of dried sauce from the hem before putting it on, which had made her feel a total slob. She wished she'd checked it earlier and had it dry-cleaned because she knew that the simple style looked well on her. But all she could think was that neither Veronica nor Kathryn would've worn a dress which had dried sauce on the hem.

As she sipped her wine she thought wistfully of laid-back barbies on the beach in Australia and of sitting, barefoot, on the step of Keith's house. She thought of the nights she'd spent around the campfire in Arizona or in the Valley of the Kings in Egypt and she wished that she was back in any of those places now. She'd never felt like a slob then, just casual and relaxed. She was a casual person at heart. And suddenly that seemed to be the biggest gulf of all between her and her family.

She chugged back the rest of her wine and put the empty glass on the coffee table. Kathryn's, also on the table, was still almost full.

Veronica glanced at her watch. 'They should be here any minute,' she said. 'And then the fun will start.'

You've got to be kidding, thought Romy. You really have.

The doorbell rang and she got up to answer it, telling Veronica to stay where she was, that there was no point in her walking more than she had to. Veronica was celebrating her family dinner by wearing her Jimmy Choos again and Romy really didn't want her to fall off them and break her neck. She might have decided to stay on in Ireland for another three months, but she didn't want to spend them all looking after Veronica!

'Hi.' Darragh leaned forward and kissed her on the cheek, which took Romy completely by surprise. She was equally surprised when Giselle did the same before both of them swept past her and into the living room.

Romy followed them, rubbing her cheek.

'You look lovely, Giselle,' said Veronica warmly as her daughter-in-law walked into the room. 'You really do.'

She did, thought Romy. And how she did it with that bump was amazing, but Giselle actually looked very beautiful. Her blond hair fell softly to her shoulders and her eyes were subtly highlighted so that they looked extra big and extra blue in her flawless face. Her silver-grey dress with its embroidered black detail was stunning and her bump was as neat and elegant as ever. And Romy couldn't help admiring her wonderful Swarovski-encrusted shoes which sparkled every time she took a step.

'It's lovely to be here, Veronica,' she said.

'I've brought some bubbly,' said Darragh. 'To celebrate.'

'Celebrate?' Romy looked puzzled.

'The fact that we're all here, of course,' he said. 'That's what this dinner is about, isn't it? The family together for the first time in years. And the fact that Mum is on the road to recovery too.'

'Lovely!' Veronica clapped her hands in delight and took some glasses from the cabinet while Darragh carefully eased the cork out of the bottle with a gentle pop.

'Here's to the Dolans,' he said when all the glasses had been filled. 'May our glasses never be empty.'

Romy glanced at Veronica, who was beaming broadly, and then at Darragh.

'And here's to the Kilkennys,' she said. 'Me and . . . well, Dad, I guess, and part of Mum. May our mugs always be full.'

Veronica said nothing but Darragh looked at Romy in irritation.

'I wasn't having a go,' he said. 'I was embracing everyone.'

'Yes, but I'm a Kilkenny,' she said simply. 'I don't need embracing.'

'We're only in the door and you're starting—'

'She's right, Darragh,' said Veronica quickly. 'She's a Kilkenny and she's entitled to be a Kilkenny and that's fine, but it doesn't make things any different. We're all family.'

Romy said nothing but gave a small smile in Veronica's direction, uncomfortably aware that she'd managed to make everyone feel awkward and wishing that she'd grow up enough not to blurt out whatever came into her head. But honestly, she thought as she swallowed some champagne, he should be more sensitive. He should know that it matters. After all, being a Dolan matters to him. Being a Kilkenny matters to me.

She sighed inwardly. Maybe she was wrong to think it mattered at all. Maybe it didn't, in the end. And how weird was it to have Veronica jumping to her defence? In fact how weird had her whole relationship with Veronica become? Especially now that they'd be living together for another twelve weeks.

She took another sip of the champagne which, she realised, was very nice. She hadn't seen the bottle but clearly Darragh hadn't bought it in the local supermarket. Maybe that was really the difference between them. Not that he had the money to splash out on expensive champagne – just that he would always choose the best no matter how much he had. While she would always think it a terrible waste when you could pick up a bottle of Asti at the supermarket for a tenth of the price. So maybe that was the difference between being a Kilkenny and a Dolan. She was sparkling wine. They were vintage champagne.

Plenty of people liked sparkling wine she told herself. Though she couldn't help thinking that most of them would go for the vintage champagne if they had the choice.

Chapter 22

Kathryn was feeling detached from it all. She knew that there was conversation going on between Giselle and Veronica about some charity ball that Giselle had been to, or was going to, but she wasn't really listening. She'd noted somewhere deep in her subconscious that Giselle was totally sucking up to Veronica and she wondered if she normally spoke to her mother like this. She'd dismissed her sister-in-law as a preening airhead before, but now she wasn't so sure. Veronica was clearly enjoying the attention that Giselle was giving her and positively revelling in it as Giselle told her at regular intervals how great she was and how fabulous she looked. Kathryn wasn't sure whether Giselle's flattery was genuine but she could sense a certain desperation in the other girl's voice which both surprised and intrigued her.

It didn't intrigue her enough, though, to drag her own thoughts away from the fact that earlier that day she'd finally told Alan (albeit by voicemail) that she wanted a divorce. Soon she'd tell everyone else. Veronica would be disappointed but she'd understand something not working out. Neither Darragh nor Romy would be all that interested one way or the other. So she didn't have to do a whole confessional thing with her family and rake over every horrible detail. It was funny, she thought, how being away from the situation had clarified it for her. Quite suddenly she didn't feel afraid any more. She'd left the message and when he eventually called back she'd just repeat it. Then she'd go back to New York and deal with it. Dealing with things was what she was good at and was something she told her clients to do. 'You might not want to believe that someone you trusted let you down,' she sometimes said to them. 'But you have to accept it and deal with it.'

She realised that until this very moment, she hadn't accepted it. But now she had. She felt proud of the sudden hardening of her heart. It seemed strange to her that nobody else around the table realised that she'd just come through a terrible ordeal by herself. Yet she was glad that they didn't know. She hated the idea of them talking about her, pitying her. She didn't need their pity because she was the strongest of them all.

She prodded at a piece of the melt-in-your-mouth beef. Looking up from her plate, she caught Romy's eye. Romy smiled conspiratorially at her and Kathryn knew that it was because she too was amused by Giselle's conversation.

'So,' Giselle said triumphantly, 'it'll be in next month's *VIP*, which is just fabulous.'

'I'm sure you'll look amazing,' said Romy.

'And then after the baby is born we'll probably do another shoot for them.'

'*VIP*?' asked Kathryn, feeling that she'd been silent for too long and should join in the conversation.

'Gossip mag,' said Romy. 'Pictures of Ireland's celebrities in their beautiful homes.'

Despite her current feelings, Kathryn stifled a giggle. Romy's tone had been irony-free, but Kathryn knew perfectly well that her sister thought the whole idea of Giselle and Darragh in a celebrity magazine was hilarious.

'You two have a gorgeous home,' said Veronica warmly. 'I'm sure it'll be fantastic.'

'Good for me,' said Darragh. 'And the company, of course.'

'Darragh, getting your picture in a glossy magazine isn't exactly good for the company,' said Kathryn.

'Publicity,' Darragh told her. 'And you can shove your nose in the air all you like but our clients read that magazine.'

This time Kathryn couldn't hide her own amusement. 'Our clients? Buyers of circuit setters and control valves read gossip magazines?'

'Oh, get down off your high horse,' said Darragh. 'Everyone reads gossip mags. And it's not gossip anyhow. It's just pieces about people. It's not scandalous or anything.'

'Not that you have anything scandalous in your life,' said Romy.

'Of course not.' Giselle glanced at them all. 'We're very, very happy and Darragh is a great husband and father and a brilliant company director and you two don't know how hard he works.'

'I'm sure he works very hard,' said Kathryn. 'The question is, is it always at the right thing?'

'Don't start!' Veronica's voice was firm. 'This isn't the time for business conversations. Later, perhaps, I might want to talk to you about it. But not now.'

Her three children looked at her in surprise.

'What—'

'Later,' repeated Veronica. She shook her head so that her long silver and blue earrings jangled. 'Right now I want to talk about nice things.'

The three of them were silent. None of them could think of a single nice thing to say.

'That new oxyjet facial.' Giselle spoke into the silence. 'Have you tried it yet, Veronica? It's absolutely fantastic.'

After they'd finished the main course, Romy brought cheese, biscuits and fruit from the kitchen. Veronica never ate desserts and neither did Kathryn. Romy was pretty sure that Giselle wouldn't let anything as fattening as dessert pass her pouting lips so she reckoned that the only two of them with a sweet tooth would be herself and Darragh. Earlier that afternoon when she realised that Veronica wasn't going to have anything sweet at all, she'd nipped down to the speciality store and bought a selection of petits fours, which she now put on the table alongside the cheese.

She was satisfied to see that she was right and that Darragh bypassed the cheese in favour of the coconut and truffle sweets.

'Gorgeous,' he said as he licked the dusting of chocolate icing from his fingers.

'Sometimes I get it right,' she told him. 'Have another.'

'Oh, look . . .' He took another sweet. 'If you think I've been a bit hard on you, I'm sorry. I think you've been pretty good overall these last few weeks and I'm sure Mum is very grateful.'

'Gee, thanks.'

'I *am* grateful,' Veronica said. 'I know it wasn't easy for Romy to come home and look after me. And I know that there were particular reasons which might have made that decision even more difficult.'

'What reasons?' asked Darragh.

'They're not important.' Veronica looked at Darragh and then at Romy, who couldn't quite keep her mother's gaze. 'The thing is that when it mattered Romy came through and she's been great.'

This time Romy felt herself blush. She couldn't ever remember being praised so fulsomely by Veronica before and she didn't quite know how to react.

'While she's been here – and I'm very glad she's staying on a bit longer – she's made me realise a few things.'

All four of them stared at Veronica.

'Maybe I haven't always treated my children equally,' she said.

'Of course you have!' cried Darragh. 'Nobody could be fairer than you.'

Beside him, Giselle stiffened in her seat and sliced her uneaten cheese into tiny squares.

'It's not that I don't try to be fair,' said Veronica. 'I always have. But sometimes maybe my idea of fair and yours could be different.'

'I don't see how,' said Kathryn mildly.

'I think you're one of the fairest people I know.'

Both Kathryn and Romy looked at Giselle with irritation as she spoke.

'Anyhow,' continued Veronica, 'being sick has made some things come into focus for me.' She leaned back in her seat, aware that they were all staring at her.

'One is that I won't live for ever.'

'Oh Mum!'

'Veronica!'

'I'm not being morbid,' said Veronica. 'I'm just stating a fact, that's all. I don't intend to shuffle off yet. I'm far too young for that.'

There was a relieved sigh around the table.

'But I did realise that I want to enjoy my life,' continued Veronica.

'I kinda thought you already did,' murmured Romy.

'You're right. I do,' Veronica told her. 'But there are things that I could be doing that I'm not. I'm rattling around in this old house – you've said it yourself – and maybe I should be somewhere smaller. I go out with lots of friends but I haven't really travelled as much as I should. Maybe I need to meet someone again.'

This time, her three children as well as Giselle looked horrified.

'I'm not saying that I will!' cried Veronica. 'Only that maybe I should look.'

'Seems to me there are plenty of men falling over themselves for you,' said Romy. 'All those bridge club guys – and you're heading off with them tomorrow . . .'

'True.' Veronica grinned. 'And maybe something will come of one of them. Maybe not.'

'Mum . . . I'm not sure we need to hear all this,' said Darragh. 'We appreciate that it's been a trying and traumatic time for you. But your life is your own. We don't mind what you do with it, although I have to say that . . . well, I wouldn't be too keen on you marrying again. It's not that I don't want you to be happy,' he added hastily. 'It's just that there are some real barracudas out there.'

'I know,' said Veronica. 'And they look at me and see the matriarch of Dolan Component Manufacturers and they think that maybe one day I'll sell the company and be an extremely rich widow.'

'You're doing OK as it is,' Kathryn said. 'The dividends—'

'Yes, yes,' Veronica interrupted her. 'It's a nice sum of money into the bank every year but I have other ideas. I can live on my pension and my investments and my savings for starters. Your dad was shrewd when it came to pensions and investments.'

'He was shrewd about a lot of things,' said Darragh quickly.

Romy stayed silent.

'Anyway, the point is this.' Veronica looked from one to another. 'First of all, I've decided that the time has come to sell the house.'

'Mum! You can't.' Darragh was aghast while Kathryn and Romy looked startled. Giselle flinched and continued to cut up her squares of cheese.

'Of course I can,' said Veronica. 'I've been holding on to it for far too long and for the wrong reasons.' Her voice faltered momentarily and then she smiled brightly. 'But it's far too big for me and I'll save money if I downsize. Plus I'll have a lump sum to add to the income from the pension and investments! Maybe I could move to one of those new little bungalows near the park. Ideal.'

'Mum – this is the family home.' Darragh was still horrified.

'I think it makes perfect sense,' said Romy slowly.

'No it doesn't,' snapped Darragh. 'We've always lived here.'

'But you don't live here now,' Romy pointed out. 'You live in your lovely *VIP*-featured home on the other side of the village. So it shouldn't matter what Veronica does.'

'Exactly,' said Veronica. 'Darragh, darling, I'm rattling around this place. There are too many bedrooms and too many reception rooms and it's a lovely, lovely house but not for a woman on her own.'

Kathryn looked at her in astonishment. 'The other day you said that all your memories were here.'

'I know,' said Veronica. 'But I was thinking about that and . . . maybe I should be concentrating more on the future than the past. When Romy goes it's going to be hard work looking after this place. I don't need that sort of stress.'

'You can get someone in to help,' protested Giselle. 'We have Magda and Jelena. I couldn't be without them. I'm sure you could get someone . . .'

'It's not that,' said Veronica. 'It's day-to-day stuff. I've thought about it a lot over the last few days. Selling is the best option.'

'But if you sell it now . . . I always thought that maybe one day Giselle and I . . .' Darragh's voice trailed off.

'You and Giselle what?' demanded Kathryn when he didn't complete the sentence.

'We thought, maybe, about buying this house.'

Giselle failed to hide her surprise at Darragh's words.

'Darling, you never said you wanted to buy the house before,' said Veronica in astonishment.

'I didn't think . . .'

'He thought you'd leave it to him,' said Kathryn. 'Son and heir and all that sort of stuff.'

'No . . . no I didn't,' said Darragh uncomfortably. 'I just never . . . it's our home, that's all.'

'Well if you want to buy it, of course that's fine,' said Veronica. 'It would be a lovely thing to do and I'm sure we could work out a price, but that's your personal decision. I definitely think that I need somewhere smaller and easier to manage.'

'I think it's a very good idea,' said Romy warmly.

'You would.' Giselle's words were muttered and Veronica didn't hear her. But Romy shot her a daggered look.

'I'll get an estate agent in to value it,' said Veronica. 'Like I said, if you wanted to buy we'd do something on the price. But selling it means that I'll have some extra money to look after myself in . . .' she grinned and looked sideways at Romy, 'in my old age.'

'Veronica! You're not old.' Giselle looked at her and frowned.

'And you're so sweet,' Veronica told her. 'But I have to do some forward planning and this is it. Sell the house, buy a bungalow – a nice one, but the fact that it'll all be on one level is good. Better for my back.'

Darragh still looked shocked. 'That part of it makes sense,' he admitted.

'Yes, it does,' said Veronica cheerfully. 'The second thing I'm doing . . .' She looked at them and then cleared her throat, while they waited in anticipation.

'I talked with my solicitor last week and I was in his office the other day, and what I've done is to divide out my shareholding,' she continued.

'What!' Once again Darragh was shocked. 'What do you mean, divide out your shareholding?'

'Equally, of course,' said Veronica. 'One third to you, one third to Kathryn and one third to Romy.'

There was total silence in the room.

And then Giselle slid off her chair and under the table.

'I'm sorry,' she said a few minutes later, after they'd clustered around her anxiously. 'I think it was the heat and the food . . . I suddenly felt weak, that's all.'

'Are you all right?' Darragh looked at her anxiously.

'Yes,' she said.

'You didn't have very much dinner,' observed Veronica. 'Haven't you been eating properly lately?'

'Of course I have.' The colour was coming back into Giselle's face. 'I've been eating healthy food for the baby. Not . . . not heavy stodge like that.'

Kathryn and Romy exchanged glances as Veronica's eyes widened.

'Stodge?'

'She didn't mean stodge,' said Darragh hastily. 'Not in that sort of way. Just, you know, different. We only have chicken and fish at home, and . . .'

'. . . and in that case it's no wonder she keeled over,' said Veronica. 'Her iron count is probably low. For heaven's sake, Giselle, you should eat properly. For the baby.'

'I *do* eat properly,' she said sharply.

'Look, the important thing is that you're all right,' said Darragh comfortingly. 'Although I guess you might have been taken by surprise and that caused it.'

'Surprise?' Kathryn said sceptically.

'Well, Mum's news is quite a shock,' Darragh retorted.

'Is it?'

'Yes,' Romy mumbled. 'It is.'

'Oh really?' Darragh said. 'Like you're surprised and you here morning, noon and night?'

'You asked me to be,' she said simply.

Veronica stared at them.

'Are you fighting over this?' she asked. 'I was hoping that there wouldn't be any fighting. This is important to me.'

'We're not fighting,' said Darragh quickly. 'Not at all. It's just that . . . you said that I'd have those shares.'

'Not exactly,' said Veronica. 'I said that I'd sign shares over to you. I never said all of them.'

'You implied it.' Darragh was keeping his voice even with great difficulty. 'You said that me and Giselle and our family were the future of Dolan's and that we should be in control.'

'But you *are* in control,' Veronica said firmly. 'You're the managing director. You're in charge, you make all the decisions. And you and Kathryn will have an equal shareholding just like always. But now Romy has something too. That's all. I don't see what the problem is.'

'Mum, you've got to be joking.' Kathryn, who'd been kneeling in front of Giselle, stood up. 'You know that Darragh and I disagree over the direction of the company. There's potential for problems.'

'Especially if she . . .' Darragh looked at Romy, who was now huddled into one of the armchairs, 'starts siding with Kathryn against me.'

'Oh don't be so melodramatic!'

Romy couldn't help smiling, even faintly, at her mother's words. Veronica, whose announcement had been full of melodrama (and who must surely have known the trouble it would cause), was now asking them to take things in their stride.

'Look, Mum.' She sat up a bit straighter. 'I appreciate what you've done, but those shares . . .'

'. . . are Dolan shares!' cried Darragh. 'They're ours, not hers. She's a Kilkenny after all. She said so!'

Veronica shook her head. 'There isn't an ours and yours and theirs and hers,' she said. 'We're all the one family and I won't have any arguments. Anyway, it's too late. I've done it. I called in to the solicitor the other day and it's sorted.'

'I'm not sure that you can,' said Darragh. 'I need to talk to him myself.'

'Do,' said Veronica. 'But he'll tell you that it's all in order. I don't want to be a shareholder any more and I don't want to be a member of the board. I want all of you to get on with making the company as good as it can be. And I want you all to get on with each other too.'

She got up and walked out of the living room. Then she

took off the Jimmy Choos which were absolutely killing her and walked barefoot upstairs to her room.

'She's lost her marbles completely.' Giselle's voice was faint.

'Oh, I dunno,' said Kathryn. 'Seems to me she knows exactly what she wants.'

'This is all your doing,' Darragh said fiercely to Romy. 'You've smarmed your way into the house and into her mind and you've warped her thoughts completely.'

'Smarmed my way into the house!' Romy laughed at him. 'Darragh, you know perfectly well I didn't want to come here in the first place.'

'Didn't you?' asked Kathryn. 'I thought—'

'It doesn't matter,' cried Darragh. 'It makes no difference how you got here but the fact is that you used it to your advantage.'

'It's not to my advantage,' protested Romy. 'I don't give a toss about Dolan shares.'

'Well in that case you can just sign them back over to me.'

'Hold on a second,' interrupted Kathryn. 'She doesn't have to sign them over to you. She can sign them over to me.'

'Oh really! So's you can destroy everything I've built up over the years. Like that's going to happen!' Darragh's face was red with anger and Giselle looked at him anxiously.

'If you ask me, this company could do with a dose of common sense running through it,' said Kathryn. 'And I can bring that. You're a dreamer, Darragh Dolan. You think you're in the mould of Dad but you're not. You'd like to be, but you never will.'

'How dare you!' Darragh was furious now.

'Stop it!' cried Romy. 'Stop it, both of you. I'll talk to Veronica in the morning. There's no need for all this.'

'You'd better,' said Darragh. 'Because I'm damned if I'm

going to have my life's work ruined by two harridans who don't deserve to have anything to do with it.'

'Watch your tongue,' said Kathryn sharply.

'Oh, sod off,' retorted Darragh. He turned to Giselle. 'Are you OK now?' he asked. 'Ready to go home? Will you be able to drive? Because obviously I've had a couple of glasses of wine and I don't want the night completely ruined by being hauled over by some jobsworth cop who should be out catching murderers or something.'

She nodded.

'We're off,' said Darragh. 'I'll talk to you tomorrow, Romy.'

'Right,' she said uncomfortably as her half-brother and his wife walked out of the house.

Neither Kathryn nor Romy spoke for a few minutes. Then Kathryn grinned.

'Good ol' Mum,' she said. 'Always throwing the cats and the pigeons together.'

'I don't know why she did this,' said Romy anxiously. 'I never wanted—'

'You deserve those shares,' said Kathryn firmly. 'I worried and worried about what would happen to them. Darragh's right, Veronica did kind of imply that he'd get them, and I reckon that let loose he'd destroy the company. I'm glad she's showing a dose of common sense at last.'

'Are you being entirely fair on him?' asked Romy. 'After all, he's been in charge all along and things are fine from what everyone says.'

'That's because I manage to rein him in sometimes,' Kathryn told her.

'But wasn't the set-up that Veronica had half and you two shared the rest? In that case wouldn't Veronica always have backed him and so what difference did your say make?'

Kathryn stared at her. 'I didn't realise you were so clued in.'

'For heaven's sake!' cried Romy. 'All you guys ever bloody talk about is that damn company. Of course I'm clued in.'

'We don't talk about it that much,' said Kathryn mildly.

'Kathryn, it's the only topic of conversation when the three of you are together,' Romy told her. 'It's the elephant in the room whenever the Dolans are around. It always was.'

Kathryn laughed.

'Seriously,' said Romy. 'I used to sit and listen to you and wonder what on earth you'd have to talk about if it wasn't for Dolan's.'

'And did you resent it?' Kathryn looked at her curiously.

'Of course I did!' admitted Romy. 'Why would I not? It was the thing that kept you together and me apart.'

'So you should be pleased at being part of it now.'

Romy groaned. 'I'm not pleased. I'm still apart. I'm the wedge between you and I don't want to be. I know there's some kind of hassle going on about a deal with an energy company because Darragh has badgered Veronica about it, and I know that you're not interested because you said so, and why on earth would you think that I want to get into the middle of that?'

Kathryn frowned. 'Perhaps that's why Mum has done this.'

'Why?'

'Perhaps she doesn't want to be in the middle of it either. And she thinks that you can cope better.'

'Me!' Romy looked horrified. 'I can cope with finding old bones, but high finance – that's not me at all.'

'Well it might be from now on,' said Kathryn. 'Besides,' her eyes twinkled, 'think of the money.'

'I don't want the money,' said Romy. 'I never wanted the money.'

'Oh Romy, Romy.' This time Kathryn laughed. 'People say that, but in the end it's what everybody really wants.'

They talked about it for a while longer, Kathryn outlining the problems she had with Darragh as managing director and with the environmental energy deal and then telling Romy exactly how much the dividend had been the previous year, something which made Romy blink in astonishment because it was more than she earned working on digs. She suddenly realised that with the Dolan money behind her she could pick and choose where she wanted to go without having to think about the money side of things and that she wouldn't have to struggle in the same way as she'd struggled up until now. Not that struggling had really been a hardship. She wasn't the sort of girl who needed to have things. She was the sort of girl who needed to *do* things.

She tried to explain this to Kathryn, who looked at her in understanding but reiterated that the dividend was their mad money and that Romy was entitled to some mad money too. Besides, Kathryn added, she was also entitled to some sort of compensation for having given up her job to come home and look after Veronica, especially if she didn't want to come in the first place.

'That's not why I did it!' wailed Romy. 'I didn't want to come because I was happy in Australia but I didn't do it to worm my way into Veronica's affections and grab the family silver.'

Eventually Kathryn told her to sleep on it, that she'd feel different in the morning. Romy had no idea how she'd feel in the morning, but she had an uncomfortable suspicion that under pressure was going to be part of it.

As she walked past Veronica's room she heard the muted hum of the TV. She knocked on her mother's door.

'Come in,' said Veronica.

Romy pushed the door open gently. Veronica was sitting up in the bed, an array of satin pillows behind her. She was wearing a soft pink silk nightgown and had an angora shawl around her shoulders. As Romy walked into the room she hit the mute button on the remote control.

Romy glanced at the TV. Veronica had been watching a

DVD and Romy recognised *Breakfast at Tiffany's*. It had always been a favourite movie of her mother's.

'About these shares—' she began, but Veronica interrupted her.

'It's a done deal,' she said. 'I want you to have them. You deserve them. You've been terrific. Like I said, I'm well provided for and I don't need the income.'

'Everyone is talking about the income, but there are responsibilities too,' said Romy. 'I don't want the responsibilities.'

'Romy, you've bent my ear a million times about how I treated you differently and how you never felt part of the family and how horrible the Dolans were to the Kilkennys,' said Veronica. 'Now you've got some Dolan interests and you can't complain any more.'

'But—'

'Besides, you're entitled to them,' said Veronica. She moved one of the pillows behind her into a more comfortable position. 'I always wanted to do something . . . to apologise . . . for . . . for everything . . . to make you realise that I never meant to hurt you.

'Look, Mum—'

'I know the divorce was really hard on you. I know that what happened at Kathryn's birthday changed everything between us. I felt awful about that. I . . . I still do. I was a terrible mother and I did a terrible thing and I don't have any defence whatsoever.'

'Even that he was too old for me?' asked Romy.

'I had to say something!' cried Veronica. 'Oh, look, I know that giving you the shares doesn't really make up for it, but . . . it's all I could think of. The truth is that I thought about it before, only you were away, and it seemed to me that if I did it you'd think I was bribing you to come home.' She sighed deeply. 'I remember wanting to give some to your father. And that's what he said. I was trying to tie him to the house by bribing him with Dolan shares.'

'He would say that, yes,' agreed Romy.

'And so for you I thought that, well, you're here. You came home anyway. So it wasn't a bribe.'

'I didn't want to come home,' Romy admitted.

'I know,' said Veronica. 'But the fact is that you did.'

'And I didn't think you wanted me here,' said Romy.

'How could you think that?' asked Veronica. 'You're my daughter. I was delighted you came.'

Romy felt tears prickle behind her eyes. 'Don't give me all that mother–daughter crap,' she said and swallowed.

'I won't,' said Veronica. 'It's not really me anyway, is it? But I've always said that I love all my children equally. And I do.'

Romy said nothing.

'You're a sensible girl,' said Veronica. 'Maybe not the sort of girl I understand in the same way as I understand Giselle, for example. But you know what you want and you have your head screwed on the right way, and I honestly can't think that you got that from Dermot, so I'm sort of hoping that inside my own bubble head there's actually some sensible stuff too and you got it from me.'

This time Romy smiled faintly. 'Whatever I got from you, Mum, it surely can't be level-headedness.'

'You'll be fine with those shares,' said Veronica. 'You really will.'

'They'll fight over it,' said Romy. 'And they'll hate me even more.'

'They won't hate you,' Veronica told her. 'They'll admire you. Like I do.'

Romy slid off the side of the bed where she'd been sitting. 'I never thought I was good enough for you,' she said. 'I thought it was because I was Dermot's daughter.'

'Oh, Romy.' Veronica looked at her. 'I'm really sorry if you thought that. I don't know what else I can do.'

Romy leaned over and kissed her on the forehead.

'Saying sorry and meaning it is more than enough,' she told Veronica. 'And I know that you mean it. I'm sorry too if I was awful to live with and always leaping to Dad's defence even if he was in the wrong. Now I'd better get to bed. I have a feeling I'm going to need all my faculties around me in the next few days.' She looked at Veronica quizzically. 'Is this why you're heading off to Cork in the morning? To be out of the firing line.'

'I wasn't thinking of it like that at the time.' Veronica grinned. 'But possibly.'

'Then you're right. Maybe if I've got any sort of sense it might be from you after all.'

'Good night, sweetheart,' said Veronica.

'Good night, Mum.' Romy felt as though she should say something more to her mother. But Veronica had already pointed the remote at the TV again. So she left the room and closed the door gently behind her.

Chapter 23

Veronica, along with some of her friends from the bridge club, had decided to take the midday train to Cork. Romy drove her to Heuston station, glad to be out of the house because she was certain that Darragh would call around to harass her about her shares and she didn't feel able to deal with him yet.

As she drove through the city she asked Veronica once again if she didn't want to change her mind, if she knew what she was doing by giving her the shares. And Veronica reiterated that she wasn't going to change her mind, that this was what she wanted to do. That Romy deserved to be a part of the company.

'I can't help wondering if "deserve" is being used correctly here,' said Romy sardonically. 'Maybe you think that I deserve to put up with the flak from Darragh.'

'It'll be short-lived,' Veronica promised her. 'He'll realise that it's only fair.'

But Romy truly wasn't so sure about that.

After she'd left Veronica at the station (her mother looking radiant in a short linen jacket, tapered trousers and her sequinned loafers), Romy continued on to the north side of the city and Dermot's house. She'd made the decision on the spur of the moment because she hadn't really been sure that she even wanted to talk to Dermot about the whole issue of the shares. She knew how he felt about Dolan Component Manufacturers. He hated the company, had always resented the hold it had over Veronica and her two children by Tom. But she had to talk to someone.

As she stood on the doorstep, her finger poised over the bell, she could hear the sound of a child screaming angrily within. She hesitated. Maybe now wasn't the best time to call. But she rang the bell anyway and about a minute later her father opened the door.

'Oh,' he said. 'This is a surprise.' He was barefoot, wearing loose jeans and a blue T-shirt stained with an unidentifiable liquid.

'Bad time?'

Erin's roars echoed around the house.

'Larissa's gone shopping,' said Dermot dolefully. 'Erin always goes bonkers when she leaves without her. She sprayed me with Fairy Liquid just now as a protest.'

Romy followed the sound of the little girl into the kitchen at the back of the house.

'Hey, Erin,' she said. 'It's me. Romy. Your . . . your big sister.'

Erin stopped crying and looked at her from enormous blue eyes which were still brimful of tears.

'Why don't we sit down together for a while and I'll read you a story?' offered Romy.

The little girl looked at her uncertainly.

'Pick a book.' Romy gestured at the selection of Mr Men and other children's books scattered around the kitchen.

'Great,' she said as Erin handed her a brightly coloured storybook. '*Farmyard Tales*. Let's go.'

She sat and read to Erin for nearly twenty minutes while Dermot changed his T-shirt and then cleared up the disaster area that was the kitchen. After that she allowed Erin to sit on her lap and twist her hair around her fingers while she talked to her father.

'I didn't think you were good at that.' Dermot was surprised at how docile Erin had become.

'Hidden talents.' Romy grinned. 'Actually, I didn't think I'd be good at it either. I must have a maternal instinct after all.'

'Whatever, it's very welcome,' said Dermot. 'It's not like I can't cope with her, but sometimes she goes off on her own wavelength and there's nothing I can do.'

'You were great with me,' Romy told him.

'You never cried,' said Dermot simply. 'If you didn't get what you wanted you just sulked instead.'

Romy chuckled.

'Anyway, it's lovely to see you.' Dermot sat down in the faded but comfortable armchair opposite her. 'How're things in Rathfarnham Towers?'

She grinned. 'The name of the house is Avalon,' she reminded him.

'I know.'

'Well, they've actually taken an unexpected turn.'

She recounted the events of the previous night and Dermot looked at her in astonishment.

'She's selling the house! And she's given you shares!' he exclaimed. 'But – but, honey, they could be worth a lot of money.'

'Only if someone wants to buy the company,' said Romy. 'Which Darragh will never let happen.'

'He might,' said Dermot. 'If he keeps on with these expansionary plans, maybe he'll need to sell off a bit to bring a new partner in.'

Romy shook her head. 'I doubt that. It's not how he sees the company. Or himself. At the moment, though, he's just enraged about the whole thing, 'cos he thought he'd get the shares. And Kathryn is quietly amused but probably delighted that he doesn't have the majority so he still has to ask her about doing stuff. And I – I'm in the middle of them.'

'An interesting place to be,' observed Dermot.

'Dad! It's a freaking nightmare, that's what it is. In fact it's such a damn nightmare that I'm not altogether sure it isn't some kind of revenge plot by Veronica.'

'Revenge for what?'

'For being a stroppy teenager. For having headed off on all those digs. For not being pretty and gorgeous like she wants.'

'A bit extreme, surely. All teenagers are stroppy, and why shouldn't you go on the digs? Plus, my sweet, I think you're pretty gorgeous.'

Romy grinned at him. 'Dads always think their daughters are lovely even when they're not. And I'm not, not really.' She ran her fingers through her hair. 'Why, why, why does life have to be so complicated? And why is it always my parents who make it that way?'

Dermot looked affronted. 'I haven't complicated your life,' he said.

'Not deliberately,' agreed Romy.

'Do you hate me?' asked Dermot. 'For the divorce and everything?'

Romy smiled warmly at him. 'Of course not,' she said. 'How could I hate you? You're my dad. And so – I love you. No matter what.'

'I'm glad to hear it.' Dermot sounded relieved. 'Because I love you too.'

'It's good to know that there'll be some loving coming my way,' said Romy gloomily. 'Because it's going to be pistols at dawn from the others.'

'Perhaps they'll agree over the company,' said Dermot.

'They never do,' Romy told him. 'And apparently there's some deal that Darragh's trying to push through which Kathryn doesn't approve of. That's why I reckon it could get messy.'

'Don't get involved,' advised her father.

'I can't not! That's the problem.' Romy looked at him in frustration. 'Apparently I have to vote on things as a share-holder, and as well as that, Kathryn said that I'll probably take Veronica's place on the board.'

Dermot laughed. 'I never thought I'd see the day when a Kilkenny would be on the Dolan board.'

'You might have if you'd taken the jobs when Veronica offered them,' said Romy.

'I couldn't do that.'

'I know.'

Dermot looked at Romy quizzically. 'You really would've liked me to, wouldn't you?'

'Sometimes.'

'I'm sorry,' he said and then smiled awkwardly at her. 'I keep having to apologise to you for things I didn't know mattered.'

'It's OK,' she assured him. 'Honestly. You wouldn't have been you if you'd started working in Dolan's. And I'd have hated that.'

'Thanks.'

'You did the right thing. And me – well, I think by coming home I did the right thing too.'

'You'll be heading off again soon. You'll be out of their way.'

'I'll still have to vote. And I'm not heading off for a few months.'

'Oh?'

Romy explained about the job in Wicklow.

'I'm surprised,' said Dermot. 'But glad that you're going to be around for a bit longer.'

'It seemed like a good idea at the time,' Romy told him wryly. 'Now I'm not so sure.'

'Never mind.' Dermot grinned. 'Let's forget about them. Are you rushing back today? Or can you spend more time with me?'

Giselle arrived back at the house from dropping Mimi to a birthday party for one of her ballet class friends. The little girl had waved her away quite happily and Giselle couldn't help feeling that already – even before she started school – her daughter was becoming independent and asserting her own personality. It was a good thing, she knew, but as Mimi ran into Flora's house without a backward glance, Giselle found herself patting the bump of her stomach and thinking that it would be nice to have the total dependence of the new baby. Even a fat new baby. It would be good to know that for a short while, someone would think that she was the centre of their universe.

Normally she liked to believe that Darragh thought that way, but since Veronica's announcement about giving the shares to Romy she'd realised that Dolan Component Manufacturers was still the centre of his universe. If she'd suddenly announced that she was leaving him she didn't think that he'd be any more devastated than he was over the idea of Romy having a say in the running of the company.

As she walked into the kitchen he looked up from the papers he had spread out over the table when they'd got home the previous night.

'I can't believe Mum,' he said for what she reckoned was about the fiftieth time. 'I don't know what she's thinking and I don't know why she's done what she's done.'

Giselle hung her bag over the back of the chair. 'She's betrayed us,' she said, feeling another spurt of anger herself as she thought about Veronica's actions. 'We've always been there for her, and by doing this—'

'She knows that Romy isn't entitled to those shares!' cried Darragh. 'My dad wouldn't have wanted it.'

'Can't you explain that to her?' asked Giselle.

'As soon as she comes back from her damn break I'll certainly explain it to her,' Darragh told her. 'For crying out loud, it's not as though Romy has any interest in the company anyhow! She's so damn snooty about it usually. So I really don't know what's going through Mum's head.'

'We don't know what Romy's been saying to her every day,' Giselle said. 'All sorts, probably. Doing us down.'

'I should never have asked her to come home.' Darragh,

who had got up from the table and begun pacing up and down the kitchen, spun around and faced his wife. 'It's my fault. I thought it was the right thing. I put her in the position where she could influence Veronica.'

Giselle looked at him miserably. 'Maybe it's my fault. I could've had your mum stay here but I thought that Romy should come home.'

'Sweetie, you couldn't have coped with her,' said Darragh. 'When she came out of hospital she needed help getting around the place and you couldn't have helped her. You're pregnant with our baby and that's really important. So don't feel as though it's your fault.'

'Even if I could've coped I didn't really want her here,' confessed Giselle. 'But I should have thought of what might happen.'

Darragh stared at her. 'What d'you mean, you didn't want her here? You said that you did.'

'That's not entirely true,' she admitted uneasily. 'It would've been very difficult but we could've worked it out. I just didn't think that I could have put up with her here all day. So when you said that it would be hard on me, I agreed with you.'

'Why?' demanded Darragh. 'Why did you agree with me if you thought you could've managed? I thought you were a bit disappointed over the whole thing actually. I thought you would've wanted her to stay if at all possible. You get on with her, don't you?'

'Of course I do. But not all day, every day.'

'I can't believe this!' he cried. 'You mean we could've had her here but because you didn't want to – and not because you couldn't cope – we made Romy come home; and now because of that she's scooped up the shares that we should have got!'

Giselle looked at him uncomfortably, wishing heartily she'd kept her mouth shut. 'It's not that I don't care about your mum,' she said rapidly. 'But she's kind of overwhelming at times. She would've interfered and I hate people interfering.'

'My mother is a great woman,' said Darragh fiercely. 'She wouldn't have interfered but she might have offered you help or advice.'

'I don't need help or advice!'

'Maybe she could have done a bit of cooking,' said Darragh curtly. 'She could have taught you how to feed me properly. And feed yourself too while you're at it.'

'On that damn pie crap?' Giselle was really annoyed now.

'There's nothing wrong with my mother's food.' Darragh was equally annoyed. 'She's a brilliant cook and she doesn't obsess about calories and cholesterol and all that nonsense. I wouldn't have minded a bit of her home cooking once in a while, and maybe if you thought a bit more about what you ate you wouldn't keel over at the drop of a hat.'

'I don't keel over at the drop of a hat!' cried Giselle. 'I'm a healthy eater.'

'Oh, come on.' Darragh looked at her impatiently. 'There can be too much of a good thing.'

'Well, thanks a bunch for appreciating how much I try to look after you and our family!' cried Giselle. 'You're such a mammy's boy, aren't you? As far as you're concerned, there's nobody in the whole world better at anything than your damn mother. Well, looks like it doesn't matter how much you defend her; she's still gone off and left us high and dry with what she's done with those shares.'

'She was entitled to do it,' said Darragh. 'She's wrong, but she was entitled to do it.'

'Oh, for God's sake! Are you forgiving her now – just because I dared to criticise her?'

'It's not a question of forgiveness,' said Darragh.

'Good,' said Giselle, 'because we've worked bloody hard for that company and if she thinks that she can just write us out of it like that . . .'

'*I've* worked bloody hard,' said Darragh. 'You haven't.'

'Excuse me!' Giselle was outraged. 'Who was it that did the

makeover and turned it into a modern company instead of some ancient creaking old firm?'

'Those were cosmetic changes,' he said. 'Expensive cosmetic changes which had the effect of depressing the bottom line. And maybe that's why Veronica is holding out on me. Maybe she thinks I allowed you to plough too much money into things that don't really matter. Kathryn probably said that to her. She's always thought the makeover was a complete waste of time.'

'Oh, great.' Giselle looked scornful. 'Just because your sister is back you get cold feet about everything. Kathryn hasn't a clue about style and fashion and how things should be.'

'We're an industrial component manufacturer!' cried Darragh. 'Not a fashion emporium! And Kathryn looks OK these days.'

'I did a good job.' Giselle was furious with him. Not just for his sudden decision that the upgrade had been a bad idea, but also because he had noticed that Kathryn looked good.

'You cost us a fortune,' he said.

'You thought it was a good idea!'

'I never expected you to go a hundred per cent over budget.'

'It was a stingy budget!'

'We're a family firm,' said Darragh. 'Not a global conglomerate.'

'And I'm family!' yelled Giselle. 'But your mother doesn't really see it like that after all, does she? Otherwise she'd have given me shares and not bloody Romy.'

'Romy is my sister,' said Darragh.

'Half-sister. And I'm your wife!' Giselle couldn't quite believe that somehow Darragh had managed to work himself into a position where – despite how he really felt – he was actually supporting his mother's insane decision.

'Oh, I know,' said Darragh. 'And I'm your meal ticket.'

Giselle's eyes glittered furiously. 'How dare you suggest that!'

'Because that's how you see me,' Darragh told her. 'Don't think that I don't know it. Don't think that I haven't realised that our relationship, our marriage, is all about you. What it gives you. What you can get out of it. You can do your shopping and your lunching and all that sort of stuff and it doesn't matter because I pay for it all. But if I couldn't . . . if we lost everything . . .'

'You're impossible in this mood,' cried Giselle. 'If you carry on like this at board meetings it's no wonder Veronica gave the shares to Romy!'

'Well thanks for your support. I'm out of here!' He stormed out of the kitchen and Giselle heard the slam of the front door as he left the house too.

'Damn,' she said as she flopped down on to a chair. 'Damn and blast and damn.'

Veronica eyed her partner over the green baize table.

'No trump,' she said.

Will Blake grinned at her and she smiled back. They had been cleaning up at the table so far, having won most of the rubbers they'd played, and she was feeling good about life again. She'd sorted things for Romy, and although it had been a shock to Darragh and Kathryn, she knew that they would have to resolve it between them. When Romy had ranted at her about the way Dolan's had always been part of Darragh and Kathryn's lives but not hers, and how it had always kept her apart from them, Veronica had realised that she was absolutely right. If Romy had been Tom's daughter there wouldn't have been any question about the shares. It was wrong that Romy should lose out. And she'd been wrong to do what she'd done at Kathryn's birthday. So giving her the shares would make things right on a whole heap of levels, even if it was a little bit awkward now. Anyway, thought Veronica as her eyes flickered over the cards on the

360

table, Romy still had less than the other two, which was fair.

She knew that Darragh didn't think so. She also knew that Kathryn didn't mind. She knew too that Romy would probably have to be strong. But, thought Veronica, if she wanted to be part of the Dolan empire, that was how she would have to be.

'We win.' Will Blake's words cut into her thoughts and she realised that they had taken yet another rubber – no thanks to her. 'Time for a break,' he said. 'Can I get anyone a drink?'

The men were on beer and the women drinking wine. Will went to the bar and Connie and Graham, their opposition, began talking about the hotel and the facilities and the enjoyment they got out of travelling to tournaments, while Veronica nodded from time to time in agreement.

It was good, she thought, to be away from them all. She loved her children, but having them around her all the time was becoming suffocating. She'd decided as much at her ill-fated dinner party – why, she wondered, had she thought that would be a good idea? Other people's families might be able to sit around the table as though they were auditioning for an episode of *The Cosby Show*, but hers never would. And maybe that was a good thing. Maybe that proved that she'd raised strong, independent children.

Or maybe they're all just totally messed up, she thought ruefully. Maybe I was a crap mother, just like Romy said.

Alan still hadn't responded to her voicemail. Kathryn felt bad about having left it but good about the fact that she'd summoned up the strength to do it. However, some of that strength was beginning to ebb away and that made her angry with herself. What's the matter with me, she wondered, that I can't deal with this the same way as I deal with everything else? Why am I being so uncertain about it when I know there's only one thing to do?

She dialled his cell again.

'It's me,' she said. 'I know you're not picking up my calls but you need to know that I'm serious. I'm sure my lawyers will be in touch soon.'

She disconnected and realised that her hands were shaking. She stared at the phone in her trembling palm, expecting it to ring, expecting him to call her this time. But it remained resolutely silent.

What was he going to do? In her mind she'd gone through a whole heap of scenarios, but she had a horrible feeling that no matter what the worst one she came up with was, he'd actually manage to top it. It didn't matter, though. She'd made the decision. She'd told him she wanted the divorce. She could get back to her life again.

She sat at Veronica's computer and logged on to her webmail service.

She scrolled through her work emails, which were automatically forwarded to her personal address when she was out of the office. Although she checked them every day and answered the ones she could, there were still a lot of things piling up. She'd have to go back soon. When she'd told them she needed some time off to visit her mum and said she didn't exactly know how long she'd have to take, they'd practically laughed at her. But then she reminded them that she hadn't taken her holidays the previous year and that she needed time and that she was going to take it. Now that time was almost up.

In more ways than one, she thought as she stared unseeingly at the screen and wondered whether she had to go back and face him at all. Whether it wouldn't be easier all round for her to remain exactly where she was now.

After all, it wasn't as though she had so much to lose by staying in Ireland. And perhaps she had a lot to save. She could get a job here. There was plenty of work. Maybe even in Dolan's. She chuckled humourlessly. There was a whole new set-up in Dolan's now, what with her and Darragh on an equal footing as far as their shareholding was concerned. Because although they might have always had the same before, the fact that Veronica always voted with Darragh had made Kathryn irrelevant. Romy wouldn't always vote with Darragh, though. Would she? Kathryn rubbed the base of her neck, which had begun to ache.

Romy was a complicating factor, really. Veronica shouldn't have given her the shares at all. Not, Kathryn thought, because she wasn't entitled to something – she'd always felt bad about the fact that Romy was excluded from the whole Dolan dynasty thing that Veronica and Darragh had going on – but because it had put her in a terrible position and Romy just wasn't interested anyway, which meant there was potential for a complete disaster.

It's all such a mess, Kathryn thought. Personally, professionally. For me. For everyone. She'd thought that coming home might have helped her to clarify her own problems, but it had only succeeded in making them seem even more complicated.

The ring of the doorbell, long and shrill, startled her and she jumped.

'Fool,' she muttered to herself. 'There's no need to be like some damned scaredy-cat.'

The bell rang again, more insistent this time. She pushed the chair back from the table and walked quietly into the hallway and opened it. Her brother was standing on the step. She released the breath she'd been holding.

'Hi,' she said as he pushed past her and went into the living room. 'How's Giselle?'

Darragh sat down in one of the armchairs and then got up again.

'I suppose you think this is great fun,' he said, ignoring her question.

'What?'

'This mess that Mum has landed us with.'

'It's not a mess,' lied Kathryn. 'Or at least it doesn't have to be.'

'Yeah right.' Darragh snorted. 'Our little half-breed sister—'

'Darragh!'

'OK,' he said, 'our conniving half-sister—'

'What are you like?' demanded Kathryn. 'Honestly, Darragh Dolan, you've always been horrible to Romy. She's our sister and that's that.'

'Half-sister,' he repeated. 'And she *is* conniving.'

'How?'

'You don't think she's engineered all this?' he asked. 'For someone who investigates fraud, you're particularly naïve.'

'Of course she didn't engineer it,' said Kathryn. 'For heaven's sake, Darragh, you're being paranoid. You know that she has no interest whatsoever in Dolan's.'

'Yeah, so why the hell has Mum given her one?'

'Perhaps Mum wanted to repay her,' said Kathryn. 'For giving up her job. That was a hard thing for Romy to do.'

'Oh come on!' He snorted again. 'Giving up faffing around in the mud? To live here in luxury? Not exactly a hardship.'

'For Romy maybe it was,' said Kathryn.

'She has the wool pulled over your eyes too,' said Darragh. 'Don't tell me that in the cold light of day you think she actually deserves those shares?'

Kathryn shrugged. 'We have more than her. She can't dictate policy. What's the problem?'

'The problem is that they were for me and Giselle,' said Darragh angrily.

'Why?'

'Because we deserved them.'

'Why?'

'Because I'm the managing director of the company and I've worked hard and so has Giselle . . .' He faltered as he thought of the argument they'd had earlier and his fury with his wife, but shoved it as far back into his mind as he could.

'I'm entitled to those shares. She told me she was giving them to me.'

'But why should you be entitled to them?' asked Kathryn. 'Why do you think that just because you're working in the company – and taking out quite a hefty salary by the way – and just because you live nearby . . . why that should entitle you to more?'

'Because I'm . . . it's my business!' cried Darragh. 'It always has been.'

'It's a family business,' Kathryn reminded him. 'Isn't that what we say on our marketing material?'

'Stop splitting hairs.'

'I'm not,' said Kathryn. 'You seem to think that you've got some God-given right to do what you like with it. Well you haven't. I'm as equal a shareholder as you. And although Mum might have agreed with everything you wanted, there's no reason to believe that Romy will.'

'You bitch!' Darragh glared at her. 'You've got a plan, haven't you? To make Romy side with you on everything.'

'No I bloody haven't,' said Kathryn. 'But hopefully she'll see sense over some things.'

'See your side of it is what you mean,' said Darragh. 'So that you can block me at every turn.'

'Darragh—'

'It's my company,' he said fiercely. 'And nobody is going to take it away from me. Not you. Not her. Not an unwelcome corporate bidder. Nobody. I'll make sure of that, I promise you.'

Chapter 24

The house was in darkness when Romy arrived home.

She'd spent the day with Dermot and Larissa even though that hadn't been her original intention. But when Larissa had got home she'd invited Romy to stay for lunch and then she'd hung around talking to her while Dermot took some studio shots of a couple who were celebrating their twenty-fifth wedding anniversary. In the end she'd stayed for dinner too, helping Larissa peel vegetables for the stew that she was preparing. As they'd worked together Romy had made some quip about nobody in her family lasting the pace for twenty-five years and Larissa had said, quite seriously, that she fully expected to be with Dermot for that long. Romy had laughed, but Larissa, still serious, told her that marriage had to be worked at and that she would work at it because she loved Dermot and she wanted her family to be happy. And then she told Romy that they were currently trying for another baby, which Romy felt was too much information but which also made her feel, once again, as though she was peripheral to Dermot's new life, even if she couldn't help feeling that he was very happy in it and entitled to be happy.

Half a Kilkenny and half a Dolan, she was thinking as she pointed the zapper at the gates to open them, and not feeling as though I belong to either of them any more. Except, of course, Veronica has done this mad thing with the shares to make me feel wanted by the Dolan half but which will only complicate my life even further.

She parked the car and then let herself into the silent house, wondering if Kathryn and Darragh were having an emergency Dolan family meeting to discuss the new shareholder set-up. She was pretty sure there'd be plenty of discussion between the two of them about her and she hadn't yet decided how to deal with it. She was half hoping that Veronica hadn't actually finalised the transfer of the shares and that she could stop her so that things could go back to the way they were. She was amused at this thought, knowing how she'd always hated the way it had been before and how she'd longed (not because of any interest in the company but only to feel accepted) to be part of it.

Be careful what you wish for. The old Chinese proverb ran through her head as she opened the door. You might get it. And having got it, she murmured to herself, I so hate it!

She went into the kitchen and poured herself a glass of water. Then she walked into the living room. She switched on the lights and then let out a startled cry as she realised that Kathryn was stretched out on the sofa.

'I didn't know you were there!' she exclaimed while Kathryn blinked a couple of times in the light. 'You almost frightened the life out of me.'

'Sorry.' Kathryn sat up. 'I was . . . thinking. I like to think in the dark.'

That was true. Romy remembered times in their childhood when Kathryn would retreat to her bedroom for some solitude. And Romy knew that she would sit there for hours as night fell but that she never bothered to switch on the lights.

'What were you thinking about?' she asked.

'Stuff.'

'Stuff like me and the shares?'

'Only partly,' said Kathryn. 'Darragh was around earlier.'

'Oh.'

'He's pretty upset.'

'I guessed as much.'

'He feels as though Mum has let him down.'

'I can understand that.'

'But,' said Kathryn, 'I think Mum has made quite a clever decision. After all, there'd be no point in giving Darragh complete control. Every company needs checks and balances. And if she'd divided the shares evenly between Darragh and me there'd be nothing but stalemate. So giving some to you was a good idea.'

'From her point of view maybe,' said Romy glumly. 'All it does for me is make me a pawn in your constant bickering.'

Kathryn laughed. 'It won't be like that.'

'Won't it?' Romy looked at her in disbelief. 'If, as you say, there'd be a stalemate between you because you want different things, you're looking to me to break that stalemate. If I go along with your wishes, Darragh will be angry. And if I do what he wants, you'll have a canary.'

'You'll just have to negotiate,' said Kathryn.

'Oh, come on!' Romy looked at her impatiently. 'I don't want to. You know that. He knows that. Veronica knows that. She's just being . . . contrary, I guess! But it's not helpful. Besides, I know nothing about the company.'

'Maybe it's time to learn,' said Kathryn.

Romy looked at her miserably. 'This is so not what I want to learn about.'

'It's not that bad,' Kathryn assured her. 'It's quite straight-forward really.'

'If that's the case, then why do you and Darragh fight over it?'

'Direction,' said Kathryn simply. 'Different vision. I think mine is better but that's only an opinion. Some of his plans aren't half bad but he usually makes a bags of executing them.

He gets sidetracked into unnecessary projects. I keep telling him that all he really needs to do is concentrate on our core values.'

'Y'see, it's phrases like that that do my head in!' cried Romy. 'Core values! That means nothing to me.'

Kathryn grinned again. 'Our core values are manufacturing high-level industrial components. We provide a quality product at a reasonable price and we also give a great after-sales service. We're not always the cheapest but we're always the best.'

'And doesn't Darragh share that core value?' asked Romy.

'Darragh wants to be a captain of industry who's loved and respected even by people who don't do business with us,' said Kathryn. 'Because of that he wants to invest in things that aren't part of the Dolan knowledge-set.'

'Maybe that's a good thing.' Romy shrugged.

'There's nothing wrong with diversification,' agreed Kathryn. 'You've just got to know what you're diversifying into and why.'

Romy made a face. 'This all sounds far too much like hard work to me. To be honest, I'm going to talk to Veronica when she comes back. I want to make her change her mind.'

'And do what?' asked Kathryn.

'Take the shares back. Everything was fine the way it was before.'

Kathryn shrugged. 'Depends on what you mean,' she said. 'If you think it's fine that Darragh gets his own way on everything, even if that's not good for the company, then by all means allow Mum to get involved again. But if you think the company should be professionally run so that the value of it goes up, then perhaps you should think again.'

'Y'see!' cried Romy. 'It's starting already. You're trying to influence me.'

'Darragh influenced Mum for years,' Kathryn told her. 'I'm

not doing anything different. And I'm going to give you an unbiased picture. I promise.'

'I don't care about the damn company,' Romy told her. 'It means nothing to me.'

'It should,' said Kathryn. 'If you own a part of it, it should mean a lot.'

Romy groaned.

'Listen to me.' Kathryn suddenly grabbed her by the wrists, surprising her. 'You've got to get something into your head. This is a business. We have employees. We have a responsibility towards them as well as towards ourselves. Maybe you'll persuade Mum to take back the shares, although I think that would be a pity. Maybe you'll want to divide them between me and Darragh so that the two of us can slug it out between us. But whatever you do, you have to know why you're doing it. And it isn't just about you. It's about everybody who has anything to do with Dolan's. You have to understand that.'

Romy had never heard Kathryn speak so passionately about the company before. She was surprised at how fervent she was and how much it really did seem to matter to her. She'd always thought it was only Darragh who really cared.

'Oh, all right,' she said in resignation. 'Give me whatever information you think I need to know. But I warn you, I haven't a clue about business and it'll probably just go in one ear and out the other.'

Kathryn smiled at her. 'I'll make it interesting for you, I promise.'

Romy suddenly realised that it was a long time since she'd seen Kathryn smile and mean it. She finds this fun, she thought. We really are totally different people! But she sat down beside her and started to listen.

Later that night, after she'd spent what seemed like hours trying to absorb everything Kathryn told her about Dolan

371

Component Manufacturers, Romy went up to her room, opened her laptop and Skyped Keith.

'Hey!' he said when they'd connected. 'Nice to hear from you.'

'Really?'

'Well, yeah, really. It's been a while. I thought that you were too busy with the new job . . .'

'I don't start that till Monday,' she told him. 'And I'm soooo looking forward to it.'

He laughed, his face in the video link crinkling up with amusement. 'I'm glad.'

'Me too,' she said contentedly. 'It'll be a bit like normal life again. It's been so weird here especially now that Mum has given me some shares in the company! I've spent the night being lectured in corporate responsibility by Kathryn.'

'Romy!' He looked surprised. 'Didn't you always say that they'd never let you get involved?'

'Yes, but—'

'So isn't that a good thing?'

'You'd think, but—'

'Doesn't it mean they accept you?'

'Oh, Keith.' She groaned. 'I know I always banged on about being accepted by them but this isn't the way I meant it. Quite honestly, all I want is my life back!'

He laughed again. 'Poor Romy. You never seem to really know what you want.'

'Probably not,' she conceded. 'Do you?'

'Know what you want?'

'Know what *you* want,' she retorted. 'You're great at giving me unasked-for advice and telling me how I should be with my family and what I should do with my life – but d'you know what you want from yours? Is it all crystal clear as far as you're concerned?'

He was silent and immobile and she thought for a moment that the connection had gone down.

'That's a fair question,' he replied eventually.

'Oh, Keith, I'm sorry, I'm not being fair at all by asking it,' she told him. 'I'm just frazzled by everything. I know that you know absolutely what you want. You've always been totally together about stuff. It's only me . . .' She shrugged. 'Anyway, maybe it'll all work out.'

'And then?'

'Then . . .' She shrugged again. 'Then I'll apply for another job on another dig somewhere else in the world.'

'Not here?'

'I don't know,' she said. 'There isn't as much available work there as in other places. I browsed the Heritage Help site earlier. They're not looking for people right now. They've got everyone they need in Melbourne and they don't have anything in Sydney. So . . . maybe I'll go back to Lisbon like I originally planned.'

'Perhaps that would be best,' he agreed after a moment's silence. 'I know that there's a new dig supposed to be starting up there in a couple of months. I bet you'd like it.'

'It might suit me. Anyway, I'll let you know.'

'Of course.'

'I'd better go,' she told him. 'I'm totally knackered. When I'm on a dig I get tired but it's a physical thing. All this family stuff just does my head in and I feel twice as tired.'

He smiled.

'So . . . g'day,' she said.

'Good night,' he replied.

She logged off Skype. She'd wanted to blurt it all out to Keith – how difficult it all seemed, how terrified she was of being in the middle of Kathryn and Darragh, how she felt as though she had lost control of her life. But she hadn't said any of these things because she knew that Keith wouldn't understand. His life was easy and uncomplicated. And by bombarding him with a list of her complaints and worries she would only mess up what friendship there was between them by appearing a perpetual moaning minnie. He was still her best friend, after all. But there was a limit to how much even best friends could take.

Giselle was in bed, worrying. It was now after eleven and Darragh hadn't come home yet. He hadn't called her either, which he normally always did if he was out late; nor had he answered the voicemail she'd left on his mobile phone. She knew that he was angry with her but it had been a long time since he was so annoyed with anything she'd said or done that he'd walked out of the house.

It had happened once before, in the early years of their marriage, when she complained about him calling in to Veronica on his way home from the office when he was already late. He was married now, she told him, and he couldn't go dancing attendance on his mother every minute of every day. It had been their only big, monumental row. Darragh had gone bright red with rage and shouted that she didn't understand a thing, did she? That Veronica needed him and that the company did too. The company, he said, was the most important thing in both their lives. Veronica was part of the company. Veronica's vote mattered. Both were important. And Veronica needed his time. If Giselle didn't understand that, Darragh raged, she didn't understand anything to do with Dolan's and their lives together. And then he'd stalked out of the house, slamming the door behind him.

Of course she'd understood it. While she readily admitted that she wasn't always the brightest button in the box when it came to the family business, she had a keen sense of what was important and what wasn't as far as the family itself was concerned. When he'd come home (he'd stayed out until the morning, overnighting at a city centre hotel), he'd apologised to her for shouting at her and she'd apologised to him for nagging. She'd told him that she loved Veronica as much as her own mother. That the company was as much part of her life as it was of his. And then she'd thrown herself completely into the role of being the perfect wife. She got involved in the corporate makeover; she took Veronica on shopping trips, and she knew that she had become closer to her than either of her two daughters and more important to Darragh than anyone else too. She began to realise that Darragh needed someone uncritical and supportive by his side. She was prepared to be that person because she knew that if Darragh was happy then the company did well and it meant more money for them all.

Giselle liked the money, he was right about that. She liked not having to worry about the cost of her clothes and her hair and her holidays or anything else that she wanted. Darragh paid her a monthly allowance for housekeeping and for herself and it was a very generous amount. All she had to do in return, she knew, was to be there for him. And although she sometimes grew impatient with him, she was happy in her marriage. She knew that he was happy too. He said so, loads of times. He told her that he loved her. And why wouldn't he? Wasn't she the perfect wife?

Only it was hard for the perfect wife to trump the perfect mother. As far as Darragh was concerned, Veronica could do no wrong even when she was clearly being incredibly stupid. Giselle wished he'd allow her the same latitude.

She looked at her watch again. She wanted to phone him and yet she didn't know whether it would be a good idea. When Darragh was in a temper, in a real rage, it was better to leave him alone. He hated someone trying to talk him out of it. He rarely lost it completely these days but when he did he usually went to the gym and pounded the treadmill until he'd worked it all off. But the gym would be closed by now and he still wasn't home.

Giselle felt sick. She hoped that she hadn't pushed him too far. She wanted him to come home. Now.

Darragh was in his club in the city centre. He wanted to be somewhere quiet and peaceful, away from Romy and Kathryn and especially away from Giselle because he knew that even the sight of her would send his blood pressure soaring. He'd taken his wife at her word when she'd said that having Veronica stay would be too difficult for her. He'd never for one second imagined that she wouldn't want to have his mother in the house. He'd loved her and he'd trusted her and she'd let him down.

Mammy's boy! That was what she'd called him. She'd spat it at him as an insult, her face contorted with anger. He'd never seen Giselle look like that before. She'd be sorry, he thought darkly. Sorry for helping to get them into this mess and sorry for calling him names and sorry for everything.

Actually, Darragh thought, they'd all be sorry. His mother too. After all, Giselle was right about one thing. Veronica had betrayed them. All those years when they'd sat together around the rosewood table in the boardroom (the table which Tom had picked up in a second-hand shop in Francis Street and lovingly restored); all those years she'd listened to what he had to say and agreed with it and he had always been right. He'd steered the company to its current levels of profitability, and instead of rewarding him all she was doing was snatching it away from him. He'd never really felt angry with her before but he was furious now.

He'd called to Kathryn that afternoon to try to talk to her and make her see that the situation was untenable. But she'd laughed at him and told him to grow up and get a life. She'd grinned and said that things didn't always work out the way you expected, did they? But they had worked out for her. He knew that Kathryn was now earmarking Romy as an ally, someone to be on her side, not his, when the big decisions had to be taken. So it had worked out just fine for Kathryn. Which was why she looked at him with detached amusement when she spoke. He'd been so angry with her at that point that he'd had to leave because he was afraid that if he stayed he'd just punch her in her smiling face.

It was a long time since he'd felt so angry. And so help-less. Probably not since the day when he'd seen Tom holding the bloodstained towel to his nose. Everything had changed then. Everything was going to change now.

Unless he did something to stop it.

Chapter 25

Romy had expected to pick Veronica up from the train station on Monday evening but her mother phoned her to say that she was going to take the option of staying on for an extra week.

'Having a good time, then?' asked Romy.

'Well, yes, I guess so,' said Veronica. 'It's ages since I came away with the bridge crowd and I'd forgotten how much fun they are. Besides,' she added, 'I don't feel like coming home yet and letting you and Kathryn and Darragh and probably Giselle too have a go at me.'

'In that case you shouldn't have given us the opportunity,' retorted Romy.

'I want you to work it out between yourselves.'

'Mum, you know that's insane,' said Romy. 'We can't.'

'I'm sure you can,' said Veronica. 'In fact, I'm not going to come home until you do.'

Romy laughed shortly. 'In that case you'd better check out the hotel rates. You might be away for a long time.'

'Talk it through,' said Veronica.

'We wouldn't have to if you'd talked to us first.'

'And let myself be persuaded out of it?'

'It might have been for the best.'

'It's not,' said Veronica firmly. 'I know what I'm doing. But I'm still staying out of harm's way for a few days. I'll call you during the week.'

'OK.' Romy replaced the receiver with a half-smile. Her mother's words had reminded her of her Agatha Christie scenario again – Veronica's battered body found in the hallway of Avalon with the entire family under suspicion. Only it wouldn't be Veronica's body now, would it? Veronica didn't own the shares any more. She shivered suddenly. Both Darragh and Kathryn wanted her shares because the majority shareholder would control the future of the company. What lengths would either of them be prepared to go to in order to get them from her?

OK, she muttered as she walked back into the living room, where Kathryn was stretched out on the sofa reading a book. I'm losing my marbles now. They might hate me but I need to keep a sense of perspective. I'm not living through an episode of *Midsomer Murders*!

'What time's her train?' Kathryn looked up from her book.

Romy explained about Veronica's decision to stay away for a few more days. Kathryn chuckled.

'Doesn't want to face us?'

'What about you?' Romy asked. 'Don't you have to get back to the States? You came to see Mum and clearly she's OK now that she's gallivanting around the place under her own steam.'

'I'll make arrangements during the week,' said Kathryn slowly. 'We'll be having a board meeting before I go to discuss everything.'

Romy groaned.

'Mum has to come back for that,' said Kathryn. 'And we have to decide on your position.'

'Do you hate me?' asked Romy suddenly.

Kathryn looked startled. 'Why would I hate you?'

'I have some of the shares. Maybe you might have got more . . .'

'Who knows?' Kathryn shrugged. 'It's not important. Besides, it's right that you should have some.'

'You think so?'

'Of course,' said Kathryn impatiently. 'I said it to Mum before.'

'You did?' This time it was Romy who looked startled.

'Yes. We do occasionally talk about you, you know.'

Romy groaned. 'I'm not sure I like the thought of that.'

'Get over it.' Kathryn chuckled. 'Mum cares about you. It's just that you never want to see it.'

Romy was silent for a moment. Is it true? she wondered. Do I constantly look for imagined slights and ignore the times when she pays me compliments or when she's fun to be with? Have I been obsessed with the wrong things all along?

'You OK?' Kathryn was watching the changing expressions on her sister's face.

Romy smiled. 'I think you've just knocked some of those chips off my shoulder,' she said. 'With one sentence.'

'Good,' said Kathryn cheerfully. 'You'll find it lightens the load. Anyhow . . . about the company. I'll talk to Darragh. See what he wants to do.'

'Will you miss it?' asked Romy. 'When you go back? All this corporate in-fighting?'

A shadow darkened Kathryn's face. 'There's plenty of in-fighting in the US too,' she said shortly.

'Bet Alan will be glad to see you.' There was a hint of a challenge in Romy's voice.

Kathryn hesitated. She still hadn't had a response to her message about the divorce. She couldn't say anything to Romy until she'd heard from Alan. Until it was official. It wouldn't be right. So she simply nodded at her sister as though agreeing with her. But she said nothing at all.

Romy was up early the following morning, excited at the thought of the Wicklow dig and finally getting back to doing something she truly enjoyed. As she got into the car her mobile beeped with a text alert. It was from Keith, wishing her good luck. She felt a lump in her throat as she read it. He was good to her, he really was. She missed him. She replied to his message, thanking him and telling him she'd call him and let him know all about it. And then he texted back to say that he'd be out of touch for the next day or two because he was investigating a site further north and the coverage was woeful but he was sure she'd be fine and he'd talk to her soon. Her face clouded over as she read the message. She couldn't help feeling that despite the fact that he'd sent the first message, he was retreating from her again.

She shoved the phone into her jeans pocket and started the engine. She was getting back to work. And even though it was in Ireland and she'd sworn to herself that she was never going to work here again, she was glad that she'd taken the job.

It took her forty minutes to get to the site. Taig was already there, wearing a grey T-shirt and cargo pants, his hair pulled back into its ponytail. For a moment she thought it was like her first dig again, when Keith had been the one to welcome her, but then Taig waved at her and shouted for her to join him and suddenly everything was very different.

The site had already been stripped back and test ditches dug. As she stood at the door of the Portakabin, pulling her hi-vis jacket on over her T-shirt, Romy looked at the various areas of land which had been marked out with pegs. Thanks to the previous week's rain it was still damp and muddy despite the warmth of the day's sun.

'I think it's possible that this is a small burial site,' Taig told her. 'The landowners are obviously hoping that if we uncover something it's not so fantastic that it delays their project. They want to build a housing development after all.'

Romy nodded. 'On the one hand it's so exciting if we find something. On the other – if we do it causes all sorts of hassle, doesn't it? It could be like Tara or Carrickmines.'

'I hope not,' said Taig grimly. All of them were well aware

of the controversies that accompanied development these days when preserving the old and catering for the needs of expanding towns and cities collided, sometimes dramatically.

'But these developers are local,' Taig continued. 'They want to incorporate any historical interest into their project.'

'Like what?' Romy grinned at him. 'A skeleton hanging from a tree?'

'Are you always this gross?' asked Taig in amusement. 'They're probably hoping for the ruins of a small church or something. Then they can put a little fence around the ruins and call the estate Church View.'

'I might be gross but I'm not that cynical.' Romy laughed. 'OK. Let's get down to it. Is there anything special you want me to do?'

She spent a happy day working with two other archaeologists as they investigated a trench along the eastern side of the site. After a few hours of work with her trowel she still hadn't uncovered anything more interesting than some old shilling coins and a Barbie doll's head. But she didn't really care. It was good to be outdoors again with the scent of grass and mud in her nostrils and the warmth of the breeze ruffling her hair. She ate her lunchtime sandwich sitting on a block outside the Portakabin, her legs stretched out in front of her as she chatted happily to Jerry and Mick about the likelihood of uncovering evidence of a burial site. Both of them were optimistic, and an hour or so before they finished up for the evening their optimism was rewarded as Jerry called out with delight and held up what they could see was a mud-encrusted shroud pin.

'Excellent!' cried Romy. 'So Taig might be right about the burial site after all.'

They continued with the work although by the end of the day they hadn't turned up anything else of importance. As

Romy got ready to call it a day, Taig came over and asked if she wanted to join them for a drink in the village pub.

She'd been going to say no, that she had to get home, but then she realised that she didn't. And that although she'd chugged back lots of water during the day she was thirsty and it would be nice to sit and talk to a whole new set of people. So she said yes instead and scrubbed her hands clean under the tap before changing into the clean pair of jeans and fresh T-shirt which she always brought with her.

An hour later she was sitting in the beer garden at the back of the quaint pub, a glass of Lucozade in front of her. Most of the team had come along and they were exchanging chat about the various projects they'd worked on over the last few years.

'My favourite was a field trip to Easter Island,' said Mai, a Finnish girl with flaxen hair and sky-blue eyes. 'We did surveys of the house sites but there was all sorts of interesting stuff. I kept unearthing mataas – obsidian spear points; had quite a collection by the time I finished. The whole atmosphere was amazing – you kept feeling as though those stone torsos were going to come alive at night. Spooky. But great.'

'I suppose my spookiest was an osteology project in Romania,' said Romy. 'Lots of interesting remains and loads of dental work and we were in a very Transylvanian setting. I kept wondering if I'd unearth vampires' fangs.'

'My worst was here,' said Jerry moodily. 'Galway, in the winter. It rained nonstop for a week. The site was one big mudbath and everything I possessed was coated in the stuff. You couldn't walk anywhere without ending up to your knees in sludge. And,' he added darkly, 'the trenches kept filling up with water. One day we arrived to find a fish swimming around in one of them.'

Romy laughed. 'You're such a liar!'

'It's true,' said Jerry defensively. 'I dunno where it came from or how it got there, but it was doing laps of our trench.'

Taig grinned. 'I prefer to do my digging in dry weather.

But that's not why I still think Egypt is the most interesting place I've ever been,' he said. 'I know it's a kind of cliché, but there's something about those pyramids that does it for me every time.'

They were all in agreement with that. And as Romy laughed and chatted with them she realised that she'd missed this over the last few weeks, the easy banter with people who had the same interests as her, people who didn't think that wanting to look at ancient bones and teeth was weird and faintly disgusting and people who didn't think that big business and lots of money was all that mattered in the world.

'I'd better get back,' she said after she'd finished her second Lucozade. 'It's not that I wouldn't like to stay here all evening, but it's a while since I've done so much digging. I need a bath!'

'Sure,' said Taig easily. 'See you tomorrow.'

'Absolutely.' Romy told him. 'Looking forward to it.'

'You look happy,' said Kathryn when Romy walked into the living room and plopped down on to the sofa.

'I had a great day.' She beamed at her sister. 'We didn't find much but it was good to be out there again.'

'You know you've got mud on the carpet?'

Romy sat upright. 'Oh, shit. No.'

Kathryn laughed. 'It's dry. We'll get rid of it. Don't worry.'

'I really don't care about stuff like carpets normally.' Romy lay back on the sofa and stared at the ceiling. 'I don't care about carpets or clothes or family companies, and you know what, I don't want to care either. But for you, sis, I'll clean it up. In a minute.'

The following day was another one in which they dug for ages without finding anything before eventually once again revealing a couple of shroud pins. Almost inevitably after that Mai called out that she'd found some bones and Romy came rushing over to take a look.

'They're clearly ancient,' she said as she looked at them and then stood back and assessed the area where they'd been found. 'Look like they're buried east to west too, which would point to an early Christian burial site. I suppose we'd better let the boys in blue know.'

The police were always advised about discoveries of bones on archaeological digs owing to the possibility that they could be relatively recent and so either spark off or bring closure to an investigation. Romy knew that these weren't recent remains, but she chatted to the local sergeant as he looked at the site anyway.

'Don't think you're going to have a major murder inquiry this time,' she told him cheerfully, and he grinned at her and said that he had enough to be doing, thanks very much.

The weather was glorious. Romy worked in her T-shirt and a pair of shorts, enjoying the feeling of sweat trickling down her chest as she carefully used her leaf trowel to clear away the earth and expose the bones before taking photographs of them. Then she got some of the revoltingly fishy-smelling permatrace paper from the Portakabin and began to make a scale drawing of her find.

Jerry and Mick came with news of some further evidence of burials and Taig said that he reckoned there might be about fifteen or twenty graves on the site.

'Not bad,' he said. 'We get to unearth them, send the bones to the museum, and the developer will eventually be able to do his building.'

'No neat little church for him, though.' Romy grinned.

'No.' Taig guffawed. 'Don't think he'll be calling it Graveyard View somehow.'

Romy laughed with him and then went back to filling plastic containers with soil samples which she thought needed further examination. She cursed when she broke a nail trying to reopen one of the containers – usually she kept them very short, but they'd grown during her weeks with Veronica and she was secretly rather proud of them now, which made breaking one more of a big deal than it would have been before. But, she told herself, she was back to her normal life again and it didn't have room for elegant nails. When she went into the Portakabin a short time later to grab a cup of tea, she caught sight of herself in the mirror and grimaced. Her hair was escaping from its plait, her face was streaked with dust and her T-shirt was damp with perspiration. She suddenly realised that during the time she'd spent with her mother, she'd taken more care than she'd realised over her appearance. Even though she'd never be a fashion plate like Veronica or Giselle, or as stunningly groomed as Kathryn, she'd lost the air of permanently looking as though she'd tramped through a field in a hurricane. But it was back again. She reached into her bag, took out her brush and replaited her hair. Then she rinsed the muck off her face. It wasn't vain, she thought, to look clean!

She didn't go to the pub after they'd finished that evening. Downing Lucozade was all very well, but during the course of the afternoon, the idea of an ice-cold beer became more and more appealing, and she knew that there were bottles of Miller in Veronica's fridge. It wouldn't be exactly the same as sharing tinnies with Keith on the back porch of his house, but she liked the idea of sitting on Veronica's deck and knocking one back.

When she arrived home, though, she saw Giselle's SUV parked in the driveway. She groaned aloud. The last two days had been blissfully Dolan-free. She'd hardly seen Kathryn and hadn't heard anything more from Darragh. It had been good while it lasted but she knew that her family had to be faced sooner or later.

It had been Darragh's idea that Giselle should call to the house to see Romy, and as far as Giselle was concerned, whatever he wanted she was going to do. She was determined to support him in every way possible so that he knew he could depend on her completely.

When he'd walked out of the house the previous Saturday she'd had the horrible feeling that maybe he wouldn't be back. The row had been their worst ever. They'd never before argued so deeply and so personally and Giselle hadn't been sure that they would be able to get over it. The logical part of her brain told her that one way or another he'd have to return home sometime – after all, he'd gone without his clothes or his toiletries or even his passport – but that didn't necessarily mean he'd be home to stay. Giselle couldn't believe that her fairy-tale marriage might break up because of Romy. Or Veronica. She couldn't bear to think of being a single mother bringing up two children on her own. And it didn't matter that Darragh would probably provide generously for them. What mattered was that it would all be over. And the thought chilled her to the core.

It can't happen, she'd thought, as she lay in bed that night praying that he'd come home soon; he loves me and he loves our life and our family matters to him. He won't – he can't – leave us.

Nevertheless she couldn't help worrying. After Mimi had gone to bed she'd sat in front of the TV and felt her stomach contract with terror at the idea of him never coming back. Although the idea of eating made her feel ill, she craved the comfort of food, just as she'd done years before. Whenever she'd felt inadequate or worried, whenever she was teased or laughed at, she'd found comfort in chocolate bars and sweets and crisps. And she desperately wanted that comfort now.

Later that night, having left four unanswered messages on his voicemail, she'd gone into the kitchen and opened the cupboards and stared blankly at the contents. Mostly they were filled with jars and packets of organic or healthy eating food. There were lots of dried fruits and additive-free bars, the guilt-free snack foods which she bought every week at the supermarket and which she thought tasted like cardboard.

And then she opened Darragh's cupboard, where he kept what he called his stash of forbidden goodies – the individual-sized tubes of Pringles and blocks of Yorkie which he loved. Her mouth watered as she looked at the Pringles, and then she'd taken two tubes of them – Spring Onion and Texas Barbecue – and brought them into the living room, where she'd eaten them both while watching *Nip/Tuck* on TV. She'd been disgusted with herself afterwards, especially when she'd gone back into the kitchen and taken a Yorkie bar out of his cupboard too. She hadn't eaten Pringles or Yorkies since before she'd met him!

She didn't really feel comforted by the chocolate and crisps. Afterwards, terrified that Darragh would come home to find the evidence of her spectacular fall from the wagon, she'd pushed the empty cartons and wrappers to the bottom of the bin. The pleasure of the food had been fleeting. The self-loathing she'd felt as she brushed her teeth to rid herself of the mingled taste of chocolate and crisps stayed with her for longer.

It was a moment of weakness, she told herself five minutes later. And it'll never happen again. Even if he has left me. She shivered violently at the awful thought and then made herself put it out of her mind before going back to bed.

She'd slept fitfully but had jolted into complete alertness when she heard a key in the front door. Then she heard the sound of footsteps walking through the hallway and into the kitchen, and heard the kettle being filled with water. A wave of relief engulfed her.

She lay in the darkness of the bedroom, eyes wide open, for what seemed like hours (but was in fact twenty minutes) before she pushed the duvet back, slid on her pale apricot satin robe, brushed her golden hair and then padded down-stairs. She wasn't sure whether going downstairs was a good thing under the circumstances. On the one hand, wearing her nightclothes accentuated her pregnancy. On the other, despite the fact that she'd bought them in Brown Thomas the previous week (and that she'd hidden the receipt in case Darragh saw it), neither the robe nor her nightdress were particularly flattering to her size. She wanted to look beautiful yet vulnerable for Darragh. She was afraid that she might actually look like a mobile pumpkin. But, having weighed it up, she felt that standing in front of him pregnant was the best thing to do.

He was sitting on the sofa, staring at the TV. He hadn't bothered to switch it on.

'Hi,' she said.

He looked at his watch. 'You're awake late.'

'I couldn't sleep. I was worried about you.'

He snorted. 'You should've worried more a couple of months ago,' he said. 'When you lied to me.'

'I didn't lie.' She looked at him helplessly and then pushed her hair back from her face in a gesture which she knew he loved. 'Sweetheart, I know I said that I probably could've coped with your mum for a while and that I sort of used being pregnant as an excuse . . . but that was only a vague kind of thing. I did honestly feel that it would be difficult and it was only afterwards, when Romy came, that I changed my mind.'

'You called my mother interfering.'

'I didn't mean it like that,' said Giselle as penitently as she could. 'I know it sounds like I thought she poked and pried and everything, but all I meant was that she has very strong views on how things are done and so have I and they're different! And I thought we might clash over that and I didn't want to because I truly do love your mum and I didn't want to fight with her.'

'Sounded to me like you hated her,' said Darragh. 'Like you've always hated her.'

Giselle took a deep breath. A single tear slid down her cheek and plopped on to the carpet. The tear surprised her. She hadn't intended to cry. 'Of course I don't. I would never do anything to hurt her and I'd never do anything to mess up her relationship with you. And, quite honestly, I would never have thought that Romy and her would end up getting on well together.'

Darragh regarded her thoughtfully. She was beautiful, there was no doubt about that. She was the loveliest thing in his life and there hadn't been a day that he'd regretted marrying her. She was the perfect wife for him. But sometimes she was as thick as two short planks.

'My mother is a softie at heart,' he said. 'And so with Romy there it was only a matter of time before she'd make a move to reconcile with her. You should've thought of that.'

'I know,' said Giselle apologetically.

'What's done is done.' He heaved a sigh. 'It's a question of retrieving the situation.'

'I'm sure we can think of something,' said Giselle, a dart of relief in her voice. She sat down beside him on the sofa.

'We have to,' said Darragh. 'I'm not having everything I've worked for destroyed by some happy-clappy girl who hasn't a clue about big business. And my not-so-happy sister who's only dying for the opportunity to make me look stupid.'

'That won't happen,' promised Giselle as she moved closer to him. 'It absolutely won't. And whatever it takes, we'll fix things together.'

He looked at her. Her blue eyes were grave and her face was completely serious. It matters to her too, he thought. For loads of different reasons. And that's why we're a great couple. Because, in the end, we want exactly the same thing.

'OK,' he said. 'Any ideas?'

They spent half the night discussing the situation and they'd eventually come up with a strategy. So when Romy arrived back from the dig and walked out on to the deck behind the house, Giselle was there to greet her. She got up from a sun-lounger and smoothed down her cleverly cut white sun-dress which flattered her bump and showed off her lightly tanned body. Kathryn, lounging beside her, had abandoned her New York chic for a pair of comfortable baggy cotton trousers and a loose rugby shirt.

'Hi, Romy.' Giselle smiled brightly at her. 'How was your day?'

'I had a great day,' replied Romy, keeping the surprise at seeing Giselle from her voice as she flopped on to one of the cushioned chairs. 'We found loads of good stuff and eventually unearthed the skeleton of a man who had clearly been hit on the back of the head. It was really interesting.'

'No!' Giselle's eyes were round.

'Yup.'

'And . . . so . . . is it a murder inquiry?'

Romy laughed. 'The bones are about fifteen hundred years old, so no,' she said.

'Oh.'

'A good result for you, though,' said Kathryn, and Romy said that yes, it was very pleasing.

'Why was he hit on the back of the head?' asked Giselle.

'Even my brilliant powers of forensic deduction don't go that far,' said Romy. 'It could've been an ancient-century mugging.'

She reached out and picked up the jug of orange juice that was on the garden table.

'I hope you've washed your hands,' said Kathryn. 'I don't like to think of millennium-plus dust in my orange juice.'

Romy laughed and poured herself a drink. She refilled both Kathryn's and Giselle's glasses too.

'And so, Giselle,' she said, 'to what do we owe the pleasure? I thought you and Darragh were far too pissed off with me to call around.'

'Don't be silly.' Giselle laughed lightly. 'We were shocked, of course, about everything, but it's Veronica's decision to make.'

'Are you here to suss out the house?' asked Romy. 'Check it out before putting in an offer?'

'Not quite yet.' This time Giselle's tone was a little cooler.

She hadn't actually discussed the issue of the house with Darragh. She knew why he wanted to live there, but in all honesty she preferred the modernity of their own home to the older design of Veronica's. But she wasn't going to get into an argument with him over it. Not now, anyway. Maybe not ever. She turned her attention back to Romy. 'No, what I was wondering was if you'd like to come to Monart with me at the weekend.'

'I'm sorry?' Romy looked at her in puzzlement while a faint smile played around Kathryn's mouth. 'Where?'

'It's a spa resort,' explained Giselle patiently. 'Very high-spec. I go there a couple of times a year with some of my friends to be pampered. It's a lovely break and you get the most fabulous treatments.'

'A spa?' Romy was astonished. 'You want me to go to a spa with you?'

'Well, why not?' Giselle smiled at her. 'It would be nice for the two of us. You could probably do with a massage, what with all the digging and stuff . . .' She glanced at Romy's scraped fingers and broken nail. 'Maybe get a manicure or something too. And I need a bit of chilling-out time before the baby comes along.'

'Giselle, I can't possibly go on a spa break with you,' said Romy.

'We'll pay, of course,' said Giselle. 'It's our gift to you for looking after Veronica so well.'

Romy stared at her. 'You'll pay for me to go somewhere and get massaged?'

'Well, why not?' asked Giselle brightly. 'It's been a difficult time for you, what with all the running around you've had to do, and I'm sure you could do with a break. Both Darragh and I really appreciate what you've done and so we thought you'd like it.'

Kathryn stifled a giggle while Romy continued to look at Giselle in amazement.

'It's in a lovely setting,' continued Giselle. 'Very restful, beautiful gardens, gorgeous rooms. You'd love it.'

'I don't do spas,' said Romy blankly.

'Oh, but you should.' Giselle was very definite. 'You owe it to yourself, Romy. You spend so much of your time out of doors that your skin is in danger of being totally dried out. You can't see it now, but there's all sorts of damage deep down. A moisturising facial plus hand and nail treatment would do you the world of good.'

'Giselle!' Romy held up her hand and then put it down again as she saw her broken nail with a track of dried mud behind it (despite the fact that she had scrubbed her hands after the dig, it was impossible to get rid of it all!). 'I don't have time to go to a spa. I'm up to my neck on the dig. And although it's very generous of you and Darragh to offer, it's totally unnecessary to bribe me like this.'

'Bribe you?' Giselle opened her eyes wide. 'We're not trying to bribe you.'

'Come off it,' said Romy shortly. 'Paying for me to go to a spa and be indulged? Look, Giselle, I know that you and Darragh aren't one bit happy about the whole share thing and that he's probably terrified I won't support him, but I'll do what's right. Regardless of spa breaks or anything else.'

'All we wanted was to do something nice for you,' snapped Giselle. 'You don't have to be so bloody ungracious.'

'And I'll still do the right thing for the company,' said Romy evenly. 'No matter how rude you and Darragh are to me either.'

Giselle got up from the table. 'You're impossible,' she said. 'I'm doing my best to be nice to you but you make it very difficult.'

'I don't need you to be nice to me,' said Romy.

'I'm going home.' Giselle pulled a light jacket over her shoulders. 'I'll tell Darragh that you've spurned his very generous offer. I doubt that he'll be so generous in the future.'

'I'll live with it,' said Romy, and poured herself another orange juice.

After Giselle had gone, she and Kathryn continued to sit in the shaded part of the deck.

'He has a deal he wants to get through,' said Kathryn, 'and he's afraid that we'll muck it up by ganging up against him.'

Romy looked at her curiously. 'Is that the way business works?' she asked. 'That you offer people stuff to vote a certain way.'

Kathryn laughed in genuine amusement. 'That's the way life works,' she said. 'Crikey, Romy, you're terribly naïve sometimes.'

'Obviously,' muttered Romy as she tried to even out her broken fingernail by nibbling at it. 'But then I'm a Kilkenny. We're like that.'

Later that night, while Kathryn was watching TV, Romy sat in the kitchen and accessed her emails. There was one from Tanya which she opened immediately.

'The dig is great,' she read. 'Really interesting with lots of potential. It's such a shame you can't be here but I'm sure you're having a great time in Ireland and not missing us at all. Pam says hello, by the way, and to give her a call if you're coming back to Oz. Though I hear you've got a job there. I met Keith the other day and he told me about it (we went to a lovely bar and restaurant near the river). That's great news. I'm sure that you'll be much happier there with your family. I know you said that you didn't get on especially well with them, but in the end, blood's thicker than water, isn't it, and I bet you've changed your tune. Well, you must have to have gone for the job. So I hope it goes really well for you. Let us know if you find anything exciting. I know I said our site was interesting but of course it isn't really that old. I do love hearing about those ancient Celtic bones!! Keep in touch. Amy and Trish send their love. All the best. Tanya.'

Romy continued to gaze at the screen even after she'd finished reading Tanya's email. So she'd met Keith, had she? But what was he doing in Melbourne? He hadn't said anything to Romy about leaving Perth. What he had done, though, was to tell Tanya about her Irish job. Which was probably why she was being so damn friendly – because she knew that Romy wouldn't be back to throw her weight around and try to muscle in on her. Well, she couldn't really blame Tanya for that, could she? She'd be the same way if she'd scooped the supervisor's job. But it still rankled with her.

And they'd gone out together. Romy stared at the email. Of course they'd all gone out as a group in the past and it was no big deal that Tanya and Keith might have met up and gone to a bar together . . . but it was disconcerting all the same. It was also weird to think that they were talking about her, discussing her career and her future. Funny how Tanya seemed keen for her to stay in Ireland. She couldn't help wondering whether that was because the other girl wanted to hang on to the supervisor's job or because she wanted to make a move on Keith.

Bloody hell, thought Romy savagely. It doesn't matter to me what she does! Either with the job or with Keith. With the job because it'll all be over by the time I get back. And with Keith because . . . because I don't care. I don't need a man in my life. Especially not Keith.

She rubbed the bridge of her nose. I don't, she assured herself. And I don't mind what Keith is doing without me. It's his life after all, and if having some kind of relationship with Tanya does it for him, then why should I worry?

She picked at her broken nail. She didn't like to think about him having a relationship with Tanya. She didn't want to think about the two of them sitting on the veranda behind his house (though obviously not while they were both in Melbourne!) and sharing tinnies like Romy had done with him. She didn't want Keith to be as close to Tanya or Amy or any of the others as he was to her. As I thought he was, she reminded herself. I'm making a big deal out of it, only there isn't any sort of deal to be made at all. I should get over him. And myself. Not that there's anything to actually get over, of course!

And yet . . . could it be a case of absence making the heart grow fonder? she wondered. Do I suddenly want Keith because he's thousands of miles away? She stared at her reflection on the glossy computer screen. I don't want him. That's horribly possessive and I'm not a possessive person.

But I miss him. I really do. And what on earth does that mean in the grand scheme of things?

Romy logged off the webmail program and put the computer to sleep. I can't possibly miss him, she amended as she closed the laptop. Not in a possessive sort of way, anyhow. I don't own him. And I should stop reading all sorts of ulterior motives into my own actions. I should stop sending him emails too. The sooner I realise that he's out of my life, the better.

She gazed unseeingly at the blank computer screen. And when, she wondered suddenly, did I ever think he was in my life in the first place?

Chapter 26

Darragh was annoyed but not entirely surprised at the fact that Romy had rejected the idea of a girlie break at the exclusive spa. The more he thought about it the more he realised that pampering wasn't her thing. He was also pissed off at her assertion that he was trying to bribe her when he'd hoped that she'd see the offer as a thank-you gift for all that she'd done for Veronica.

In the end he decided to shelve the problem of how to deal with Romy and instead arranged for a trip to the London offices of the Swiss energy company to talk about the deal that he was trying to put together with them. He was going to present it at the next board meeting and he wanted to chase down every last detail of the proposal so that when it came to the crunch he would be able to face Kathryn over the rosewood table and tell her that whatever objections she had to his deal she was totally wrong.

The new idea for sweetening Romy came to him as the cab he was in swung by London Wall. He suddenly had a flashback to his history books and Mr Kelly talking to him about the Romans and London (though what the lesson had been all about he couldn't for the life of him remember). But he'd had an image of the Romans strutting through London two thousand years earlier and he'd wondered whether it was images like this which had inspired Romy to busy herself with digging up the past. And then the idea of offering her a grant to do just that had come to him. Corporate responsibility, he'd thought, that's how to package it. Dolan's often got requests from community projects for some kind of sponsorship. Well, they would sponsor Romy. The dig in Wicklow would end in a couple of months' time, and after that she'd be looking for somewhere else. She'd complained that a commercial dig, like the one she was doing now, that a local authority or developer had to have carried out as part of their planning permission process was more rushed and less thorough than the more detailed studies of academic digs. But academic digs often meant volunteering your services or even paying to be involved. Darragh was astonished at that. And so his plan, courtesy of Dolan Component Manufacturers, was to provide her with some funding to go to whatever location and dig appealed to her most. He would put up a link to the dig on the Dolan website and say that they were supporting archaeology. Maybe he'd tell her that she had to wear a T-shirt or a baseball cap with the Dolan's logo on it too. It was good for companies to be involved in cultural projects and it made perfect sense to be associated with something that the family had an interest in. Not that anyone other than Romy gave a toss about broken pottery and clunky skeletons, but it would look good all the same. As a result, she'd be so grateful to him that she'd support whatever he wanted. Why the hell shouldn't she? What did she know about industrial components anyhow?

The meeting with the environmental energy people went better than he expected and he returned to Dublin on Friday afternoon full of enthusiasm for the project and his potential sponsorship of his half-sister. He went straight to the office to work through the sets of figures again, trying to decide how he would present the business deal to them and at the same time frame the sponsorship proposal to Romy so that it looked philanthropic instead of just like a bribe. Supporting her career – now that was a wholly different matter from luxurious spa breaks!

Kathryn wouldn't agree, of course, but he didn't care what she thought. However, he was sure that Veronica would understand. And in the end, Romy would be back overseas where she belonged and things would return to normal.

He heaved an enormous sigh. Maybe it would all work out. He'd put the business deal together and it looked like a good one. It had been easier to do by himself, without roping in Alex and Stephen, who'd have made it all so much more complicated. He'd surprised himself with the amount of time and energy and hard work he'd invested in it and the amount of satisfaction he got from doing it on his own. He realised that over the last few years he'd let them do more and more of the nuts-and-bolts sort of stuff and now he thought that might have been a mistake. They were younger guys and better qualified than him. But, he told himself, they didn't have as much passion for the job or for the company. They saw it as a game. It was his life. He'd forgotten how much difference that made.

The only major problem facing him was the financing, which wasn't entirely cut and dried. He'd spoken to the bankers and the feedback had been cautiously positive although they'd told him that they'd need a lot more details on the proposal. However, the fact that they didn't dismiss him out of hand had spurred him on. He'd gone through the figures carefully and he knew that over time the returns from the deal would boost the company's profitability and that the diversification into other areas of business would insulate them from people like Jim Cahill who allowed themselves to be lured away by predatory pricing. It was clear and straightforward to him but the problem was the women on his board. And women were always so bloody difficult to deal with. All emotional and hormonal and seeing slights where there weren't any and fighting over things that they didn't need to fight about . . .

He wondered how his father would have dealt with it. But, of course, Tom would never have had this particular situation to cope with. If Tom had lived there wouldn't have been emotional women on the board in the first place. Veronica would still have been a director but she probably wouldn't have bothered turning up to the meetings, and could have happily lived her life as the socialite wife. Kathryn wouldn't have been made a director and so she wouldn't have been such a thorn in his side. And Romy wouldn't have been born at all. Which, thought Darragh, would have been just peachy.

Only other things might have happened too. He'd never thought about it before – what life would have been like if Tom had lived. His first instinct was to think that it would have been so much better, but how the hell did he know that? Maybe Tom wouldn't have invested in the new machinery that Veronica had agreed to back in the nineties when the then managing director, Christian, had called around to the house with the plans and talked them through with her. He remembered sitting in the corner while Christian explained about the plant and machinery and Veronica said that she'd get back to him on it because Christian was talking about ploughing a lot of money into this whole upgrade and it was a huge decision when the economy wasn't doing well. Afterwards Dermot had looked at the plans with her and said that investing in the company by upgrading the plant seemed the right thing to do, but that he knew nothing about it really and she had to trust the advice of people who knew what they were talking about. And Darragh remembered her saying that when it came to the company Tom was the only man she'd ever trusted and how did she know that Christian wasn't a complete moron?

Dermot had offered to meet Christian with her and they'd gone to a meeting with the bank too and in the end they'd carried out the refit. It had worked out perfectly because they'd been ready for the boom that had taken hold of the country afterwards while rival manufacturers had been left behind.

If Dermot hadn't been there for her to lean on, Darragh

thought, his mother might not have agreed to the refit. The company had had to borrow a huge amount for the work and Veronica hated borrowing money. She was still of a generation that was uncomfortable with debt, even if it was the company's debt, not her own. Maybe Tom wouldn't have done the refit either (although Darragh was pretty sure that he would). But the point was that it had happened and Dermot had supported it and so, much as he'd like to think otherwise, Darragh knew that his stepfather had put the interests of the company first.

Maybe I didn't like that about him, he thought suddenly, as he felt a sudden knot in his stomach. Maybe I didn't like the fact that he did the right thing but he still wouldn't get involved because he just wasn't interested enough. I didn't like to think that he wasn't interested in something my father had built up. But perhaps I wouldn't have liked him taking over either.

Darragh sighed. He reckoned that looking at things in hindsight always changed your view. He should stop looking back and think of the future. Which, right now, concerned the fact that Veronica had done an incredibly stupid thing by allowing Romy to have a say in what would happen to Dolan's. Which was why it was important to do something to get her on side. Because, and his stomach knotted again as he thought about it, when it came to the crunch he knew that without any reason not to, she would always give her support to Kathryn. That was how women were. They had this whole feminine thing going on so that they supported each other no matter what. And then, abruptly, he remembered that wasn't always the case. Veronica usually supported him, not Kathryn, because she agreed with how he ran the business. She didn't let any kind of feminine solidarity thing get in the way of her business decisions. But Romy was different. She'd always been different.

He got up from his desk and walked along the narrow corridor and down the stairs. He pushed open the heavy door that divided the offices from the factory. The noise hit him straight away and Donie, the foreman, came over to him, hard hat in his hand. Darragh put on the hat and walked around the factory floor. It was a good business, he thought. A strong business. But they still had to diversify, whatever his sister might think.

His jaw tightened. He wasn't going to let Kathryn push him around. He wasn't going to let her manipulate Romy. He would get his own way on this issue. He really would. No matter what it took.

Kathryn had made up her mind to go back to the States the following week. She'd been away for much longer than she'd expected and there had been increasingly agitated email messages from everyone in New York asking her when she intended to return. The most recent was from Henry Newman, suggesting that if she didn't get her ass back to her desk within the next week she mightn't have a desk to come back to.

Kathryn phoned Henry and told him that she was arranging her flights and that she'd see them all soon and that she appreciated very much their patience and understanding at what had been a stressful time for her family. Although, she thought, as she replaced the receiver, they'd hardly be too sympathetic if they knew that right now Veronica was cavorting around Cork in high heels with her bridge club friends! However, her mother would be back before the board meeting which Darragh had called for the following Monday morning. Kathryn intended to go to the board meeting and say what needed to be said, and after that she'd go back to the States and deal with her own problems and leave Darragh to deal with his. Maybe she'd come back to Ireland at some point. Maybe she'd manage to resolve everything so that she felt secure about staying in New York. She didn't know. But what she did know was that lounging around at home wasn't helping anything.

She was sitting at Veronica's computer, checking on flight times to the States, when the doorbell rang. The only person who rang the doorbell these days was Darragh. Although he had keys to the house he never simply walked in, something which surprised Kathryn, given his stated desire to own it. Instead he usually rang the bell and only used his keys if he didn't get an answer.

She went to the front door and opened it, then stood back in shock, his name frozen on her lips. She gasped as she was pushed to one side.

And she knew that she should have gone back to America before now.

It had been another good day at the dig. By now they'd all agreed with Taig's conclusion that the site was an early Christian burial ground and had identified potential plots that they felt were worth examining further. Romy had begun the excavation of another skeleton. She'd also broken two more nails and had skinned the side of her leg when she tripped and fell over a present-day concrete block which was obscured by long grass. But she didn't care. She'd enjoyed the painstaking work and she'd also enjoyed advising Jerry and Mick as they worked alongside her.

'You'll come for a drink this evening?' Taig asked her. 'It's Friday after all.'

She nodded. 'I'm dying of thirst,' she told him. 'I think I deserve it.'

Half an hour later they were all in the beer garden of the village pub again, chattering happily about the dig and the findings they'd made and proposing various theories about the demise of Romy's favourite skeleton, the victim of an ancient mugging (or just plain murder!).

'Would you like to come to dinner afterwards?' asked Taig, turning to Romy, while the rest of the group talked about a variety of methods of bashing people's heads in. 'There's a lovely restaurant in town. I'm sure you'd like it.'

'Gosh but things have changed on digs in Ireland,' she told him. 'Drinks after work. Dinners too. D'you do this every day?'

'It's nice to come and socialise,' said Taig. 'But I was asking *you* to dinner. Not everyone else.'

'Oh.' Two pink spots appeared on her cheeks. 'Just the two of us, then?'

'Well, yes. Unless you don't want to?'

'I . . . I hadn't thought.' She smiled at him. 'Sorry, you've taken me by surprise.'

'You're not appalled by the idea, are you?' His voice was suddenly anxious.

'Of course not,' she said, although her mind was working furiously. It's only dinner, she told herself. It doesn't have to be the start of some intense relationship. Women are always getting the wrong end of the stick on things like this . . . although if he doesn't want to date me, why would he ask me to dinner? But it's good to know – it confirms things in my own mind – that I can go out to dinner with people who aren't Keith. It means that I was right all along about him and it was only absence making the heart grow fonder and all that sort of thing.

She looked at Taig again and realised that he was regarding her quizzically.

'Dinner would be great,' she said. 'Thanks.'

And indeed it would be, she thought. Better than going back to the house and sitting around with Kathryn who, she was now convinced, either had an eating disorder or an alcohol problem or both. She was just too skinny to be true and she would sometimes throw back a glass of wine in a couple of gulps while on other occasions she would look at it as though it contained poison. She was jumpy and unlike herself a lot of the time and she had a perpetually worried air which bothered Romy. Anxiety and Kathryn had never gone together, and there was the whole thing about Alan too. Romy had noticed that Kathryn never seemed to talk about him or bothered to call him. Whenever she or Veronica had asked about him, Kathryn had always said that he was fine. Busy, she'd add. Really busy. And she would immediately change the subject. Romy felt sure that there was something wrong in the marriage, and what that might be worried her too. However, Kathryn wasn't telling and Romy didn't want to ask. Part of her felt that she should, and yet they never interfered with each other's lives. So maybe, she thought, it was better to keep her own counsel and say nothing. Anyway, she was looking forward to an evening out and about on her own, not having to be concerned about her family.

And it was nice to be able to say that she was on a date. Perhaps she'd put that in an email to Tanya later. She could talk about the site and say how friendly everyone was and how Taig had asked her to dinner out of the blue. Maybe Tanya would tell Keith that and he'd know for sure that she wasn't pining for him and that the comfort kiss had long since worn off.

Of course Tanya might take the fact that Romy had a date of her own as a green light to keep meeting Keith in the bars and restaurants of Melbourne. Romy wrinkled her nose at the thought. But the fact of the matter was that they were both six thousand miles away and there was nothing she could do about them and everyone had to get on with their lives.

She dragged her chair closer to Taig. Getting on with her life was exactly what she was going to do.

Chapter 27

Kathryn stared at him. She couldn't believe that he was here, in Ireland. She felt her heart begin to thud in her chest.

'Alan,' she said.

'Indeed.' He looked well. He was wearing one of his favourite navy Armani suits and a smooth white linen shirt.

'You'd better come in.'

But, of course, he was in already. She hadn't been able to stop him. She wondered how he'd got past the electric gates. Everyone in the family either had a zapper or knew the keypad number to open them. She'd thought at first that the electric gates might actually provide a certain level of security. An early-warning system. She should have known better.

He walked through the hallway, instinctively turning into the elegant living room.

'Nice.' He raised an eyebrow. His face was hard. 'I thought you said to me that you came from humble beginnings.'

'I never said humble,' Kathryn told him. 'Ordinary, that's what I said.'

'This is a lovely house,' he told her. 'Very tasteful. Obviously not cheap.'

'Ireland isn't a cheap country any more,' she told him.

'So the Upper East Side is slumming it as far as you're concerned.'

'Of course not!' She kept her tone as even as she could.

'All the same, you don't need me, do you?' he asked. 'You've clearly got a good family behind you. You've got a great career – although I'm astonished at how long you've managed to stay away . . . doesn't anyone here think that's astonishing too? And don't they think it's strange that you haven't bothered to come home?'

'They knew I rang,' she said. 'I rang lots of times and I emailed you and you didn't answer.'

'No. Because I was too busy taking stock,' he told her. 'After all, my wife walked out on me and left a cell message asking for a divorce.'

'I didn't walk out on you,' she said. 'I left you a note.'

'You didn't say anything about a divorce then. You lied.'

'Oh, Alan, you know that . . .' She moistened her lips. 'I had to come home to my mum, but while I was here I realised that . . . that we can't go on like this.'

'You decided. Not me. And you did it by leaving me a fucking voicemail.'

She winced. 'You hadn't called me back. And I thought—'

'What did you expect?' He interrupted her. 'That I'd ring you and say, oh wonderful, that's fine, call my lawyer!' His face was red and angry. 'Did you really think that I wouldn't want to fight for my marriage? Fight for you?'

Her heart was beating so fast that she thought it might actually explode out of her body.

'There is no marriage,' she said as calmly as she could. 'What we have isn't a marriage.'

'How dare you say that!'

She knew that she was shaking. But she didn't want him to see how scared she was.

'Alan – you have to see that . . . that it's all wrong. That I have to divorce you.'

'I don't see that at all,' he told her. 'I see that my wife has got a bit antsy over things and that she's run away, using her mom as an excuse.'

'That's not true,' she said.

'I think it is.' He walked around the room while she stood in the centre. 'You said that you didn't think it was working out.'

'Alan . . .'

'I think it can work out,' he said. 'I think it's just a question of setting boundaries.'

She swallowed the enormous lump that had suddenly come into her throat.

'I don't think so,' she said, and she could hear her voice shaking. 'It's more than that, Alan. I can't live with you. I . . . I don't want anything from you. I don't even want to go back to New York. I don't want to press charges or . . . or anything.'

'Press charges?' He spun around.

She could see that his eyes were glittering. She wished she hadn't said anything about pressing charges. That was stupid. Stupid. Stupid.

'I mean, divorce stuff,' she said quickly. 'I don't want anything from you.'

'You're my wife,' he said. 'You're entitled.'

'I don't need anything from you,' she told him. 'Not at all. I'm fine the way things are.'

'You think so?'

Her eyes flickered around the room. 'Totally,' she said.

'I don't think you're fine,' said Alan. 'I think you're a mouthy, ignorant bitch.'

Kathryn felt sick. She realised that she was wringing her hands. She'd never quite understood what that meant before. But she was doing it, her fingers and hands wrapping themselves around each other over and over again in a quiet frenzy of movement.

'I'm sorry if you think that.' She was still trying to keep her voice calm but she knew that she wasn't one bit calm. And she was afraid that she was going to start to cry. Of all things, she didn't want to cry in front of him. 'We can just walk away from this,' she said. 'It doesn't have to go any further.'

'You want me to walk away from my marriage?' he asked. 'You want me to pretend that those vows I made didn't matter? That I don't care about you? That I can't make it work?'

'It's not you,' she said quickly. 'It's me that can't make it work.'

'Oh, Katy.' He smiled sadly at her. 'I know that. I know you have problems. Drink problems. Other people know that too. But I'm going to help you to make it work. You have the wrong attitude, is all.'

'Alan . . . Alan, you have to leave.' She was losing it. She could feel the tears in her eyes and she knew that her voice was cracking.

'No I don't,' he said.

'You do,' she told him. 'You have to leave because I don't want you here.'

'I'm sorry?'

'Get out,' she said abruptly. 'Get out, Alan. This is my mother's house.'

'Honey, I don't give a fuck whose house it is.'

She was faster than him. She didn't think that she could be but she was. She managed to bolt out of the door before he reached her and she ran up the stairs more quickly than she'd ever thought possible. She could hear him following her as she slammed closed her bedroom door and turned the key in the lock.

Veronica had looked at her curiously the day she'd asked whether there were keys for the bedroom doors, and she'd said that yes, there were, all on a ring under the stairs. Kathryn had waited until Romy and Veronica had gone shopping one day before testing them all to find the ones to her bedroom. She'd taken both of them off the ring, put one in the lock and the other in the drawer of the bedside locker. She hadn't thought she'd need them. Or maybe, she said to herself now, as she looked in fear at the locked door, maybe she'd always known that she would.

'Open the door, you bitch!' He was banging at it now and she was terrified that it would give way. She looked around her anxiously, wishing she'd had the wit to bring her phone with her, but of course she hadn't.

'Kathryn! Open the fucking door!'

She opened the French doors to her Juliet balcony and closed them behind her.

'You can't get away from me, you know that.'

Yes, she knew that. She'd always known that. She'd known it from the first day he hit her.

That day wasn't the first day she knew that she'd made a mistake in marrying Alan. But it was the first day she realised things were worse than she'd originally thought. Before that she'd managed to rationalise it. There had been doubt and she'd allowed that doubt to confuse her thinking.

Kathryn had always assumed that discovering your husband was violent would occur straight away in a marriage. (In fact she'd assumed you'd know a person's character before you married him and so, in reality, women who married men who abused them would know that there had been the possibility of problems from the start.) But she'd seen nothing in Alan's character to make her think he was anything other than kind and loving and courteous. And she'd been sure that they'd have a great life together.

Their marriage had been idyllic at first. Nothing was ever too much trouble for him – he used to treat her like a fragile piece of china. Sometimes she would laugh at him and tell him that he didn't need to keep her wrapped in cotton wool, that she'd been living in New York for years and that she was a streetwise kind of gal. She reminded him that she testified in corporate criminal trials and that she could look after herself.

And he would always respond by telling her that she didn't have to look after herself now, that he would do it for her. She'd actually thought that sweet.

These days, when she looked back at that time, she wondered whether she'd been living some kind of fantasy. Everything had seemed so perfect that she hadn't noticed how much her life was coming under his control and how much she was changing to accommodate him.

It had happened gradually. He always phoned her at work every day, but suddenly she realised that he was calling her five or six times for no apparent reason. When she was out of the office he'd leave a message to call him back and he'd leave a message on her cell too if she didn't answer. She was amused, if a little irritated, by the fact that he always wanted to know where she was. But she hadn't been concerned. She hadn't thought that it would lead to anything more serious.

The first day there'd been trouble it had all seemed innocuous enough too. She'd been home late from work even though she'd told him earlier that she wouldn't be. And when she'd arrived back at the apartment he'd been sitting there, surrounded by the cartons from a Chinese takeaway, watching TV.

'You're late,' he said.

'I know.'

'You told me you'd be home early.'

'I'm sorry. I got tied up at work.'

She leaned forward to pick up some of the empty cartons and he suddenly grabbed her by the lapel of her jacket.

'What made you late?'

'Alan!' She looked at him in irritation. 'You'll crease my jacket. And you're practically choking me.'

'What made you late?' He stood up as he spoke, still holding on to her jacket, and she found it hard to keep her balance in her high-heeled designer shoes.

'I had to meet with Henry about a client,' she said. 'Honestly, Alan, you're—'

'In a bar? You were drinking?'

'Well, yes. We decided to meet out of the office. I had a glass of white wine.'

'I hate the fact that you go to bars and drink with other men.' His grip on her jacket tightened. 'It's not right, Kathryn. You're my wife.'

And then he'd abruptly let go of her jacket so that she stumbled and fell, catching her arm on the side of the glass table as she hit the ground, which made her cry out in shock and pain.

'Oh my God! Kathryn! Katy. I'm so sorry.'

He'd cradled her in his arms then, telling her that he'd overreacted and that he'd been under pressure that day and that he'd been surprised when she wasn't home and then worried about her because she hadn't called; and all the time he'd stroked her hair and told her that he loved her.

She *had* called. She'd left a message on his cell and on the answering machine in the apartment. He'd certainly listened to the apartment message because the machine was switched off. So why would he think that she hadn't called? What the hell was wrong with him?

He apologised the next day too, especially when he saw the bruise on her arm. He told her that he didn't know what had come over him, that he was a fool, that he didn't deserve her.

She said it didn't matter.

But it did matter. She'd seen a side of him that she hadn't known existed and she'd wondered how big a mistake marrying him might have been. But in the days that followed he'd been so attentive, so loving, that she began to think that she herself was overreacting to what had, after all, been a very minor incident. It hadn't been his fault that she'd hurt her arm, and grabbing her jacket the way he did – well, it had been rough but sometimes guys were rough without meaning to be. All the same, it was very unsettling. As unsettling as his sudden desire to meet her after she'd been out with friends, to pick her up and bring her home. She told him that he was being overprotective and he reminded her that there'd been an outbreak of muggings in the city and that he didn't want anything to happen to her. She was his wife, he told her. He had to protect her. She tried to tell him that she was capable of looking after herself but he didn't listen. And something about the way he spoke made her feel that it was the wrong time to tell him that she was feeling suffocated by his attention and needed a bit more space.

The next incident wasn't quite so minor and worried her even more. It had been a few days before she'd gone to the trendy nightclub with the rest of the staff. The two of them had been at home in front of the TV and she'd been bored with the nature programme that was showing. So she'd picked up the remote and started flipping through the channels.

'What the fuck are you doing?'

She looked at him in surprise. 'Changing channels.'

'I was watching that.'

'I'm sorry,' she said. 'I didn't realise. You had your head in a book.'

'I was still watching it. And it's the height of bad manners to channel-hop without asking me first.'

'Chill out.' She laughed and pointed the remote at the TV again.

He grabbed her by the wrist so tightly that she nearly yelled out.

'Are you laughing at me?'

'Of course not.'

'It sounds to me like you're laughing at me.' He tightened his grip even though she hadn't thought that possible.

'Alan . . . I'm not.'

'You don't just come here, move into my apartment and then start acting as though you own the place.' Now he was twisting her arm behind her back.

'Alan, for God's sake!'

And then he released her and grinned at her. 'Just so's you know.'

She rubbed the weal on her wrist. 'You hurt me,' she said.

He looked at her in consternation. 'I hurt you?'

'Of course you bloody hurt me! Look!' She held out her arm.

'Oh jeez, Katy – I'm sorry.' He stared at it in dismay. 'I didn't realise. I'm sorry.'

But she didn't think he was sorry. And that night, after he'd kissed her and made love to her (she hadn't really wanted that to happen, but she hadn't wanted to antagonise him by refusing either) and after he'd told her that she was the only woman in the world for him, she'd wondered if grabbing her by the jacket and then grabbing her by the wrist was . . . well, abuse? It was so hard to think of it like that. He hadn't beaten her up or anything. It wasn't as though she was lying in bed with a broken arm, for heaven's sake. He'd hurt her but it wasn't terribly serious, was it? Was it? She'd lain in the darkness and wondered and worried about Alan and about herself, and the next day she'd been totally distracted at work and not thinking straight at all. He phoned the office ten times and the final time she told him that she was really busy and could he please stop calling; that evening when she got home, he was in a foul mood but he didn't say or do anything other than ask her how her day had been. After a week where she didn't go out after work and where she allowed all of his calls to go to her voicemail, she was beginning to feel besieged by him. Which was why, even though she hadn't really wanted to, she'd gone to the nightclub with the rest of the people from work.

She'd drunk far too much because she'd been trying to put him out of her mind, despite the fact that she was worried about him and about her marriage and trying very hard not to think that she could be a woman whose husband beat her. Because he hadn't beaten her. Not yet.

It was when she'd thought 'not yet' that she knew that she was in big trouble. Because not yet implied that some day he would.

But, she kept telling herself, this was Alan. A successful businessman. A person who was respected in the city. He wasn't some drunken lout who came home and thumped her because his dinner wasn't on the table. And she wasn't some downtrodden woman with no other place to go. So whatever she was thinking about abuse was all wrong because it didn't apply to Alan and it didn't apply to her, and whatever was wrong between them wasn't as bad as all that. Possibly, she thought, he had anger management issues. They could deal with that. There were plenty of places he could go to learn how to deal with his temper. They could check them out together. It wasn't the worst thing in the world that could happen. And, she reminded herself, he still hadn't hit her.

And then he did. When she'd come home from the club and walked into the bedroom he'd been sitting there waiting for her. She'd hoped, when he'd put his arm around her, that it would all be OK. But then he'd become angry. He'd ranted about her drunken state, her clothes, her make-up and the high-heeled shoes she was carrying in her hands. He said she looked like an off-duty hooker. And he told her that she was letting him down and herself down and it was about time she saw sense. He'd pushed her away from him and she hadn't known what to do, and then, suddenly and without warning, he'd slapped her – a stinging blow across the side of her face which had left her with a cut over her left eye where the diamond set into his wedding ring had caught her.

She'd been so shocked she hadn't been able to speak. This time he didn't instantly tell her that he was sorry. He told her that she'd have to mend her ways, that this was what women who flaunted their bodies around the city deserved. She'd known then that she'd have no option but to leave. She knew that she should have walked out right away and checked into a hotel. But she was afraid to do anything in case she triggered the rage in him again. And so she'd lain on the bed and he'd lain beside her and then he'd started to talk, saying that he knew he shouldn't have hit her and that it had been a mistake. She thought she might be able to sneak out of the apartment while he was sleeping, but every time she moved he moved too, and so she stayed.

She'd gone to work the next day wearing sunglasses to hide the cut (and the bruise that had come up around it) and she'd told herself that she had to get out. She could, she knew, file a report on him for spousal abuse. But she didn't want to do that. She didn't want people to know what had happened. It sounded so dramatic and so seedy and so awful . . . and she couldn't help thinking that this was something she should deal with herself. The social services that came with being an abused wife – well, they were for people who were seriously abused. Who were less educated than her and who didn't have great careers in the city. They were for women who were afraid of their husbands because they didn't know their rights. She knew her rights. She knew what she should do. She was just inexplicably reluctant to do it. She didn't want to believe that this was happening to her, to Kathryn Dolan, who was a strong, independent woman and who wasn't afraid of anyone or anything.

He phoned her at work. He said that they needed to talk, that last night had been a horrible accident, that he hadn't meant to actually hit her. And she'd said that she didn't want to talk about it yet, that she was coming to terms with the fact that he'd hurt her. She needed to make up her mind about that.

And then, that evening, when she came home, nervous because she didn't know what sort of mood he'd be in and wondering whether she should have come home at all, she found the apartment decked out with dozens of red roses. There was a bottle of champagne on the table and a jewellery box beside it. There was no sign of Alan. She looked at the flowers and at the champagne and then she finally opened the jewellery box, which contained a diamond bracelet. And as she looked at the bracelet, the phone rang.

'I know you think I'm a shit,' said Alan. 'I'm sorry. I've been under pressure and I've taken it out on you. This is my way of saying that nothing like it will ever happen again.'

She looked around the room and the door opened. Alan had been in the guest bedroom waiting for her. He had his cell phone in his hand.

'Alan . . . this is all . . .'

'. . . no less than you deserve,' he said. 'That's the thing, Katy darling. You deserve the best and I'll always give you the best. I love you.'

'We need to talk, though.' She exhaled slowly. 'You know, you've really scared me these last few weeks, and—'

'I promise it won't happen again. I give you my word.' He smiled at her, his eyes dark and emotional. 'I've been a shit and I don't deserve you.'

She looked at him. He came into the room and put his arms around her, holding her closely to him.

'You're my girl,' he told her. 'You always will be.'

She leaned her head on his shoulder. She knew that she wasn't his girl at all. She never had been. She never would be.

But although she kept thinking about leaving him, she didn't do anything about it straight away. Even though she knew that she had to do something. It didn't matter how wonderful he was being now, it was how he could be that counted. But except when she was at work (where he continued to phone her regularly, although not as often as before), Alan always seemed to be around. It was as though he was watching her, waiting for her to make the wrong move. When she left she wanted to leave quickly and quietly, packing her bags and going before he had the chance to stop her. But that opportunity never seemed to be there. And there was a part of her that worried about flitting off like that too. It would make him very angry. And she was scared of what he might do.

She told herself that she was being feeble and useless and then she told herself that she wasn't, she was being clever, biding her time, waiting to see how things turned out. She was in control of the situation and there was no need to do anything rash. She would go, she knew that. She didn't love Alan any more and she certainly couldn't trust him. Nevertheless, she had to be careful about it. She had to pick her moment. But it wasn't until the night of the awards ceremony that she realised she couldn't pick a moment, that she wasn't in control of anything, that if she stayed she'd be making an even bigger mistake than she had already. That night when she'd walked into the bedroom after listening to Romy's message, thinking he was asleep, and realised that he wasn't. And that the drink and the disappointment of his client not having won an award was all too apparent. And that for some reason, he blamed her.

She didn't like to remember what had happened. She'd tried to give him time to fall asleep, hoping that the amount of alcohol he'd consumed would knock him out. But it had been a vain hope. When she'd come into the room and he'd shredded her cigarettes she'd known that things were moving out of her control. And then he'd accused her of holding hands with his client and refused to believe her when she'd denied it. That was when she knew that she should have left him. That was when she decided that she couldn't wait any longer. She'd picked up her bag and told him that she was leaving. And he'd moved so quickly that she hadn't even had time to react, slamming the bedroom door and telling her that she was his wife and that she wasn't going anywhere. She told him that he'd promised to treat her well and he'd said that that clearly depended on how she behaved and that she'd been a tramp that night, flaunting herself. Which, he said, was OK now because she was home. And because it had worked. And he'd pushed her on to the bed and the next thing she knew he was on top of her and . . . She'd always thought before that people who were raped should have tried harder to get away, but she'd been frozen with fear and hadn't done a single thing to stop him.

She should have reported it to the police. She knew that. But hours later, when he'd passed out from the exertion and from the drink, she'd showered and changed and left a note saying that she was going home to be with her mother for a while. And she'd got the next available flight to Ireland, where she was too ashamed to tell anyone what had happened.

'Open the goddamn door!'

Standing on the Juliet balcony she could still hear him. She knew that the bedroom door would break open eventually. She knew that if she was on the balcony when it did he'd probably throw her off. She couldn't quite believe that she was in a situation where she felt that she was in real danger. This was the sort of scene that she felt should be in some kind of gritty TV drama, not in real life. But it was her life and it was being threatened by her husband. It was incredible, she thought, how helpless women were when men were really angry. She'd always thought that she was a match for any man, but she wasn't. She was weak. And scared. It was pitiful. She despised herself.

She took a deep breath and then kicked off her shoes before throwing them over the balcony so that they landed on the grass beneath. And then she did something that she hadn't done since she'd been at school. She climbed on to the rail and swung herself sideways until she was grasping the pipe that ran down the side of the wall. But instead of climbing down it, she went upwards, grabbing hold of the gutter and hauling herself into the valley between the double roof. She didn't cry out even when she scraped her knees and her fingers.

It was the first time she'd ever done that in getting on to the roof, which had been a place where she'd come as a child to hide from everyone else in the family. Her private place that nobody knew about. She used to come there with her books so that she could read in peace without Veronica muttering that she was ruining her eyesight and telling her that she should get out more. She'd always felt safe there, tucked away behind the stack of the chimney, out of view of everyone.

Her heart was hammering in her chest and every breath rattled in her ears. She tried to inhale and exhale more quietly because she felt sure that he could hear her. She still didn't feel safe. She wasn't sure she'd ever feel safe when Alan was around.

She heard the bedroom door finally give way and she heard him ransacking the room looking for her. Then she heard the slamming open of the French doors and the sound of him on the Juliet balcony. And she hoped that he was seeing her shoes on the grass below and thinking that she'd jumped from the balcony (although how she could have managed that without breaking her legs would be a mystery). She decided that if he hadn't been fooled, if he'd guessed that she'd come to the roof and if his head appeared above the parapet, she would kick his face in. She didn't care if that meant he fell from the pipe himself. She didn't care what happened to him any more.

She pushed herself closer to the chimney stack and tried not to whimper out loud.

Chapter 28

When Darragh opened the door that evening, the aroma of sautéed onions wafted out to greet him. He walked into the kitchen expecting to find Magda in front of the cooker, but it was Giselle who turned around at the sound of his footsteps.

'I'm glad you're home,' she said. 'I was beginning to think that I'd have to eat this myself.'

'What is it?' He sniffed appreciatively.

'Steak and onions and mashed potatoes,' she said.

He raised his eyebrows even as he felt his mouth water. 'Why?' he asked.

'You like it,' she told him.

'I know, but that never meant I got it before!'

She lowered the heat under the grill. 'True. But I've been thinking that maybe I've been a bit selfish on the food front. I appreciate that perhaps tofu and green bean salad isn't ideal for everyone.'

'I thought the smell of red meat made you sick,' said Darragh.

She shook her head. 'I exaggerated. I'm not fond of it myself,' she added hastily. 'I'm having some fish. But I thought that you might like a steak.'

He walked over to her and put his arms around her. 'Are you working on the way to a man's heart being through his stomach?'

'Um. Yes,' she admitted. She turned around. 'Look, I know

you're still mad at me about Veronica and I know we're in a dodgy situation and I know it's partly my fault.'

'You apologised already,' said Darragh. 'I accepted your apology.'

She nodded. 'I know that, but I also know that you're still mad at me,' she told him as she regarded him steadily. 'We're a good team, Darragh. We belong together.'

'I haven't gone away,' said Darragh.

'I don't want you to,' said Giselle.

'Why would you,' he asked, 'when there's so much at stake?'

'They don't think you're smart enough,' she said fiercely. 'And they think that I'm a blonde bimbo. But you are and I'm not and we'll make it all work out. You've worked too hard to see Kathryn and Romy take the company from under your nose. It's your inheritance. And mine, Mimi's and Muf— the baby's too, no matter what anyone says. And I'm not going to let any of us be done out of it.'

'And for that you're cooking steak?'

'I'm doing it to show you that I care,' she said fiercely. 'That it all matters to me.'

'What matters?' he asked. 'The house? The clothes? The car?'

'The family,' she said. 'The business. You. I'm a Dolan and I always will be. Because I married you. And we come first.'

'And if we were penniless?' he asked.

'That's irrelevant,' she said firmly. 'We're not and we won't ever be because that's not what we are.'

'But would you leave me?' he asked. 'If I lost everything.'

'If you lost everything, I'd help you get it back,' she said simply.

He looked at her thoughtfully. He wanted her to put her arms around him and tell him that she loved him and would always love him no matter what. But perhaps that wasn't true. Maybe there were things that would stop her loving him. And yet she was a hundred per cent behind him, like she'd always been. Wasn't that more important than mere words?

'You're right,' he said. 'It won't happen because Dolan's is a strong company, so even if Kathryn and Romy started throwing their joint weight around – not that Kathryn has a pick on her these days – they wouldn't be able to do too much damage. Anyhow, I've come up with a plan and it's going to work.'

He told her about sponsoring Romy, and a big grin broke out on Giselle's face.

'Clever boy,' she said. 'Clever, clever boy.'

'Killing all my birds with one stone,' he said with satisfaction.

'That definitely deserves steak and onions,' she told him as she took a plate out of the oven. 'Go inside and sit down and I'll bring this in to you.'

Romy was enjoying dinner with Taig. It wasn't, of course, in as spectacular a location as the last dinner she'd eaten with a guy – it would have been hard to top the trendy Sydney restaurant that Keith had brought her to – and nor was it half as exclusive, but the food was good and the atmosphere relaxed, which made her feel relaxed too. This is so much more my thing, she thought. I'm really not a starched tablecloth sort of girl.

Although I could be. She thought again of her extra income thanks to the company dividends she was now entitled to, and she wondered just how much her involvement with Dolan's would change her life. She didn't want anything to change. But she had a feeling that it would whether she liked it or not.

Well, it would all depend on the board meeting on Monday. She'd had to ask Taig for time off so that she could go, and he'd looked at her in astonishment and said that he hadn't realised that archaeology was just a hobby to her. She'd retorted fiercely that it absolutely wasn't, it was her career, and that the board meeting thing was family stuff which was really just a pain in the arse. But she'd seen him look at her speculatively throughout the day, and after he'd asked her to dinner she'd wondered briefly whether it was because he thought she was some kind of rich heiress. Over their main course she'd made it very clear to him that she wasn't, and in the end he'd laughed and said that he hadn't really pegged her for a real-life Lara Croft but that was OK because he wasn't interested in money.

Leaving the money out of it (and it wasn't really heiress stuff, she reminded herself, nice and all though it might be), she was still having difficulty getting her head around the idea that she was going to go to a company board meeting. It would be held on the premises – she'd asked Kathryn why on earth they couldn't just have it around the kitchen table at home, but Kathryn said that they always did things properly. Tom had held all his meetings in the boardroom and Darragh wouldn't do it any differently. Besides, Kathryn had said, it made them feel more serious about what they did. It reminded them that even though it was a private company, they had responsibilities to everyone who worked there.

Romy was impressed by Kathryn's sense of responsibility. She didn't think that Darragh felt the same way. In fact she rather thought that Darragh's only sense of responsibility was to himself and his own family. And to some intangible notion of Tom's memory.

'Do you think you'll stay on and do some post-ex work with us?' asked Taig, cutting into her thoughts and bringing her back to her present surroundings.

'I'm not sure,' she told him. 'My original plan was to go back to Australia. And then I thought perhaps of Lisbon again. But now . . .' She shrugged. 'I have to have a think about what I really want.'

'I'll be going to a site near Mayo after this one,' said Taig. 'If you were interested in coming along, there'd definitely be a position for you.'

She smiled. 'That's nice to know.'

'Hey, you're good,' he said. 'But it's not the only reason I want you to come to Mayo.'

'Oh?'

'I like you, Romy. There's a connection between us. Don't you think?'

'You've only known me for a week,' said Romy. 'Maybe you're getting a bit carried away.'

'We click,' said Taig. 'Don't you feel it too?'

She did. He was right. There was something between them. The same easy-going friendship that she'd had with Keith. Only Taig was more proactive than Keith. Taig was prepared to say that he wanted more from her than friendship. After only a week! She'd known Keith for years. And he didn't want anything from her at all.

'We get on well,' she admitted as she picked up her spoon and dug it into her dessert.

'Hell, you sure know how to make a guy feel special,' said Taig.

She looked at him over the huge spoonful of tiramisu. 'It's only been a few days,' she reminded him. 'But you've definitely made me feel special.' She grinned at him. 'And it's a really good feeling.'

Kathryn had never noticed the lights before. But from her vantage point on the roof she could see them as they started to appear through the dusk; city lights sparkling in yellow and white stretched out in the distance below her. It was very beautiful. How weird, she thought, as she huddled beside the chimney, that I can look at something and think about how lovely it is when I'm afraid of being beaten to a pulp.

She looked at her watch. She'd been on the roof for nearly a quarter of an hour and he hadn't thought of looking for her there yet. She'd heard him bellowing and roaring in the house and the sound of more breaking wood – she didn't know whether he'd knocked down a door or turned over Veronica's furniture, but it had sounded horrific. And she couldn't help thinking – what if it was her in the house, what would he do to her?

He was unrecognisable to her as the man she'd married. The person who'd wined and dined her in the Four Seasons and brought her for a carriage ride around Central Park had gone completely. She couldn't believe that he'd changed so much. But of course he hadn't really changed. He'd been the same man all along. He'd just hidden one side of his character.

And that, she supposed, was why Naomi had left him and had started over in Dallas. She wished she could call her now and ask her about her time with Alan. She wished that there was someone, anyone, who could advise her in her current predicament. But she'd always been the person who'd done things on her own, and like it or not, she was doing things on her own now.

She stretched out and peeped over the edge of the roof, then drew her head back quickly. He was standing in the garden, her shoes in his hand, looking around. Even seeing him made her feel sick with fear.

'Kathryn!' At first she thought he'd spotted her and her heart tripped in her chest, but then she realised that the branches of the apple tree had hidden her from his view. He was just calling out loud. 'Kathryn, I know you're still around here. I know you haven't left the house or garden. I want to talk to you, is all.'

She realised that she was shaking more than ever as she pressed herself against the chimney stack again.

'Come on,' he called persuasively. 'It doesn't have to be like this. I know I scared you. I was angry. I'm sorry. Come out from wherever you are and let's deal with this like adults.'

She swallowed. Like adults? Like adults beating the crap

430

out of each other? She squeezed her eyes closed, like a child playing hide-and-seek, as though by not being able to see she was making herself invisible to him.

'Kathryn, I love you! You know that.'

She put her fingers into her ears. She didn't want to hear him say that. But then she took them out again because it was better to be able to hear him. She opened her eyes again too. That way she knew where he was. She knew how safe she was.

'Kathryn, we can work this out!' cried Alan. 'You went off and left me. I was hurt and angry. But it's OK now. Come on, Kathryn. Let's get this over with.'

Surely one of the neighbours would hear? He was yelling loudly enough. But the nearby houses were detached and well away from Avalon. People might hear him yelling but they wouldn't necessarily know what he was yelling about. Besides, nobody ever interfered in each other's business around here.

'I'm waiting for you,' he said. 'You know that.'

He can't stay there for ever, she thought. He's going to have to leave sooner or later. And then I'll come down. Much later. Hours later. She rubbed her eyes and realised, to her astonishment, that she was crying. She never cried. Ever.

'Kathryn!'

She wished she had her mobile phone. If she had it, she could ring the police and they'd know to take her seriously because they'd hear the terror in her voice. And they'd see whatever he'd done to the house. Why hadn't she kept it with her? Why had she been so damn stupid when she was supposed to be so damn smart?

Taig had suggested to Romy that she might like to go for a drink after dinner but she refused. She didn't mind one or two soft drinks in a pub but she knew that at some point she'd cave in and ask for a beer and then she wouldn't be able to drive home. Which was not how she wanted things to turn out tonight. And so she told Taig that she really appreciated the meal but she was going to have to go.

He didn't try to change her mind but walked her as far as Veronica's Golf, and after she'd opened the door and said good night, he'd reached out and tilted her head upwards and kissed her. It wasn't a comfort kiss. It was the kiss of someone who wanted to kiss and be kissed. A good kiss, she thought as she released herself from his arms. A really good kiss.

'See you Tuesday?' He smiled at her.

'Of course,' she said as she got into the car. He stood and waved as she drove out of the car park and headed back towards Dublin.

And so, she thought, as she switched on the radio and listened to 104FM, I've found someone who'd like to be my boyfriend. My life in Ireland is taking on an ever more permanent feel. Another job offer, shares in Dolan's, a bloke who thinks we click . . . what more could I want?

She thought about Australia and sitting on the deck in companionable silence with Keith. That was over now. And even if she was ever to go back and see Keith, she didn't think that the companionable silence would return. Regardless of how he felt about her, she knew that her feelings had changed completely. Before he was Keith, her friend. Now he was Keith, the guy she'd kissed. And she couldn't take that back. It was a pity she'd ruined their friendship for the sake of a kiss that hadn't been even half as good as the one she'd just shared with Taig. But the big difference, she supposed, was that unlike Taig, Keith hadn't wanted to be kissed.

Dammit, she thought as she pointed her zapper at the double gates, I wish I could get over that kiss.

And then she completely forgot about kisses as she turned into the short driveway and realised to her surprise that all the lights in the house were on. Kathryn was very eco-friendly and never left the light on in a room when she'd gone out of it. Romy suddenly wondered whether Darragh had shown up with some mad plan about how brother and sister could take the shares away from her. She pictured him pacing around the house, telling Kathryn that whatever else, they had to wrest the shares from Romy. She felt herself bristle at the thought and then asked herself why she cared. She'd kept saying that she didn't want the damn shares, hadn't she? But she didn't want them ripped from her hands either.

She opened the front door and called Kathryn's name, then Darragh's. But there was no reply. She frowned as she walked into the living room and then shrieked as she saw an unknown man sitting on the large sofa reading a newspaper.

At her exclamation, he lowered the paper and looked at her.

'Hi,' he said. 'Romy, I presume?'

She looked at him warily. 'And you are?'

'Alan. Alan Palmer.' As he spoke, he folded the newspaper and put it on the coffee table beside him.

'Kathryn's husband.' Romy had guessed as much. After all, Kathryn had sent her wedding photos. But the man in front of her now seemed a lot grimmer than the smiling groom of the glossy photographs. 'What are you doing here?' she asked him. 'What's going on? And where's Kathryn?'

'I came over to see my wife,' he said. 'To collect her and take her back to the States because she seemed to be abandoning me.'

'It's been a while,' agreed Romy.

'She'd left a message saying your mother was seriously ill. Where is your mother now, by the way?'

Romy looked at him cautiously. She didn't entirely feel at ease with Alan, which was strange because he was smiling at her. Yet his smile made her feel uncomfortable.

'She went on a trip with some friends.'

'Hardly the actions of a sick woman,' remarked Alan. 'Bit of a waste, Kathryn rushing over to see her while she's off on a trip somewhere.'

'Mum is on the mend,' said Romy. 'She's due home

tomorrow. I know that Kathryn was talking about returning next week.'

'Was she indeed?' asked Alan. 'What else did she talk about during her very extended time here?'

'Oh, you know Kathryn.' Romy shrugged. 'She's not very chatty. And she never confides in me.'

His eyes narrowed. 'Never.'

'Nope.' Romy shook her head and then looked round her again. 'So where's she gone?'

'Well, you know, I'm not too sure about that,' said Alan. 'She wasn't really all that happy to see me.'

'No?' Romy could feel an increasing tension in the air between them. She didn't know whether it was him or her. But it was there and building.

'I know she's your sister,' said Alan. 'But she can be a bit annoying.'

'Sure she can.'

'There are times when I wonder how I put up with her.'

'I know the feeling,' said Romy, although she was really only replying to keep a dialogue going between them. She was feeling more and more afraid in his company.

'In that case, maybe you're the one who can persuade her to come and join us,' said Alan.

'Persuade her?' Romy frowned. 'She's in the house somewhere?'

'Did you think she'd left me here?' He laughed. 'On my own? She only leaves me in America.'

'Have you two had a fight?'

'What sort of fight?' His eyes darkened.

'An argument. Did you row about something?'

'I never row,' said Alan. 'Your darling sister does, though. All the time.'

'She's actually my half-sister,' said Romy, watching him carefully.

'Aha. So she is.' He put his head to one side. 'Does that mean you don't care about her?'

'Not exactly,' she said.

'That she doesn't care about you?'

'Possibly not.'

'I find that hard to believe.' He stood up, the movement so quick that Romy hadn't budged by the time he'd moved beside her. He was too close and she edged away from him.

'Would you like a cup of tea?' she asked. 'I'm sure wherever Kathryn is she'd want you to have a cup of tea.'

He smiled at her. 'Good idea. Kitchen it is. But coffee for me if you can manage it.'

Romy had wanted to be in a different room from him. All her shadowy suspicions about him and his marriage to Kathryn were bubbling to the surface of her mind. Where the hell was Kathryn? she asked herself. Surely she'd heard her come home? Why hadn't she joined them? Romy filled the kettle, thinking furiously.

'You're not like I imagined.' Alan was sitting on one of the bar stools watching her.

'No?' She clicked the kettle on and took three mugs from the cupboard.

'Kathryn said that you were a plain little thing who liked digging in the mud. You don't look plain to me.'

Romy had no idea what to say.

'But you're not like Katy, that's for sure.'

'What d'you mean?'

'Poor Kathryn. She hasn't been well either, you know. She's been working too hard.'

'Really?'

'I keep telling her there's no need. That I'll look after her. I'm her husband. That's my job, isn't it?'

'Kathryn can look after herself,' said Romy as she spooned coffee into the mugs. The spoon clattered off the ceramic and she realised that her hand was shaking.

'So she says.' Alan chuckled. 'But all of us need someone, don't we?'

'Where is she?' Romy turned to look at him.

'You know,' said Alan. 'I haven't the faintest idea.'

Veronica was in her hotel room, sitting on the bed and watching a movie on TV. Will, Graham and Connie, who'd all decided to take advantage of the hotel's special deal and stay on for the extra few days, were down in the bar. But Veronica had wanted some peace and quiet after dinner. She had been (so Will told her) the life and soul of the party all week, keeping them amused with stories and anecdotes about her life and her marriages and her children. She'd enjoyed herself, both with her friends and occasionally with other visitors to the hotel. The previous evening she'd struck up a conversation with a couple of German tourists, backpackers in their twenties, and had chatted happily with them never once feeling old or ridiculous or past it despite the fact that they were two good-looking young men. And then they'd said good night to her and she'd asked where they were going and they'd told her that they were going to bed because it was getting late and they had a full day tomorrow and they wanted some quiet time. It was then she realised, with a sudden lurch, that the two guys were together, that they were partners. And she hadn't known whether to laugh or to cry at the idea that she'd thought she was flirting with them.

Maybe I am past it, she'd thought, as she glanced at the mirror behind the bar. Or maybe I'm just past spotting the right signals!

When she'd told the others that she was going to her room after dinner they'd fussed around her, asking her if she was OK, and she'd told them that she was absolutely fine. But Connie had looked worried and said that it wasn't like Veronica to want a quiet night and that she only had to say if her back was hurting her – Connie had some great painkillers that her doctor had given her. They'd worked wonders on her own dodgy knees.

Veronica had assured them that she just wanted some time to herself, a little irritated to think that people didn't expect her to be on her own at all. And yet she understood that because she knew that on many occasions they were right. She wasn't really good on her own. She preferred being out and about. It meant that she didn't have time to think.

She wasn't generally an introspective person. She didn't think a lot about anything. She often felt that other people thought far too much. But she had spent a number of hours wrestling with her decision about the shares for Romy and about how it was the right thing to do. She hadn't, in all honesty, given a lot of thought to how Darragh would feel about it, but now she had to concede that perhaps he might be feeling a bit let down. They would all have to get on with it, she decided. In the same way as she was getting on with it in making the decision to sell the house and move somewhere more suitable. It had suddenly occurred to her that rattling around in Avalon was rattling around with memories of Tom and of a life she hadn't lived. And that she was somehow always harking back to it, always wanting it to have been how she'd expected it to be. Her marriage to Dermot had broken down because she'd wanted him to be another Tom, only he wasn't. She'd wanted him to put her before everything else and he hadn't. She'd liked that about him at first, but – and it had come to her with a horrible jolt – she realised that she always wanted people to put her first. She liked being the centre of attention. Tom, despite the business, always made her feel the centre of attention because he told her that everything he did he did for her. It had been hard to adjust to Dermot's insistence that he loved her but that his career was important to him and he wasn't going to change just to keep her happy. She'd expected him to change but she knew that was silly. Men didn't. Probably nobody did. They compromised, but that was different. The problem for her and Dermot seemed to have been that they hadn't been able to keep compromising. And Larry, her third husband . . . She'd certainly been the centre of attention until they'd married but after that he hadn't been one for compromise at all.

She put down the remote and picked up her mobile. She wanted to check that Romy was going to meet her at the station. She hesitated for a moment before dialling. Did ringing her daughter to confirm their arrangements constitute wanting to be the centre of attention again? Should she just assume that Romy would remember?

Oh for God's sake, she said to herself as she pushed her blond hair out of her eyes. I need to be rational here. Everyone rings to check arrangements. It's not that important in the grand scheme of things!

Romy jumped as the phone in the kitchen started to shrill. She looked at Alan, who was still standing opposite her, a slightly mocking expression on his face.

'Leave it,' he said.

'I'm not going to leave it.' She looked at him in annoyance. 'For heaven's sake, it's a ringing phone. I'm going to answer it.'

'I said, leave it.'

She went to push by him and he grabbed her by the wrist. She gasped and twisted away from him but his grip only tightened.

'What the hell do you think you're doing!' she cried. 'Who d'you think you are?'

'I'm your brother-in-law,' said Alan.

'Where's Kathryn?' asked Romy once again as the phone continued to ring. 'What have you done to her?'

He laughed. 'I haven't done anything. Not that she wouldn't

deserve it, by the way, bitch that she is. However, I haven't laid a finger on her.'

'Not this time,' said Romy slowly. 'But you did before.'

'Y'see, I knew she'd tell you sooner or later.'

'She didn't.' Romy tried to wriggle her wrist free but his hold made it impossible. 'But clearly, the way you're treating me now, you must've treated her like this in the past. No wonder she came home.'

'She's my wife,' said Alan. 'She had no right to leave me. And you have no right to keep her from me.'

'I'm not keeping her from you,' said Romy. 'Now let go of me, you bastard.'

He released his hold so suddenly that she stumbled. And then he hit her across the face.

'Oh my God.' Romy was conscious, through the blinding pain of his blow, that the kitchen phone had stopped but that her mobile, buried deep in her bag, had now started to ring instead. She put her hand to her cheek, which was burning hot. 'You hit me.'

'And I'll do it again if you piss me off,' said Alan.

'You think?'

'You know, you're a feisty little thing, aren't you?' Alan took two steps across the kitchen and picked Romy up by the hair. 'Kathryn said that you were annoying. Now I know what she means.'

'Let me go!' she cried.

'Shut up,' commanded Alan. 'Shut up or I'll give you something to roar about.'

Romy shut up. She realised that her mobile had stopped ringing too. The sudden silence in the room was even more threatening.

'This is ridiculous,' she said after what seemed like an eternity when the only sound was her own laboured breathing. 'We can't stay like this for ever. Look, let's call a truce here.'

'Call a truce?' He laughed. 'Were you in the girl scouts or something?'

'There's no point in us trying to beat each other up,' said Romy. 'That's not going to solve anything. What do you want?'

'I want my wife,' said Alan. 'I want her home. And I want you to stop shielding her.'

'Obviously I'm not shielding her,' said Romy. 'I don't know where she is.'

'I know how to find her.' Alan smiled and Romy shivered. He was crazy, she thought. He really was. And she didn't know how to deal with someone who was totally irrational. She didn't know whether there was anything at all that would defuse the situation, whether the rage might suddenly leave him. She didn't know whether he was mentally ill or whether he was just a thug. She had no idea what on earth she was supposed to do.

He caught her by the wrist again and she winced.

'Come on,' he said and dragged her out of the house and into the back garden.

'What are you doing?' Tears of pain were stinging her eyes.

'Call her,' he demanded. 'Call Kathryn.'

'What good will that do?'

'She's hiding,' said Alan. 'Coward that she is. Call her and tell her that you want her.'

'If she's hiding from you it's because she's scared,' gasped Romy. 'Me calling her won't make any difference.'

'It might,' said Alan, 'if when you call her you tell her that I'll break your neck if she doesn't come out.'

Romy looked at him in horror. 'This is insane,' she whispered. 'You can't do that. That's murder. It's silly. You've got to look at this logically.'

'Shut the fuck up!' He jerked her arm so that it was suddenly behind her. 'You're the mouthiest girl I've ever met.'

'And you're not a murderer,' she said unevenly. 'Clearly there's a problem with Kathryn and it needs to be solved, but saying that you'll break my neck won't help matters.'

'Maybe I won't,' agreed Alan. 'Maybe I'll just break your arm.' He jerked it again and she couldn't help screaming out with pain. 'Maybe I'll break your leg. Doesn't much matter really, does it? Now call her.'

Kathryn heard Romy's first shriek of pain. She moved to the edge of the roof and saw them both, through the leaves of the apple tree, bathed in the light of the living room which spilled out into the garden. She looked in horror at her husband and at Romy. How had she let things get to this state? How? She was cowering on a roof. Romy was being held down by her husband. This wasn't how her life was supposed to be. This wasn't what she'd expected when she'd married Alan. This was tabloid newspaper stuff. It wasn't what happened to people like her.

She'd had those thoughts before, in the States, when she'd been worrying about what to do. But she hadn't done anything because the whole idea of reporting Alan for being a bit rough with her had seemed outlandish. And she'd had a feeling that nobody would believe her. Why would they? As far as everyone else was concerned she was, as they so often put it, part of a New York power couple. It would have been humiliating and awful to tell people anything else. And then she'd have to drag the police into it. She wasn't the sort of person who went to police stations and talked about someone beating her up. She was the sort of person who discussed white-collar crime with guys who wore sharp suits and didn't look as though they had anything to do with law enforcement. But now, because she hadn't done anything, Romy was in danger. She'd let that happen because she'd been weak and feeble and unwilling to admit that there was a problem. Because she hadn't been able to say to herself that her husband was a violent man and that he was dangerous. Because she'd always believed that violence

441

happened to other people, not people like her. Because she'd been a fool. Because, despite always thinking that she was strong, she was weak. She was a failure. And because she was a failure, her sister was in danger.

'Kathryn.' Romy had decided to call her anyway. 'Kathryn, I'm fine, don't worry, I'm sure this is something we can sort out. Alan's upset. I understand that.' She swallowed hard. 'You know you can stay wherever you are if you want. It's OK.'

She gasped as Alan twisted her arm again.

'I want her out here in front of me in five minutes,' he said. 'Or it gets broken.'

'For God's sake!' she cried. 'What d'you think you're doing? You're talking about breaking my arm as though you were some cheap criminal. You're a successful businessman! You don't need to be doing things like this.'

'I'm a success because I'm strong,' said Alan. 'I let my first wife get away with stuff and in the end she divorced me and took me to the cleaners. Nobody is going to mess me around this time.'

He was off his trolley, Romy thought. There was no reasoning with him and she didn't think there was any point in trying. She understood now why Kathryn had come home, why she hadn't wanted to talk about it. The whole experience was beyond anything she'd ever known. Just like Kathryn, Romy couldn't help thinking that being hit by a man wasn't something that happened to people like them. They were strong women, in control of their lives. They weren't dependent on a guy for anything. They could make their own way. And yet she was here, in the back garden, in the dark, not knowing what to do because a man had complete control of her right now.

'Kathryn!' Alan called out this time. 'Kathryn, get your skinny ass out here now or I'm telling you both you and your sister will be sorry.' He tugged at Romy's arm again, and even though she didn't mean to, she yelped in pain.

'I'm here.'

Neither of them had seen Kathryn ease herself off the roof and down on to the balcony. So they were both taken by surprise when she stepped out into the garden. Romy blinked away the tears and looked up. Kathryn's face was paper-white, a defeated expression in her eyes, which were ringed with dark shadows.

'Well, well, well.' Alan looked at her mockingly. 'So you do care for someone after all.'

'Let her go,' said Kathryn. 'Please.'

The three of them faced each other in silence.

And now what? thought Romy. What the hell does he think he can do?

The same thoughts must have been going through Alan's mind, because he held on to her even as he watched Kathryn carefully.

'This is all your fault,' said Alan. 'You made it happen.'

'No you didn't,' said Romy quickly. 'Kathryn, this has nothing to do with you. It's all because of him— Ow, ow!' This time when he wrenched her arm she couldn't help the tears sliding from her eyes.

Kathryn bit her lip as she looked at Romy.

'Let her go,' she repeated.

'I don't think I will,' said Alan. 'I think it's important to have the two of you where I want you.'

Romy wished that she had one of the shroud pins from the dig in the pocket of her jeans. Or her trowel. Or anything she could use as a weapon. Because it seemed to her that the only way of getting out of this situation was by doing something herself. Kathryn looked like a ghost. It was as though all her spirit, all her strength had been sucked away. The girl standing in front of them wasn't the Kathryn she'd grown up with. She was someone else entirely. And Romy knew that she couldn't depend on her.

Kathryn's eyes flickered between Romy and Alan. She saw the tears on her sister's cheeks. She saw the defiance in her husband's eyes. I let this happen, she thought. How could I? How?

'You've got to let her go.' Somehow she managed to keep the quaver out of her voice.

'Why?'

'Because this is about you and me,' she said. 'It's nothing to do with Romy.'

'You made a fool of me,' said Alan. 'You married me for my money and now you want to take me to the cleaners in a divorce. But you're the one, Kathryn, you're the one who's the problem here, what with your drinking and your carousing and your affairs . . .'

Romy looked startled.

'You know that's not true.' Kathryn swallowed hard. 'You know I never had an affair.'

'Out with all those people from your office all the time,' he said, ignoring her. 'Throwing yourself at them in your disgusting dresses . . .'

'No,' said Kathryn.

'Defying me.' As he spoke, his grip on Romy tightened again and she blinked back more tears of pain.

Kathryn looked at Romy, who, quite suddenly, smiled through her tears.

'I'm OK,' she mouthed at Kathryn. 'Don't worry.'

Kathryn took a deep breath. 'Alan, we're not talking about anything, we're not going anywhere until you let her go.' There was a sudden authority in her voice and Alan looked at her in surprise.

'Why should I let her go?' he asked. 'Why should I believe that you'll talk to me?'

'Because I've never lied to you,' said Kathryn. 'What do you want, Alan?'

'I don't want anything,' he scoffed. 'Except my wife back at home where she should be.'

'I'm not going to come home in these circumstances,' said Kathryn.

'How else will I make you?' demanded Alan. 'How else will everything work out?'

'You've got to let Romy go for starters,' Kathryn told him. 'Then we can talk.'

'No.'

'Alan.' Kathryn's voice was steady. 'This is about us. Husband and wife. Not Romy. She doesn't count. She's not even my sister. She's only my half-sister.'

Romy had kept her gaze fixed on Kathryn during the exchange. It was extraordinary, she thought, how positive her sister had suddenly become. Ever since she'd come home, Romy had felt as though Kathryn was in some way a shadow of the girl she'd known. There had been something hesitant and uncertain about her. But now, quite unexpectedly, she was turning into the Kathryn of old. Determined. Cool. Suddenly in control again. Romy wasn't sure whether it was a good thing or not that Kathryn seemed to have regained some of her strength right now.

'We can work it out together,' said Kathryn. 'You know we can.' She held out her arms to him and, abruptly, he released his grip on Romy, who stumbled to the ground. 'Get out of here!' cried Kathryn as Romy picked herself up. 'Get out of here and get help.'

Romy darted forward, and as she did, Alan grabbed hold of Kathryn.

'You sneaky bitch!' he cried. 'You're trying to con me.'

'I'm not,' said Kathryn frantically. 'She needs help. She's in pain.'

'You want to get me arrested! So that you can have an excuse to divorce me!'

'No!' cried Kathryn as this time it was her arm that was suddenly locked in Alan's vice-like grip.

We've achieved nothing, thought Romy helplessly. He's got Kathryn now instead of me and we're back to where we were before, only he's probably even madder. And I'm not leaving her here with him.

A familiar sound attracted her attention. Neither Kathryn nor Alan had heard the muted metallic thud, but Romy knew that the electronic gates had been opened. And now she could hear the murmur of a car engine. She turned and ran in the direction of the house.

'You see!' Alan's voice was triumphant. 'You only have me, Kathryn. She's run away. You always only had me.'

Romy ran through the kitchen and the hallway and hauled open the front door. Darragh was getting out of his BMW, an annoyed expression on his face.

'Oh Darragh, thank God you're here.'

He looked at her in surprise. Romy had never seemed pleased to see him before.

'I'm here, you're here,' he said irritably. 'Which I knew you would be. Honestly, Veronica rang me because nobody was answering their phones and she got worried and panicked – why, I just don't know.'

'Darragh, Darragh . . .' Romy had to work hard to slow down her words. 'Alan's in the garden and he's got Kathryn and he's absolutely crazy. He could kill her.'

'What are you talking about? Alan who?'

'Alan! Her husband!' Romy looked at Darragh in frustration. 'He hit me.'

'What?' Darragh stared at her, taking in her dishevelled look and the red weal on her face. He'd noticed, of course, that she'd looked messy and unkempt but as far as he was concerned that wasn't anything new for Romy.

'Oh Darragh, he's completely mad.' To her horror, Romy

felt herself start to cry. 'He nearly broke my arm and he threatened to kill me and we have to do something.'

'Are you serious?'

'Of course I'm serious.'

Darragh took his phone out of his pocket. 'In that case,' he said, 'let's do the right thing and call the police.'

He hit the switch to open the front gates again before walking through to the back garden followed by Romy.

Alan was still holding Kathryn in his grip although he had forced her to her knees on the damp grass. Romy bit her lip and wiped her eyes with the back of her hand.

'What the fuck do you think you're doing to my sister?'

Darragh strode across the lawn, and before either girl knew what had happened, he had punched Alan Palmer in the face. An explosion of blood shot from Alan's nose as, stunned, he released his hold on Kathryn. She scrambled away from him, towards Romy, who rushed to her and put her arms around her.

'You bastard,' said Darragh and punched Alan again.

He'd gone to boxing lessons. Romy remembered it now. Anger management, Veronica had once called it, an outlet for Darragh's fiery temper. But he'd learned to control his temper over the years and Romy never remembered him utterly losing it. She was afraid, though, that he'd lose it now.

But he was standing in front of Alan, not touching him, just watching as the other man shook his head slowly and wiped the blood from his nose.

'You hit me.' Alan looked at Darragh in astonishment. 'You hit me.'

'And I'll hit you again if you lay a finger on my sister.'

'You'll be sorry.' Alan blinked a couple of times. 'Do you know who I am?'

447

'Sadly, yes,' said Darragh.

'She asked for it,' said Alan. 'She's nothing more than a slut and she—'

Darragh hit Alan for a third time. And this time he fell to the ground and didn't move.

Chapter 29

Kathryn had been sick in the garden. After Darragh hit Alan for the final time and she'd seen her husband crumple to the ground, she'd thrown up, retching violently on to the grass so that Romy had rushed over to her and held her hair from her forehead, murmuring that everything was all right, that Kathryn would be fine. Meantime Darragh stood apart from them, watching them and watching Alan too, waiting for him to move again. When the other man finally stirred, Darragh had frogmarched him back into the house and pushed him on to the long sofa in the centre of the room. Which was when the doorbell had rung and the guards had arrived.

Now they were all sitting in the living room. Kathryn was in one of the armchairs while Romy perched on the arm beside her. Darragh stood behind Alan while the two gardai took stock of the situation.

'So.' The tall, well-built garda who'd introduced himself as Richard Carr looked at Alan. 'Are you saying to me that you want to make a complaint against Mr Dolan?'

Alan looked up at him, his face red and angry but also bruised. 'He beat me senseless,' he said. 'He punched me with no provocation whatsoever and knocked me out. That's assault.'

'And what you were doing to my sister wasn't?' Darragh walked around the sofa and faced him. 'You worthless piece of shit—'

'Mr Dolan, please.' Richard Carr looked at both men. 'This

has been a domestic dispute and I'm not at all underestimating the seriousness of the alleged attack on Mrs Palmer or Miss Kilkenny. What I want to find out is whether or not any of you people are taking things further.' He turned back to Alan. 'Bearing in mind that both Mrs Palmer and Miss Kilkenny allege you assaulted them, are you intent on proceeding with a complaint against Mr Dolan?'

Quite suddenly Alan deflated. Kathryn, watching him, saw the anger disappear from his face, replaced, she thought, with fear.

'What's the point?' he asked. 'I'm the foreigner here. You'll rig it so that I come off the worst.'

'That most certainly will not be the case.' The garda's voice was firm.

'If they don't press charges against me I won't press charges against them,' said Alan sullenly. 'They don't know how lucky they are.'

'You don't know how lucky *you* are, you bastard,' said Darragh. 'If it was up to me . . .'

'Mr Dolan.' Richard Carr sounded a warning note and then turned to face Kathryn and Romy. 'Ladies?'

Kathryn looked at the garda despairingly. She desperately wanted it all to go away, to pretend that it had never happened. She wanted Alan to disappear back to America so she would never set eyes on him again. She wanted to go to bed tonight and forget about him, forget that any of this had ever happened. But if she formalised it . . .

'I want to make a complaint.' Romy's voice was shaky.

Alan looked at her with loathing and she took a deep breath. 'He assaulted me and he shouldn't get away with that.'

'I didn't fucking assault you,' he said. 'If I had, you'd know all about it.'

Romy scrubbed at her eyes, surprised that she was crying because she didn't feel that there was anything to cry about now. She realised that she was shivering and rubbed her hands along her arms.

'I want to make a complaint too.' Kathryn's voice was un-expectedly steady as she reached out and took Romy's hand. 'I absolutely do.'

'You fucking bitch!' cried Alan. 'You'll be sorry. You know you will. I'll get you . . .' His voice trailed off as he realised that the two policemen were watching him carefully. 'This is a family argument,' he said. 'She's a slut, you know she is, and she deserved it.'

Kathryn said nothing at all. And then Richard Carr arrested Alan Palmer.

Alan was remanded in custody. Back at the house, Kathryn couldn't quite believe that he was in jail. But the gardai had told the judge that they considered him to be a danger to Kathryn and to Romy as well, expressing their concern that he would leave the jurisdiction. The judge agreed. And to everyone's amazement (because none of them had any experience of seeing someone arrested, charged and remanded in custody all within the space of a couple of hours), Alan Palmer was led away to a cell.

'Why didn't you say anything before?' asked Romy as they sat in the kitchen back at Veronica's house.

'I was too ashamed,' admitted Kathryn. 'I couldn't believe that I'd let him hit me in the first place.'

'Surely you must have guessed that he was violent?' Darragh adjusted the ice-pack on his hand, which had swollen up dramatically over the course of the evening. 'I mean, someone doesn't suddenly turn into an animal like that.'

'It wasn't sudden,' Kathryn agreed. 'But I didn't realise how it was happening.' She sighed deeply. 'At first he was just possessive. And I thought it was kind of cute because nobody ever seemed to care about me like that before. But then he got more and more . . . well, still possessive, I guess, but jealous too – every time I went out with someone he asked who it was and where I was going and when would I be home . . . I used to joke with him about it and he'd laugh and say that he cared too much. But it was a bit weird. He'd grab hold of me and make jokes about how much he cared, but he hurt me . . . and then one night he hit me.'

'Y'see, I don't know why you didn't leave there and then,' said Romy. 'It was abuse, for heaven's sake, Kathryn. Why on earth did you stay?'

'Because he said he didn't mean it,' she told them. 'And I believed him.'

Darragh shook his head.

'It seems as clear as anything now!' cried Kathryn. 'But when it was happening, it didn't. And yes, I was worried about our marriage and how domineering he was becoming but I thought it was just . . . I thought it was something we would work through. I thought he liked being in charge, being the one to say what was what – you know, the alpha male. I thought he was threatened by the fact that I was a successful person too. Men are,' she added wearily. 'They don't like women telling them what to do.'

Romy glanced at Darragh, whose face had darkened slightly at Kathryn's words.

'Not all men resort to hitting women,' he said. 'No matter how annoyed they might get with them. No matter how domineering they might want to be. Most men wouldn't even dream of it.'

'I know.' A tear rolled down Kathryn's cheek. 'I know. I was fooling myself and in the end that put Romy in danger too. I'm sorry.'

'Hey, that's OK.' Romy hugged her. 'Besides, you did a really silly big-sister sort of thing. You made him let me go and grab you instead.'

Kathryn smiled weakly. 'I couldn't have let him hurt you any more,' she said. 'I'm really, really sorry, Romy.'

'The important thing is that he's locked away, at least for now,' said Darragh. 'There'll be a hearing, I suppose, and goodness knows what else. I'll get in touch with the family solicitor and get some advice on our situation. Because however this is played, we want that bloke behind bars.'

'He'll probably be extradited back to the States,' said Romy.

'I don't care where he ends up,' said Kathryn. 'As long as he doesn't bother me again.'

'What are you going to do now?' asked Romy. 'Stay here or go back?'

'I have to go back,' said Kathryn. 'I need to get some advice myself. I'd already decided to divorce him. But I left a message, which probably wasn't the wisest way to go about it. It just seemed an easy way out.' She massaged the top of her arm. 'I need to move out of the apartment, of course, and—'

'You shouldn't have to move out,' Darragh interrupted her.

'I can't possibly stay there,' Kathryn told him. 'It's his apartment, after all. And I'd feel . . .' She shuddered. 'No, I want out.'

'Make sure you get a good settlement,' Darragh said. 'You're entitled—'

'I don't want anything from him,' she said quickly. 'Nothing. I don't need it and I don't want it.'

'You deserve something,' said Darragh. 'With what he put you through . . .'

'I don't know what I deserve,' said Kathryn, 'but I'd puke if I thought that anything I had came from him. In fact . . .' She suddenly wrenched her gold wedding ring and her magnificent diamond engagement ring from her finger. 'Take these. I never want to see them again.'

'Don't you think that's a bit extreme?' asked Darragh.

'No,' said Kathryn. 'It's about time I got to grips with my life again. As Kathryn Dolan, not Kathryn Palmer.' She smiled shakily at her brother and looked at her ringless hand. 'And you know, without those weighing me down, I feel better already.'

It was the early hours of the morning by the time Darragh got home to his own house. He'd phoned Giselle to tell her what had happened and Giselle had been the one to call Veronica. She hadn't been able to give Veronica much information other than that Alan had turned up at the house and there'd been some kind of row but that everything was OK now, so she was dying to know exactly what had happened. She sat up in bed as she heard Darragh walk slowly up the stairs.

'You're still awake?' He looked at her with concern.

'I couldn't sleep,' she told him. 'It's hard now anyway with the size of me. I wake up all the time. What's the story?'

He'd phoned her a second time from the police station and so she knew that Alan had been arrested. He filled her in on the rest of it.

'So he's in prison?' she gasped.

'In custody,' Darragh amended. 'He still has to have his case heard. But, my God, Giselle, it was unbelievable. The whole process . . . awful.'

'How's Kathryn?'

'Teary,' he said. 'Upset.'

'Crikey. I don't think I've ever seen Kathryn upset before.'

'I've seen her upset,' Darragh said. 'But usually she's just angry upset. I've never seen her cry.'

'Maybe she's softening up,' suggested Giselle.

'I'll tell you something.' Darragh eased his shoes off his feet. 'The whole thing would make anyone want to cry. What sort of bloke would do that to his own wife?'

'Lots of men,' said Giselle.

'Go on,' Darragh said. 'Tar us all with the same brush.'

'I didn't mean it like that,' she protested. 'Just that there are violent men out there and there are women who accept

454

it and it's not right. What astonishes me is that it happened to Kathryn. I mean, she's such a determined sort of woman herself. I couldn't imagine anyone getting the better of her in an argument and I still can't imagine her staying around long enough to get hit.'

'I know.' Darragh looked grim. 'She said it happened gradually.' He repeated to Giselle everything Kathryn had told him as he undressed and finally got into bed.

'Your hand!' She gasped as she saw it. 'Omigod, Darragh, you look like you've been in a real fight yourself.'

'I'm not proud of thumping him,' said Darragh. 'Meeting violence with violence isn't right. Dad always told me that. But there wasn't any choice.'

Giselle took his bruised hand in hers. 'My hero. The family hero, in fact.'

He snorted. 'Don't worry, she'll have forgotten it all by Monday when we're having the board meeting. She'll have the knife out for me and the company again then.'

'Maybe not,' said Giselle comfortingly. 'Maybe she'll realise that you know what you're doing after all.'

He shook his head. 'She's already made a few comments about the energy deal and about Switzerland and Germany. She says that the German company is a good option and that she has ideas about funding . . . How she had the damn time to check all this out when her husband has been thumping her around the place I just don't know.'

'Maybe it kept her occupied,' said Giselle. 'Took her mind off it.'

'Maybe.' Darragh yawned suddenly and burrowed down into the bed. 'I'm exhausted,' he told her. 'I've been running on adrenalin for the last few hours but I think my engine is empty.'

'Get some sleep,' said Giselle. 'You deserve it.'

'Thank you.' He closed his eyes and within a couple of minutes he was snoring gently.

Giselle lay beside him for a few minutes and then got out of bed. She was wide awake and knew that it would be ages before she felt tired again. She pulled her silk robe around her and walked softly into Mimi's room. Her daughter was lying on her back, her arms flung over her head and her golden curls fanned out on the pink pillow. She was heartbreakingly beautiful, thought Giselle. And one day she'd meet a bloke and perhaps he'd be the one for her and they'd live together or get married and . . . Well, if he touched a hair of her head, if he hurt her at all . . . Giselle was shocked at the rage she felt tremble through her body. She would never let anyone harm her gorgeous daughter and neither would Darragh. She was immensely proud of how Darragh had sprung to Kathryn's defence. She hadn't for one minute ever imagined him actually punching someone. She knew that it wasn't something that should be recommended, but it made her think that she was really lucky to be married to someone who would do something like that. And if he'd reacted like that to a threat to Kathryn, who let's face it wasn't his favourite person in the world, Giselle could only imagine what he'd do to anyone who threatened her or Mimi or Muffie. Her heart swelled with love for him. They were a strong family, she told herself. And Muffie would be part of that too.

Poor Muffie. Giselle rested her hands on her bump. She still couldn't help thinking negatively about her potentially fat daughter. What would her life be like if she was a hefty kind of girl? If she wasn't pretty and gorgeous like Mimi? What if she hated pink? Giselle wondered how on earth she would cope with someone truculent or bookish or just plain weird like Kathryn or Romy? Most especially Romy. How would she deal with an outdoors kind of girl?

The baby suddenly turned over inside her and Giselle felt a rush of guilt at her thoughts. What if Muffie had sensed how she felt? What if she was already feeling unwanted? What if she felt unloved because she wasn't pretty enough?

She sat down abruptly on the chair in the corner. There was no point in pretending that pretty girls didn't get more opportunities, but look at Romy – she'd travelled the world and she actually seemed to be very happy with her life. Could you be happy without being pretty?

Giselle hadn't been happy when she'd weighed fourteen stone. She'd been miserable and she'd been bullied and she'd hated her life. She didn't like to think that all the good things that had happened to her had only happened because she'd managed to slim down to a size ten. She didn't like to think that Darragh only loved her because she was one of Dublin's Glamorous Socialites.

'Are you all right?'

She turned around, startled. She hadn't heard him coming into the room.

'Couldn't sleep.'

He looked at her and frowned. 'What's the matter?'

'Nothing.'

'You're crying,' he said. He walked across the room and put his arms around her. 'Why?'

'I . . .' She rested her head on his shoulder. 'I guess I was panicking.'

'About what?'

'About the fact that our baby is a girl and that she might not be beautiful and that you might not love me.'

Darragh lifted her face and looked at her. 'A girl? Are you serious?'

She looked at him anxiously. 'You wanted a son and heir and I'm not giving you one.'

He kissed her on the forehead. 'And who says my daughters won't want to run the business? Maybe one day we will have a boy, but you know what, I don't really care! I love Mimi and I love you and I love the new baby just as much. She'll be the most beautiful baby on the planet. As well as Mimi. Why wouldn't she be? Doesn't she have you for a mother?'

'I'm a crap mother,' said Giselle. 'I want everything to be perfect for them and I want them to be perfect too.'

'All mothers want that.'

'I was afraid that Muffie would turn out like Romy,' confessed Giselle.

'Muffie?'

'It's my nickname for her,' confessed Giselle. 'After Miss Muffet. Eating curds and whey.'

Darragh roared with laughter and Giselle smiled uncomfortably.

'Please promise me that it's only a nickname,' he begged. 'I don't think I could go through life calling my daughter Muffie.'

'Of course it is,' said Giselle. 'But . . . well . . . when I thought she'd be fat and awful or maybe all outdoorsy and self-sufficient like Romy and turning down trips to exclusive spas . . . I kinda felt it suited her.'

'We'll talk that particular issue through when she's born,' Darragh told Giselle. 'And in all honesty – don't for God's sake ever tell her this – there are probably worse things that could happen than her turning out like Romy.'

Giselle's smile was watery. 'You think?'

'That bastard Palmer nearly broke her arm,' said Darragh. 'And she was really scared of him. But she said she was making a complaint against him and there was no stopping her and I was really quite proud of her.'

'And Kathryn?'

'I was surprised at what happened,' admitted Darragh. 'She just didn't seem to be the kind of person to allow it. But if Muffie grows up like Kathryn she'll be smart and bright and obviously a bit vulnerable under the surface but she'll still be a great girl.'

'And me?' asked Giselle.

'If she grows up like you she'll be perfect.'

Giselle smiled at him. 'I love you.'

Darragh felt a lump in his throat. She'd said it. For the first time in ages she'd told him that she loved him.

'I really do,' she added. 'More than anything.'

He put his arms around her and held her close to him. They stood without moving for a few moments and then Giselle yawned involuntarily.

'Sorry,' she said.

'You're tired,' Darragh told her. 'It's late and you must be exhausted.'

'Not as exhausted as you,' she said. 'I haven't been defending the family honour.'

'But you are carrying the next member of the family. And I know you haven't been sleeping well. Go to bed now and I'll bring you something to help you sleep.'

'I can't.' She looked horrified. 'I can't drink alcohol or take tablets.'

'I'm not talking about that,' Darragh told her. 'I'm going to make you a cup of cocoa with full-fat milk and you're going to drink it and enjoy it.'

'Oh, yuck.'

'I won't take no for an answer,' said Darragh. 'If I've got you cooking steak and onions for me, the least you can do is drink milk.'

She laughed suddenly. 'You're so macho. But you're talking about hot milk!'

'I know.' Darragh shrugged. 'I'm also in touch with my feminine side. But for God's sake don't tell anyone. Now here.' He handed her a tissue. 'Blow your nose, go back to bed and I'll bring it up to you in five minutes.'

She did as she was told. But when he came up the stairs with the mug of steaming cocoa, she was already fast asleep.

Chapter 30

Although the sun was blazing down from a china-blue sky the following day and temperatures were reaching into the mid-twenties, Romy wore a long-sleeved top over a mid-length denim skirt when she went to pick up Veronica from Heuston station. She arrived early and parked in the car park before strolling into the relative cool of the old station building, where she ordered a mango smoothie and sipped it until the train lumbered up to the platform. She left the remains of the drink on the counter and walked out to meet Veronica.

Her mother was instantly recognisable in the crowd, her blond hair gleaming and her face perfectly made up as always. She was wearing a tailored blue skirt, plain white top and blue shoes – though Romy saw that the shoes had a very low heel and looked considerably more comfortable than Veronica's usual favourite footwear.

Will, Graham and Connie walked with her. The two men were in casual shirts and trousers and Connie was dressed in a cool pastel pink dress with a floral pattern. It was a pretty dress, conceded Romy, and Connie was an attractive woman, but there was absolutely no doubt that Veronica (despite the lower than average shoes) had returned to form with a vengeance and looked positively stunning.

'Hello there.' Her mother enveloped her in a hug, leaving a haze of Chanel around her. 'How are you? How's Kathryn? What's the story about that bastard Palmer?'

Romy disentangled herself from Veronica's hold and assured her that everything was fine. She sneezed a couple of times (her mother's perfume always had that effect on her) while Veronica said goodbye to her friends. Romy noticed that she lingered a little longer over her farewell to Will, who kissed her on both cheeks and told her to give him a call later.

'You had a good time then?' remarked Romy as they walked to the car park while the others went in search of a cab. (Veronica had offered them all a lift but there wasn't really enough room in the Golf for an extra three people plus luggage, so Romy had been relieved when they'd declined.)

'It was OK,' said Veronica impatiently. 'Good to be away. But then this happened and all I wanted to do was get back. Was it awful?'

Romy unlocked the boot and hefted her mother's case inside.

'Scary,' she admitted. 'But then Darragh turned up and whacked Alan on the nose and it was like being in the middle of a movie set.'

'Fair play to Darragh,' said Veronica. 'I'd never have thought he'd do something like that.'

'Well to be honest I was terrified that he'd be the one ending up in the clink,' said Romy. 'He knocked Alan out, you know. And goodness knows, when the dust settles and Alan gets legal advice, he might still press charges against him.'

'Let him try,' said Veronica grimly.

'Hopefully he won't.' Romy pulled out into the traffic and headed back towards Rathfarnham while Veronica settled herself more comfortably in the passenger seat.

'And you're sure that both you and Kathryn are all right?' Veronica asked.

'I'm fine. My arm hurts a bit.'

That was an understatement. Romy had taken a couple of

Nurofen earlier because of the incessant throbbing in her arm and she'd chosen the long-sleeved top to hide the imprints of Alan's fingers and the bruising which covered it. She really didn't want Veronica to see it and fuss over it.

'I think it's the same for Kathryn. She's got some other scrapes too but they're not from Alan; she climbed on to the roof to hide from him and tore strips off her knees.'

'The roof!' Veronica looked at Romy in horror. 'The roof! She could've been killed getting up there.'

'Chill out, Mum,' said Romy. 'She used to shimmy up the drainpipe all the time when we were kids. She didn't think anyone knew but I saw here there sometimes leaning against the chimney stack with her Chalet School books.'

'The roof.' Veronica shook her head. 'How come I never knew about that before?'

It was half an hour before they reached the house. Once again Romy helped Veronica with her case and then both of them walked out to the back garden. Kathryn, wearing Bermuda shorts and a long-sleeved top similar to Romy's, was stretched out on a sun-lounger. Her eyes snapped open as she heard their steps on the deck.

'Oh, Katy!' Veronica sat down beside her and put her arms around her before patting her scraped knees and making Kathryn wince. 'My poor, poor Katy.'

Kathryn allowed herself to be held for almost a minute before she pushed Veronica gently away.

'I'm OK,' she said. 'Really. Everything's OK.'

'It's not OK,' said Veronica fiercely. 'How on earth did this all happen? Why didn't you say something before?'

'I didn't . . .' Kathryn hesitated. 'I didn't think that it was important.'

'Kathryn!'

'I know it sounds daft now.' Kathryn looked defensive. 'But

like I said to Romy and Darragh, when it happens over a period of time it becomes sort of normal. You justify it, make allowances.'

'Did he ever really hurt you?' asked Veronica, her eyes dark with anger.

'Last night was the worst,' Kathryn told her. 'And you know, he hurt Romy a lot more than me.'

'You said you weren't badly hurt!' Veronica looked accusingly at her younger daughter.

'It wasn't that bad. Honestly.'

'Stop trying to pretend!' cried Veronica. 'Both of you! It was a terrible, awful thing and he deserves everything he gets, and I'm just sorry, Kathryn, that I was blinded by his looks and his success and thought that he was the perfect husband for you.'

'Hey, I was blinded too,' said Kathryn. 'The thing is, Mum, that it was all about jealousy really. He needs help, he does really.'

'He needs to be locked up for ever,' retorted Veronica.

'I want to get in touch with Naomi, his first wife,' said Kathryn. 'I want to find out if it happened to her too.'

'It's so awful,' repeated Veronica. 'It really is.'

The sudden silence between them was broken by the sound of the buzzer at the gates.

'I'll get it,' said Romy. 'It might be the police again.'

But when she went to the door, she recognised her father's ten-year-old Focus outside. She opened the gates and went down the steps to greet him.

'What are you doing here?' she demanded as he got out of the car.

'Darragh phoned me,' said Dermot. 'He told me about last night. I came straight away. My God, sweetheart, are you OK?'

Romy swallowed hard. 'We've just gone through it all with Veronica,' she said. 'I can't go over it all again, but I'm fine.' She looked at him hesitantly. 'D'you want to come through? We're in the back garden – me and Veronica and Kathryn.'

'I guess she won't freak out too much today,' said her father as he stepped over the threshold and then stopped abruptly. 'Goodness, it's changed.'

'You haven't been here in years,' Romy reminded him. 'It's gone through a few makeovers since then.'

'Rather like Veronica, so.' Dermot grinned at her then followed her on to the deck (another design feature of the house which hadn't existed in his time there), where Kathryn and Veronica looked at him in surprise.

'Dermot!'

'Dad!'

Romy blinked at hearing Kathryn's exclamation. She'd forgotten (how, she wondered, how had I forgotten?) that Kathryn had, until about the last year that Dermot lived with them, always called him Dad.

'Sweetheart.'

She'd forgotten, too, that Dermot used the same endearments to both of them.

'Oh, Dad.'

Suddenly Kathryn was crying, huge tears coursing down her cheeks while Dermot held her to him. He rocked her gently in his arms until her sobs had subsided. Then, still holding her close to him, he looked at Veronica.

'Hi,' he said. 'Long time no see. I hope you're feeling better. You look amazing. As always.'

Veronica had been waiting to hear him speak, waiting for the expected mockery in his voice, the mockery she'd grown used to when she was married to him. But his voice was warm and she bit back the riposte she'd been about to let fly.

'I'm feeling a lot better, thanks,' she said. 'Though obviously this has been a bit of a shock.'

'If I could get my hands on the bastard . . .'

'Oh, stop with the violent thoughts!' cried Romy. 'You and

Darragh both. And Mum too. Much better that things have worked out the way they have. Violence isn't nice. It's messy and horrible and just . . . terrible.'

'It was an expression,' said Dermot.

'Please don't use it.' Romy was really distressed. 'Please.'

'You're right,' her father said. 'And I won't.'

'Neither will I,' said Veronica. 'But that won't stop me wishing all sorts of awful things for him.'

'Me neither.' Kathryn's words were muffled by Dermot's embrace.

'You OK, hon?' He loosened his hold on her, allowing her to nod.

'I just feel such a fool.' She sniffed and Veronica took a tissue out of her neat handbag. 'I should've known better and I should've done something sooner.'

'Should've, would've, could've,' said Dermot gently. 'Darling, we'd all probably do things differently in hind-sight. But that's not how life works. You do things and you hope and pray that they're going to work out for the best, but sometimes they don't. It doesn't mean that it's your fault.'

'It was *his* fault,' said Veronica.

'I know,' said Kathryn. 'But obviously he has problems. So . . .'

'So nothing,' Veronica said.

'But Dad has a point,' Kathryn told her. 'Sometimes stuff isn't anyone's fault.'

Veronica said nothing, but looked at Dermot. He smiled at her and, after a moment, she smiled back. 'At least we never beat each other up,' she said.

'I wouldn't have dreamed of touching a beautiful hair of your head. Ever,' he added. 'Even in our worst moments.'

'I know,' she told him. 'You were a . . . a decent man.'

'Thank you,' said Dermot. 'But . . . well, I accept that I possibly wasn't the best husband in the world.'

'No,' said Veronica. 'You weren't.' She shrugged. 'Still, you weren't the worst. And when you were around, you were good to me and the children.'

'We were wrong for each other,' Dermot reminded her. 'Some of it was great, though, wasn't it?' He grinned suddenly and so did Veronica, who had an amused gleam in her eye which made both Romy and Kathryn wonder exactly what the great parts were.

'Yes.' Veronica laughed. 'It was. And some of it was shit, but it was a long time ago and we've moved on, haven't we?'

'Totally.'

'That's good to hear,' said Kathryn. 'It's not as though we ever need to get together on a regular basis, but it's nice to think that if we did there wouldn't be skin and hair flying.'

'We've seen enough of that.' Romy shuddered and Dermot, still with his arm around Kathryn, reached out to her too.

'Happy families.' Veronica almost smiled.

'C'mere, Mum.' Kathryn moved along the sun-lounger so that there was room for them all.

And that was where they were still sitting when Darragh, who for once hadn't bothered ringing the bell but had just let himself in with his own key, walked out of the kitchen with Giselle, holding Mimi by the hand, behind him.

'A reunion.' Darragh looked at Dermot warily while Giselle regarded him curiously and Mimi hung back.

Dermot stood up and extended his hand. 'Thanks for phoning me.'

'You're welcome.' Darragh turned to Giselle. 'This is my mum's ex-husband, Dermot,' he told her. 'Romy's dad.'

'Oh.' Giselle blinked a few times. 'You never said he was so hunky.'

There was a stunned silence and then Veronica laughed. Kathryn and Romy joined in too, their laughter a release from the anxiety of earlier.

'Well he is,' said Giselle defensively. 'And now I see where Romy gets it all from.'

'Um . . . I dunno if I should be thanking you for that,' said Romy. 'Hunky?'

'Well you're not at all like Veronica,' Giselle pointed out. 'But you're so totally Dermot's daughter it's unreal. Not pretty, Romy. Just – you know, strong.'

'Right,' said Romy. 'Strong. Thanks.'

Kathryn grinned at her and suddenly Romy was overcome with a fit of giggles while Giselle looked at her helplessly and tried to tell her that it was a compliment, honestly, and she didn't know what was so funny. Mimi started to laugh too and then rushed to Veronica, who put her arms around her.

'I've been in touch with the gardai,' said Darragh. 'Palmer hasn't said anything about charging me with assault and they can't pursue it unless he does . . . but they still don't know when he'll go to court again or anything.'

'He's still in custody, though?' Kathryn looked anxious.

'So far,' said Darragh.

'I'm going home on Wednesday,' Kathryn told him. 'I called Sybil, a friend of mine in New York, and I'm going to stay with her for a while. Then I'll try to find somewhere of my own.'

'So you're not coming back?' Veronica looked disappointed.

'Not yet,' said Kathryn.

'Are you still OK for the board meeting?' asked Darragh. 'That was the original plan.'

'Of course,' replied Kathryn steadily.

Dermot glanced at both of Tom's children. He'd heard the sudden hardening of their voices and he wondered just how the board meeting would go. And how Romy would cope with it. She'd said that she didn't want to be caught in the middle of the two of them and he'd dismissed her fears. Now he wondered if she wasn't right to be concerned. Darragh might have been a conquering hero the previous night, but he was perfectly capable of being a different sort of person entirely when it came to the company.

'I brought some stuff for you both.' Giselle broke the edgy silence and handed a big L'Occitane carrier bag to Kathryn. 'There's creams and bath oils and other pampering bits and pieces,' she added. 'I thought you and Romy might like them.'

'Oh.' Kathryn peeped inside. 'Thanks, Giselle, that was really nice of you.'

'It's good stuff,' Giselle told her. 'I use it myself all the time.'

'In that case I'm looking forward to trying it out,' said Romy. 'Even if I haven't got the looks, I could have the skin!'

'I didn't mean . . .' Giselle broke off in confusion while Romy grinned at her.

'It's OK. I understood. I really did. And I appreciate it, Giselle. Thank you.'

'Would anyone like tea or coffee?' asked Veronica. 'Mimi, would you like juice?'

'Yes please.'

Veronica poured some juice for Mimi while Dermot shook his head. 'I'd better be going,' he said. 'Larissa is going out later and I need to be back in time to take over my baby-sitting duties.'

Veronica snorted and he smiled ruefully at her. 'Yes, I know. I was useless before. Sorry. Sorry to you too, Romy.'

'You apologised to me already. But you're right to apologise to Mum.'

'There's no need to say sorry any more,' said Veronica. 'There was a pair of us in it, I think. Anyway, the bottom line is that we've been in touch and we can be civil to each other and so something good came out of something terrible.'

'Exactly.' Kathryn stood up. 'And it was nice to see you again. It really was.'

'You too,' said Dermot. 'I know this part of your life was dreadful, but the rest – well, I've kept track and you're doing so well . . . I saw that article about you and the fraud trial on the internet – well done.'

'Thanks.' She looked surprised.

'Keep in touch, Kathryn.' He hugged her again and then turned to Darragh. 'Thanks for being so great last night,' he said as he extended his hand.

'No problem,' said Darragh, shaking it.

'And – well, good luck with the business.'

'Thank you.'

'Nice to meet you too.' He smiled at Giselle. 'I can see why Darragh was bowled over.'

She blushed.

'I'll walk you to the door,' said Romy. She linked her arm with his as they left the others outside. 'You really are an awful old charmer, aren't you?'

He laughed.

'You are,' she repeated. 'Flirting, kind of, with Giselle. Being nice to Mum. Shaking hands with Darragh!'

'I didn't do all that to be charming,' said Dermot. 'I meant what I said. Veronica is a phenomenon. And Giselle is a cracker.'

'You'd better not let Larissa hear you say that.'

'Larissa is the love of my life,' he said simply.

'Is she?'

They stood beside his car.

'Next to you,' he told her, and she punched him gently in the stomach. 'She's right for me,' he added. 'We work in a way that Veronica and I didn't. I'm happy with her, hon.'

Romy nodded. 'I know. And I'm glad you're happy. Honestly. I'm glad you have her and Erin, and if you have another kid I'll be glad about that.'

'Such gladness,' he teased her.

'Last night put things in perspective,' she said.

'Good,' Dermot told her. 'But listen, sweetie, just because Darragh was a knight in shining armour when it came to Alan Palmer doesn't mean that he won't have all sorts of issues when

470

it comes to the company. So – watch your back at that board meeting. Blood might be thicker than water, but a business is a business and you know how the Dolans feel about that.'

She grinned. 'Only too well.'

'OK then.' He hugged her lightly again. 'Give your old man a kiss and let me know how things go.'

She kissed him on the cheek and watched as he drove away, then turned back into the house.

Darragh was in the kitchen, taking a beer out of the fridge.

'Thanks again for being our real-life hero,' she said as he popped the tab.

'You're welcome.'

'It was surreal,' she told him. 'I didn't believe it was happening.'

'I guess Kathryn didn't either.'

'I guess not.'

She wanted to walk outside again, and yet she got the feeling that Darragh didn't want her to leave. She stood hesitantly beside the sink.

'You haven't forgotten about the board meeting, have you?' he asked.

'How could I possibly?' She smiled slightly. 'I'm taking the day off to be there.'

He laughed. 'Surely your job doesn't matter so much now,' he said. 'With the dividend and everything.'

'The dividend is nice,' she agreed. 'But of course my job matters.'

'Are you enjoying it?'

'It's OK,' she told him. 'Not a hugely exciting site despite my murder victim, but they can't all be.'

'Where would you find one more exciting?' he asked.

'There are lots.' She grinned. 'But they're often ones where you end up going as a volunteer because there's so much there and more people wanting to work on them than they need. When I went to Arizona it was as a volunteer.'

471

'How did you afford that?' he asked curiously.

'I'd saved. And it's not like I could spend a lot of money where we were.'

'So where would you go?' he asked. 'If you didn't need to earn a heap of money?'

'Oh, I don't know.' She shrugged. 'I like going to different places. Central America maybe; there's a site in Panama that I was thinking about last year, but I couldn't afford it then.'

'There's a way that perhaps you could,' said Darragh.

She frowned, and then he told her of the plan he'd discussed with Giselle. Sponsoring her on a dig. Partly sponsoring the dig itself, perhaps. Her eyes widened as he spoke.

'You'd pay me?' she asked. 'To go away?'

'Not to go away,' he said. 'To do your job. Make things easier for you.'

'Do Veronica and Kathryn know about this?' she asked.

'I haven't talked it through with them yet. I don't need to,' he added. 'The amount of money is within my own personal authorisation. The board has to sign off on bigger projects, but this is small beer really.'

She smiled. Small beer to him. But not to her.

'Just as well the board doesn't have to say anything,' she mused. 'After all, it would be a big conflict of interest for me, wouldn't it? Voting on money for myself.'

'I'm sure nobody thinks about it like that,' said Darragh, and this time Romy rocked with laughter.

'You can't really be that naïve,' she said. 'And you can't think that I'm that naïve myself.'

'It's a reasonable offer.'

'Yes,' she said thoughtfully. 'It is.'

Later that afternoon, after leaving Veronica, Kathryn and Romy sitting in the sun, Darragh brought Giselle and Mimi to the Yellow House for some pub grub. Giselle had suggested it, saying that she couldn't be bothered to cook, and Darragh and Mimi had clapped their hands delightedly.

After her kid's portion of lasagne, Mimi had curled up on the seat and fallen asleep while the adults had tea and, in Darragh's case, a pint of lager.

'This was a great idea,' he said.

'Glad you liked it,' Giselle told him. 'Maybe we can do it a bit more in the future. Though heaven knows, when Muffie arrives . . .'

'Look around you,' said Darragh. 'The place is crammed with families.'

'True.'

'And the food is good. You ate all yours, I see.' He glanced at her empty plate. She'd chosen the salmon but she'd eaten it all.

'I was hungry.'

'Must be Muffie,' he teased.

'Must be.' She smiled back at him.

'We'll have to start calling her something else,' he said sternly. 'Otherwise you're going to lumber her with that name.'

'I know. I thought of Chantelle. Or Shania.'

He looked doubtful and she grinned at him. 'You don't like modern names, do you?'

'I guess I'm a plain guy at heart,' he said. 'I'm more of your old-fashioned, unreconstructed man.'

'You can choose her name,' she told him.

'I can?'

'Absolutely.'

'What if you hate it?'

'Give me three vetoes.' She grinned at him and he laughed.

'OK. But I need time to think.'

'There's a few weeks to go yet,' she reminded him.

'Indeed. And during those few weeks, you need to keep your strength up.'

'With everything that's been going on lately, I tend to

agree.' She sipped her tea. 'I'm going to amend the healthy eating regime. It wasn't really about being healthy; it was about being thin. So there'll be a few changes. Though not burgers and chips every day,' she added hastily as she saw his face light up.

'That's OK,' he told her. 'And in return I'll cut back on the Pringles.'

They both laughed.

'So . . . how do you reckon the board meeting is going to go?' she asked after a moment's silence.

He looked thoughtful. 'I think that Kathryn is going to be extra tough just to show that nearly being beaten up hasn't upset her. So I think she'll be as obstinate as ever. And I don't know about Romy.'

'But the sponsorship,' said Giselle. 'Have you told her about that yet?'

'She thinks it's another bribe.'

'Well,' said Giselle, 'it is, isn't it?'

'No.' Darragh looked affronted. 'I'm helping her out.'

'It's all so messy,' said Giselle. 'All this change.'

'It wouldn't have been if Mum had spoken to me first,' he said. 'We could have arranged it differently.'

'The sponsorship is a great idea, though,' said Giselle.

'It's got to be a very tempting offer.'

'Of course it is,' agreed Giselle. 'And it makes perfect sense, Darragh. Romy hasn't a clue about anything, and this way she's out of your hair.'

He exhaled slowly.

'I'm sorry,' said Giselle.

'What?'

'I know I said it before but I really am. Sorry about the whole Veronica thing.'

'Oh, it doesn't matter,' said Darragh. 'Perhaps her guilt about Romy would always have come through.'

'I've made things more difficult, though,' said Giselle. 'Maybe her guilt wouldn't have come through until after you did the deal you want to do.'

Darragh smiled and then hugged her. 'It wasn't your fault. Not really. Regardless of everything, I think it probably would have been too much to have Mum stay. So it's fine.'

'Really?'

'Yeah, really. I know I flew off the handle, but . . . it's a challenge, that's all.'

'We can't afford to be too soft with them.' Giselle looked at him seriously. 'Maybe you'll go easy on Kathryn and maybe you don't want to stick the knife in too much, but she isn't the managing director and she doesn't know the ins and outs of what's going on and you have to be firm with her. Veronica too.'

'I will be,' said Darragh.

'They might have messed around with it, but it's still your inheritance,' said Giselle.

'Don't worry.' His voice was suddenly harder. 'I'll never forget that. No matter what.'

Chapter 31

Romy had spent a lot of time going through the papers that both Kathryn and Darragh had given her ahead of the board meeting. She'd had to read them over and over to get an idea of what they were all about, and even then she still wasn't sure if she'd grasped things properly. She felt a rush of sympathy for Veronica, who'd obviously had to read this kind of stuff for years when it clearly wasn't something she was hugely interested in either. And now she completely understood why Dermot had been so against getting involved in the company too. You were either business-minded or you weren't, she thought. And she wasn't. Having shares in Dolan's and a responsibility towards its future was daunting for someone who was happier delving into the past. She was dreading the board meeting which, she was sure, would reveal to Darragh and Kathryn just how stupid she was about this sort of stuff and make them even more annoyed with Veronica for having handed over the shares.

Until the day of the meeting, she had never visited the offices of Dolan Component Manufacturers. There hadn't been any need. She'd never even seen the building, although she knew more or less where it was. It had seemed really weird to her that morning to get into the car with Veronica and Kathryn in the knowledge that she was going there for the first time. And knowing that she was suddenly part of something she'd never expected to be part of.

As usual, she was the one who drove, turning on the radio as soon as she closed the car door and so preventing them from talking much during the journey. She didn't want to talk, didn't want them to mess with her head, even by accident. She nodded briefly when Kathryn spoke for the first time, telling her to take the slip road off the motorway (even though Romy had already got into the correct lane to exit it) and a couple of minutes later she turned into the industrial estate where the company building was located. She knew that when the estate had first been built the area around had been fairly desolate and the estate itself was more an aspiration than anything real. But now there were plenty of factories and office buildings all apparently thriving and busy, if the amount of haulage trucks and cars was anything to go by.

She pulled into the Dolan Component Manufacturers car park and hesitated briefly before Veronica told her to park beside Darragh in what she said was her usual spot. Romy turned into the space near the door and they all got out of the car.

'Well,' said Veronica. 'Here you are. The family firm.'

Romy could see that most of the building was taken up by the factory and that the office area was a two-storey redbrick structure to the front. A large blue sign pointed people towards either the reception area to the left or the delivery and collection area to the right. There were a number of racing-green vans lined up outside the delivery and collection area, all emblazoned with the company name and logo. (The logo, Kathryn had told her when she asked, was a representation of a pressure valve. Apparently Giselle had wanted to change that to go with the new green colour but Darragh hadn't allowed it.)

Veronica led the way towards the reception area, which was bright and airy, with mushroom-shaded carpets and neutral walls. Colour was introduced by abstract prints and by the green of the receptionist's jacket.

'Hello, Mrs Dolan. All ready for the meeting today?' She beamed at Veronica.

'Indeed we are, Jo,' Veronica replied. 'Is Darragh in his office?'

'Yes he is,' she said. 'I'll let him know you're on the way up. He's expecting you, of course.'

Kathryn and Romy followed their mother up a narrow flight of stairs and along an equally narrow corridor. The high-pitched whine of machinery penetrated through from the factory. Romy was thinking that it might be interesting to have a walk around the shop floor itself when Veronica stopped outside an opaque glass door and knocked briefly before pushing it open and walking in.

Romy had expected something a little more extravagant for Darragh's office. But it was a small room containing only a big oak desk, a pedestal to one side and a low bookshelf running beneath the window which overlooked the car park. Darragh was sitting in a black leather chair behind the desk and he was scribbling something on a Post-it note.

Romy had always imagined that Darragh's office would have oil paintings on the wall and maybe a few sculptures dotted around the place; a drinks cabinet too, perhaps, and a few armchairs . . . She realised that she was basing her ideas on the movies she watched, where big businesses were always housed in prestigious buildings and where the CEOs had chauffeurs and limos. Despite the fact that Dolan's was paying out that dividend every year, it was still a relatively small family company.

I had him pegged as a mogul, she thought as she watched him stick the Post-it to the front of the leatherbound diary on his desk. But he's not really. He's just someone doing a job.

'Hi.' Veronica perched on the edge of his desk. 'Are we early?'

He shook his head. 'I'm just finishing up one or two things. D'you want to head off into the boardroom and wait for me?'

Perhaps the boardroom will be a bit more luxurious, thought Romy, as she followed Veronica and Kathryn down the narrow corridor again. Perhaps it will have the drinks cabinet and loads of different clocks telling the time in the world's major cities.

It wasn't. Like Darragh's office it was a small room, although in this case totally dominated by the rosewood table that Tom had bought years earlier. Eight high-backed chairs were arranged neatly around it, three on each side and one at each end. A manila file lay in front of four of the places. There was a large bookshelf in one corner of the room (although there were very few books on it) and a tall potted plant in the opposite corner. There was also a portrait photograph of Tom on the inside wall. Romy stared at it, taking in his determined face, his strong jaw and his piercing blue eyes. Those features had all been passed to both Darragh and Kathryn, she thought, although Darragh's jaw wasn't as strong and Kathryn's eyes were a softer blue. But she could see him as the patriarch of the family and the owner of the business, and, quite suddenly, she shivered.

I've no right to be here, she thought. Even if Dolan's is a small, family-owned company it's way beyond everything I know about. It's ridiculous that I should have any kind of influence on what goes on. Ridiculous that I should have shares in it at all.

'You'll be fine.' Veronica smiled at her and Romy was startled to realise that her mother had guessed what she was thinking.

Kathryn was leafing through one of the files, frowning every so often and then, occasionally, smiling slightly as she made a note.

There was a knock on the door and Romy jumped. Susan, the PA Darragh shared with Alex and Stephen, walked in carrying a tray with tea, coffee and an assortment of biscuits. Veronica poured coffee for them all, even though Romy was far too nervous to drink it.

Why am I feeling like this? she asked herself. I don't care about this business, I don't care about the Dolans and it doesn't matter to me what the hell goes on here today.

'Sorry about that.' Darragh arrived a couple of minutes later and took a seat beside Veronica and opposite Romy. 'Had to take a call from one of our customers. He's reordering.' He smiled as he said this and shot a glance at Kathryn, who was sitting beside Romy. 'He's very happy doing business with us.'

'That's good,' said Kathryn noncommittally.

'So first things first,' continued Darragh. 'At this meeting we welcome Romy as a shareholder and a board member and we thank Veronica for all her efforts in the past.'

As he spoke, the door to the office opened and Susan walked in again carrying a huge bouquet of flowers which she handed to Veronica.

'From all of us,' she said. 'The staff. To say good luck in the future and that we appreciate everything you've done for us.'

'Oh.' Veronica looked surprised. 'Thank you. Thank you all very much.'

Susan's cheeks were pink and she smiled at Veronica.

'Thanks, Susan.' Darragh smiled at her and she left the room. 'They wanted to do that,' he told Veronica. 'You're liked a lot here. They were sorry to hear that you were standing down.'

Romy could hear the edge to his voice and she began doodling on the corner of the notepad in front of her.

'I shouldn't really be at the meeting today, I suppose,' said Veronica.

'Well, actually, although you've signed over the shares to Romy, we still have to do the paperwork regarding her member-ship of the board,' said Darragh.

'I did that,' said Veronica. 'When I was with the solicitor.'

'Romy hasn't signed her B10 form yet, though,' said Darragh. 'So technically . . .'

'. . . I shouldn't be here.' Romy looked pleased and relieved, while Kathryn frowned.

'You should,' said Veronica. 'The way I see it, technical-ities don't matter. If something needs a vote you can tell me which way to vote.'

'Mum, I'm not sure that—'

'Sounds fair.'

Kathryn and Darragh spoke at the same time and Romy groaned internally.

'Now,' said Darragh. 'The results for the last quarter.'

As he spoke, Romy felt her mind begin to wander. She knew that the results had been OK but were down on the previous quarter. There were reasons for this; she'd read them all in the papers that Darragh had given her. He was talking about clients and competition and a whole range of things and it kind of made sense to her, but the truth was she wasn't sure that she could sort out the useful information from the useless.

When Darragh finished talking Kathryn asked him a couple of questions and he seemed to answer them to her satisfaction because she just jotted down a few numbers on the corner of her folder. Veronica didn't ask anything at all.

'Romy?' Darragh looked at her. 'Anything you want to add?'

She shook her head.

'OK,' said Darragh. 'In that case can we come to the issue of our investment in Biovert?'

'Are we going to talk about it side by side with the proposed investment by Hemmerling?' asked Kathryn.

Romy knew that Biovert was the energy company Darragh was interested in doing business with while Hemmerling was the German company that wanted to buy a piece of Dolan's.

'If you want, we can go through the pros and cons of each,' said Darragh. 'I think you'll find, though, that the Biovert proposal offers us the best long-term prospect for sustainable business.'

'There is the question of a return on our money,' said Kathryn.

'We'll get that.'

'It might take a long time,' said Kathryn. 'Environmental energy isn't mainstream yet.'

'But it will be.'

'And, of course, it's not an area we have any expertise in whatsoever.'

'But everyone knows that the environment is important,' said Darragh.

'Important, yes. Profitable, no.' Kathryn regarded him thoughtfully. 'You're asking us to sink money into this company, yet they haven't provided us with a clear strategic plan for the future. And the thing is, you're asking us to do it with borrowed money because our own reserves have fallen over the past couple of years.'

'We have to take a long-term view,' said Darragh.

'Don't you think that with Hemmerling we might be doing that?'

'They want to buy us out!' cried Darragh. 'I'm not having some foreign company come here and rip the soul out of Dolan's. Dad worked too hard for that to happen.'

'Their proposal isn't about ripping the soul out of Dolan's,' said Kathryn calmly. 'They're talking about an investment which will help us gain a foothold in other markets.'

'No,' said Darragh. 'They want to get into our market and wipe us out.'

Romy listened as the argument raged back and forwards between them, not reacting but thinking that both of them made good points. Darragh had clearly spent time costing out the whole Biovert deal. Kathryn made Hemmerling sound like a great company with only their best interests at heart. She had no idea which was best for Dolan's and she felt panicked that she might make the wrong choice.

She glanced at her mother. Veronica's eyes were moving from one to the other as she followed the arguments too. It suddenly occurred to Romy that Veronica knew a lot more about the business than she let on. In which case, thought Romy, she's generally supported Darragh because she really believes that he's right. And the company has done well, so it's been a good decision by her. The only thing about that is that perhaps Kathryn might be just as right. And maybe the company would've done even better if they'd followed her advice. She sighed inwardly. How was anyone to know?

They were talking now about capital and gearing and using jargon that was floating way above her head. She was trying desperately to keep focused on the discussion but her mind was down in Wicklow, at the dig, and she was thinking that she'd much rather be there than here on a glorious day like today, arguing about the provenance of a piece of pottery or a shard of bone rather than things like projected cash flows. That was what was so great about her job. It was about people and their way of life. It was about things she could really understand. And it had the benefit of being in the open air. She wasn't stuck behind some overladen desk in some stuffy office. Her work was so much more exciting than this. A sudden gust of wind rattled the window and reminded her that occasionally the open air was cold and wet. But it was still, she thought, a lot better than being indoors.

'. . . break for coffee.'

They'd been talking for ages, Romy realised, but she hadn't heard half of it. Her presence here was a joke. Veronica must know that already. And surely by now she was having second thoughts about those shares.

They all pushed their chairs back from the table, and as if by some kind of magic, Susan appeared again carrying another tray with fresh tea and coffee and more biscuits, even though nobody had touched the first plate.

'So what do you think so far, Romy?' asked Veronica as she poured tea for herself.

'Oh, I dunno.' Jeez, thought Romy, how pathetic does that sound?

'Coming down in favour of one proposal or the other?' Kathryn's eyes glittered with amusement.

She's enjoying this, Romy thought, suddenly realising that this was what Kathryn did, this was what interested her. In the same way as finding a skeleton excited Romy, finding flaws in the figures, working out the best solutions, excited Kathryn.

'I'm sure Romy will see what's good for the company,' said Darragh. 'And for her too, of course.'

'I explained all about the company,' Kathryn informed him. 'Let her know about her responsibilities to our staff, that sort of thing.'

'Oh really?' There was a degree of sarcasm in Darragh's voice. 'You've explained it? That's all right then. She's totally clued in so.'

It was like being at home again, Romy realised. When they were kids and Darragh and Kathryn would clash over everything. Whatever Darragh was doing, whatever he had, Kathryn wanted to do or to have too. At half Darragh's age she'd been twice as determined and utterly convinced that she was as capable as him no matter what. She'd want to know why he was allowed to use the electric shears to cut down the hedge at the back of the house while she wasn't. Or why he could get driving lessons and she couldn't. (She'd complained about that when Darragh was eighteen and she was a mere twelve.) And when she wasn't allowed to do something that he was she'd make some comment about how stupid and useless it was anyway and how stupid and useless he was too.

It must have been very annoying for him, thought Romy, knowing that Kathryn always had to have the last word and always had to be right. Even when she was wrong. (Darragh had passed his driving test on his first attempt. It had taken Kathryn three. She said that it was because they were biased against women and that they had quotas of passes and failures and that her tests had clearly been scheduled at the wrong times. Darragh had muttered that it had more to do with her inability to reverse around a corner than anything else.)

They finished their tea and coffee and came back to the table.

'We can't sit still and do nothing,' said Darragh. 'As you've seen, there are areas where we are being priced out of the market and that's a big problem. And as you pointed out already, Kathryn, our reserves are down too, which I'm not comfortable with. But there are opportunities for us and I'm keen on the Biovert option. I think that it would be worth pursuing and I'd like your agreement to do that.'

'And Hemmerling?' asked Kathryn.

'I don't think that any of us want to dilute the holdings that we have,' said Darragh. 'We don't want outsiders on our board and that would happen with Hemmerling.'

'You don't think it would be a good idea to have some new board members?' Kathryn looked at him quizzically. 'After all, I'm going to be in New York again soon and Romy . . . well, goodness knows where she'll be. And so it will be difficult to have regular board meetings.'

'We have them every two months at the moment,' said Darragh. 'But there's nothing to say that they couldn't be quarterly. Or three times a year.'

'I don't think it would be a good idea to have infrequent meetings,' said Kathryn. 'I know that technology means we can hook up, and maybe that's how we should play it in the future.'

'Videoconferencing?' It was one thing that Romy did actually know about. They'd often done it at Heritage Help when they'd been talking to people in different parts of Australia.

'Excellent idea,' said Darragh. 'So that blows your worries out of the water, Kathryn.'

His sister smiled. 'From that point of view. But we should really be thinking about fresh blood on the board.'

'We have fresh blood. Romy.'

Romy looked uncomfortable.

'And I'm sure she'll make a positive contribution in the future,' said Kathryn equably. 'But we should think about other people too. Non-executive directors who would be able to help and advise us. The company has grown but we haven't grown with it and that's holding us back.'

'You mean I'm holding us back?'

'No,' she said. 'I don't mean that at all.'

'We can always think about people for the board in the coming weeks,' said Darragh. 'That shouldn't stop us from voting on the proposal now.'

'We need to talk a bit more,' said Kathryn. 'I wanted to ask some questions first. About Romy's conflict of interest, for starters.'

Romy, who been drawing diagrams of skeletal feet on her notepad, glanced at Kathryn.

'Conflict of interest?' Darragh looked at her warily.

'Oh, come on!' Kathryn snorted. 'The sponsorship plan, Darragh. Paying her to go away. And you don't think that could influence her?'

'It won't,' said Romy.

'How did you know about that?' asked Darragh at the same time.

Kathryn smiled slightly. 'She told me.'

Romy looked at Darragh guiltily. 'I had to,' she told him. 'It wasn't fair not to.'

'What sponsorship?' asked Veronica.

Romy filled her in on Darragh's proposal.

'Interesting idea,' said Veronica. She looked at Romy. 'Don't you think so?'

'Of course,' said Romy. 'The idea of having some money and not having to worry about which job I'm going to is fantastic.'

'I know,' said Darragh sourly.

'But the thing is, if I voted for something that you proposed and nobody knew about the sponsorship and they found out at some other time, then there could be trouble, couldn't there?' she asked. 'And that wouldn't be right. My vote would be sort of suspect.'

'Are you thinking of voting for my proposal?' Darragh glared at her.

'You're angry with me for telling,' she said. 'You shouldn't be.'

'No,' he said. 'I suppose I shouldn't. It's all a game to you. To Kathryn too. But it's my life, mine and Giselle's. I've worked like crazy for this company and nobody seems to understand that. I've tried to do a good job, to look out for everyone's interests . . .'

'Darragh.' Kathryn's voice was firm. 'Nobody is saying that you haven't done a good job. Or, indeed, that you haven't looked after our interests. You've done that in a whole heap of ways. Especially the other night, with Alan. You were great.'

Darragh looked at her in surprise.

'Nobody thinks that you haven't got great skills in managing the company,' she said. 'And nobody thinks that you aren't a strong . . . strong head of the family.' The last words came out in a rush.

'But you still want to mess things up,' said Darragh. 'Because you can't stand it when I'm successful. Because you have this thing about being the girl, about Dad not leaving the business to you.'

'He hardly could,' said Kathryn, 'and me a baby at the time. And of course him having been brought up in a world where it was men doing all the work.'

'And in your world it's women doing all the work and men being nothing but useless twats,' said Darragh angrily.

'I have thought that,' admitted Kathryn. 'But come on, Darragh – I never said that you were useless.'

'Regularly,' said Darragh. 'You said it regularly.'

'Not recently,' amended Kathryn.

'At the last board meeting,' he told her.

'No,' she said. 'I said that the pricing strategy was useless. You didn't come up with that. Alex and Stephen did. And, darling brother, they *are* useless!'

'They've been with the company for a long time.'

'Hum.' Kathryn looked at him knowingly. 'That's why

they're useless. They're comfortable and complacent and they don't think . . . well, to use that awful expression, they don't think outside the box.'

'Whereas you're never in the bloody box,' said Darragh.

'You do, though,' said Kathryn. 'That deal with Romy was very out-of-the-box stuff.' She grinned suddenly. 'I was impressed by it.'

'You were?'

'Sure. It proved to me that you can be just as ruthless as the next person.'

'Thank you.'

'You're welcome.'

'So . . .' Romy looked at them both. 'What now? Are we going to vote or not?'

'I want to talk about something else first,' said Kathryn. 'Then you can vote.'

'Look, it's a vote about Biovert or Hemmerling,' said Darragh. 'No matter what you say, it won't make a difference to that.'

'Of course it will,' said Kathryn. 'The company needs funding and it needs to diversify. You're right about those two things. I just think you're going the wrong way about it. Romy, can I have your laptop?'

She'd borrowed it the previous night and spent ages tapping at the keyboard while Romy had asked her what she was doing. 'Working on things,' was all Kathryn had said, but now she plugged the laptop into the data projector and projected a graph on to the white wall.

'Restructuring,' she said. 'The way forward for Dolan's.'

She spoke for twenty minutes, during which nobody else said a word. She homed in on numbers in the accounts which, she said, showed the strengths and weaknesses of Dolan's and which, she told them, could be their salvation. Then she outlined a plan in which the company would restructure its debt to take day-to-day pressure off them and enable them to price their goods differently. It would be a favourable deal for the banks – she'd done a similar one in New York a few months earlier. And it would mean that Darragh could invest in Biovert – but not as much as he wanted to do now. Finally, she said, they could go back to Hemmerling and talk about a possible partnership without ever being in the position of feeling as though they were going to be bought out.

When she'd finished talking there was complete silence. Then Darragh clapped his hands slowly.

'Thanks,' he said. 'Thanks for making me look like a complete moron.'

'What d'you mean?' she asked.

'All the talk earlier. All the plans. But you had this up your sleeve the whole time.'

Kathryn looked at him edgily. 'We needed to hear all the other stuff,' she said.

'So's this deal could look even better?' His tone was harsh.

'Does this mean you think it's a good one?' she asked.

'You've found another way,' he told her. 'You must have had this planned all along.'

'I wasn't sure,' she told him. 'I needed to talk to one of my banking contacts to see if it was possible. It's more diffi-cult with a private company, you see.'

'But you came up with it all the same. Not me.'

'It's my job, Darragh,' she said. 'It's what I do.'

'No,' he said. 'What you do is put people in prison because they cooked the books.'

'That's only part of it,' she told him. 'I also look at deals like this. And I'm telling you that this is a good one for us.'

'You know,' said Darragh, 'you were right all along. You are better at this than me. You should be the one in charge.'

Kathryn shook her head slowly. 'You're wrong about that,' she said. 'I couldn't be. I didn't find Biovert. I didn't find Hemmerling. You did. You went out and met people and talked about the business with them. You're good at that.

I just looked at the numbers. Which is what I'm good at. Different strengths, that's all.'

'But if you were the managing director you'd find those deals and run the ruler over them yourself and everything would be so much simpler.'

'I wouldn't,' she told him. 'People come to me with problems and I solve them. I can think . . . well, differently about them. But not about the business part. I wouldn't have thought of environmental energy as a proposition for us, but having looked at all the papers I think it has some really interesting potential. And it is a diversification thing and I agree that we need to do that. I have to admit that, yes, I always wanted to be managing director. But lately I've realised that . . . that I'm not quite tough enough.'

'If you're saying that just because a bloke hit you . . .'

She smiled crookedly at him. 'That's not it at all,' she said. 'What it is . . . well, I haven't got the same passion as you for this, Darragh. I thought I had, but the passion I had was proving that I could do it. Always wanting to be right. Sticking it to the other guy. But then when Alan . . . when I . . .' She swallowed hard. 'I stayed with him because I didn't want to be wrong. Because I couldn't admit that I'd made a mistake. And because of that he nearly killed me and he might've killed Romy too . . .'

'It wasn't that bad,' interjected Romy.

'. . . and it made me see that I'm bloody obstinate,' said Kathryn. 'I've had this notion about running Dolan's for ever, but it's just an obstinate notion. I don't want to be the MD of the company. I'd be a crap MD. You're a great MD. You need someone better on the numbers side than that pair of clowns you have working with you, but with smarter people I don't see why the company can't continue to do well.'

Darragh and Kathryn looked at each other in silence. Veronica and Romy were silent too.

'Go through the proposal again,' said Darragh eventually. 'Line by line.'

Romy and Veronica exchanged glances while Darragh and Kathryn continued to talk about her restructuring proposal. Neither of them joined in the conversation but Veronica suddenly winked at Romy, who winked back in return. And then, when Kathryn had finished talking it through for the second time, Darragh leaned back in his chair and looked at Romy.

'OK,' he said. 'Did you get all that?'

'I got the fact that you two seem to be working together,' she said. 'Which is probably a good thing?'

Kathryn grinned. 'Probably.'

'I knew you could work it out.' Veronica looked satisfied. 'I always knew you had it in you.'

'I hope you didn't plan this,' said Darragh. 'Because it went down to the wire.'

'I didn't plan it,' said Veronica. 'I don't have the brains to plan these things. But I knew that you two could work together better. And you have.'

'If Darragh approves of the plan,' said Kathryn. 'If he wants to go ahead with it.'

'So vote,' said Veronica. 'You and Darragh and Romy.'

'The vote will be about this restructuring?' asked Romy. 'Kathryn's idea. We do some refinancing and we extract value out of the assets?'

Veronica looked startled and both Darragh and Kathryn stared at her.

'Did you understand what they were talking about?' asked Veronica.

'Well, sort of,' said Romy. 'Kathryn explained it very well. She's good at that. And it sounds fairly reasonable to me. It gives us that kind of cash-flow thing you were talking about, doesn't it? And means we can stay as Dolan's without needing someone else's money. So if you're asking me to vote, I'm saying yes.'

'Um, right.' Darragh continued to stare at her. 'You did understand it.'

Romy shrugged.

'Crikey,' said Veronica, as they all agreed on the plan. 'Maybe it *is* me with the business gene after all, and I've passed it on to Romy as well as the two of you. Maybe it wasn't Tom's brains at all.'

Darragh and Kathryn roared with laughter.

'What about Romy's sponsorship?' asked Veronica. 'Is she still going to get that?'

'That was to support Darragh,' said Romy. 'And it's OK. I never really expected it anyway. Besides, I've still got the dividend money, and if this plan works then it should be even better next year, shouldn't it?'

'We could still sponsor you,' said Kathryn. 'It wasn't a bad idea, actually.'

'Oh, but . . .'

'Let's talk about it later,' said Darragh. 'Like I said before, it's within my marketing budget.'

'You two can work it out,' said Kathryn. 'Maybe we could give you some money for one of those voluntary digs you go on. And you could do a blog about it on our website or something.'

Romy nodded. 'Maybe.'

'Excellent.' Kathryn closed the file in front of her.

'Well, if everyone is finished,' said Darragh, 'I want to thank you for coming to the board meeting and thank you for your hard work. I guess in the end all I've ever wanted was a strong company. I thought there was only one way to achieve that but I was wrong. And . . . so . . . thanks. To you all.'

'You're welcome,' said Veronica. 'I'm glad to see that Dolan's is in good hands and that I made the right decision.'

'We would have worked it out without you standing down,' said Kathryn.

Veronica grinned. 'Maybe. But it sure focused your minds.' She turned to Romy. 'Yours too.'

'I guess.' Romy laughed.

They smiled at each other and began to tidy their papers away. Kathryn clicked on Romy's computer.

'I like your screensaver,' she said. 'I was afraid it might distract us from the task in hand.'

'Balmoral Beach,' she told her. 'Near Sydney. I used to go there a lot.'

'Will you go back there?' she asked. 'With or without the sponsorship?'

'I don't know,' said Romy.

'What about the boyfriend?' asked Veronica. 'Won't he be waiting for you?'

'I lied about him.' Romy shrugged. 'He's just a friend. I needed an excuse both not to come and to want to go back.'

'And now?' asked Kathryn.

Romy smiled slightly. 'I have plenty of reasons to stay in Ireland and maybe just as many to go to other places too.'

'But not Australia?' Darragh looked at her questioningly.

'I have to think about it,' said Romy. 'But then I've had to do loads of thinking lately, so that's nothing new.'

Chapter 32

It was the hottest day of the year so far. Driving to Wicklow earlier that morning, Romy had already felt the heat of the sun through the windscreen; by midday, when she'd finished uncovering the bones of the latest skeleton, she was coated in a sheen of perspiration. She sat on the block beside the main Portakabin and pushed a damp wisp of hair from her eyes.

'Warm work?' Taig stood beside her and offered her a bottle of water.

'Thanks.' Romy gratefully accepted it and glugged back half the contents. 'I needed that.'

'Are you feeling OK?'

Taig had seen the marks and bruises on her arm when she'd come back to the site the day after the board meeting. She'd glossed over the incident with Alan but he'd been absolutely horrified and told her to take it easy, insisting that she didn't push herself too much. The bruises had faded but her arm still ached after a day's work.

'I'm sore,' she replied cheerfully. 'But that's from work, so it's an OK kind of pain. We should just about get everything uncovered in our time span.'

They'd finally estimated that the burial site contained twenty graves and they had a tight schedule before the developers moved in. Taig had been in touch with them and they were anxious to get moving on their project as quickly as possible, but Romy expected that they'd manage to excavate all the skeletons before then.

'Fancy dinner tonight?'

It seemed like a long time since their meal in the local restaurant on the night that Romy had come home to find Alan Palmer in the house.

Alan had been released on his own bail although he was prevented from returning to the States. Romy had shivered when she heard of his release, but he was staying at a hotel on the other side of the city and didn't come near Avalon. Kathryn, who'd gone back to the States herself, had begun divorce proceedings. Veronica wanted her to return to Ireland as soon as possible but Kathryn said that she needed to find her feet in New York again. Besides, she'd added in the hour-long phone conversation the previous night, she'd been given a really interesting case of suspected corporate fraud to look at and it would be completely involving for the next few months.

She was still staying with her friend Sybil in her apartment, which was closer to downtown and to Kathryn's office. It was a nice apartment, she told them, and she felt safe and relaxed there. Veronica worried that she wouldn't feel safe and relaxed if Alan got back to New York and Kathryn said that it was something she'd deal with if and when it happened. But, she told her mother, if that was the case, she was ready to take out a legal order preventing him from coming near her. Her friends and close colleagues already knew about the abuse, and although they'd been horrified, they'd been supportive.

'I thought they'd think I was a failure,' Kathryn admitted. 'But they don't. They just think I was unlucky.'

'Romy?' Taig spoke again and Romy stopped thinking about her sister.

'Sorry,' she said. 'Daydream.'

'You keep doing that,' Taig complained.

'I know, I know.' Romy looked at him apologetically. 'It's

just that I seem to have a lot of stuff to think about these days and I haven't quite managed to put it all into context.'

'Well, maybe having dinner with me would help.' He grinned at her. 'What d'you say?'

'I can't tonight,' she told him. 'My sister-in-law has invited me and my mum over for dinner. She's never done that before and so we think we have to go.'

'Oh.' He looked disappointed. 'Friday?'

She looked at him regretfully. 'I can't on Friday either,' she said. 'I'm really, really sorry, Taig, but I'm baby-sitting for my dad and his wife.'

'For heaven's sake!' He looked at her sceptically. 'Just how close is your family?'

She chuckled. 'Not that close at all,' she said. 'It sounds as though we're in each other's pockets all the time, but we're not usually. In fact, after I finish at this dig we'll be scattered again.'

'Why?' he asked. 'Where are you going?'

'I haven't made up my mind yet.'

'Aren't you going to stay on for the post-ex work?'

'I don't think so.' She looked at him regretfully. 'It's a fun site but it's small and . . . well, I'm looking at the prospect of something in Central America.'

'Oh.'

'Sorry,' she said again.

'What about the kiss?' he asked.

She looked startled.

'Last time. After dinner. It was a good kiss. I thought perhaps we could try it again.'

'Tempting,' she said slowly. 'But the truth is . . . I know it's a cliché, but I'm not quite ready yet.' She looked at him apologetically. 'I think I'm a good kisser, Taig, but not quite so good at afterwards. I like you and I liked the kiss too. But I'm not sure about the rest. I'm sorry. I really am.'

His smile was philosophical. 'That's a pity. But you never know, do you, how things might pan out.'

'No, you don't,' she agreed.

'In the meantime . . .' He gestured at the site. 'Can you keep control of this for the rest of the day? I have to go into town, and if we're not meeting up tonight I might stay there.'

'Sure,' she said. 'No problem.'

'OK.' He nodded at her and strode off across the field, a tall, rangy man who still in many ways reminded her of Keith.

Was that why she was so reluctant to go out with him again? she wondered. Was it that every time she talked to Taig she thought of Keith instead? Even though Keith had changed so much from the first time she'd met him?

She hadn't heard from him in over a week. She'd called him after the whole fracas with Alan but the message about being out of touch was still on his phone. She hadn't left a message of her own but she had emailed him and given him the lowdown on the story. As she typed she'd realised that she was trembling and that she was crying again, and she'd been shocked at how deeply she still felt about it all. And she'd got up from her computer and knocked at the (now repaired) door of Kathryn's room and surprised her sister by breaking down and hugging her fiercely. Kathryn, who had been packing at the time, hadn't cried at all.

'I think I'm getting better,' she'd told Romy. 'Though probably as soon as I get to New York I'll end up in therapy.'

'You shouldn't have had to go through it,' said Romy. 'You should have said and we'd have supported you. Never, never feel that you have to be so brave that you can't say when something has gone wrong in your life.'

'Right back at you,' Kathryn murmured, still holding Romy in her arms.

It was weird, Romy thought now, how much closer they all were. It wasn't that all the issues between them had been suddenly brushed away, but that night, coupled with the successful board meeting the following week, had suddenly made them realise that they had more things in common than there were differences between them. And although she didn't think that she'd voluntarily choose to spend a lot of time with Kathryn (who was still far too self-possessed no matter what) or Darragh (who couldn't help being bossy), she didn't feel as though she was somehow inferior to them any more.

'You never were,' Veronica told her the night that Kathryn left and the two of them were sitting alone in the house together. 'You were the only one who thought that. I never did. Neither did they.'

'You're wrong there,' Romy said. 'But perhaps we agree that we can't all be good at the same things. And that those different things can be complementary.'

'I'm glad about that,' said Veronica. 'I want you to complement each other. I want you to get on.'

'It takes time,' Romy said. 'But maybe we will.'

'And us?' Veronica looked at her quizzically.

Romy exhaled slowly. 'I thought we agreed to put it behind us.'

'I know. But I want to feel as though you mean it. I want to believe that I didn't ruin your life.'

'Oh, Mum!' Romy shook her head. 'Of course you didn't. Nobody can ruin someone else's life. You can let it be ruined, and maybe I nearly did – maybe I wanted to blame you for the stuff that went wrong for me – but it doesn't matter any more.'

'Really?'

'Really,' Romy assured her. 'Let's face it, Perry Fitz and I weren't going to be for ever. And yes, it was all horrible as far as I was concerned, but you were drunk or stoned—'

'You make me sound so irresponsible!' wailed Veronica.

'If I accept that I was moody about it, will you accept that there *were* times when you were *wildly* irresponsible?' Romy looked at her mother hopefully and Veronica laughed.

'All right,' she said. 'I was an irresponsible mother and I nearly made a hash of bringing you up, but obviously I didn't quite because you've turned out all right in the end.'

'Excellent,' Romy told her. 'Now, how about giving my poor archaeologically wrecked hands a massage with that gorgeous cream Giselle gave me? I could do with the pampering.'

Veronica had laughed at that, but she'd given Romy a lovely massage and then they'd watched a rom-com movie on TV before going to bed.

It was all a lot more peaceful than it had been before, Romy thought as she watched Taig get into his Jeep and drive away. And in a couple of months' time she'd be in Central America away from them all again, but this time not running away and this time not being afraid to come home.

'Hey, Romy!' Mai called to her. 'Looks like we've got another skellie here. Wanna take a look?'

And so she stopped daydreaming and got back to work again.

By the time they were finishing off for the day, she was utterly exhausted. She'd spent the majority of the afternoon supervising the unearthing of an almost complete skeleton which they identified as being a young woman. As always, Romy wondered about her and her life and how she'd died, and she hoped that the girl's short life had been a happy one.

She stayed at the site even when some of the others had left, lost in the past and comforted by it, until she suddenly realised that she had to get home and shower and change before heading over to Darragh and Giselle's. She wasn't entirely looking forward to an evening with both of them – it was all very well, she thought, to have a kind of *rapprochement* with her brother, but Giselle still drove her nuts. And the last couple of weeks, instead of being glamorous and girlie, she seemed to have come over all earth-mother and caring, which, Romy thought, was probably even worse. All the same, she would cope with Giselle.

She wouldn't sigh loudly or make nasty comments like she used to, and she promised herself that she'd try to be interested if and when Giselle talked about her clothes and her spa treatments and the imminent birth of her baby.

She stretched her hands above her head and looked across the field. In a few months it would all be given over to housing. It was a shame that it had to happen, but it was inevitable too. People had lived here before and they'd live here in the future, she reminded herself, and that was what life was like. It was a cycle. And sometimes you had to remember that you were only a part of it. It didn't revolve around you. It never would.

'G'day!'

She'd been so engrossed in what she'd been thinking of as her meaning-of-life stuff that she hadn't heard him walking across the dry field. She whirled around and stared at him.

'Keith!'

'That's me.' He grinned at her, his blue eyes bright in his tanned face. 'How're you doing, Ro?'

'I'm good,' she said. 'But . . . but what are you doing here? I thought you'd gone trekking in the outback or something.'

'I went to Taz for a few days,' he told her. 'Got the chance for a bit of diving and stuff.'

'Oh.'

'And then I thought, why don't I come and see my old friend Romy, who seems to have been going through the mill a bit.' His eyes darkened. 'I read your email. Jeez, Ro, what a crock.'

'It wasn't the best ever night of my life,' she admitted. 'Kathryn's either. In fact I've never been so bloody scared.'

'I'm not surprised,' he said. 'But then your brother rode to the rescue . . .'

Romy grinned. 'I know. He was amazing, he really was.'

'So you're OK?' He looked at her anxiously. 'You said that bloke hit you and I was worried.'

'I had a bruise.' She touched her cheek. 'But it's gone. It could've been a lot worse.'

He reached out and touched her cheek too. She didn't move.

'Seems to me that I can't let you out of my sight,' he commented. 'Remember when you went off to Egypt on your own and fell and twisted your ankle?'

'That wasn't so bad,' she protested.

'And in Romania you had to get a tetanus jab when you were bitten by a dog.'

'OK, that was a bit more scary. I thought he might be a vampire dog.'

'You need looking after,' Keith told her.

'I can look after myself.'

'Yeah?'

'Yeah.'

'So I've wasted my time coming here?'

'If you came to look after me, then yes!'

He laughed. 'Actually I came to see if . . .'

'If what?'

'If . . .' He leaned forward and kissed her. It wasn't a comfort kiss. It was as good a kiss as she'd ever had in her life before. Better, much better, than the one she'd shared with Taig. It wasn't the kiss of someone who just wanted to be her friend. It was a kiss from someone who was already a whole lot more than just a friend. It was a kiss from someone special. And that made all the difference.

I love him, she thought suddenly. I really do. I always have. She dropped the trowel she'd been holding in her hand and put her arms around him, pulling him close to her and feeling his hold tighten around her.

'Oh,' she said when he finally released her.

'Yup. It was.'

'What?'

'As blindingly good as I thought it would be.'

502

'I thought that I'd scared you with that kiss,' she said. 'I didn't mean to and—'

'Hey, you told me a million times you didn't mean to,' he said. 'Over and over. All the time! And so I kept thinking that you regretted it. Only *I* didn't. I was shocked when you did it. Because . . . well, because I'd been thinking about doing it myself for ages. But I didn't because you never let me think . . . We were friends, Ro, that's all. I didn't want to mess it up. Then *you* kissed *me*! And I thought maybe it was because you were leaving and you were so unhappy. Not because you really wanted to kiss me. And every time we talked afterwards you were at pains to point out that it didn't mean anything. Then one day I met Tanya and I told her and she said that I'd be crazy not to come over here and scoop you up in my arms because she reckoned that you and me were just meant to be.'

'Tanya said that!' Romy was shocked.

'She did,' confirmed Keith. 'So did all the others too.'

'You've been talking to them about me?'

'About us.'

'You think there's an us?' Romy looked at him questioningly.

'I'm kinda hoping that after that kiss there is.'

She let out her breath. 'You know, Keith, after that kiss there'd bloody better be!'

She was later than she'd planned in getting back to Veronica's house.

'Nice place,' said Keith as she zapped the gates and turned into the driveway. 'Look, are you sure your mum won't mind me crashing out here? I can stay somewhere else.'

'Believe me,' said Romy as she got out of the car, 'she'll be so pleased to see that I really do have a boyfriend, that someone actually finds me attractive, she'll be putting out the red carpet for you.'

Keith flung his backpack over his shoulder and followed Romy into the house.

'I'm home!' she called. 'Sorry I'm late.'

She walked into the kitchen and stopped abruptly so that Keith almost clattered into her.

Veronica and Will Blake were standing side by side. Veronica's hair was mussed and she was frantically straightening it. Will looked guiltily at Romy.

'Hi, Mum,' she said cheerfully. 'You haven't forgotten, have you, that we're going over to Darragh and Giselle's tonight?'

'No,' said Veronica. 'Will was just leaving.'

'Yes,' said Will quickly. 'I'm off. So, um, Veronica, I'll be talking to you again soon, and I'll bring those brochures over for you to look at.'

'What brochures?' asked Romy.

'Brochures about houses, of course,' said Veronica. 'Will is helping me to house-hunt.'

'Ah,' said Romy.

'Yes,' said Will again. 'House-hunting. Well, yes. See you soon, Veronica.'

He made his way out of the kitchen while Veronica continued to smooth down her hair.

'You could've seen him out,' said Romy as they heard the front door close behind him.

'I know,' said Veronica. 'But he's very shy.'

Romy snorted.

'He is,' said Veronica defensively. And then, as though she'd only just seen him, she looked at Keith. 'And you are?'

'Mum, this is my boyfriend,' said Romy. 'The one I left behind in Australia.'

'The boyfriend!' Veronica's eyes widened. 'I thought you said he didn't mean anything.'

Keith looked quizzically at Romy.

'I was wrong,' she said simply. 'He means everything.'

'Oh.' Veronica's eyes widened even more.

'Hello there.' Keith held out his hand to her. 'It's really nice to meet you. Though I never would have guessed you were Romy's mum. You two could be sisters.'

And Romy couldn't help smiling as Veronica beamed with pleasure at her boyfriend's words.